Mediterranean Sea

Black Sea

Caspian Sea

Nile River

Red Sea

Tigris River

Euphrates River

Indus River

Ganges River

Arabian Sea

Indian Ocean

Alexandria

Antioch

Jerusalem

Palmyra

Petra

Dura-Europos

Ctesiphon

Ecbatana

Bukhara

Myos Hormos

Seleucia

Merv

Kashgar

Berenice

Charax

KUSHAN EMPIRE

Begram

Mathura

PARTHIAN EMPIRE

Barbarikon

Muza

Kane

Balygaza

Arikamedu

N

trade routes

tenth stone

BOOK TEN

A.D. CHRONICLES®

tenth
stone

Tyndale House Publishers, Inc.
Carol Stream, Illinois

BODIE & BROCK
THOENE

Visit Tyndale's exciting Web site at www.tyndale.com

TYNDALE and Tyndale's quill logo are registered trademarks of Tyndale House Publishers, Inc.

A.D. Chronicles and the fish design are registered trademarks of Bodie Thoene.

Tenth Stone

A.D. Chronicles series designed by Rule 29, www.rule29.com

Interior designed by Dean H. Renninger

Edited by Ramona Cramer Tucker

This novel is a work of fiction. Names, characters, places, and incidents either are the product of the authors' imaginations or are used fictitiously. Any resemblance to actual events, locales, organizations, or persons, living or dead, is entirely coincidental and beyond the intent of either the authors or the publisher.

Library of Congress Cataloging-in-Publication Data

Thoene, Bodie, date.
  Tenth stone / Bodie & Brock Thoene.
    p. cm. — (A.D. chronicles ; bk. 10)
  ISBN 978-0-8423-7534-4 (hc)
  1. Jerusalem—Fiction. I. Thoene, Brock, date. II. Title.
  PS3570.H46T46 2009
  813'.54—dc22   2008049107

Printed in the United States of America

15 14 13 12 11 10 09
 7   6   5   4   3   2   1

For Sarah Palin—America's Northern Light
Psalm 20

Yeshua did many other things as well. If every one of them were written down, I suppose that even the whole world would not have room for the books that would be written.

JOHN 21:25

Prologue

London was cloaked in the perpetual dusk of January. The sky was heavy from midday on. The leafless trees of Regent's Park scraped the gloomy underbelly of the clouds.

Shimon Sachar, wrapped in his heavy Burberry overcoat, sat on a cold bench outside the ticket booth of the Outdoor Theatre. The bushes of Queen Mary's Rose Garden, which bloomed in the summer months, were pruned back to stubs.

Shimon adjusted his hat and tan plaid scarf until only his nose and eyes were visible.

He glanced at his watch—3:37 p.m.

"Late," Shimon muttered, wondering if the old man would show up.

Shimon missed the sun and warmth of Jerusalem. Even in winter the weather of Israel was as comfortable to him as his own skin. It was during the cold weather like today that he especially regretted agreeing to fill the guest lectureship at the University of London left vacant at the death of his father.

Soon enough he would be home again.

This clandestine meeting with an old colleague of his father's was his last London duty as the son of Moshe Sachar before he boarded the El Al jet and flew south like a sensible bird.

But where was the old man?

Shimon had never met "Abe" Golah before, but he had grown up hearing Moshe tell stories about him during World War II. Moshe had never missed the opportunity to meet with Abe every time he passed through London. Abe had been unable to come to Moshe's funeral in Jerusalem. A letter of condolence had arrived two weeks later and, with it, an intriguing note in Moshe's handwriting . . . rather, half a note. The paper was torn in two but contained instructions to Shimon to contact Abe and meet with him in London before the year was out.

So. Here Shimon was, with a torn slip of paper in his pocket and no idea why his father had commanded him from beyond the grave to travel to London to meet with Eben Golah.

It was getting dark. Shimon decided he would wait only until 4:00. If Abe did not appear by then, they would both be lost in the early winter twilight in Regent's Park.

Shimon pulled his folded copy of the *Times* from his coat pocket and scanned the latest war news from Iraq. Violence had escalated in Fallujah. The count of British and American casualties continued to rise.

Depressing news. Not meant to be read on a lonely park bench on a freezing cold afternoon.

A stiff breeze picked up errant leaves that skittered across the sidewalk. From somewhere across the park, Shimon heard what he thought was the piercing cry of a hawk. Raising his chin, he caught sight of the aviary in the London Zoo. He regretted that he had not been to visit it and now probably never would.

Shimon opened the newspaper and covered the slats of the bench with it for insulation.

A voice behind him spoke. "Fallujah. In the news again."

Shimon spun around, expecting to see a wizened old man. Instead, he found himself face-to-face with a tall, well-built man probably in his midthirties.

The hawk called again. From the aviary? Or closer?

Green eyes glinted with amusement and crinkled at the corners. "You're Moshe's boy." It was not a question.

"I'm Shimon Sachar." He extended his hand.

Firm grip. Strong shake of the hand. "You look just like him," said the stranger.

"Thanks. I mean, I was expecting to meet a friend of my father's. . . ."

The stranger replied as he sat down on the headlines, "Your father was a great man. Always."

Perhaps something had happened to the old man, Shimon thought. Perhaps the cold had kept him indoors, so he had sent someone in his place.

"And you are . . . a friend of Mister Golah?"

Again the smile flashed. He tugged at his gloves. "Sit, Shimon. You look so much like Moshe at the same age."

Shimon remained standing. Suspicious now, he glanced over his shoulder at the thought that perhaps the meeting was not as it was supposed to be. "You've seen photos of my father."

"Anyone who studies biblical archaeology has seen photos of Moshe Sachar."

"Where is Mister Golah?" Shimon instinctively centered his balance as though he expected an attack.

"Here." The stranger patted his chest. "I am Eben Golah."

"What's the joke?" Shimon asked. "My father has known Mister Golah since . . ."

"1941. The political coup against British rule in Iraq. Moshe and I fought against the Nazi-trained Muslim nationalists together. The grandfathers of the very same chaps who are fighting in Fallujah today. Same war, really. Ancient war." He tapped the bench. "Do sit down, Shimon. Your father wanted me to meet with you after his death." He produced the other half of Moshe's letter and placed it in Shimon's gloved hand.

Yes. It matched. But how had this fellow come by it? What did he want? Where was the old man? Eben Golah, the exile. His father's friend.

"You're too young to be . . ."

The stranger smiled gently. "Age one way or the other is a foolish supposition from a man who knows the secrets beneath Yerushalayim."

Shimon's breath caught. "What . . . what are you saying?"

"You know what I'm saying. The tunnel that leads from your father's study. The grooves in the roof of the tunnel." He held up his fingers. *One, two, three.* "Shimon . . ."

"Where is Eben Golah? He must be at least eighty-five years old."

"At least."

Shimon stared at him, refusing to believe. Yet there was something about his eyes—behind his look of confidence. He knew the secret. But how?

"What do you want from me?" Shimon asked.

The stranger produced a padded envelope. "There is something in the Chamber of Scrolls that you must see."

"I don't know what you're talking about."

"Open it. Take out the page."

Shimon complied. A fragment of what appeared to be ancient papyrus was sealed in a plastic sleeve. Ten Hebrew words were written on it in what appeared to be first-century script, interconnected by lines forming the geometric pattern of the Star of David.

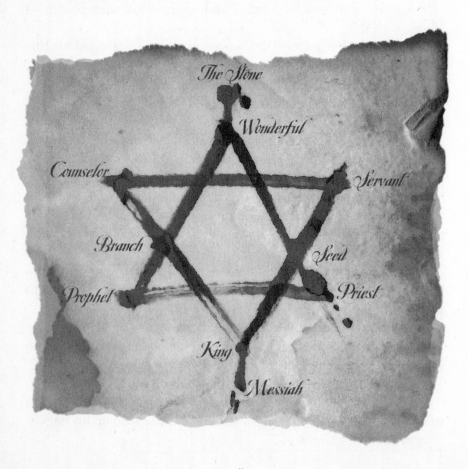

The stranger said, "You know this pattern."

"The foundation stones." Shimon nodded. "Fallujah. 1941. My father was taken to the site by a man. . . ." He raised his gaze.

The stranger was smiling. Confident of what he knew and who he was. "Eben Golah," he whispered.

Could it be? Shimon wondered, scanning the youthful face and strong white teeth.

"There was a story Papa used to tell," Shimon said slowly. "At least I always believed it was just a story . . . the reason the battles were so fierce in that location."

"You are the guardian of the truth now. It dates from the exile from Eden."

"How can this be?"

"He healed them all."

"Healed . . . but for how long?"

"I'm not alone. There are others."

"You say you want nothing from me?"

"Read what your father wrote. . . . Go on. A few words to ponder, but they explain the headlines, eh? Go ahead. I've got time. He knew this day must come."

Shimon fit the two halves of the note together. Moshe's blocky Hebrew handwriting was unmistakable.

Shimon,	my dear son,
Meet	
Golah	Geulah
ALEF	NUN
BET	BET
NUN	ALEF

The stranger squinted at the lowering sky. At the top of a giant plane tree a hawk swayed on a dancing branch. "It will be dark soon. I have never become accustomed to the long nights of these northern winters." He stood. "You're going home? Israel?"

Shimon nodded and tucked the thick envelope beneath the protection of his coat. "Yes. Tomorrow."

"When you return, there is a jar. Tenth on the tenth row in the first room. You'll find all the proof you need there." He extended his gloved hand and clapped Shimon on the back. "Your father asked me to look in on you from time to time. I'll see you again . . . soon."

Eben Golah turned on his heel and walked briskly back through the park the way he had come. The hawk launched from its lofty perch and soared above him.

It was dark by the time Shimon reached the Baker Street tube station and descended into the depths beneath the city.

PART I

"When you enter a town and are welcomed, eat what is set before you. Heal the sick who are there and tell them, 'The Kingdom of God is near you.'"

LUKE 10:8-9

CHAPTER 1

And so it had come to this.

It was the night when Rabbi Ahava's shofar echoed in the Valley of Mak'ob, summoning the lepers of Israel. All that remained of the child's life could be counted in a thousand heartbeats. She was the smallest of all the lepers in the Valley of Sorrows. Born in a cave to a diseased mother four years before, she began her life with the certainty of death on her horizon. Her mother died giving her life.

Rabbi Ahava named the baby girl Ya'el but called her Yod, after the smallest letter in the Hebrew alphabet. "*Yod*," he said to the children in his Torah school, "is the most important letter, after all.

"The letter *yod* hangs above the other letters like a little bird. *Yod* begins the word *Israel . . .* Yis-ra-el." The old man held up a gnarled forefinger to inscribe the *yod* upon the air in a single crooked dash. "So Israel begins with what is smallest. As it is written in Deuteronomy, *The Lord did not set His love upon you and choose you because you were more in number than any other people, for you were the least of all the people.*"[1]

Rabbi Ahava taught them, "Israel begins with the smallest stroke, *yod*. Israel ends with the largest letter, *lamed*. This proves that the

Almighty, blessed be he, loves all of Israel from the smallest to largest. From the youngest to the eldest. And everyone in between."

Yod was a good name for the child. She had never known any world but the leper colony, so she was happy even in the midst of suffering. Little Yod was indeed the smallest citizen of the Valley of Sorrow. She was nursed by three women who had lost their children to the disease. Yod thrived on the milk of her surrogate mothers, though she was a tiny infant when the spot of leprosy appeared on her right hand.

Each of her mothers perished before her third birthday. All the lepers of Mak'ob, from the eldest to the youngest, were her mothers and her fathers and her brothers and sisters.

She loved the kind young man named Cantor and his wife, Lily, most of all. Perhaps she imagined that they were her true father and mother and that they could live a long and happy life as a family. Cantor praised her spirit. Fearless. Quick to learn. Yod fed Cantor's hawk and was not afraid even when children twice her age cowered in fear of the fierce raptor. *If I am a brave girl, Cantor will want me to be his daughter*, she thought.

But it was not to be.

Cantor, handsome and kind, became sick one night and died suddenly. When he was buried, Yod hung back from all the other children who had loved him. She wept the tearless grieving of a leper . . . and became blind.

The death of Cantor shattered all hope in the Valley but one.

A baby boy was born to Lily's friend Deborah. His name was Isra'el. Like his name, beginning with *yod* and ending with *lamed*, his life somehow represented all the dreams of the lepers of Mak'ob. From the smallest to the largest, it was decided that the baby boy must not remain in the Valley, where he would surely sicken and die. So Cantor's grieving widow, Lily, had carried the newborn up the steep path to the Outside in order to save him.

When Lily had topped the rim of the Valley and turned to look at those who remained, Yod began to weaken. Only days passed before Yod was carried to the Dying Cave. There she remained until, at last, only one thousand heartbeats remained before the end of her life.

It is told that the last sense to leave before death is the sense of hearing.

Yod did not know how long she had been in the Dying Cave. She could not see. She had no sense of touch or taste. She could not speak.

1,000 heartbeats . . .

Yod heard the call of Rabbi Ahava's shofar. Suddenly around her there was stirring. Voices. A whisper of excitement.

"Lily's back!"

"The Great Healer!"

"The One we have been waiting for!"

"He's coming!"

"The Light!"

"The Prophet? Help me. Oh, help me!"

"Someone get me my stick."

"Yes! Messiah! Healer of Lepers!"

"Let me help you. He is here! On the stone of the bema. Teaching! Healing!"

"He has come to heal us all!"

"Hurry! Please!"

Yod heard the shuffling of feet near where she lay. Did they not see her?

There was a rustle of tattered blankets as those who shared the darkness with her moved toward the light. Had they forgotten her?

Yod tried to speak. Tried to ask for help. She could not move her hands. Her mouth, a festered sore where lips used to be, would not form even one word.

There was silence in the Dying Cave.

818 heartbeats remained.

Then a single voice called, "Anyone else? Anyone still here?"

Yod's thoughts raced. She could not form the words, *Me too! Though I'm the least! Don't forget me!*

The sounds of faraway excitement filtered in.

But Yod was alone. Forgotten. Left behind in the darkness.

749 heartbeats . . .

Outside the bonfire blazed. Torches streamed toward the source of light like molten metal about to be remade.

670 heartbeats . . .

"Me first!"

"Please, Lord!"

"Heal me first!"

But Yeshua of Nazareth commanded that the children of Mak'ob be brought to Him before any others.

612 heartbeats . . .

Rabbi Ahava identified each faceless boy and girl by name and guided them toward the arms of the Great Healer. All were thin and gaunt. Some were blind, all lame, and a few so eaten away that they were unrecognizable as human. Their faces were a mass of sores and rotting flesh. They were atrophied specters of what boys and girls should have been. Those who gathered round Yeshua were from ages twelve to six.

572 heartbeats . . .

Yeshua saw them all. He saw them each. One by one He passed down the line of thirty-two, from the tallest boy to the smallest . . . and He healed them all.

"Tell no man," He said to Ahava. "These children are in danger. You must take them all to the synagogue of your brother." Then He asked, "But is this every one of us? All the lepers of Israel?"

The old rabbi frowned and scanned the ranks. "Everyone?"

Yeshua questioned him. "One little lamb is missing. Counting from the smallest to the largest. *Yod* to *lamed*. All of Israel."

400 . . . 399 . . . 398 . . .

Ahava's eyes widened. "But where has she gone? There is a little girl, you see. Yod is her name . . . you know. But where is she?" The old rabbi peered into each face, behind each boy and girl. "Where is your sister?"

336 heartbeats . . .

"In the Dying Cave," Lamed, Yod's oldest brother, replied sadly.

Ahava stretched his hands out to the congregation. "Our little one! Our youngest child! She was in the Dying Cave. Did anyone carry Yod here?"

No one answered. A moan rose up from the congregation. Had the littlest in Israel perished just before the moment of deliverance? Had they left this one precious soul behind?

212 heartbeats . . .

Yeshua tucked His chin. Snatching a burning brand from the fire, He strode alone toward the face of the cliff. He ducked and entered the low limestone entrance of the Dying Cave.

"Yod," He cried as her pulse raced toward the end.

All the people of Mak'ob watched in silence as the light of Yeshua's torch fell on every rag and mound of blankets in His search for the child.

100 . . . 99 . . . 98 . . . 97 . . .

The Great Shepherd cried, "Yod! It's Yeshua! I have been looking for you, little one! Searching . . ."

The light paused, illuminating the smoke-scarred stone of this last refuge. Yeshua planted the torch in the ground and stooped beside the tiny body. He drew back the tattered rag that covered her.

Ahava whispered, "Does she still survive?"

77 . . . 76 . . . 75 . . .

Yeshua gathered Yod into His arms and held her close.

35 . . . 34 . . . 33 . . .

He kissed her bloody cheek and stroked her hair. Tiny stubs that had been feet protruded from His arms. Moments passed as He held her.

16 . . . 15 . . . 14 . . .

The flame of the torch flickered in a sudden wind, then was extinguished.

5 . . . 4 . . . 3 . . . 2 . . .

The smallest of all Israel. The dearest of all in Israel. Yod . . . floating like a little bird above the others. . . .

Three days had passed since Yeshua of Nazareth had gone down into the Valley of Mak'ob to heal the lepers. Of all the 612 afflicted, only Lily and Cantor, healed and whole and waiting, remained now, watching, on the rim high above the valley floor.

The hawk spread his wings and swung in a lazy circle over the place of separation. There was only one man left below of all who had entered that exile of loneliness: His common name was Yeshua, which means "God is Salvation." The prophets who foretold His coming to this valley of suffering called Him the Great Leper. They wrote what the God of Israel had commanded them concerning Messiah: *A Man of Sorrows. Acquainted with Grief.*[2]

But other words of prophecy had come true for the people of the Valley of Mak'ob: *By His wounds we are healed.*[3]

From the top of the precipice Lily and Cantor gazed at the floor of the canyon, where the outcasts of Israel had tended gardens and lived until they died.

The Valley of Israel's Sorrow was vacant. Smokeless, blackened pits punctuated the spaces where only one day before, men and women without hands or feet or faces had spent all their energy keeping the watch fires lit.

Lily stared at the mounds of the cemetery. She fixed her gaze on the open grave where Cantor had lain. She said, "What was here . . . and who we were before he came . . . it will be forgotten, I suppose."

Cantor nodded, testing his voice. "When the time is right, he will call them each by name, like he called me. And they will also hear and come forth healed from their graves. Better than healed. They will walk up the steep path to where we stand now." He stretched his hand up to Hawk in a signal that it was time to go. "Or maybe on that day we will all know how to fly."

Lily smiled softly. "Will you tell me . . . everything?"

Cantor nodded. His eyes reflected light from a distant place. "There is no death there."

"And where he is sending us now? The land where Eden once existed? The land he said is waiting to hear our story—that the Redeemer of Eden has come back?"

Cantor frowned for the first time since he awakened from the long sleep. "It was perfect once. I saw it as it was . . . before. There was no death until there was a murder of brother by brother."

Lily asked, "What was it like?"

"Too much to tell. Beyond beauty . . . beyond fear. Lily, I will never be afraid again. They are all there, waiting for us, and waiting for him to return home." Cantor inclined his head toward Yeshua.

Yeshua sat alone on the broad flat stone where Rabbi Ahava had led the minyan of ten lepers in prayers each morning. Now Yeshua, the Great Leper, healer of all, prayed alone.

Lily wondered aloud, "Cantor, do you think Yeshua will stay here? Do you think since he has healed us all and has taken our disease upon himself . . . do you think he will remain in the Valley? Will he suffer here in the place of those of us who are free?"

Cantor answered, "There are too many lost living in Israel for him to stay here for long. It is written: *He sent forth His Word and healed them; He rescued them from the grave.*[4] And so he still has work to do. It must be fulfilled while he is on earth."

Cantor looked up at the hawk he had trained to hunt—so very long ago it seemed. The arc of the bird's flight grew ever higher, almost to the top of the cliff.

The bird was rising on the prayers of the Messiah, Lily thought. Flying upward with a single purpose: to do the will of the Master.

Through the unbroken spiral of the raptor, a high, shrill cry tore the fabric of the sky.

Yeshua lifted His face, ravaged by the sickness of others. He held up leprous hands in farewell to Hawk. And then He waved to the silent observers who perched on the rim of His suffering.

Cantor cupped perfect fingers around his mouth and shouted down, "Shalom! Yeshua! HaMashiach!"

The stones of the surrounding hills echoed in antiphonal song:

"*Yeshua!*"

"*Mashiyah!*"

"*Shalom!*"

"*Shalom!*"

"*Yeshua!*"

"*Shalom!*"

And there followed on the breeze a scattering of voices, living stones, who watched over the Great Leper from secret places in the cliffs.

"*Give thanks . . .*"

"*To the Lord!*"

"*For He is Good!*"

"*His Love endures forever!*"

"*Forever . . . forever . . . forever . . .*"[5]

Lily whispered, "Though the place is empty except for him, even the stones cry out to praise him!"[6]

When the last echoes died away, Lily and Cantor turned from the Valley of Mak'ob and left that place. Hawk came along, flying from stone to stone, alternately following and preceding the newly created couple as they walked toward the place where Eden had been, to the far country where Yeshua had commanded they must go.

Melchior of Ecbatana leaned against the parapet surrounding the rooftop terrace of his home. The sunset breeze from Mount Alvand was cool on his face. The carved sandstone grapevine atop the balustrade was warm to his touch.

Stretching away to the west were fields and orchards that all belonged to Melchior. Olive trees lost their individuality as a cloak of twilight wrapped them, but the precisely placed rows of the vineyard still pointed unerringly toward the distant peaks and countries beyond.

Though formerly court astronomer to King Phraates of Parthia, Melchior had been a wealthy merchant for the last three of his six decades. Still, his heart frequently wandered among the stars. Moonless nights found him lingering in this spot long after his family was asleep.

More than ever, recently, though Melchior's gaze drank in the heavens, his thoughts went elsewhere. He returned in memory to a journey made years earlier, to someone he had met once, decades before. "It's happening now," he murmured aloud, though alone on the platform. "It must be. He is in his thirties. By now he must be about his Father's business."

"No need to ask who you mean," agreed a familiar soft voice from behind him. Melchior did not have to turn to recognize the intruder.

Esther's arms encircled Melchior, as did the sweet aroma of her lavender perfume when she pressed herself to his back. As she often had over thirty years, Melchior's wife slid round his side to tuck herself beneath his right arm. He drew her close.

"And are the wandering stars as expressive tonight as when they led us to Beth-lehem?"

"See for yourself," Melchior replied, his voice betraying his excitement. He gestured with his free hand toward the dwindling cone of pale blue evening. "By now you can name them as well as I."

Esther peered at the horizon. "Venus, just there," she reported. "Rightly named Splendor, as my grandfather taught you to call it, even before you embraced our faith."

"Go on," Melchior urged.

"The New Moon, of course," she continued. "Which is why we cannot linger here for long. It's New Moon night, and we have guests for supper. I came to fetch you."

"A minute more." The quiver in his words betrayed some as-yet-unexplained significance.

"That faint dot beside the Holy Spirit Moon? Is that Mercury, The Messenger?"

Melchior nodded. "And both The Adam and The Lord of the Sabbath hover just above them," he concluded eagerly. "Mars and Saturn have joined Mercury and Venus in the evening sky. And just for tonight, the New Moon is with them as well."

Now his words tumbled out. "A month ago they were together . . . all except Venus. That vision was my warning to be watching. And see! Tonight four of the five wandering stars and the Moon have all gathered. Close! So close! Half my fist covers them all! Try it." Melchior raised Esther's outstretched arm, urging her to lift her delicate hand beside his own.

"But as Grandfather would have demanded," Esther added, "'what does it mean?'"

Melchior's words turned grave. "I have been studying . . . that," he said, his voice betraying hesitation.

"But you're not yet ready to tell me?"

Melchior shrugged. "Soon, I think." Recognizing his duty to his guests, he said, "We should go down. Unless—" he brightened—"they'd like to see this rare event. I especially want Daniel to see it."

Esther frowned, trouble visible on her features even in the growing shadows. "Joshua's family is here with the others, but Daniel hasn't come home yet. And he sent no word where he'd be."

Daniel ben Melchior squinted out the window at the increasing darkness. The fat, greasy innkeeper of the Jeweled Peacock tavern bustled about. He touched a lit broom straw to the wicks of the oil lamps hanging in the corners of the room. How late was it? Surely sunset had been only moments before.

The slender twenty-two-year-old paused to push a hank of dark hair out of his eyes. "I'm late," Daniel observed. "Better make this my last game." Loading the dice into the throwing cup, he shook out a pair of fours and moved his counters forward on the board.

"You can't quit now," Karek, the thick-lipped ruffian who sat across the table, growled. "It's still early." He poured amber fluid into Daniel's cup, spilling some in the process.

There was a pile of silver tetradrachms in front of Karek and only a half dozen of the coins in front of Daniel.

Daniel shrugged. "Should have been home already. But you're right. Luck's bound to change soon, eh?" His words were slightly slurred. He took a swallow of barley wine and passed his hand across his eyes again.

"Not afraid your wife will lock you out?" Karek sneered.

"No wife," Daniel retorted. "But my—"

Daniel's friend Bartok interrrupted hastily. "He means he has important business early tomorrow. He'll have even more money for you to win off him if this deal goes through."

Staring stupidly at Bartok, Daniel tried to recall what business he had tomorrow. At the moment he could not even remember what day tomorrow was. He grunted. Tomorrow would take care of itself. For now he was behind a month's allowance in his winnings.

Given that fact, why should he quit early? *"Be home in time for the New Moon supper,"* Daniel's mother had warned him. *"Important visitors coming. Rabbi Hasdrubal from Babylon will be here."*

Daniel snorted, then wiped his nose with the sleeve of his robe. Important? Stuffed and pompous, probably. All his father's visitors ever seemed able to discuss were politics, astronomy, and religion. Boring beyond belief. No music. No women. It was bad enough to be stuck here in a backwater place like Ecbatana. But when guests arrived from someplace exciting like Babylon or Ctesiphon, did they ever talk of exciting things? Never!

"You gonna throw or should I do it for you?" Karek demanded.

"Throw? Didn't I just?"

"A double," Bartok hissed. "Go again."

Daniel pursed his lips and rattled the dice cup toward the ceiling as if summoning the goddess Fortune, the way he had seen Karek do. The room swam in front of him, and the lamp flames danced.

Perhaps it was time to go home.

"Tell you what," Daniel said loudly, rubbing the birthmark on his cheek. There were times it seemed to throb. "I'm tired of this game. Stake everything on one throw. What d'ya say?"

"I don't think that's . . . ," Bartok suggested.

"Not up to you," Daniel shushed his friend. Then, to Karek, he demanded, "So?"

Karek frowned. "I go first," he said at last.

Daniel extended the dice cup. Karek snatched it away, then slammed it, mouth downward, on the table. "Six and three," he noted as he removed it. "Now you." Karek retrieved the dice and cup with a flurry of fluttering sleeves and handed them to Daniel.

Carelessly Daniel tossed the bone cubes back onto the table. They landed in a puddle of beer. He leaned forward to peer at the result.

"Dogs!" Karek chuckled at the pair of single dots facing upright. "You lose." He raked over the last of Daniel's coins.

Gaze fixed on nothing, Daniel slurred, "You cheated me. You're a cheat."

"No, no! You don't mean that. . . . He didn't mean that," Bartok corrected urgently. Leaning close to Daniel's ear, he hissed, "Apologize . . . quickly! He'll cut your heart out and eat it. He's killed men for less!"

Daniel shoved his friend away, then looked around to see many unfriendly eyes focused on him. Belated caution struck him. He waved vaguely. "Sorry. Meant nothing by it. Just the drink talkin'." More brightly he added, "Win it back tomorrow."

Karek smirked and said nothing.

Leaning heavily on his friend, Daniel staggered his way out of the inn.

As soon as they were out of earshot, Bartok warned, "Don't ever do that again! You'll get us both killed."

"But he was cheating. I saw it." Birthmark, forehead, and stomach all suddenly churned at once. Daniel was not disposed to argue further. "Feel sick."

"Losing all that money," Bartok guessed.

"No matter. Old man'll give me more. You'll see. Nothing to worry about. But get me out of the street. Gonna be sick for sure."

By the time Bartok assisted Daniel home, the wandering stars had long since vanished into the west. Beneath the torches outside the archway of Melchior's estate, Bartok inspected his friend.

Daniel was now sober enough to correctly interpret Bartok's worried expression. He must look like he'd been drunk for the entire day, which was almost true.

"Maybe I should take you to my house," Bartok offered.

The second son of the House of Melchior the Magus knew what a spectacle he presented: greenish pale, sweaty, stinking of beer and woodsmoke, his eyes bloodshot and his clothing stained. Still, he waved away the cautious suggestion. "Jus' take me to the servants' gate," he instructed. "I'll go straight up to bed. Sick, see? Like the other times. They always believe me. Why not? Iss true. But not see anybody tonight."

"Then they'll worry."

"They don't worry about me!" Daniel argued. "'Sides, just tell Cook you brought me home sick. She'll tell Mother. Good enough." Bracing himself on the wall and wondering if he could make it upstairs on his own, Daniel added, "Father won't even notice I'm gone. Jabber, jabber. He sits up talking. Jabbering," he repeated. He was confused to see a third torch appear between the two flanking the portal. Were his eyes playing more tricks on him?

"Planning to lie your way out of this one too?" a gruff voice demanded impatiently. "Go away, Bartok. I'll take him from here."

Scarcely pausing to call out a "good night," Bartok scurried off.

Daniel groaned. This was the worst possible development: being found by his older brother, Joshua. Father would express disapproval, and Mother would act grieved, but Joshua! His self-righteous sneering was more than Daniel could bear.

"Leave me alone," Daniel asserted, drawing himself upright and lurching forward. "Don't need your help."

Joshua snorted and grabbed Daniel firmly by the elbow. "And let you embarrass Father in front of his guests? You're right. We're going around the back." He sniffed and shook his head. "I should make you sleep with the goats . . . you smell bad enough! Only then I'd be in trouble with Mother, so I'll see you get into bed. But I won't lie for you."

"And you'll so enjoy telling them the truth," Daniel added.

Joshua squeezed a little harder than necessary and dragged his brother a little faster than Daniel's stumbling steps could match. "I don't understand you," he scolded. "Ten years ago, when I was your age, I—"

"You were already running the family olive oil business . . . had a wife . . . went to synagogue every morning . . . I know, I know. Stop talking, won't you? My head is splitting."

With Joshua's greater height and greater strength it was easy for him to grab Daniel's other elbow and shake him. "You embarrass *me*!" he hissed. "Why can't you grow up?"

Daniel felt as if the dice were now inside his head, rattling around. "Why? Just because you were a grumpy old man at age thirteen, should I give up my friends?"

"Your friends?" Joshua sneered, dragging Daniel again. "Your friends only care about you because you buy them drinks and lose money to them. How much did you lose today, anyway?"

Daniel tried to ignore the question, but when Joshua threatened to shake him again, he answered, "Nothing. Ten silver pieces."

It was another lie. The real number was nearly double that figure, and they had been tetradrachms, each worth four denarii. So the true loss was eighty silver pieces.

The fictitious lower figure was already enough to scandalize Joshua.

"Ten silver pieces? Nearly two weeks' labor for a skilled workman? Do you think money grows on trees?"

Daniel thought of a clever remark about how for an olive oil merchant, money did grow on trees, but he wisely refrained from uttering it.

Besides, Joshua's conversation had already moved on as they reached the servants' entry. "I think Father should cut off your allowance until you prove you deserve it. You need to be taught a lesson. This is the last time you'll come home drunk!"

"Just . . . just stop shouting, will you?" Daniel asked. "Let me go to bed. Fix my miserable life tomorrow, but tonight leave me be."

igh Priest Caiaphas strode along the parapet of Nicanor Gate. The terrace atop the building was for the private use of the high priest in his reflections and prayers. From its summit he viewed the sacrifices being carried out in front of the sanctuary to the west. He could also observe the monetary offerings brought to the courtyard in the east.

But on this nighttime occasion it was the north that drew his attention. Just beyond the northern rim of the Temple Mount reared the flaming torches outlining the Antonia, the Roman assertion of authority over all things Jewish.

As Caiaphas kept watch over his flock, so too, in turn, Rome supervised him.

He clasped and unclasped pudgy fingers as he probed his father-in-law's opinions. "More and more of them show up here each day."

"Frauds," Annas asserted forcefully. "No leper is really ever healed. This wild tale of the Valley of Mak'ob being emptied, of all the lepers cured—it's nonsense."

"But the Valley is empty! If they aren't healed, if they're still diseased, there will be panic. Fear of plague coming here."

"And if you agree they are truly healed, then you admit the claims of this healer, this Nazarean."

Caiaphas nodded grimly and shook a forefinger toward the Antonia. "And that message we cannot allow to reach the ear of Rome. But how do we stop it?"

Annas' bushy eyebrows drew together in thought before he announced, "Simple. When any of the so-called healed appear here, let them be arrested. That news will spread quickly enough. Then, no more claims." He brushed his hands together briskly to demonstrate how easily the matter could be resolved.

"But others'll still carry the tale elsewhere!"

Annas did not look perturbed. "Send a message to Lord Antipas. The Valley is in his territory. Let him handle it. You worry about Yerushalayim. Everywhere else is his problem."

Melchior was in his study. With him were his guests, Rabbi Sheramin of Ecbatana; Melchior's friendly business competitor, Solomon ben Levy; and the famous Rabbi Hasdrubal of Babylon.

Hasdrubal was speaking. The stout scholar had a shock of white hair combed back from his forehead. Quizzical blue eyes regarded Melchior from over a prominent hooked nose.

Hasdrubal spread his hands in deprecation. "With all due respect to our host, surely we have seen messianic pretenders before this. Always they come to a bad end. Always they cause tumult. Always misguided and foolish commoners lose their lives to no purpose. Why does the good Magus think this occasion any different?"

Ben Levy spoke up on behalf of his friend. "Have you forgotten what occurred thirty-some years ago? It wasn't only Melchior who followed the miraculous conjunction and saw the babe, but also Balthasar of this city—a great Magus and man of great faith. Joining them were men of many distant lands . . . the Indies, Africa, Tarsus in Pamphyllia. . . . Surely you do not say they all agreed on the same false tale or dreamed the same dream?"

"No, no," Hasdrubal argued. "I mean no disrespect to Melchior, or to the others you name. But where is the proof the one they found survived? Did you not say Herod the Butcher King murdered the babies in Beth-lehem? How do you know if the one you met still lives?"

Melchior tapped his chest. "I know it . . . in here."

"But where is he, then?" Sheramin demanded. "Why has he not declared himself?"

"Perhaps he has," ben Levy added quietly. "Reports have come from Judea of a man . . . some say a prophet . . . preaching repentance and baptizing in the Jordan."

Hasdrubal shook his head dismissively. "Your news is old. His name is Yochanan. Prophet or not, he has fallen into the clutches of Herod Antipas. They say he's already dead." The rabbi sounded doubtful anyone ever escaped the grasp of a Herod. "But tell us, Melchior, what you saw in the sky tonight. I heard wonder in your voice as you described it to us. I confess I am no student of the stars, though I honor their Maker. What does it mean?"

"More than ever," Melchior returned thoughtfully, "I miss the wise counsel of my wife's grandfather, Old Balthasar. He was a true sage . . . a wise man in the tradition of the ancients. But since you ask, here are my thoughts: The amazing conjunction we saw tonight—five of the seven lights of the menorah—was entirely contained within the sign of the Bull . . . what the Egyptians call Apis and the Greeks Taurus. What we call Shor. Disregarding what the heathen do, what use do we make of bullocks?"

"They are sacrificed as thank-offerings," Sheramin replied. "When the Almighty has answered our prayers, delivered us from danger, forgiven us great wrongs and restored our lives, or when a task of great importance is complete, then we give him a bullock as a thank-offering."

"Just so," Melchior agreed. "When something of great significance has been completed, there is still a sacrifice to be made."

"I do not understand," Hasdrubal argued. "What has this to do with Messiah?"

"I think his mission is already coming to its climax," Melchior said. "He who is the Splendor of the Almighty, The Lord of the Sabbath, the Heavenly Adam, and the Divine Messenger, empowered by the *Ruach HaKodesh*—combining all those titles in himself, just as we saw tonight—for him, the thank-offering of conclusion is coming soon."

"But, good friend," Sheramin disagreed, "your sign would seem to say not that the Chosen One would make a sacrifice, but that he would *be* the sacrifice."

"I know," Melchior replied softly. "I do not yet understand, yet I see the same conclusion myself. What does the prophet Isaias say? *He was pierced for our transgressions, He was crushed for our iniquities. . . . By His wounds we are healed.*"[7]

"But this Yochanan, called the Baptizer. He's already been killed," ben Levy said flatly.

Melchior put his hands flat on the table in front of him. "I have had word . . . of another. Let me tell you about him."

Rabbi Hasdrubal was up early. It was still half an hour until sunrise, but today he was returning to Babylon. His caravan would leave shortly after morning rays lit the peak of Mount Alvand.

Just now he, Melchior, and Rabbi Sheramin were again on Melchior's rooftop, this time looking east. Floating above the plain that stretched dawnward from Ecbatana was Jupiter—Tzadik. The Righteous.

"*The sun of righteousness will rise, with healing in its wings,*" Melchior murmured.[8]

"Eh? What's that you quoted?" Hasdrubal inquired.

Motioning with his right hand, Melchior drew an imaginary circle around the wandering star called The Righteous. "The Prophet Malachi," he explained. "You recall I told you last night that only Tzadik and Holy Fire—the Sun—were missing from the menorah we all saw in the sky? But see where the Sun and Righteousness rise together!"

While the trio of scholars peered toward the east, the rim of the world paled, then grayed, then silvered, with the coming day.

"I have heard it said that when the prophet wrote *wings*, he was speaking of the fringes of Messiah's prayer shawl," Sheramin put in.

"So the sages agree," Hasdrubal concurred. "The Anointed One, the Messiah, will have such power and authority that just touching the hem of his garment will cure disease. But Melchior, once more I must ask: How do you know that these signs in the heavens show us that Messiah is here now? It seems dangerously close to fortune-telling and sorcery."

Sheramin made the sign against the evil eye, spitting over the parapet between two fingers, but Melchior was not disturbed by the implication.

"It is true that Jupiter and the Sun have often risen together without blessing the words of the prophet Malachi," Melchior agreed. "But see where they are?" He gestured again toward the sky. "Both Sun and Righteousness are in The Two Fish—symbol of the nation of Israel. The same constellation in which we followed his Star thirty years ago!"

"So it is a definite sign?" Hasdrubal demanded.

"It is a definite reminder," Melchior offered, "or so insisted Old Balthasar. 'Test every spirit,' he said. 'Search the Scriptures and see if everything—every single signal—agrees with all the prophets have said. If he fails in one thing, he is a false prophet and not Messiah.'"⁹

"And this Yeshua of Nazareth, of whom you spoke—does he have the gift of healing?"

"Miracles follow him wherever he goes," Melchior confirmed.

"Someone must go and investigate," Sheramin ventured. "This matter is too important to rely on the gossip of pilgrims and the hearsay evidence of camel drovers."

"Why not you, Melchior?" Hasdrubal suggested. "You were witness to him as a baby. Shouldn't you be the one to seek him again?"

Melchior frowned as he tugged his beard thoughtfully. "I intended to leave a year ago, but I am not allowed to. King Artabanus says he needs my advice in dealing with the civil unrest in Media, and as envoy to the Lords of the Marsh . . . that he cannot spare me for such a long journey."

"You think this is an excuse to keep you from going? Why?"

Raising his chin, Melchior stared at Jupiter. "The king read my report of the babe. He knows I am a convert to our Jewish faith. He knows I went to worship beside the cradle three decades ago. Herod, may his name be blotted out of all memory, is not the only king who fears for his throne. Artabanus knows Messiah will command the loyalty of all the Jews in Parthia when he comes."

"And he's right," Hasdrubal agreed. "Though I think Lord Caiaphas, high priest in Jerusalem, looks more to Rome than to heaven for his obedience. I will pray on the matter," the rabbi concluded. "And for you. Tell your son Daniel I'm sorry it didn't work out. Perhaps another time."

4

CHAPTER

ily had not seen Hawk for some time. He had soared in lazy circles above them, only to suddenly fold his wings into a powerful dive and disappear behind a knoll. She was not concerned over his absence. Hawk always reappeared, or was found to be waiting for them on branch or boulder, as if he knew in advance exactly what path they'd follow.

This time was no exception, but Lily and Cantor found more than Hawk when they next saw him.

His russet feathers catching the sunlight in a sheen like burnished bronze, Hawk perched on the highest of a pile of ten stones. The heap marked one of the boundary points defining the Valley of Mak'ob.

Beside the warning mound was another stack, but not of rocks and stones. Inside a makeshift hutch of fallen branches and ragged cloth was a supply of unleavened bread, dried fish, preserved figs, and a round of hard cheese.

It was one of the donations friends of those condemned to Mak'ob sometimes left outside the Valley for those confined within.

"Look, Cantor," Lily exulted. "There's no one left in the Valley now! We can use this as provision for our journey."

"Too much for us, really," Cantor noted. "We can't even carry that much."

The clatter of hooves picking through loose stone made them turn. The newcomer was only a man leading a donkey on which rode a small boy.

The man was puffing, as if he had been hurrying for some time. The donkey appeared footsore, making him pull back against the lead rope and double the man's effort.

Without even pausing for breath, the man launched into an inquiry. "Did you . . . see him?" he panted. "Is he nearby? Yeshua, the Healer? Do you know where he is?"

Lily was surprised and disconcerted. "You were on the main path into the Valley? And you didn't see him?"

The man, energy seemingly spent, put hands to knees and bent over, gasping. Cantor took the lead rope from the man's hand, receiving a jerking nod of thanks.

Cantor smiled at the boy. He was about eight, Lily thought. Then Lily saw her husband's smile freeze on his face. Following the line of his wrinkled brow, Lily's gaze took in the child's legs. One was sound and whole.

The other was withered and the foot turned inward.

"Oh, Cantor, no!" Lily gasped. "He must still be here! He must!"

"We're too late," the man said miserably. "I hurried . . . fast as I could. The donkey turned up lame, you see. And when I came . . . to the fork . . . I didn't know. . . . I chose wrong," he concluded apologetically. He stretched with a heavy sigh, then stood beside his son and ruffled the boy's hair. "Aaron. Just let me . . . rest a little."

Aaron patted his father's arm, the child doing the consoling. "It's all right, Father. You'll see."

I'm praying again, God of All Mercies. You see how much this father loves his son. Is there no miracle left for them?

Why did Cantor not say something?

Cantor's eyes were locked on Hawk's unblinking golden stare, as if reading some message there. Abruptly he said, "Lily, come here and stand beside me." When she complied, wondering what was in his thoughts, he suggested, "Didn't Yeshua commission us to be his witnesses?" Without waiting for her response, he said, "But we were wrong about our duty beginning in Narda. Our job begins . . . here. Hold my hand. Put your other hand on Aaron's left shoulder and I'll do the same on the right."

Their fingers interlocked, Lily felt tingling warmth flowing throughout her body and into Aaron's thin frame. Her spirit was timid at first, then soared as she heard Cantor pray: "O Lord, God of the Universe. In the Name of the Healer of Israel, Yeshua of Nazareth, we bring Aaron before you now. We ask for your straightening, strengthening touch. Yeshua heals lepers and raises the dead. Yeshua would not refuse this request. This family's need is not too great, or too big a demand. See the father's faith and make his journey as if he had met Yeshua on the way. This we humbly ask."

"Pins and needles, Father," Aaron said. "Prickles."

I'm praying again, God Who Made Me Whole, you who raised Cantor from the dust of death. Won't you show your mercy yet again?

Before Lily had completed her prayer, Hawk launched himself skyward with pulsing wings and a great triumphant cry that rang over the hills.

Aaron's father stepped back from his son, stumbling over a fist-sized stone. "Aaron! You . . ."

The boy looked down at his now perfectly strong, matching limbs and a wide, gap-toothed grin spread across his features. "See, Father! Pick me down."

And then, as if to prove it was no dream, Aaron jumped from the donkey's back and ran a quick circle around the animal before rushing to give his father a hug. "Thank you. Thank you for believing what I said about Yeshua! Thank you for taking me."

"But, Son, thank these . . ."

Cantor shook his head. "Not us. Give glory to God and praise him in Yeshua's name. But tell no one outside your village," he cautioned. "It might be dangerous for the boy."

"I understand . . . yes, certainly. But what can I do for you? Is there no need of yours I can meet? Anything at all?"

Cantor began to shake his head again, then stopped abruptly. Lily followed his gaze to where it rested on the beast of burden.

Minutes later, from the top of the next knoll, Lily turned back to wave to the father and son as they skipped and danced the path toward home. Lily walked alongside as Cantor led their new donkey, loaded with all the provisions of Mak'ob—a donkey now perfectly sound, and not lame at all.

There was an annoying bird chirping outside Daniel's window. He could not understand what the creature found to be so cheerful about this morning, and he wished it would stop. Daniel's head felt twice normal size. The bedclothes were glued to his body and his eyes were gummed shut. Orange light illuminated the insides of his eyelids. Daniel had heard carts going in and out the courtyard gate long before, so he knew it was late morning.

He groaned. The memory of last night's drinking and gambling came back with a rush. So did his encounter with Joshua. How much trouble was he in?

Cautiously he turned his head away from the light and arched his neck to see if the kink would go away. That's when he heard someone clear his throat. The sound came from the direction of the chair beside the window. The single muffled rasp was enough for Daniel to identify the source: his father.

There was no use pretending to still be asleep. Father might not say anything, but he would remain rooted until this confrontation was over.

Might as well face it and be done. Daniel turned toward the sound. "Good morning, Father," he said, scratching his beard with both hands and opening one eye.

Melchior sat facing him, chin resting on interlocked fingers. "I checked on you last night. You looked then like you might die. You don't look much better now. How much did you drink?"

Daniel shook his head carefully. "Just enough to go with a friendly game of Twenty Squares."

Melchior snorted. "And how much money did you lose? Joshua said ten silver pieces, but I'm guessing you lied to him."

Turning his face away, Daniel muttered, "Joshua . . . couldn't wait to tell you, eh?"

Melchior said nothing for a moment, then remarked, "Rabbi Hasdrubal said he was sorry to hear you were sick and sorry to have missed seeing you this trip."

Adopting a penitent tone, Daniel said, "I'm sorry, Father. I lost track of the time. You know how it is."

"No," Melchior corrected, "I don't know how it is. But I do know this cannot go on."

This level tone worried Daniel. There was no anger in Melchior's voice, just frustration and firm resolution.

"You are old enough to take an active role in the family business, but can I trust you with the simplest duty? Your sisters are married and provided for. Joshua is proving that when the time comes, he will preserve the two-thirds of my estate to which he is entitled. But what about you? How long would it take you to go through your third of the property?"

This was serious. His father was talking about dying. Daniel turned over and sat up, propping his head against the wall. "You aren't . . . you're not sick?"

"Nothing like it," Melchior replied. "Unless worried sick about you counts as an illness. Ever since losing the twins, your mother and I have doted on you. Clearly we've done you more harm than good."

"Don't say that, Father," Daniel begged. "I can do better."

"I'd like to believe that," Melchior said doubtfully. "What happened to the boy who was stuck to my side every observation night? The one who could name all the constellations without missing any? Where has he gone, and who is this . . . drunken lump who has taken his place?"

There was no response to this, and Daniel did not offer one.

Melchior continued, "Rabbi Hasdrubal had asked if you'd like to accompany him back to Babylon, to study there for a year. We were going to surprise you with it last night, but . . ."

Daniel groaned again. A chance to get out of Ecbatana, to see something of the world. "Can't I catch up to him? They can't be farther than the first caravansary up the mountain."

Melchior fixed a stern eye on his youngest child. "If you cannot be trusted within a mile of your home, what makes you think I would trust you in a big city? No, Daniel. You'll have to prove yourself to me. Starting today, starting now. I've thought it over, and I know what is needed."

"Anything. Tell me what it is."

"Get washed and dressed and come down. We'll discuss it then."

It was nearing the noon hour by the time Daniel was clean, dressed, and able to make his way downstairs. He hoped the house would be empty. This was market day. His mother and the servants should be away shopping while his father and brother pursued business.

Daniel recalled something his father had asked him to do yesterday, before Daniel had stopped off in the tavern. He felt at first embarrassed and then bitter at the recollection. He really had intended to follow his father's instructions. It wasn't his fault the ale had been stronger than usual or that the time had slipped away so unnoticed. Anyway, he could make up for that error today. Father wanted him to inspect the grapevines in the wadi at the far west of the property and report on this year's growth. If Daniel could just grab a bite and get out of the house unseen, by tonight he'd be able to reappear in a more virtuous light.

The kitchen, where Daniel expected a handful of bread and dried figs, was through the dining room. Pushing aside the curtain covering the portal, he barged ahead . . . straight into an assembly of his father and mother, brother and sister-in-law.

"Sorry," Daniel apologized, trying to back away. "Didn't mean to interrupt."

"Come in, Daniel," Melchior instructed. "We've been waiting for you."

Of the four pairs of eyes studying him, Daniel saw sympathy in only his mother's. She stood and came to his side. "Here," she said. "Sit and have something to eat." She poured water into a mug for him and selected two slices of muskmelon from a platter to slide across on his plate.

"What's this about?" Daniel made the effort to sound unconcerned while knowing he had failed. He took a sip of water but pushed the dish of melon away.

Joshua regarded him coldly, but his wife Vashti's face displayed self-satisfied amusement. From the arched eyebrows and mocking smile with which she greeted him, Daniel imagined she had recently offered one of her favorite expressions: "I told you so."

"I've let you down, Daniel," Melchior asserted. "I don't know when it happened, but you've lost direction in your life."

"It's not . . . I mean, I can do better. . . ."

"Please don't interrupt," Melchior said sternly. "I see now that giving you tasks to do for me but not supervising the results has brought you to this point. You think it's all pointless make-work and can be ignored. I hoped by sending you out on different errands you'd find the part of my business you liked best and wanted to pursue. Instead you have gotten lazy, careless, and foolish. All that will stop today."

"Whatever you say, Father," Daniel agreed.

"I am opening a new trade in woven goods. I will not have time to supervise everything here as I have before, so I'm promoting Joshua to be over all operations in Ecbatana."

"So?" Daniel said. "Then congratulations, Joshua." The elder brother scowled; his wife smirked. "But what's this to do—"

"You're to be his assistant. You'll report to him every morning and every night; you'll also learn accounting from Vashti."

"Accounting? Father, I have no head for—"

"In six months we'll see if you are capable of more responsibilities, but for now this is how it must be. No more allowance. You get paid every Sabbath eve, like the others. If you fail at a task, it comes out of your weekly income. Do you understand?"

Daniel was stunned. He was to work for his brother? Joshua and Vashti could tattle to Father about whatever they pleased . . . and Daniel's spending money depended on keeping those two happy?

"But . . . but . . . the others will see me taking orders and they won't obey me."

"Already thought of that," Joshua snapped. "Lono will accompany you. He'll act as your steward in giving out orders. Just remember: You don't do anything unless I tell you to first!"

And Lono would also keep ever-present watch on Daniel. The household slave had never been known to lie and he could not be bribed. This was a disaster!

Daniel looked from face to face, trying to find some wiggle room in this mess. His mother dropped her eyes to her lap. Melchior regarded him thoughtfully. Joshua's and Vashti's outthrust chins appeared to dare him to argue.

Daniel swallowed his pride. "I'll do whatever you ask, Father. And I'll make you proud."

"By the way," Melchior added, his stern tone softening slightly, "you told the truth about being cheated. That tavern rat Karek bragged about it and was caught with weighted dice."

Remembering what a dangerous character Karek was, Daniel was not sure whether to feel vindicated or worried. "What will happen to him?"

"Not our concern," Melchior said. "Stick to your own business only . . . starting today."

It was almost Sabbath. The sun was low on the western horizon. Lily looked over her shoulder. "The sun is still shining in Yerushalayim." She was already longing for home, for Israel. Even the hawk had seemed reluctant to leave the familiar terrain of Judea. Now he hunted, bringing back quail from the wilderness, one at a time.

"No one in my family has ever been so far from home," Lily said. "Not since the time of Jeremiah."

"We follow the path of the exiles," Cantor said.

"May it please the Lord, who sent us out to bring good news to the exiles of Israel, to also bring us home one day soon!"

Lily and Cantor made camp on the bank of the Jabbok River, at the place where the patriarch Jacob wrestled the Angel of the Lord throughout the night.

Hawk did not fly over the river to hunt in the wilderness beyond the border of ancient Perea. At least this side of the Jabbok was governed from Jerusalem. Beyond the placid waters of the Jordan's tributary was the land of the Gentiles. The demon gods Marduk and Ba'al ruled the hearts of men beyond the water.

Hawk perched on a broken stump and observed his master and Lily as they prepared for the coming day of rest.

Cantor stacked wood and built a roaring fire. Lily roasted quail, enough to last from evening through the next day.

"Our last watch fire within sight of Israel," Cantor said with satisfaction. "After Sabbath we'll cross over."

Cantor took Lily's hand and led her to the water. A great mound of stones stood on the opposite shore. "The name of this place is Peniel, Face of God. It was at this very place when Ya'acov was returning home ʽer his exile that the Lord changed his name to Isra'el."

"I've never been outside, Cantor. I'm afraid."

He squeezed her hand. They stooped beside the flowing steam. Pebbles, worn smooth by thousands of years beneath the current, glistened in the water.

"When Ya'acov, now named Isra'el, came home, his feet touched those very stones. He was returning to claim his birthright at last. A different man than when he left. He crossed over and, just here, he laughed and stood knee-deep in the water. Before he took his last step onto the land, he plucked pebbles from this very shore to give to his sons. These small stones that remain in the Jabbok contain the joy of seeing the Lord face-to-face. They were witnesses of the blessing of our father Isra'el."[10]

Lily gave Cantor a sideways glance. "How do you know such things?"

Cantor smiled wistfully. "One day I'll tell you."

Lily's hair prickled as she saw some distant light in Cantor's eyes. "Soon? I want to know . . . everything."

Cantor brushed aside her curiosity. "It's almost twilight. Our last Sabbath on this side. Gather our blessings from the shore of our home, Lily. To bless tonight and carry away with us."

She hesitated, then nodded and plunged her hands into the water. By the last glimmer of sunlight she selected ten smooth stones of Israel's blessing.

I'm praying again, Namer of Isra'el, I'm asking. I'm praying for every descendant of Avraham, Yitz'chak, and Ya'acov. I am praying again for me and Cantor. For every exile from the land of your covenant. May we carry your promises to Isra'el with us in our hearts. May we bring them home again to praise you in Yerushalayim and in Eretz-Israel soon.

Variegated colors shone rich and vibrant in her dripping palms. The stones where Jacob rejoiced. The promises of God to Eretz-Israel, more precious and beautiful than jewels!

Cantor placed his hands over hers as the sun slipped away. Together they recited the Shema, as Jacob must have heard it from the Angel of the Lord when he saw God face-to-face and lived to tell about it. "Hear, O Israel: The Lord our God, the Lord is one. The Lord is one."[11]

Hawk sprang from his branch and soared high above them for a time. The rays of sunlight over Eretz-Israel still shone on his wings, seeming to bear him up, as the shadows lengthened below.

Lono's constantly cheerful disposition was in direct contrast to his name, which he translated "rain." He was taller than Daniel, as tall as Joshua in fact, but much broader and much thicker. Add to that bulk his mound of unruly, wiry black hair, and Lono filled any doorway in which he stood.

Captured by Arab slave traders from some distant eastern isle while still a small child, Lono could not recall ever being free. He had been with Melchior's family from before Daniel's birth, had always been part of the household as far as Daniel was concerned.

Daniel had never seen the slave's tattooed face angry, but he had seen ample demonstration of the islander's immense strength. When Daniel was eight, Lono shepherded him at play in the family oil warehouse. As Daniel darted in and out of the rows of stacked amphorae, Ecbatana was struck by one of the earthquakes that frequently rattled the Zagros Mountains. Daniel froze in terror as several piles of empty clay jars, each as tall as he but stacked six high, tottered and leaned toward him.

Heedless of the pots already crashing around them, Lono held up a heap of swaying jars with one beamlike arm. With the other he swept

Daniel to safety beneath his chest while he braced another collapsing stack with his back. When the tremor subsided, Daniel emerged from beneath an archway formed of the only unshattered jars in the room.

Daniel had many reasons to be grateful for Lono's presence in their household, but sometimes the slave's willingness to accept whatever life brought was too much for Daniel to endure.

Today was one of those days.

"Putting me under my brother and sister-in-law," Daniel griped, "makes me like a scribe instead of an heir."

"But Mastah Melchior say you get bettuh place soon. Show Mastah Joshua what you can do."

"If I have to please my brother in order to impress my father, it'll never happen," Daniel moaned. "Don't you understand? I can't do anything right as far as he is concerned. And having Vashti check my accounts? That woman chews silver and spits copper! Money runs in her veins, not blood."

"This no good way to start," Lono rumbled. "You smart. You learn quick; get bettuh job soon, eh?"

Daniel shook his head. "I'll do it, but I won't like it."

"So," Lono said with satisfaction, "we go now?"

"We're going to visit Mina first. She hasn't seen me in days, and the way Joshua and Vashti spread stories about me, there's no telling what she's heard."

"You do pretty good job spreading stories 'bout yourself," Lono corrected. "Bad idea to make brudda angry for you come late."

"You're not my brother or my father," Daniel corrected angrily. "And we're wasting time. Come on."

Herod Antipas grabbed a handful of scruffy beard and flabby cheek. "I know what he's up to. Caiaphas will use these wild tales of healed lepers to discredit me with the governor. He'll make it my fault that the lepers have all escaped the Valley of Despair. What can I do?" The goblet shook in his trembling fingers, slopping wine on his chin and chest.

"Calm yourself," Herodias instructed her husband. "No matter what Caiaphas says, any lepers who arrive in Yerushalayim are his problem, not ours."

"But what about the rest? We don't know where this Yeshua hides out. What if he's forming a rebel army right now? What?"

Antipas' wife had sharp features—an angular nose, chin, and cheekbones. When she was plotting, she became even more vixenlike in appearance . . . and ruthless.

"Kill them," she said bluntly. "Double the guard at the border crossings from your territory to anywhere else. Demand 'where from,' 'where to,' and 'why' from every traveler. Arrest any who mention leprosy, Mak'ob, or Yeshua. Arrest them and make them disappear. Honestly, Antipas, you make things much more difficult than they really are. By taking such forceful action, you will look good to Rome . . . not feeble, like the high priest."

"Thank you, my dear," Antipas returned. "You comfort me."

She kissed his forehead.

The Herodian guard sergeant was not pleased with the Syrian nags he had been allotted for this scouting mission. The mounts were fractious, sawing and biting at the bits, skittering sideways at every scrap of weed blowing in the wind. Here on the rim of the Valley of Mak'ob the horses pranced about even worse, making it nearly impossible to survey the scene below.

With a savage yank on the reins he fought his stallion to a standstill. Removing his conical helmet and wiping his brow on the sleeve of his green tunic, the sergeant reflected on his fate. Officers always expected their sergeants to do the impossible with the unmanageable. The two troopers detailed to ride with him—both raw recruits, one Samaritan and the other Idumean—were as bad as the riding stock.

"Get on down there," the sergeant commanded. "One to the north end, the other south. Search the caves especially. Round up and detain anyone you find."

"There's nobody down there, Sergeant," the Samaritan noted, peering into the depths.

"No smoke, no fires, nobody movin'," his Idumean comrade agreed.

"So? Then what are you waiting for?"

"Well, it's this way, see," the Samaritan whined. "It ain't natural, like."

"Yeah. Where'd they all go? Up in smoke?" the Idumean added doubtfully, his neck twisting about as if he expected the former inhabitants of Mak'ob to rematerialize right beside him.

"Lepers don't just vanish," the sergeant scolded. "Our job is to bring Lord Antipas a report."

"But. . . . lepers?" the Idumean repeated, gnawing his lower lip.

"Are you afraid?" the sergeant demanded, his voice an angry shout. The back of his own neck prickled as a faint echo from the valley replied, *"Afraid . . . afraid . . . afraid . . ."*

"Not of no Jew livin'," the Samaritan replied stoutly. "But don't they call lepers 'the living dead'? And now this. It ain't natural, I say."

"All right," the sergeant said, slashing his mount with his crop. "We'll go together. Come on."

6

It is written that he who has heard the music of *olam haba* and returns knows how to praise all things extravagantly.

A patch of blackberries grew beside the highway. "Just for us," Lily said as they waded into them.

Cantor plucked one and held it up to examine the geometric pattern of the berry. "A miracle." He held it to his nose and inhaled the scent, then brought it to his ear as if it could whisper a message.

"What is the berry saying to you, Cantor?"

He did not hesitate. "Fear not. Fear nothing. Fear no man. Fear no moment. That is what the miracle of one blackberry or one blade of grass or . . . well, look." He swept his hand across the horizon. "Fear not."

Cantor had not seen all of The World to Come. He admitted this. Only a glimpse. A fragment on the edge of what was Everything. But he had seen and heard and smelled and tasted enough to know. . . .

This world? A reflection in a pool. One stone and the image is shattered; the vision ripples away.

And yet, it seemed to Lily that every sense in this world now seemed immense to Cantor.

Berry. Plum. Pear. Apple and pomegranate. Cantor savored flavors like visions of color, rejoiced in the simple things as much as in a cloud-burst when the sun breaks through or the rolling of thunder before a rainbow arches across the sky.

"Heaven is so much . . . more," he said, tasting a single blackberry, pausing as if to consider the sensations dancing on his tongue for the first time. He grinned from among the blackberry vines. "Wonderful. Wonderful. Yes, Lily. It is written in the juice of a blackberry. Inscribed on my tongue. Fear not."

An hour later, as they drew near the border crossing, Lily clutched Cantor's arm. Her anxiety increased with each passing step. Why was she so frightened? Was it because her only previous trip out of the Valley had been so filled with danger and heartache?

But then she had still been a leper. That journey, fearful as it was, ended in triumph, not tragedy, at the feet of Yeshua of Nazareth.

Yet she could not, by any act of her will, make her pulse stop racing or slow her breathing. Could Cantor feel her heart pounding in the touch of their hands?

"Don't be afraid," he said. "We have done nothing wrong. He who sent us knows every step we take before we ever took the first."

Lily nodded. *I'm praying again, Lord of All the Angel Armies. You would not bring us this far to abandon us, would you? You are the Good Shepherd. You rescue from danger, and all your paths are true. As David, the man after your own heart, wrote: I will fear no evil, for you are with me.*[12]

A piercing cry from overhead drew Lily's view upward. Hawk, circling on unseen currents of air, drifted in lazy spirals above their heads.

Lord of All the Angel Armies, Lily added, *do we have angel guardians as real as Hawk? Do they circle above us, seeing farther than we are able to see?*

Though Lily heard the noise of a group of travelers coming behind them along the trail, ahead of them the crossing was empty. A guard, wearing armor but no helmet, lounged against a lean-to shelter, taking advantage of the only shade. He looked bored and barely straightened from his slouch at their approach. He did not bother to retrieve his spear from where it lay in the dust.

"Where are you going?" he demanded perfunctorily.

Cantor replied for them both. "My wife and I are going to Narda."

"Narda, eh?" the guard repeated. "Why Narda?"

"To show ourselves to the priest there," Cantor replied truthfully.

The guard shrugged. There were priests much closer than Narda, but pilgrims sometimes made unaccountable vows. Besides, the guard was not a Levite. He was a civilian employed by Herod Antipas to curb smuggling. These two souls had nothing worth stealing, let alone worth smuggling. It was no business of his what awkward oaths they had made.

"Pass," he said, jerking his thumb over his shoulder.

Beyond the checkpoint the road rose into the hills in a series of switchbacks. At the midpoint of each traverse, the shape of the natural bowl carried the sounds from below as well as a distant view.

On the third crossing of the slope Lily heard the approach of a galloping horse. A rider, dressed in Antipas' livery, scattered the band of pilgrims with the violence of his arrival. With a savage tug on the reins, he skidded his mount to a stop beside the guard, who jumped to attention.

"New orders," Lily heard the courier bark. "Pay attention to anyone mentioning Mak'ob or leprosy. To anyone talking of healing or miracles or such claptrap."

"And do what?" the border sentry demanded, hastily donning his helmet and grabbing his spear.

"Detain them and notify your captain. Fail and it's your neck."

Then the messenger clattered off to the north, in the direction of the next crossing point.

I'm praying again, Great Leper. You who have our names engraved on the palms of your hands.[13]

Bartok was out of breath and panting as if he had been running. "Daniel," he said urgently, "I've been looking everywhere for you." Bartok leaned on the doorway of the office, wheezing.

"So?" Daniel returned, not raising his eyes from the column of figures he was reviewing. He could not seem to reconcile the remaining inventory of last year's oil amphorae with the total of a recent shipment to Ctesiphon, a number of jars broken in a warehouse mishap, and a few containers that had turned rancid and had to be discarded.

The amount left on hand was higher than it should be. Not long ago Daniel's attitude would have been to be pleased with a positive discrepancy and ignore the conflicting sums.

Now he was rabidly pursuing the errant figures. Daniel would not give up without correcting the mistake. This time, he was certain, he would find both problem and solution before Vashti ever noticed the error.

"So?" he repeated. "I've been here in the countinghouse all day. What's the urgent news? Is Rome invading Ecbatana? Has Queen Esther come back from the dead? Is a new Haman threatening us? What, Bartok? Speak!"

Bartok managed to look wounded despite the sweat pouring down his face. "What's happened to you? Here I am, bearing the most exciting news ever to reach Ecbatana, and you can't be bothered? If I'm wasting your time, just say so!"

Drawing in a deep breath and letting it go with a prolonged sigh, Daniel flung the stylus onto the floor and pushed the wax tablet away. Fingering the birthmark on his cheek, he stretched neck and shoulders before facing his friend. "You have my attention. But this better be good."

"Aren't you the one who says nothing exciting ever happens here?" Bartok demanded. "You remember when we heard a trader was bringing an elephant for delivery to some Armenian warlord? You and I watched the caravansary for days! Remember? Well, this is bigger than the elephant."

"I seem to recall that the elephant was scrawny and frightened of chickens," Daniel suggested dryly. "But go ahead. What?"

"Hannel is here!" Bartok pronounced triumphantly.

"Who?" Daniel returned absently. His gaze strayed back across the last tally of oil jars. He spotted a place where he had made an extra mark. Was that five or six?

"Lord Hannel of the Marshes, that's who. The greatest Jewish warrior since Zamaris . . . maybe since Judah Maccabee."

"The one who rules Narda between the rivers?" Daniel queried, his interest growing in spite of himself.

"Pay attention now," Bartok urged, speaking slowly and distinctly as if addressing someone hard of hearing or slow-witted. "Lord Hannel, brother to Lord Tannis, who gathered an army of Jews, built forts in the marshes of the Euphrates, and beat the governor of Babylon in battle . . . that Lord Hannel."

Daniel's face flushed, emphasizing the dark spot. "He's here? In Ecbatana?"

The Jewish brothers, sons of a weaver-woman, had carved out a kingdom for themselves. Instead of eradicating them, King Artabanus, the Parthian monarch, bribed the Hebrew warriors to keep a check on his Babylonian subjects' ambition. For ten years the brothers had plundered and robbed passing caravans, but for the last decade they had been paid—handsomely, it was said—to provide protection for those same trade routes. They lived like kings, defended by handpicked Jewish archers, multistoried stone walls, and a network of canals and embankments that augmented the natural swamp. The story ran that no one, not even King Artabanus himself, could enter their domain without their permission. It was also said that no one could find his way out again unassisted.

Bartok retrieved the stylus and presented it to Daniel with a flourish. "Give the man a prize. He can be taught to listen after all! Who knows? Maybe he will speak intelligently someday too. Listen! Hannel is here. He's at the Jeweled Peacock. Do you want to meet him or not?"

There was just an instant when Daniel's gaze fell across the wax tablet and he frowned. It wasn't like the accounting error he was pursuing was his fault. It would keep just as well until tomorrow. He had been working long hours for many days, after all.

"Let's go," he said.

7 | CHAPTER

The Jeweled Peacock was packed with people eager to see and hear Lord Hannel. Jews and Medes from Ecbatana mingled with Parthian merchants and caravan travelers from Bactria and beyond. Ecbatana lay on the Silk Road connecting the artisans of the Orient with the commerce of the Mediterranean, so the mix of cultures and languages was no surprise.

What was of interest to Daniel was the setting. The tavern was no mansion. The provincial governor had a home inside Ecbatana's seven-walled citadel. The king's summer palace was at the top of the ringed fortress. But this public house, just inside the outermost wall, on the lowest level of the city, catered to the most common of common folk. Why would Lord Hannel choose such a venue? What was his purpose here?

There were no women in attendance, but the windows were festooned with boys as young as ten, anxious to see the renowned warlord. The crowd outside the two entries was already six deep.

"We'll never hear a thing now!" Bartok fussed.

"Don't give up so easily," Daniel cautioned. Spotting the tavern keeper pushing his way through the throng, Daniel hailed him. A moment later, after a silver coin bearing the profile of King Artabanus had changed palms from Daniel to the Peacock's owner, the two friends were led through the crowd and placed at a table near the fireplace. In the center of the table was a bowl of apples.

Standing on a stool, so as to be raised above the heads of the audience, was a sharp-nosed, middle-aged man. A sky blue silk robe, shot through with gold thread, hung from shoulder to ankle. The line of his pointed beard emphasized his high cheekbones. A thin gold band rested on his brow, matched by a gold hoop that dangled from his right ear.

Encircling Hannel—or so Daniel guessed him to be—was a ring of men all dressed in black, from black turbans to black cloaks and black leather boots. On each back was a Parthian bow and quiver of arrows. Hanging at each side was a curved sword. Thrust into each sash was a dagger as long as a man's forearm. Daniel rightly guessed this was Hannel's personal bodyguard.

The tavern owner, as self-appointed chamberlain, banged the bottom of a pot with a wooden spoon instead of ringing a gong. "Quiet! Quiet, please," he implored. "My lord Hannel will speak."

The hawk-eyed chieftain peered around the room, judging, considering, discarding. Briefly the disturbing stare probed Daniel's face, then moved on. "I greet you in the name of the Almighty, whose servant I am," Hannel intoned. "I am here seeking brave men who wish to join with me and my brother in defending the caravan routes. I need archers, swordsmen, and cavalry—fearless men who will die for me if I order them to do so."

Once more Hannel's stare encountered Daniel's gaze; the young man shivered in spite of himself and the stifling interior of the room.

"You ask why I do not recruit from the soldiers in the citadel? Because I don't want garrison soldiers who draw their pay and grow fat walking in perfect safety atop high walls. I want men who can live rough and not complain, chase bandits into their desert lairs and come out alive.

"I don't want men whose loyalty can be bought. If they'll take pay to leave one master, they'll do so again when a greater sum is offered. I want only those who'll pledge their lives to me, personally. I promise you, those who do will be amply rewarded. But first you must prove your worth. Ezekial, show them."

The tallest of the black-robed guards gestured for Bartok to toss an apple into the air. As Daniel's friend did so, both sword and dagger flashed out. The sweep of the sword cleaved the fruit in two; the warrior caught both halves on the point of the knife before they hit the floor.

A murmur of admiration coupled with fear rippled through the crowd.

"Tomorrow I have business elsewhere. But watch for me. Soon I will make camp near the olive press a mile outside the eastern gate. Then those of you who think you're worthy should come there to prove it."

Daggers drawn, the bodyguards instantly cleared a path for their master. The onlookers tumbled backwards to get out of the way. With a flash of his robe that glittered with the light reflecting from the golden threads, Hannel stalked from the room.

The evening air brought pleasant relief from the heat of the day. On the path back toward the countinghouse, Bartok bubbled with excitement. "Did you see the gold he wore? And his guards? I tell you, not even Artabanus has warriors as fierce as those. They say in Narda an officer over ten men is treated like a prince and a captain of fifty lives like a king! All the villages for a hundred miles around pay tribute to the brothers. They send their daughters to Narda so Hannel's men can choose the best to be their wives."

Daniel laughed and shook his head. "And this appeals to you?" he teased. "To achieve this great reward? All you have to do is survive dying of thirst in the desert. And miss having a bandit's wife cut out your tongue and feed it to you. And avoid being caught over the border by the Romans and nailed to a cross. And then you can have your pick of all the women in Mesopotamia! But no thank you, Bartok. If I even looked at another woman, Mina would skin me alive anyway."

There was an uncomfortable pause, which Bartok covered with a cough. Bartok looked at his friend up and down, as if viewing a complete stranger. "What's happened to you?" he inquired again. "You who never let one day pass without griping about being stuck in Ecbatana. Now we meet someone who has really lived. Seen the world! Had adventures! And all you can think about is—" he gestured toward the countinghouse door—"scribbling little marks on wax? And they aren't even tallies for gold or jewels. Oh no! You're tallying olive oil jars!"

Daniel frowned. "Good night, Bartok," he said coldly.

Even before he left for heaven, Cantor could name the stars for children of the Valley of Mak'ob who gathered round him. But since Cantor's return from the land beyond death, he cherished the sight of the stars almost as much as he loved the daylight.

"Let's not build a fire tonight," he said to Lily as they pitched their camp beside a river.

"It will be cold."

Water rushed over the rocks. Cantor hummed softly as if he heard a song. He pulled Lily down next to him. They leaned back on the boulder. "I'll keep you warm."

"How will I cook the fish Hawk caught for us?"

"It'll keep 'til morning. We'll eat the bread instead."

"Bread."

"Fire dims my view of the stars."

Lily was still more attached to earth and fire and warmth than to the distant stars. She stared at the place where the fire should have blazed. "Cantor? It's getting cold already."

Cantor pointed up at the sky toward the gathering of wandering stars. They clustered close around the New Moon like a band of pilgrims who meant to travel together. He snuggled Lily under his arm and named each wandering star for her. "Splendor, The Messenger, The Adam, and The Holy Spirit in their midst. Their congregation speaks of Messiah's presence, you see? It means something. . . ."

"I'm glad to hear your voice, Cantor." She absently stroked his arm, then raised her face to kiss him. "And you do keep me warm."

"Oh, my love. Yes, you are the only fire we need tonight." Cantor returned her kisses.

It was close to midnight again when Daniel at last gave up his attempt to locate the accounting mistake. After another week's effort, he still had not found the error and his thoughts wandered so far from extra jugs of oil that at last he quit trying.

Despite his protest to Bartok, Daniel could not stop reviewing what he had heard about Lord Hannel. There was a man feared by his enemies but courted by them as well. He was known at the palace in Ctesiphon, followed by mobs of children through the streets of Babylon, and respected as a negotiator by the Romans at the border. He and his brother had not only founded a kingdom for themselves but found a place in history as well.

Bartok was right. Daniel had changed. It was no more than months since Daniel would have been lost in admiration for such a champion. Now he was confused.

He tiptoed into the house so as not to awaken anyone but saw a light gleaming from his father's study and turned aside to say good night. To Daniel's astonishment Melchior was not alone. Seated opposite him, in a matching X-shaped chair drawn close to his, was Lord Hannel.

"Ah, Daniel," Melchior greeted his son. "Come in. This is Lord Hannel of the Marshes. Perhaps you've heard of him?"

"I . . . indeed. An honor, sir."

An instant of the earlier knifelike stare was succeeded by a broad smile. Hannel made no reference to Daniel's attendance at the tavern. For a moment Daniel considered keeping the matter secret from his father. Where had that notion come from? Was he embarrassed to have been again at the Peacock, or was something else preying on his thoughts?

Daniel rejected the lie. "I saw Lord Hannel earlier, Father. When he was recruiting. Bartok and I were there together, but of course his lordship didn't know who I was."

"But how stupid of me not to recognize you as your father's son," Hannel said. "You are very like him. Probably the exact copy of him at the same age."

Melchior gestured at Hannel's empty glass with a half-empty bottle of wine, but the warlord shook his head. "It's late and I must be up early, winnowing the wheat from the chaff; intolerable amount of chaff for very few grains of wheat, I expect, but what else?" A starker, colder tone came into his next words: "You'll think about what I said? Perhaps you'll change your mind?"

Melchior shook his head. "I'm satisfied that I won't," he replied firmly.

"Ah." Hannel shrugged as Daniel looked from face to face but found no clue to what had been discussed.

"And you, young ben Melchior," Hannel said abruptly. "I'm honored you came to see me. Perhaps you'll visit my camp?"

"I . . . no, I don't think so. I have my duties."

"And no doubt you perform them admirably. Good night, then. Thank you for the wine and the conversation. Don't trouble yourselves," he said with a negative gesture toward Melchior and Daniel. "I can find my own way out."

Surprisingly Hannel gave a sharp whistle as he exited the room.

Even more surprising . . . and disturbing . . . were the half dozen guards who appeared out of the darkness as if black-robed phantoms had simply taken on solid form out of transparency.

The group disappeared just as mystically.

"Father?" Daniel inquired. "What was that about?"

Melchior rubbed his beard with both hands and adjusted the prayer shawl around his shoulders. "Lord Hannel is a dashing figure, eh?" he said, avoiding the question.

"But what did he want?"

Melchior sighed. "He came to offer me a position. He wanted me to move to Narda and be his court astronomer. He said he'd make me fabulously wealthy."

Daniel's thoughts leapt ahead. "So this story of recruiting more guards is not his real purpose here? He came to see you? Will you do it?"

"Settle down," Melchior urged. "He said 'astronomer,' but he means 'astrologer.' He wants me to be a fortune-teller. Of course I won't do that! Amazing how that notion still hangs around my name after all these years."

"But why now?"

"It's complicated. Hannel and his brother think another war between Parthia and Rome is inevitable. They're probably right. When it does come, they want to be able to jump nimbly to the winning side, which they believe might be Rome. If they switch allegiance, Hannel thinks Rome will let him replace Herod Antipas as tetrarch of Galilee and make his brother ruler of east of Jordan. They want a magic way to know when to jump. If you're planning treason, it's best to time it correctly."

"But Lord Hannel . . . his brother . . . they're honorable, surely? admired?"

Melchior sighed heavily. "They were successful bandits. Then they managed to trap a fatheaded Babylonian governor in the swamps, and ever since they are 'the greatest Jewish warriors since Judah Maccabee.'"

Daniel felt himself blush, but in the darkened room his father did not notice.

Melchior continued, "Of the two, Tannis has some military savvy. Hannel is all bluster and show. They will come to a bad end one of these days. But, praise the Eternal, it will happen without me. Now, let's go to bed."

8

erod Antipas paced up and down the length of his council chamber. Without conscious thought he stepped only on the white squares of the tessellated floor, avoiding the black marble tiles as if his life depended on it.

"You say the Valley is completely empty?"

"Sire," the captain of the guard returned, "my sergeant and his men searched thoroughly. There's no one in the hovels, no one in the caves. Untended graves . . . nothing more."

"Could they have all died?"

The captain bowed his head respectfully before replying, "If so, who buried them?"

Antipas glanced toward the hall outside this chamber, where the sergeant and the two troopers of the scouting party stood shuffling their feet. They had been in the place of lepers. Antipas would not allow them near him, whether they had found lepers or not.

"Absurd," Antipas snorted. "Where did they all go? No one's ever heard of a whole group of lepers suddenly being healed. No one with real leprosy is ever healed, *ever*. Could they have been shamming all along?"

The guard captain mentally reviewed the gruesome images and

nauseating smells of the noseless, fingerless, stinking-with-corruption wretches he had previously seen staggering about in the Valley of Despair. The place was a sewer, an open grave. That was no shamming. "Not all of them, sire. It's not possible."

"Then someone must have seen them go! Find them! Follow them! Search all the nearby villages, but get to the bottom of this. And kill them when you find them! Since lepers can't be healed, they have all violated the law of separation. Kill them all."

The captain struck his chest with a clenched fist in a salute of obedience, then whirled and left without another word, gathering his soldiers as he passed.

As Daniel lay in bed that night, once again sleep would not come. He reviewed what he had heard. He pondered which opinion of Hannel was correct. Was he a great hero, or was he all swagger?

Daniel had also discovered there was more to his father than he had previously suspected. The story of the triple conjunction that drew wise men from all over the world to a village in Judea had been brought out and reviewed every Hanukkah since Daniel's childhood. It was near Hanukkah, his father said, that the miraculous child had been born in Beth-lehem, even though it was several months later when Melchior arrived there.[14] The story had grown familiar with the telling, and familiarity . . . Well, Melchior had imparted his love of the heavens to his sons, but somehow Daniel disconnected the signs in the sky Melchior described from events in the real world. Now, tonight, someone famous, whether deserving of that reputation or not, had come seeking Melchior's advice. Hannel might not be everything that he appeared, yet he was still important to kings and kingdoms, to governors and caravans, and he had come all the way to Ecbatana to consult Daniel's father.

The young man got up and stared out the window. There, hanging due south between zenith and horizon, was Jupiter, Tzadik, The Righteous. Tonight it was planted in the midst of the sign of Israel, The Two Fish, just as in Melchior's tale of long before.

The Righteous held its own against the glare of the rising three-quarter moon looming in the southeast. When Daniel moved to the eastern casement, Saturn, Shabbatai, The Lord of the Sabbath, also appeared there, just peeking over the rim of the world. At this angle Daniel could not recognize the constellation in which Shabbatai was lodged. His father would have known instantly; a handful of years earlier, so would Daniel . . . but he had forgotten much.

When he finally slept, it was not an easy rest. Daniel's dreams were a confused mosaic of flashing swords, piles of treasure, chains shackling him to a counting table . . . and a man standing beneath a blazon of stars, his arms outstretched in welcome.

9

CHAPTER

The heap of dry brush crackled merrily and the bigger logs were alight. The donkey grazed nearby. Lily toasted bread for their supper. Soon enough the coals would be right for roasting a pair of spotted sand grouse already spitted on sticks. Lily recounted for Cantor an experience she once had with roasting quail in the wilderness.

Hawk was already enjoying his share of the meal, which was only fair, since he had fetched it for them. Gravely he had accepted a raw drumstick from Lily's fingers, then turned away from the firelight to stare into the dark.

"Hello the camp," a man's voice called. "May we share your fire?"

"Come in and welcome," Cantor returned. "Warmth . . . and food too, if you need."

The travelers were a family of four: mother, father, twelve-year-old son, and young, towheaded child wrapped in a blanket and sleeping against her mother's shoulder so that only a blond mop of hair protruded.

"Pilgrims heading for Yerushalayim," the father explained. "We're from Hamadan. My children have never been to the Holy City. Wanted them to see it before my son is apprenticed next year, so may not get leave again to make the journey for some time. Of course," the man added ruefully, "my daughter still won't see it."

Cantor looked but did not speak his question.

At a nod from the father the mother tugged the blanket down from the girl's face. The girl's eyes were wrapped in a cloth. Even by the firelight Lily saw the yellow stains on the bandage.

"They never get completely well," the man said, leaning forward. "Worse in spring and summer; some better in winter. But when they get as bad as this, she cannot stand the light. Cries somethin' fierce with the pain. Like gravel in her eyes, she says. I fear she will be altogether blind soon. Breaks my heart . . . and her mum's; she's such a cheerful child."

Beckoning Cantor to lean toward him, the father explained, "Truth be told, that's the other reason we're going to Judea now. There's been talk of a healer . . . not that I put much stock in such myself . . . but I says to my wife, I says: 'What'd it hurt?' So. You've come from there, I take it. Have you heard aught of him, this fellow from the Galil?"

Lily did not wait to be asked. Stretching her hand out, she grasped Cantor's fingers and said to the mother, "Would you mind if we . . . if we prayed for your daughter?"

The girl stirred beneath their combined touch, pushing herself back from her mother's embrace.

Cantor laid his hand directly over the blindfold and she quieted. "Almighty King of the Universe," he prayed, "a journey begun in hope may move into faith with your help. You see this child; you see the hearts of her parents; you see their need. In the Name of Yeshua of Nazareth, we humbly beg you to intercede and heal."

I'm praying again, Lord of Compassion who loves children best of all. Your mercy does not depend on our promising to make a thousand-mile journey, but only that we open our hearts to trust your love.

A low hum came from the child, almost like the purring of a cat. Her hands reached for the bandage, encountered the crusted surface and recoiled, then grasped Cantor's hand eagerly.

While mother and father held their breath and the brother hung back, almost as if afraid, the child pushed the bandage upward onto her forehead . . . and stared at Hawk with clear, bright, shining eyes. "Bird," she said. "Pretty bird. Deb'ra hold 'im?"

The father fell at Cantor's feet. "Yeshua! That's the name! You're he?"

"No, no," Cantor corrected hastily, pulling the father upright. "Listen: Yeshua is the Messiah of Israel, sent by the Almighty. We're only his servants, sent by him to do whatever he commands. When you go to Yerushalayim, offer a thank-offering of praise. Remember that it's in the Name of Yeshua this happened. But tell no one until you're safely back home. You understand?"

The man wrung Cantor's hand as the mother clutched the girl between herself and Lily 'til the child squawked.

"Aye!" the father acknowledged. "Jealousy! Priests and Pharisees! News of that even reached Hamadan. But listen: if we meet—" here the fellow lowered his voice and whispered dramatically—"meet Yeshua? What message shall we give him for you?"

Cantor nodded. "Tell him we are carrying out his instructions."

Daniel's duties took him beyond the eastern boundary of Ecbatana, into his father's olive groves. He was to supervise the pruning of a stand of seven-year-old trees. Olives bore their fruit only on shoots receiving full sun, so shaping the trees allowed for maximum production. It was also time for this grove to be topped, or limited as to its height. The wooden ladders used by the laborers reached only to fourteen feet above the ground; trees allowed to grow larger than this were a waste of effort.

Lono accompanied Daniel as his foreman. The islander understood olive cultivation, so Daniel would make no mistakes. As Daniel considered the rows of trees he consulted with Lono as to how each should be trimmed, and his notions were approved or corrected. Then Lono instructed the workers, issuing Daniel's orders.

Echoing from the next canyon eastward from the plantation were loud shouts and the clash of metal on metal. It was the location of the abandoned olive press referred to by Hannel as the position of the warlord's camp. Daniel had not intended to visit the recruiting effort . . . at least he told himself he had no such intention.

The truth was, he had ordered his day so as to go to this spot early. It had been in Daniel's thoughts that Hannel would still be conducting his trials when Daniel could witness them.

All the workers had been assigned their respective rows to prune. It would be several hours before Daniel's "orders" would again be needed.

In a nonchalant manner he remarked to Lono, "I'm going over there to see what's going on."

"You already know what noise is," Lono said with accusation. "You think you fadda approve?"

Taking advice about pruning valuable trees was one thing; being scolded by a slave was quite another.

"My father would go if he were here," Daniel argued. "Anyway, I'm going."

"Then I go too," Lono asserted, and with that statement there was no arguing.

From the rim separating the olive grove's plateau from the canyon Daniel saw a flurry of activity. A stone wall lining an ancient watercourse had been pressed into service as part of a training ground. At intervals atop the barrier melons had been placed.

A line of men, each holding the reins of a horse, stood well back from the embankment, watching.

From the far end of the dry creek bed Daniel heard another shout. A rider robed in Hannel's black livery urged an equally black horse into a lope, guiding it with his knees. The pointed hood of the man's Parthian robe was thrown back and he was grinning as he directed his mount down the row of targets.

Approaching the first melon, he nocked an arrow from a handful held along with the reins in his right hand. His left held the short, recurved bow. The bowstring twanged and the arrow plunged completely through the target and out the other side. This action was repeated five more times, until the supply of arrows was exhausted. Each of the five melons had been struck, two of them split by the impacts.

The last target had received two direct hits, the second fired over the archer's shoulder after the horse had already galloped past.

Besides the horsemanship and the accuracy of the shooting, something else impressed Daniel: the incredible speed with which the warrior fitted and shot each successive arrow. There had been no fumbling, no wasted motion. It was as if man and beast formed a perfectly attuned killing machine.

Daniel plainly envisioned the result of a battle against such troopers. A row of accomplished riders could gallop across the front of an enemy formation, loosing their bolts each in turn. The flight of arrows would decimate any rank of men armed only with swords or short-range spears, and they would have no chance to respond.

Now it was time for the potential recruits to demonstrate their skill. The first rider fired one shot that went nowhere near the target and fumbled his arrows, dropping them. Then his mount shied at some brush and plunged away from the course.

The second fared little better.

The third was bucked off into a pile of rocks, knocking him senseless. There was some delay while he was carried out of the way of the others and propped against a palm tree to recover his wits.

Daniel recalled Hannel's words about how much chaff would be sifted to gain a little wheat.

Near the tumbledown parapet encircling the old olive press was a large tent sporting a yellow banner that floated on the thin breeze. Under an awning erected at the front sat Lord Hannel.

"I'll go down and greet him. And no argument from you."

Lono inclined his bushy head, but his tattooed features bore a scowl of serious disapproval.

His vision seemingly as keen as his piercing stare, Hannel had recognized Daniel long before the young man and Lono arrived in the camp. The warlord rose from his chair and strode forward in welcome, cuffing a pair of bodyguards out of the way and bellowing for servants to bring another chair and some wine.

"Young ben Melchior, you honor me," Hannel said, brandishing a horsehair fly whisk in his right hand. Leading the way back to his pavilion, he gestured for Daniel to be seated.

Daniel explained that he had been nearby and overheard the tumult of the camp.

Hannel grimaced. "It's worse than I feared. Those of Ecbatana who fancy themselves fighters would probably lose a match with a one-armed blind man. The only worthwhile recruits are dagger men, border ruffians, and the like. They are caravan robbers and smugglers, more given to cutting throats in the night than standing up to an enemy. I would not trust them."

"So you've found no recruits?"

Hannel waved negligently. "A few. That one there by the far palm tree has no fear, and he's a decent man with a knife."

It was Karek, Daniel's gambling opponent. The man wore an odd-shaped turban, lumpy on one side, bound tightly to his head.

As Daniel watched, Karek took on one of Hannel's guards in a combat with wooden swords. The tavern tough was clumsy, but the strength of his blows caused the guard to give ground. Karek maneuvered his rival toward a patch of rocky ground, where the footing was uneven. As the guard stumbled, Karek pressed his advantage, batting the enemy's sword aside, then rising under his arm with a knife thrust that stopped just inches from the man's throat. The chief bodyguard signaled a halt and declared Karek the victor.

"He forced the battle onto ground of his choosing," Hannel said approvingly. With raised eyebrows he added, "And he struck hardest with the weapon he knows best, instead of fighting on terms imposed by the other. Both are good tactics to remember, Daniel ben Melchior."

Remembering the previous conversation with his father, Daniel doubted Melchior's judgment of Hannel. This man commanded well-disciplined troops and supervised their training. He spoke with familiarity of weapons and men that could only come from battle.

Melchior had to be wrong about Hannel.

"And that fellow Karek—more reason than most others to leave Ecbatana for my service," Hannel noted.

At Daniel's questioning look, Hannel gestured toward the lumpy turban and continued, "Lost his ear. Given a choice between that or imprisonment. Says he was falsely accused of cheating at something, but he's probably guilty." Hannel shrugged. "His past is of no concern to me, as long as it makes him more loyal to me."

Daniel shuddered, grateful the mock combat took Karek too far away for him to recognize Daniel.

"But tell me about your servant here," Hannel said, gesturing with the whisk toward the impassive Lono. "He is from the Indies?"

"Far beyond them, I think," Daniel said, summoning Lono to come closer. "He says at his home the sun rises out of the sea every morning."

"Ugly brute, isn't he?" Hannel pointed toward the wavy lines on Lono's chin and cheeks. "Can he fight?"

Daniel was surprised at the question. "He's never had to, except once when some drunks tried to break into our home. Lono grabbed two of them and smashed their heads together. The rest fled."

Hannel nodded. "And loyal to your family beyond doubt. I would love to see him wrestle Ezekial, my captain."

Since Ezekial was a foot shorter and appeared a hundred pounds lighter than Lono, Daniel protested that it would not be a fair fight.

"If you think that, why don't we put a wager on the outcome and you can give me odds. . . . Say I put up four drachmae to your five?"

Lono shook his head vigorously.

Daniel's thoughts spun. Would he let his decisions be dictated by a slave? Daniel scrubbed his birthmark vigorously.

"Perhaps the sum is too great to risk," Hannel said, spreading his hands.

"I . . . I don't have time," Daniel replied grudgingly.

"Some other occasion, then," Hannel said dismissively. "Now, you'll excuse me?"

10

The area through which Lily and Cantor traveled was rich and fertile. Hawk soared above groves of date palms and pomegranate orchards. Fallow fields, recently shorn of barley, bloomed instead with shaggy sheep grazing among the stubble. Soggy plains of rice, watered by one of the many canals crisscrossing the region, formed a patchwork of blues, greens, and browns.

Lily fingered the stones of Eretz-Israel in her pocket.

Cantor walked in silence for a time, then said, "The old men say Gan Eden once was here."

"Gan Eden." Lily repeated the Hebrew words that meant "Garden of Pleasure . . . Paradise."

Lily and Cantor traversed one of the most bountifully productive regions on earth, while headed toward the great River Euphrates. Was this the ground where the Lord planted a garden for the first man and woman? Was this the ground where Adonai walked in the cool of the day and fellowshipped with the first humans? And was it here that the Serpent tempted Eve to disobey the Lord's one command not to eat of the fruit of only one tree?

In that very field where sheep now grazed, had the blood of Abel cried out news that brother had murdered brother?

Lily keenly felt the weight of spiritual oppression as she and Cantor walked on toward the city of Narda. The air was thick with some ancient evil. Cantor's face showed the strain of that awareness as well.

Hawk disappeared for a moment in a blinding flash of sunlight.

Lily breathed, *I am praying again, Lord, who formed us from the dust of the earth, you who so loved the first man and woman that you laughed with joy when you planted a garden for them and set them in it to live untroubled for uncounted ages. Does the blood of their murdered son still cry out from these fields? Oh, Yeshua! Blind, dire breakage! The shattering of all perfection!*

Hawk floated down to the shaggy branches of a date palm. A tiny rabbit struggled in his talons. Hawk tore it apart while it shrieked and fought. Within seconds Hawk gulped half of it down and let the rest of the carcass fall onto a thornbush.

"It's unlike Hawk to kill for sport," Cantor said, responding to the scent of evil in the air. "Lily, I think death first entered the world nearby. Do you hear it?"

Lily held her breath but heard nothing but the wind rustling the palm fronds.

Cantor whispered, "Our father Avraham was called out from this land where the battle began. . . ."

Perhaps they walked where the shadow of Eden's gates fell upon the highway. And yet beyond the gates and the presence of the Lord, brother had killed brother.

Lily thought of how rich the city of Narda was reputed to be. Narda lay on the westernmost angle of a triangle formed by Ctesiphon to the northeast and Babylon to the southeast. This region was the very center of Mesopotamia . . . truly "The Land Between the Rivers."

"Cantor?" Lily held tightly to the stones of home.

"Yes, Lily?"

"We could not have misunderstood him?"

"He said we would find ten stones of Yerushalayim on the foundation where Eden used to stand. He said, 'Show yourselves to the priests there and tell them what you have seen and what you have heard. The blind can see. The lame can walk. Lepers are healed. The dead are raised.'[15] He said, 'Tell them the wonders you have witnessed.' He said, 'Tell them I am here.'"

"Did he mean for us to return to the beginning of the world . . . to the place where human Exile began?"

"We're almost there."

"Death is as heavy here as it was in the Dying Cave of Mak'ob. I know you feel it too. The evil past and the twice-evil future."

Cantor stopped and groped for a place to sit beside the road. The sun beat down on their backs.

Cantor cradled his head and muttered, "Lily! The eyes of my heart see soldiers from a distant time . . . future sons beloved by future mothers. I hear battle sounds like thunder and fire streaking down to earth where Hawk has flown. So many sons from a distant land will fight and die in this very place one day. And what message must we give their grieving mothers? . . . What?"

Lily answered carefully, certain that if she tempted Cantor now, he would turn back. "Though death remains on earth, for a short time you saw heavenly Eden with your own eyes. It is a real place. Yeshua has come to heal lepers like you and me. He raises the dead to life. He has also come to redeem creation. Even here his Garden for us will be restored. We will walk with him in the cool of the day and talk with him every day."

Cantor pressed her hand with his as they got up and resumed their journey.

The village of Taibi was a scant four miles from the Valley of Mak'ob. Like a beggar clinging to life on handouts and castoffs, Taibi tenaciously wrested a living from thin soil and too little rain. But hardship had not stolen the joy of keeping mitzvot from its villagers.

Ten years earlier one of Taibi's elders—a well-liked and much-respected man—had developed leprosy and been sent to Mak'ob. The village resolved to never forget him as often happened with those who contracted the separating sickness. While the candle of his life flickered and was slowly extinguished, Taibi never ceased to supply what he needed to ease his existence in the Valley.

The elder had died years ago, but Taibi kept alive its promise to his memory. The women of Taibi were among the few in all Israel who delivered extra rations of food to the boundary stone marking the border where the whole and clean recoiled from the living dead.

This service they had performed every Sabbath eve for the past half decade . . . until this year.

Tonight, this beginning evening of Sabbath, they gathered in Taibi's synagogue to discuss yet again what had happened to the lepers. The wind out of the desert curled around the eaves of the building and sighed through the rafters.

The rabbi, a young man only newly come to Taibi, who had not known the elder, tried to make sense of the queries.

"We went again today," a woman called out from the gallery, "to the boundary stone. To the burned remains of the guard shack. To the rim of the canyon. There's no one there. What's happened, Rabbi? Where did they all go?"

"It's a miracle," another of the good wives of Taibi shouted. "They're all healed."

"Not even the prophet Elisha healed a whole valley full of lepers," the rabbi corrected.

The breeze, strengthening, buffeted the east wall of the synagogue until it creaked and groaned.

A shepherd remarked, "The food is gone. It's said some of the *tsara'im*, the lepers, went to Yerushalayim to show themselves to the priests. Yeshua of Nazareth—"

"Do not speak that name!" the rabbi instructed harshly. "Whatever he does is done by the power of devils!"

The rabbi was a Pharisee, bound by his beliefs to a myriad of laws that maintained his ritual purity but left him scornful of those who did not.

"But what then? Where did they go?"

"I heard," ventured the wife of the village carpenter, "that some of them are going east, to our brothers in Babylon. They fear for their lives if they stay in Israel."

"How do you know this?" the rabbi demanded.

"I met them."

A buzz of interest permeated the synagogue.

"I wished them safe journey. It's true . . . they are afraid."

The flexing of the east wall was joined by a hammering on the entry door.

A newly bar mitzvahed man of thirteen spun round and pointed toward the disturbance. With bulging eyes, in a cracking voice he shouted, "It's them!"

An uproar erupted among the villagers.

The shammash, the synagogue attendant, forever after regarded as the bravest of men, answered the knock.

A green-tunicked captain of Herodian soldiers confronted him. "This building is surrounded, so no one try to leave. I want information and I want it now. Where are the lepers of Mak'ob?"

It was a Sabbath, by Cantor's reckoning. He was not entirely certain, he remarked to Lily, but it felt like a Sabbath day. Cantor said he believed Yeshua would agree that honoring the Almighty who made the Sabbath and ordained it was the crucial part of keeping it holy.[16]

So they rested beside a watering hole, eating a cold meal remaining from what Lily had prepared the afternoon before. The donkey nibbled carefully at spiky, dark green stalks.

Though nearing Narda, the only other travelers they saw were Gentiles. The absence of Jews on the highway reinforced the notion that Cantor's calendar keeping was correct.

As the day waned into late afternoon, another band of walkers approached the oasis. Lily thought she saw prayer shawls on the shoulders of some of the men and fringes on their garments, as if they were Jews, but in the growing shadows, she could not be certain.

Hawk was spiraling overhead, keeping watch. Observing him was a full-time pleasure for Lily. He soared with so little effort and swooped with such grace that he was a joy to watch. Just now he dove abruptly, flaring his wings at the last second to alight on Cantor's outstretched arm.

"Will he do that again?" Lily asked. "I love to see him."

The main body of pilgrims had already passed the rocky outcropping and bowl-sized pool beneath the rock face where Cantor and Lily rested, but the last in the line, a woman dressed in black, stood as if transfixed.

The spell was broken when Cantor stood erect and cast Hawk into the wind.

The woman shrieked something incomprehensible to Lily, pointed at Hawk, waved frantically to her companions, and began to run toward them.

Still some distance away she shouted, "You're he. The man with the hawk. The healer. It's you!"

Hawk veered off from this noisy intrusion to land on the topmost frond of a palm that sagged under his weight.

Lily stood beside Cantor and dusted off her hands.

Arriving directly in front of them, the woman said, "I found you! You will heal them, won't you? Even though it's Shabbat? I heard of you, the man with the hawk, and I've been looking for you."

Eagerly, still without giving Lily or Cantor time to speak, she summoned the rest of her party and pulled twin boys from behind the skirts of an elderly woman.

The boys clung to each other, wide-eyed, without speaking.

"Deaf!" the woman announced. "Deaf as posts since a fever hit them both last year. Fever took their father's life, left me a widow, left them unable to hear. They don't speak now either. Look: Reuven! Benoni! Look at Mother."

The boys studied Hawk and Cantor and the heap of dried figs on a platter but made no move to respond to their mother's call.

"But we've heard of you. You can heal them, eh?"

Cantor patiently explained that he was not a healer, just the ambassador of one. "Yeshua of Nazareth is my Master. He is the Messiah of Israel. He is the Master of life and death."

"Yes," the woman said with assurance. "But ambassadors are empowered to make treaties that even bind their masters, aren't they?"

Cantor said simply, "As long as you understand, it isn't done by me."

"Please," the woman begged intently. "In the Name of Yeshua, then, only let them have their hearing back again."

I'm praying again, Almighty who chooses even poor, weak vessels like me to be your ambassador. Your Name is glorious at all times, but in your mercy, won't you touch these little ones so they can sing your praises and hear your hymns in wind swirl and bird call? As you taught us: In the Name of Yeshua, who makes all things new again.

"May we have . . . ?" one of the brothers asked.

". . . some of those figs?" the other concluded. "Yes, Mother, may we? We're hungry."

"Thank you! Thank you!" the woman said, stopping to raise outstretched hands in surrender. "Thanks be to Yeshua and the power of his Name. You are true ambassadors. He must be pleased with you."

11

CHAPTER

It was an early meeting. The hour of morning sacrifice had come and gone, but much of Jerusalem was still drowsy. Caiaphas, the *cohen hagadol*, was used to being an early riser. He looked alert and neatly dressed, as did the lone scribe who accompanied him.

Antipas, tetrarch of Galilee, was unused to being up before noon. He appeared hungover and resentful, and was both. At a snap of his fingers his single attendant poured him a cup of warm, spiced wine.

Antipas had suggested this unpleasant hour so as to preserve a degree of secrecy about the encounter. Not that anything of a political or religious nature was ever truly secret in Jerusalem, and in the Holy City *everything* was both political and religious.

For reasons more related to ill will than to privacy, they chose to meet on neutral ground: beside the still-uncompleted aqueduct running up the Kidron Valley from near Hebron, far to the south.

Antipas had nothing to do with the project.

Caiaphas had weathered a storm of protest over the use of Temple monies for the construction, but most of the criticism had fallen on Roman governor Pilate . . . to the satisfaction of both tetrarch and priest.

Ambition for more power motivated the two men. Both recognized that increased authority could only come at Pilate's expense. It was easy to encourage hatred of the Romans.

Antipas thought the *cohen hagadol* a pompous, preening, hypocritical, self-righteous fool . . . and he was correct.

Caiaphas believed the tetrarch to be a cruel, licentious, dissipated, mocking, half-heathen fool . . . and he was right in his assessment as well.

Only unusual circumstance made them partners of a sort. Besides Pilate, there was one other figure whom both saw as an obstacle to their aspirations: Yeshua of Nazareth.

"Any more so-called healed lepers arrive, asking to show themselves to the priests?" Antipas inquired. "Pious frauds you neither detained nor followed?"

Caiaphas shook his head ponderously. "No. Have your men succeeded in tracking down how over six hundred lepers could just disappear? If you had . . ." He raised an admonitory finger, then subsided at the warning in Antipas' bloodshot eyes.

"I have had a report," Antipas said. "I think some of the so-called healed ones have fled to Narda and are taking refuge there."

Before the high priest interrupted with his opinion of what should be done, Antipas continued, "It is again time for the semiannual transporting of the Temple tax from Narda to Yerushalayim, yes?"

Caiaphas grudgingly acknowledged this fact. Antipas had no claim to any of the Temple revenue. The high priest hated discussing Temple finance with him.

"You will want a squadron of my soldiers to accompany your men, as usual?"

Once more, Caiaphas had to agree. Roman legionaries would protect the Temple treasure from Duro-Europa to Jerusalem, but the territory from Narda to the border town belonged to Parthia—no Roman troopers allowed.

"This time we will send envoys to the Lords of the Marsh, telling them to be on watch for any fugitive lepers or any wild stories about mass healings, or any troublemakers seeking to use Narda to plan rebellion."

"No one *orders* the Lords of the Marsh to do anything in their own lands," Caiaphas corrected stiffly.

"Everything has a price," Antipas responded.

So that was the reason for this private discussion. Tannis and Hannel gathered, stored, and guarded the Temple funds from all of the east . . . for a percentage of the revenue. Caiaphas justified this expense as needed to protect the balance from bandits. Now Antipas wanted him to give up a greater share.

"And what is the cost to you?" the high priest demanded.

Antipas ignored the issue. "For a small increase the brothers of Narda will not only locate any rebels, they will imprison and eliminate them. Solves problems for both of us and will get us good reports with Caesar. All without the aid or assistance of Lord Pilate."

Caiaphas pondered this bit of plotting. "All right, I agree. But my envoy will do the negotiating."

"Done."

Lily and Cantor sat beside the spring. At the top of the lush green pasture, a flock of sheep grazed placidly beneath the watchful eye of a shepherd.

Cantor made the blessing, then tore off a piece of bread and offered it to Lily. The couple ate in silence, punctuated by Cantor's soft prayers as each item of the meal was unwrapped and blessed.

Lily prayed in silence. *I am praying again, you who were with Cantor's soul when he left. You who know well what is on the other side. Help him speak of it. Give him the words. . . .*

No sooner had her thoughts flown to heaven than Cantor squinted into the sunlight and cleared his throat. "Lily?"

She replied, "Yes, Cantor?"

"No need to be afraid."

"I'm not. As long as you and I are together."

"I mean, even if we were ever not . . . together, I mean." He chewed his bread slowly, savoring the flavor. "It's not what you think it is."

"It?"

"*Olam haba.* The World to Come. A strange name for it, because it already exists. It is not the world to come. It is . . . already." He inhaled deeply.

"Why can't you tell me?"

"There are no words. None."

"But what did you see?" She tried to guide his memory of Paradise.

"I . . . it's easier if you ask me *who*. I can put an answer to that."

"All right, then. Who?"

"So many. From the Valley. There to welcome me. All well. Beautiful. All about the same age. No matter how old they were when they flew away, they seemed to be my age. They came and gathered around me. Embracing. Laughing. Singing. It was a celebration. You know?"

Lily named a dozen she had known in the Valley of Mak'ob. Some, Cantor had seen. But not all.

He continued his story. "Music. Songs I knew mixed in with some I had never heard. They could not be sung on earth because they are too beautiful. There was light. And color all around. Like this . . ." He swept his hand up from the water toward the sky. "Only much more . . . much more."

Lily leaned forward eagerly. "And who else? Anyone else?"

He nodded. "They walked with me. We were on a path the color of sapphire. The Lord loves color. Greens and blues. And water—the water has a scent, so wondrous. Beyond . . . oh! I don't know what it's like."

"Who else? Any of the old ones? from the stories?"

"Yes. Many. Abel, who died at the hand of his brother. And Enoch, who never died at all. Noah in the midst of a herd of deer."

"Animals too?"

"Oh yes. But not like they are here. They spoke and I understood."

"What did they say?"

Cantor held up his hand to slow her torrent of curiosity. "I can't. I can't, Lily. Too much and—"

"Maybe you could write it down?"

"Maybe. Maybe writing it down would be easier." He closed his eyes as if he could see it all again. "Anyway, where was I?"

"Noah. Deer."

"Oh, yes. His family all around him. Still work to do, you know. And they worked."

"Work in *olam haba*?"

"But not as we work here. Joy in their work. And Avraham and Sarai. All the patriarchs. At a great distance I saw Mosheh too, among a council of the prophets. King David . . . all of them. I heard a voice say,

'Those who by faith subdued kingdoms, administered justice, obtained blessings, closed the mouths of lions, extinguished raging fire . . .'"[17] Cantor paused. "Maybe I should try to write it. The journey. It seems like I was gone a lifetime and . . . if I could write down what I saw and heard. If I could try."

"When we come to Narda, we'll find ink. You must set it all down. Everything you saw. From the first to the last until you heard Yeshua's voice call you back."

Cantor cleared his throat and continued now with more confidence. "Some who were tortured for their faith had suffered greatly. Their wounds were still on them, but they were like shining gems. Battle awards. Heroes and heroines. I knew them, though they did not say their names at first. And they knew me. From first to last. There were so many. They kept coming. I would think of one great one and suddenly—" he snapped his fingers—"suddenly I would see him and know. I understand why we will need eternity."

"And what was the last thing—before Yeshua called you back?"

Cantor smiled. "It will surprise you."

"What?"

"It was the smallest in the Valley. She entered. I saw her, but it seemed just moments before I left there. Yod. Her red hair thick and shining. The clearest eyes. Beautiful . . . Yod. And she was still a child . . . still . . . our little girl."

"What did she say?"

"She told me that Messiah had come to bear our sorrows and heal everyone in the Valley. She said she had been forgotten, but now that she was with me, she didn't mind."

Lily frowned. "There was such confusion. Longing. Everyone pressing in."

"Then I heard his voice call my name. I heard your voice. And the great wind blew and I . . . woke up . . . again. Opened my eyes, and there you were beside him—your face and Yeshua's, smiling down at me."

Silence. Lily and Cantor replayed their moment of earthly reunion.

Cantor kissed her fingers. "Before he called me back, I was waiting for you, Lily. In the faces of everyone I saw who lives there, still I was searching for you. Knowing you would come soon and join me. I was waiting."

Sheep grazed and bleated in the pasture. The herd dog barked.

Cantor finished, "Something else. One more thing. They are all waiting too. Waiting for Yeshua to come back. Messiah's crown, his royal robes—all are laid aside while he is here among the lost sheep of Israel. Near the crown, there are great angels who . . ." He hesitated and winced. "Oh, Lily, I can't speak it. Maybe if I had a quill. Ink and papyrus. Maybe I could . . ."

"It's all right, Cantor. I can't take it all in. But Yod, you say? You saw her there? Just before you left?"

"She was the last . . . in her mother's arms."

PART II

"See!" Joshua said to all the people. "This stone will be a witness against us. It has heard all the words the LORD has said to us. It will be a witness against you if you are untrue to your God."

JOSHUA 24:27

12

CHAPTER

The area abounded in creeks and man-made waterways. Many of the bridges were toll crossings. Though Lily and Cantor were without coins to pay, the toll collector accepted payment in duck eggs Lily gathered from the marsh.

Narrow canal boats plied the waters. The farther into the region they penetrated, the more Cantor remarked on the defensive possibilities. Burn a few bridges and hide the boats, and an invading army, no matter how well equipped, would be stymied before going a handful of miles.

At one crossing, the way forward was barred by a brace of sentries wearing uniforms that bore the Star of David. The officer of the guard picked out Cantor from among a long line of travelers waiting to cross.

"You!" He pointed at Cantor. "Of an age to be a soldier. Or a spy. What's your business in Narda?"

"I am a messenger," Cantor answered truthfully.

"From where do you hail?"

"Mak'ob. In Judea."

"And what's your destination?"

"The synagogue of Narda. The academy. To show myself to the priests in exile."

"Another scholar, then? One of them." The officer's eyes narrowed. He checked a list. "How many of you are there from this place— Mak'ob? We've counted more'n thirty lately. All the same purpose . . . messenger you say . . ."

Cantor did not reply. He smiled pleasantly as the officer grumbled over so many Jewish scholars arriving at once in Narda. Such a flock of holy men within the fortress of Narda was enough to spook a man. He had little doubt the commerce of the city would be affected when the brothels closed their doors and gambling ceased.

The officer eyed Lily with interest. "Your wife or your sister? Or something else?"

Lily tucked herself close to Cantor.

"My wife," Cantor replied. "She is the favored daughter of the Prince of Judah."

The soldier swept off his head covering, mocking the information. "Well. All right, then. Go ahead. And stay out of trouble."

Daniel heard heated conversation before he ever reached the counting-house. It was easy to recognize Vashti's shrill, biting tones. Daniel had been on the receiving end of her sarcasm often enough. The other was a bass rumble, punctuated by angry denials. It had to be Joshua.

"What do you mean we can't fill the order?" Daniel's brother demanded. "It's a standing requirement! Has been for ten years. A dozen jugs of the best oil every week the king is in residence here."

"I can't create olive oil out of thin air, can I?" Vashti shrieked. "Go see for yourself. You're the one who let that buyer from Kermanshah have a hundred amphorae. I heard you myself. 'We can let you have all you want,' you said. 'We had a great year,' you said. Now where are we? The king will take his business to Solomon ben Levy!"

Daniel considered retracing his steps to the house. This raging argument was particularly bitter and one of which Daniel wanted no part. On the other hand, if he failed to appear, they would report him to Melchior for being lazy. While in their present mood there was no telling how bad they would paint Daniel. Perhaps it was better to just sneak in, get to his desk, keep his head down, and let them find him later, already at work.

He climbed through a window, hung up his hood, and noiselessly drew over a stool. Extracting a scroll from its pigeonhole, Daniel unrolled the production figures of an orchard in the neighboring village of Malayer.

He was not undisturbed for long. The argument migrated down the hall toward him. "Do you see these figures?" he heard Joshua demand of his wife. "Can't you tell just by looking that something is wrong with them?"

"Why me? Why is it my fault?" Vashti shot back. "You can't hardly count on your fingers, and you accuse me of making a mistake? Don't make me laugh!"

Both rounded the corner to Daniel's cubbyhole, claws out and teeth bared, as if ready to pounce on the nearest victim.

"You!" Joshua yelled. "What do you know about this?"

"About what?" Daniel replied, keeping his tone level despite the barbed accusation he perceived coming his way.

"You were working on the accounts of the First Pressing Oil, weren't you?"

Daniel admitted this, adding, "Vashti asked me to double-check some figures and copy them over into the permanent record."

Husband and wife exchanged a look Daniel immediately interpreted as meaning trouble.

Mumbling to himself, Joshua stormed past Daniel. Savagely he grasped the inventory scroll and elbowed Daniel out of the way. He continued to mutter as he unrolled with the left hand and rolled up with the right.

"Aha!" he said, jabbing a forefinger like a knife. "Two months ago! Look!"

This demand was not addressed to Daniel, so he moved aside.

Vashti shot Daniel a withering look. "Exactly!" she confirmed with a note of triumph. "I told you I couldn't make such a stupid mistake. Stupid!"

Joshua rounded on Daniel. "Do you know what you've done?" Then, without awaiting a reply, he bellowed, "Can't you do anything right? You wrote this, didn't you?"

Since the column of figures was in Daniel's small, neat script, he saw no reason to deny it.

His teeth almost audibly grinding, Joshua said, "You transposed the count! See that? Instead of 135 you wrote 531! Idiot!"

"Wait just a—"

"You don't understand, do you?" As if Daniel were not even present, Joshua faced Vashti and announced, "He doesn't even know what he's done wrong. How can anyone be so careless? so brainless? You! You? You are to have a third of Father's estate? Ha! Your error made me sell oil already promised to someone else . . . to the king! Don't you understand? Our jars wear the king's seal! Suppliers to the royal household. It's worth thousands of drachmae . . . and now we'll lose it because of your carelessness!"

Still far from the city, Cantor and Lily were halted at another checkpoint by a thin, sour-faced little toll collector. "I have no need of duck eggs. Nor do I have pity. If you cannot pay to pass over the bridge, how will you prevent yourselves from becoming beggars and a burden to the government? You may not pass until you have the money. I would take the donkey."

Cantor shook his head.

"Then you'll never pass, because you will never have the money."

So Lily and Cantor dangled their feet in the water and remembered days and nights of waiting in the Valley of Ma'kob, when they had no provisions and no hope except in God.

I'm praying again, Provider for the Birds of the Air. Dresser of Flowers. You have no need of my praise. It adds not one measure to your glory. Still, for the sake of my own heart I praise you in my poverty. If you feed the birds and clothe the flowers, as Yeshua teaches, and you heal the lepers of Mak'ob, then surely you will make a way to the city where Yeshua commanded us we must go.[18]

Lily's prayer was answered suddenly. It was the hawk that gained them favor and passage through a whole series of toll gates. A charioteer on the highway riding with a single attendant noticed Hawk as he swooped down at Cantor's command. The man, strong and in his mid-forties, with grizzled hair and beard, reined up his fine team of horses. He grinned broadly as Cantor scratched the top of Hawk's head.

"I favor falcons m'self," commented the charioteer.

Cantor answered, "I raised him from a fledgling. He fell from the nest and . . . well."

"Not from these parts. Falcon's the thing for hunting here."

"A common hawk. Judea."

"Uncommon hawk, more like. He keeps one eye on his master. I saw him stoop."

"He works for love. All of it . . . for love. You know how they are."

A deep laugh answered. "Aye. Spend my days in the mews talking to my birds. Where are you going?"

"To Narda. The synagogue." Cantor did not mention his need for the toll payment.

"Well then. I'm not the religious type. No arguing Torah and the like. But I can use the company of a fellow who appreciates falconry. Will you and your woman ride along to the city? My man here will bring your donkey."

Lily and Cantor joined him gladly. Hawk circled lazily above. The man did indeed talk falconry nonstop, even through every checkpoint. Tolls were waived for him. Officials greeted him, bowing as he passed.

Cantor discussed the care and training of birds of prey. Lily managed to shut out their boisterous male voices.

I'm praying again, Lord Who Opens Gates When Every Way Seems Barred. Thank you for sending this brash fellow to us. A pleasant enough sort. A fine judge of men and of hawks.

She closed her eyes and dozed. The air was filled with the scent of flowers. The sun was warm, but the breeze kept the temperature pleasant.

Lily sensed the city of Narda before she saw it. As the chariot approached the Nehar Malka, "King's Canal," the widest and deepest of the man-made waterways in the area, the breeze shifted. From due north the zephyr swung round to blow out of the west, instantly perfuming the air with lavender. The aroma was so rich Lily almost anticipated an atmosphere tinged with color to match the fragrance.

Once across the canal, her imagined confusion of scent and sight was nearly fulfilled. The road climbed out of a small valley to reveal the town of Narda spread before them, but it was the nearer scenery that drew Lily's attention. The fields were carpeted with lavender flowers. Millions of stalks, acres of blossoms, gave the region its name.

Pure nard was one of the most costly of all scents. The lavender from Narda, distilled to its most potent form, then combined with balsam, became the most expensive unguent in two empires. A single alabaster bottle cost as much as a month's wages. It could support a beggar for a year.

The charioteer inhaled appreciatively and thumped his chest with a clenched fist. "Smell that?" he demanded unnecessarily. "No wonder they say this is where Gan Eden stood."

The guards at the entrance to the city bowed deeply and stepped aside for the charioteer.

Wanting to make a showy entry into the city, the driver whipped up the team. "Between the rivers. Lavender growing wild. Gan Eden. Easy to see why."

13

The scene at home in front of his father was every bit as unpleasant as Daniel expected. He had been practically dragged there by Joshua and Vashti. Their nonstop, alternating torrent of verbal abuse prevented him from offering any defense; eventually he stopped trying.

The flood of criticism subsided briefly when the trio reached Melchior's study. For a moment Daniel hoped they had worn themselves out, but this optimism proved illusory. His brother and sister-in-law merely gathered their strength to redouble their efforts.

"He has really done it this time," Joshua pronounced.

While Vashti offered scathing commentary in the background, Joshua proceeded to explain how Daniel had cost the family the royal patronage and uncountable lost revenue.

"Calm down," Melchior ordered after the first outburst was spent. "It's not as bad as all that. We will go to Solomon ben Levy and buy what we need from his supply to resell to the king."

"But he'll charge us full price! We'll lose money on every jar," Vashti protested.

"Yes, but we'll keep the patronage. More importantly, we'll keep our integrity. We will make good on our promises. In the end, that's more important than a few jugs of oil or a few coins more or less."

Vashti scoffed and repeated the word *few* but bit her lip when Joshua glared at her.

"What is also important is to understand how this happened so we don't repeat it."

Daniel saw this as his moment to redeem himself. "I knew there was something wrong with the figures, Father. I knew the inventory didn't match the records."

"You knew there was a problem, yet you did nothing?" Joshua said scathingly.

"I hunted and hunted for the error," Daniel protested. "I just could never find it."

"And you told no one else?" Melchior questioned.

This comment seemed terribly unfair. "This was not a mistake anyone told me to correct," Daniel said. "I noticed it by myself. Then, when no one else said anything about it, I thought I was mistaken."

"Lazy," Joshua said under his breath. "Careless and lazy."

"Son." Melchior addressed Daniel, but his eyes rested on Joshua. His tone was not unkind. "Mistakes can happen to anyone."

Vashti and Joshua snorted in unison.

"To anyone," Melchior repeated pointedly. "But if you couldn't locate the trouble yourself, you should have told someone else."

How could Daniel explain that to announce such an error would seem critical of Joshua or Vashti? Why would his father not understand the insults Daniel would have endured if he had suggested any such thing? So Daniel said nothing; such an explanation seemed pointless and childish.

"You could always have come to me."

As kindly as this was meant, it was no real answer. If Daniel had gone to his father, Joshua would instantly claim Daniel was trying to make him look bad—that he was tale-bearing, that he was blaming Vashti for his own mistakes. Probably all of those lies would have been used against him. The self-righteousness of his elder brother knew no bounds. While Daniel's motives were always suspect, Joshua could never admit any wrongdoing of his own. By definition, anything he or Vashti did was always correct.

"Joshua and Vashti, you may go. Make the arrangements with ben Levy and the difficulty is resolved. Daniel, stay a moment more."

With an inward sigh and a carefully neutral expression, Daniel waited.

"I know there was no intentional wrongdoing," Melchior noted. "This was an error of omission only. But our business is very complex. This year's cultivation of the trees affects next year's crop and the reputation of our family a year after that . . . if you take my meaning."

"I do, Father," Daniel agreed. "All our decisions have consequences, good or bad. But this wasn't my fault! I—"

Melchior raised his hand to halt the protest. "We'll say no more about it. Remember: this training is all to benefit you. Not just counting amphorae—I can hire a clerk to do that—but also schooling in how the business works . . . and in dealing with people too. Someday one-third of all I own will be yours . . . yours and your children's after you. You are laying the foundations now for your children's children, eh? Now go along. We both have other chores to attend."

Daniel wanted to say more, wanted to talk about the timing. The hunt for the mistake had occurred just as Hannel of the Marshes arrived in Ecbatana. After that few days' excitement, locating an obscure arithmetic blunder did not seem important enough to pursue. A few days later still, Daniel had forgotten all about it, until today.

In the end, though, that sequence of events was all an excuse.

Daniel merely nodded and backed out of the study. By then, Melchior's attention was again devoted to a letter he was reading and not toward Daniel at all.

Every eye was on them as they drove through the city of Narda. The wealthy nodded. The poor bowed low. Who was this fellow? Lily wondered.

The charioteer pulled up his team and allowed them to drink at the fountain in the central square. He scowled and searched the faces of the crowd, as though he was looking for someone.

Moments later a herald and five armed servants dressed in elegant blue livery pushed through the crush of citizens, approached, and bowed at the waist.

"Lord Tannis."

"You're late," the charioteer growled. "You were told to be here when I returned."

"Only a minute or two."

Tannis cuffed the herald on the side of the head, then mounted his chariot again. Two servants took position on each side of the vehicle and two behind.

The herald cried, "Make way for Lord Tannis! Gracious and terrible. Elder brother, to be feared among all warriors. Coruler of the province of Narda!"

Cantor considered their host with renewed curiosity. Lily almost laughed.

I'm praying again, Lord Who Knows All Things. Where and When and Who and How. So you sent one of the infamous rulers of this place to help us enter. The kinder of the two brothers, they say. You know such details. Things we could not know.

Lord Tannis brought the reins down on the backs of his team of horses. It was not difficult to picture a whip in his hand snapping on the backs of the servants who ran beside them.

Tannis sneered as he drove, and now people scrambled out of the way. "So. This is my city. Now you know it. These are my slaves. I am their master. Though they are late."

Lily was certain Tannis had kept his identity a secret until he could impress and surprise them with an entourage.

"Now you will tell me," Tannis demanded, "what your business is here."

"We have come to offer a sacrifice of thanksgiving," Cantor answered.

"Why here? I can tell from your accents you are Judean. So, tell me. Why have you left the territory of our . . . friend . . . Herod Antipas?"

Cantor and Lily exchanged glances of caution. "We are . . . have lived our lives as exiles within Judea, Lord Tannis."

Tannis narrowed his dark eyes. "Our city has seen a flood of exiles from Judea these months past. Many are accused of heresy by the council in Yerushalayim. Are you heretics?"

"No, Lord Tannis."

He fixed his fierce gaze on Lily. "Then why do you come here to offer your sacrifices? I expect the truth."

"We were lepers in the Valley of Mak'ob," Lily replied.

Only an instant of surprise registered in his expression. "Were . . . you were . . . lepers? So you claim to be among those healed by the prophet we have heard so much about? This Nazarene prophet?"

Lily nodded.

"I'm not a believer. I am a Jew, but unwelcome in the synagogue of my own city. But I tell you, it is well you have fled from Herod Antipas. He beheaded the Baptizer . . . the prophet who proclaimed doom upon him for adultery. And he will kill the Nazarene as well before the story is finished."

Cantor replied, "We hope not, Lord Tannis. We pray not."

"Pray all you like. Politics and Money are the twin gods who rule Yerushalayim, Rome, and the whole world." The reins cracked down on the horses. "And the sword and the whip in the hands of men are the voice of the gods."

Cantor said, "Yeshua is stronger than death."

"No mere man is stronger than death. Death requires that all men must pay the sacrifice." He shook his head. "So . . . you claim to be former lepers of Mak'ob. Healed by a prophet. And he sent you here with the others? Where are your sacrifices, then? What do you bring to the God of Avraham, Yitz'chak, and Ya'acov?"

"The Lord will provide our sacrifice."

Tannis snorted. "The Lord is a businessman. Two doves and a lamb, is it? That is what is required? Money must first be produced before God provides such an expensive thank-offering. You will stay at my home. Inspect my raptors. Tour my mews."

The invitation of Lord Tannis was a command.

"The synagogue. Pressing business," Cantor explained.

"It can wait, I think." Tannis gazed appreciatively at Lily. "You're concerned about entering the house of an apostate? accepting my hospitality? No, don't deny it. I see it in your eyes. *Apostate*, you're thinking. But never mind. You will sleep in a tent . . . like Avraham and Sarai. All silk and brocade. A pavilion like the patriarchs. You'll not be defiled by entering my home."

Lily and Cantor had no choice in the matter. It was settled in the mind of Lord Tannis, and Lily knew that to object or refuse his offer would be dangerous.

The chariot slowed as Tannis turned onto a broad street lined with cypress trees. Armed guards at their stations stiffened in salute as Tannis passed. A walled palace loomed ahead. Lily spotted soldiers patrolling the walls. Double gates swung wide at their approach. Without missing a stride, the horses rattled into the courtyard.

Tannis stepped from his vehicle with the bearing of a hero in a Greek myth. At once servants flocked to take charge of the horses and present their master and his guests with water for washing and wine to drink. The certainty of who and what he was filled Lily's mind as she watched him in the midst of his people.

I'm praying again, Lord Who Knows the Hearts of All Men—rich and poor, proud and humble. See how he surveys his slaves and sweeps his hand over all and says, "Mine." Tannis is a lone tree, claiming every wind that touches him is his own. He is lonely, I think, Lord.

Tannis blustered, "Yes. We'll set up the pavilion there for you. Beside the fountain." He snapped his fingers and a trio of slaves set to work fulfilling his command. "But now, come with me. My falcons. My hawks. The mews where we house the birds are extensive. Bigger than the houses of most men. Even rich men. But my birds are worthy. More to be trusted than men, wouldn't you say?" Tannis strode toward a long, low building opposite the stable.

Cantor did not reply. When he raised his arm, Hawk swooped down. Cantor placed the raptor on his shoulder.

Hawk blinked at horses peering out from stalls and men at work. He cocked his head when they entered the main structure of the mews. Perches lined three sides of the room. Tethered there were twenty birds: falcons, hawks, an eagle, and four owls of varied sizes.

Hawk seemed unperturbed in the presence of such a noble company of feathered hunters. He fluffed his feathers and observed his brothers with detached interest.

Tannis reached up to stroke Hawk's head. Hawk opened his beak and struck so fiercely that Tannis would have lost a finger if the bird had connected.

"Ah, well," Tannis said. "I see your hawk belongs only to one master."

Cantor lifted the bird and Hawk stepped easily onto Lily's arm. She held him close beneath her chin without fear.

Tannis raised his eyebrows appreciatively. "You aren't afraid of his beak? Or his talons? Take your nose off like that?" Another snap of the fingers.

Lily tossed her head. "No. Not afraid."

Tannis continued, "He is an unusual hawk. Belonging to your family, eh? I had brought you here because at first I thought I might buy your hawk."

Cantor replied, "He's never been tethered. He comes and goes as he pleases. I can't sell him."

Tannis laughed. "I have enough birds. Like women, eh? For some men, one hunter is enough. These are mine. All of them belong to me." Then to Lily, "Are you afraid of them?"

They looked fierce and threatening.

Lily replied, "I respect them. They don't know me."

"Wise answer. So . . . your hawk. Does he belong to you also?"

"Do they ever belong to anyone?" Lily asked.

Tannis shrugged. "Debatable. A question for Greek philosophers, not for me. Perhaps I belong to them."

Cantor admired the raptors, passing down the line and stopping to comment upon each and to question their qualities, talent, and countries of origin. "The owls?"

Tannis brightened. "So! Have you never seen an owl hunt? I fly them at night. Remarkable." He snapped his fingers twice, and the largest of the owls opened his eyes and swiveled his head toward his master. "We must go night hunting. My owls are most intelligent fowl. Even as Greek myths portray them to be. Unusual birds. Gentle companions, even for a lady. And so silent! This one can brush the top of my head with his wing tips; I will feel a puff of air but hear nothing." There was a long silence as Tannis scratched the owl's head. Then he asked, "You like them? My little family?"

"Very much," Cantor replied.

"Good. I am in need of a falconer. A trainer. These birds are only the best. Acquired by me from around the world." He paused. "There is a falconry competition each year. Renowned. Romans. Greeks. The ruler of Parthia himself. My falconer died unexpectedly last month. He was a wise old bird, but now he's dead. So, it may be the fates at work. I find you on the road . . . and here you are."

Lily considered Tannis' words. Even the dead falconer had been "his."

Cantor replied cautiously. "I-I'm flattered, but I must have some time to consider."

"There are quarters above this room. A dwelling above the mews for a man with a family. A salary for a freeman. A good place to live. I have slaves who learned enough to carry on, yes, but I need a man who will live here . . . work with my birds for the love of the sport."

Lily caught a flash of some unnamed emotion in Tannis' eyes. It was dangerous. Somehow the offer of employment implied ownership.

Cantor smiled. "I can't accept such an offer without time to consider."

Tannis reached out in another attempt to pet Hawk. Once again the great speckled bird snapped at him. "Your bird does not like me, it seems. Well, if I cannot own your hawk, perhaps you will at least accept the gift of my hospitality. Your tent must be erected by now. Come along."

They just would not let up! Joshua and Vashti picked on Daniel constantly. Any progress he had made in being properly treated, respected as an adult, was all lost because of one stupid error that was not even his fault.

Daniel brooded sullenly for several days. His father seemed to think the matter closed, but neither Daniel's brother nor his sister-in-law did. They found fault with everything Daniel did, one of them saying one thing and the other ordering something completely different . . . then both of them lambasting him for failing to follow instructions.

After taking the abuse much longer than he thought anyone else would endure, Daniel finally stormed out of the countinghouse. His first thought was to find Bartok. He needed someone to whom he could pour out his troubles or he would explode. Daniel briefly considered enlisting the aid of his father or mother but discarded both notions.

If he wanted to be treated as a man, capable of making his own decisions and being respected for such, he could not go to his mother for help. As good as her counsel was, Joshua would never let him forget such a course. The accusation of "crying to Mama" stung Daniel's pride before he ever heard it uttered.

Melchior would listen carefully and judge fairly, but he was always too interested in reconciliation to ever actually settle disputes. Having everyone get along was his highest motivation; he would never do anything to redress Daniel's grievances or take Joshua to task for his injustice.

In fact, the farther Daniel charged along the road toward Bartok's home, the more convinced he became that his father didn't really love him. Or at least his father didn't respect him. Melchior consulted Joshua as with an equal. Toward Daniel he was more indulgent, but not in a good way. Every action, every comment, seemed intended to remind Daniel how young, how immature, how incapable he was!

Bartok would listen!

Daniel reached Bartok's home on the fourth, or "Mercury," level of the city. The city walls in this sector were painted pale blue, like a twilight sky. Melchior had once explained to Daniel that the planet Mercury—Kowkab, The Messenger, to the Hebrews—only appeared just after sunset or just before sunrise, so was always seen against a lighter blue backdrop. Magi who lived before the days of Daniel's namesake, Dani'el the Prophet, had organized Ecbatana as a constant visual reminder of the Sun, Moon, and five wandering stars.

Tonight the recollection made no difference to Daniel. Great scholar, famous man, successful merchant—none of Melchior's well-deserved reputations impressed Daniel tonight. Daniel was tired of being disrespected and disregarded, and he blamed his father for allowing it to continue.

He hammered on Bartok's door, then excused himself to the housemaid for the uproar. No, none of the family was home, she replied to Daniel's inquiry. Bartok's parents had gone to a circumcision, but Bartok was not with them. No, she did not know either where he was or when he would return.

Biting back a retort about her uselessness, Daniel left a message for his friend, saying that he was being sought, and left again.

Now what? It was still too early to go home.

Daniel realized that in his present mood he would not be good company for Mina, but perhaps she could bring him out of this black humor. If he was careful about how much griping he did to her, it should be all right.

His face brightened when he thought about seeing her. Because he had been working so hard lately, he had not visited her much, and it had been over a month since their last lengthy conversation.

Daniel's mood lightened with each step. He should have thought of Mina before this.

Between a guard station and a spice merchant's shop were steps ascending to the next level of the city. The staircase curved as it followed the sweep of the wall. Halfway up the flight, the color changed from blue to rust, signifying that he had reached the height of Mars, or The Adam, in the layout of the city.

Mina's family was wealthy. Only well-to-do citizens could live within the fifth ring of Ecbatana. Only nobles and royalty could live any higher.

It was late for Daniel to come calling, but he pressed on anyway. He had known Mina forever. They had been children together. For as long as Daniel could remember, he had expected to marry her someday. There had never been a formal betrothal, but Mina never seemed to expect that. . . . It was just an understanding. Perhaps that situation was something else that needed to change in his life, Daniel thought. He should ask his father to formally request Mina's hand on Daniel's behalf and set a date.

That would prove to his parents and his brother that he was serious about adult responsibility. He would get married and have a household of his own. Then they would have to give him the respect he deserved.

Now that his mind was made up, Daniel decided he should share the news with Mina first. It would not do to sit in her front room, making idle conversation with her parents while he was bursting with such a significant announcement.

At the side of the multilevel home was a gate leading to a terrace. Fruit trees in large clay pots ringed a flagstone courtyard where a fountain chuckled into the night sky. Jupiter, The Righteous, hung like a lantern in the south, tucked between The Waterbearer and The Two Fish. The waning moon had not yet risen, but Daniel was so familiar with Mina's courtyard that he stepped unerringly in the dark, avoiding a curb and a drainage channel without even trying.

His thoughts raced ahead to what he would say to her—how it was past time for him to suggest this step. She, though a few years younger than he, would certainly agree.

As Daniel stooped to gather a handful of pebbles to toss at Mina's window, he heard voices. From just ahead, around the next corner, came whispers . . . furtive, secretive conversation.

Robbers! It had to be. Perhaps Mina's parents had gone to the same *Bris* as Bartok's family. Sneak thieves watched homes for just such an opportunity.

It could be even worse: Perhaps Mina was home alone!

Daniel did not consider raising an alarm. He would surprise the burglars, rout them in his fury, be acclaimed by Mina and her family.

What if they were armed? What could he use for a weapon?

Based on remembered visits, Daniel's fingers searched the rim of the fountain. It was there: a clay jug just the right size and weight to be swung as a club. Now let them try to resist him!

With a loud cry Daniel charged, raising the pitcher high above his head as he hurtled forward. Just around the corner he barreled into two people standing close together, started the flask swinging forward, and nearly brained Bartok . . . who was locked in a tight embrace with Mina.

CHAPTER 14

How Daniel arrived at the Jeweled Peacock that night he could never remember. Neither did he immediately know how he came to be propped in the corner by the fireplace, soaking wet, though that came to be clear soon enough.

He remembered hitting Bartok in the jaw and seeing him fly backwards into a wall and slide down it. He had a perfect recollection of Mina screaming, then yelling that she never, ever wanted to see him again.

After that Daniel knew he had stumbled away into the night, run blindly into a potted palm, and fallen headlong into a drainage ditch. From the fact that one sleeve of his robe was in tatters he must have been in a fight, but with whom? Not Bartok, certainly.

Somehow he could not account for much else. His memory of the full tale was a pitch-black night, illuminated by rare, streaking stars of pain, chagrin, and grief.

Gingerly Daniel touched the mass of feverish, lumpy flesh that was his face. The cheek opposite the birthmark was scored and gravel-pocked, as if he had rested for a while facedown on the ground.

There were also vague memories of another tavern . . . or was it two more? Daniel's left eye would not open, but out of the right he saw movement.

An instant later a bucket of water was flung against his head. The deluge forced its way into his mouth and nose, making Daniel sputter and cough.

He waved his right arm feebly and clumsily. "Enough! Wanna drown me? I'm awake."

A pair of legs like tree trunks swam in front of his vision; then someone's broad, brown visage approached his until their noses almost touched.

Lono.

"What're you doing here?" Daniel heard himself ask. Even in his own ears it was nonsensical. "Help me up."

Why was Lono hesitating? Daniel stretched out his hand with a groan at the effort. "Help," he repeated.

There seemed to be a three-way conference going on across the room. A heated voice: the tavern keeper. A stern pronouncement: an officer of the city guards. A placating, soothing tone: Daniel's father!

Daniel groaned again, wishing he could crawl away somewhere . . . anywhere. He tried to shut his ears against the trio discussing him, but their words landed on his head like hammer blows.

"There's at least a hundred drachmae damage," the innkeeper demanded.

"I'll make it good," Daniel heard Melchior say.

"Don't forget he assaulted four of my men," the guard captain added. "One of them has a broken nose."

When had that occurred? Daniel wondered. And how had he managed to best four of the town watchmen single-handed?

"He should be locked up," the captain added.

"I'll take full responsibility," Melchior said. "It won't happen again."

Of course it would never happen again! Daniel wanted to explain about Joshua and Vashti, about Bartok, about Mina . . . about how Daniel's life had suddenly gone up in smoke like a magician's conjuring trick.

It was no good. Nothing seemed to be working. Not his body . . . not his brain . . . not his mouth.

"Come on, Lono. We'll have to carry him," Melchior observed. "Let's get him home."

Gratefully, Daniel sank back into a dazed stupor where no explanations were either demanded or attempted.

Before first light, Cantor and Lily awoke to the bleating of a lamb outside their tent. Lily pulled back the flap and emerged to find the tiny creature tethered to a stake beside two turtledoves in a cage. Nearby was the required oil and flour to complete their offering.

Lily looked toward the big house, where Tannis lived. There was the glimmer of a light and stirring behind the curtain of his bedchamber. Was he watching to see their response?

"The Lord has provided our sacrifice, Cantor," Lily said quietly. "Everything we need."

Cantor joined her in the cool morning air. He stroked the head of the lamb. "He means us to offer this sacrifice . . . not only for ourselves . . ."

Lily nodded. "If he met Yeshua, he would know."

"It is written in Leviticus that the Lord dwells with his people even when they are unclean with transgression.[19] It is the haughty and proud he cannot endure."[20]

Lily gazed toward Tannis' window. "Better a sinner in need of mercy than an arrogant man."

I'm praying again, Provider for Our Needs. You command us to fulfill the law of lepers, and you provided the sacrifice.[21] I'm praying for Lord Tannis, so far from your courts, but near to your heart. Ashamed of his sins—not proud. What word did you whisper that made such a man give the gifts of a leper to offer back to you? He is not proud, Lord, and so, I'm praying. Asking. Look at the healing sacrifice we offer today for our own leprosy as healing also for the leprosy of sin in the soul of Lord Tannis.

Hawk observed them from his perch on the olive tree. He did not follow as they gathered up the offerings and made their way to the gates of the great synagogue of Narda.

The gates swung wide and Lily and Cantor entered the courtyard of the synagogue.

Two priests accepted their offerings. "What sacrifice do you make today?"

Cantor answered, "For the cleansing of leprosy."

There was not even a glimmer of surprise in the eyes of the younger priest. He led the lamb away to be slaughtered.

Sacrifices were made at the altar, and the prayers were offered. Blood from Lily and Cantor's lamb was collected in a bowl. Then Lily and Cantor were brought into the great hall to await presentation and absolution.

The president of the Synagogue of the Exiles, to whom they were presented, was named Nehemiah, after the one who returned from Babylon to rebuild the Second Temple in Jerusalem.

The House of Study and Worship had been erected five hundred years before by the exiled craftsmen of Israel. It was a replica of Solomon's Great Temple, but occupying only one-quarter of the area. Clusters of golden grapes hung from the gilded rafters. Hebrew letters from the Torah intertwined the gold leaf vines at the top of the walls.

Known as the treasure house for Jews of the East, it was here that the half-shekel Temple tax, destined for Jerusalem, was collected. For those Jews who could not make pilgrimage to Jerusalem in order to present their tithes and offerings, Narda provided an officially sanctioned substitute.

Here was the eastern branch of the Yeshiva School of the Great Hillel, taught by disciples of Gamaliel the First. When Herod the Butcher King had crucified members of the Pharisees by the thousands, many scholars had fled here, deep into the territory of Parthia. Most, knowing that the sons of the Butcher King were the image of their evil father, had never returned to Jerusalem. News of the death of Yochanan the Baptizer had confirmed that the danger of Herodian rule was still fierce.

Each Passover Rabbi Nehemiah was heard to say, "Maybe next year in Yerushalayim, nu? Maybe next year Messiah will reveal himself and we can all go home."

Lily and Cantor were escorted to a private chamber near the storerooms of incense. The air was redolent with the aroma of nard and spices. Light streamed from a high narrow window onto a floor paved with stone the color of sapphire. They stood together hand in hand and waited to be pronounced whole and welcomed back into society.

Though the ritual of purification for lepers had been first given to Moses, before now, Lily thought, it had never been practiced.

Long moments passed.

I'm praying again, Lord Who Has Brought Us Out of Darkness. I thank you for the color blue beneath my feet. The sea. The sky. My eyes can see everything now . . . clearer than I ever saw before. I'm praying again for Life. . . . Thank you for returning Cantor to my side. I'm asking that those exiles we meet here now may see you, the God who invented color and gave us back our eyes.

The elderly Rabbi Nehemiah was stooped from years of study. A grandson of Hillel, he shared blood ties with Gamaliel the Second in Jerusalem. His eyes were cloudy with cataracts, and he was nearly blind. His twenty-five-year-old grandson, who would inherit his position one day, guided Nehemiah's shuffling steps and read Torah to him.

With quaking voice the old man asked, "Children, what are your names?"

"Lily."

"Cantor."

The old man chuckled low. "A flower and a song. Names that praise HaShem in their speaking. And from where have you come?"

Cantor replied for them both. "The Valley of Mak'ob in Judea. The ancient City of Refuge where we lived our lives as lepers until the Healer came. He told us to come here. To present ourselves to you."

The old man was not surprised, nor did he question further. He raised his eyes to the light streaming through the window. Then he raised his hands and proclaimed, "Blessed are you, O Adonai, who has let us live to see this day. You alone have sent us Yeshua . . . your Salvation. . . ."

I'm praying again, Creator of Vision. Though the old man cannot see us with his eyes, his heart sees clearly our healing. He knows the Name of your Salvation. Our request is not met with doubt.

It was the young man who examined the hands and feet of Lily and Cantor and confirmed, "There is no sign of any disease, Grandfather. Their skin is perfect. Smooth like that of a newborn baby. Perfect. As it is written of Naaman, the Syrian leper who came to the prophet Elisha and was healed, blessed be HaShem! Smooth like the flesh of the children."[22]

"So the number of the Lamedvov . . . the thirty-six righteous souls . . . is now fulfilled," Old Nehemiah declared. "Thanks be to HaShem."

The young man guided Nehemiah's trembling finger from the bowl of lamb's blood to anoint Lily and Cantor. Tip of the right ear. Thumb of the right hand. Great toe of the right foot. Then seven times he sprinkled them with the oil of thanksgiving for their healing.

Following the pattern of the blood from the guilt offering, he anointed ear, thumb, and big toe with the remaining oil.

At last old Nehemiah pronounced the end of their long ordeal: "This is the law of him who is healed from the plague of leprosy. Blessed are you, O Adonai, who heals all our diseases![23] The One called Yeshua of Nazareth has sent you to us, nu?" Nehemiah smiled a toothless smile. "You are not the only miracles who have been sent to our place of refuge. No Romans here. No Herodians. I am grandson of Hillel and brother of Simeon ben Gamaliel, who told me of the Holy Child he blessed in Yerushalayim . . . all those years ago."

Cantor replied, "We have both traveled from a far place by his word."

"After such a long journey, you must be hungry. Will you come? Follow my grandson and me. We have many guests. Though they are small, they are exiles like yourselves, who will be sharing a meal."

The laughter and voices of children echoed in the long corridor of the school as Rabbi Nehemiah and his grandson led the way. He tapped his temple as if he knew a great many things. Then he told them, "I had a vision many years ago. The Cantor and the Lily. You see, Cantor. I know the name. Trainer of hawks. Searcher of stars. Singer of songs. One who made the long journey into *olam haba* and now has returned."

Then he said to Lily, "And Lily. I know the name. Teacher of children. Seeker of the Messiah. She who had the courage to venture Outside the Valley to find and bring him back."

Lily and Cantor exchanged astonished glances. How did the rabbi know so much?

The din of young voices grew louder.

The old man stepped over the threshold of a large sunlit classroom, paused, then spread his arms as if to embrace the students and the elderly teacher in their midst.

Hawk perched on the highest window ledge of the classroom. A flock of children laughed and pointed and called out. One cry rang like a bell above the others: "It's Cantor's hawk, I tell you!"

Lily recognized the voice of little Yod, child of the last thousand heartbeats! But she did not recognize the little girl—with curls now the color of cinnamon and bright, clear eyes a slightly darker shade of brown.

Lily gasped with joy. Cantor grasped her hand.

Yod exclaimed, "It is! Cantor's hawk come all the way from Sorrow!"

A boy a year or two older agreed. "Hawk! He's followed us here and found us!"

Children, beautiful and perfect, discussed the identity of the speckled raptor who observed them solemnly. The flock of youngsters had not yet seen Lily and Cantor framed in the doorway. Somewhere in their collective memory Cantor remained in a lonely grave and Lily lived alone.

I'm praying again, You Who Are the God of the Living . . . you who love us in this world and love us in olam haba. *You saw these children always. You knew what they looked like beneath their ragged flesh and suffering. You remade them what they would have been if . . . if only there were no sickness or sorrow or death. Beautiful!*

Lily said to Cantor, "I shall have to learn to recognize them by their faces now. I only know them by their voices."

Cantor nodded, then clucked his tongue and raised his hand. Hawk spread his wings and, with one easy flap, glided over their heads to Cantor's arm.

Heads swiveled to watch Hawk float down. Cries of joy and amazement filled the room. These were the little ones who had huddled beneath Lily's arms like chicks in need of protection. How many had been destined for the Dying Cave before the evening Yeshua entered the Valley of Sorrows? Blind from leprosy, they had lost the ability to see. Robbed of speech, they had been unable to laugh until Yeshua commanded laughter to return.

Yod's eyes widened. She stood up and spread her arms as though she could fly into Cantor's arms over the heads of her companions.

They had all seen Cantor . . . dead! They had grieved as the wicker bier had passed by them. They had wept beside Cantor's grave. But *now*!

Silence fell as they gawked at Cantor holding his hawk.

They murmured the questions. Were their eyes deceiving them? A dream? And yet, Hawk perched beneath Cantor's chin . . . Hawk, who had followed Cantor's voice to the window ledge.

Yod whispered, "Cantor?"

"Rabbi Ahava? Could it be him?"

"Look! The hawk flew right to him!"

"Is it . . . ?" Everyone but Yod hung back, terrified by their joy. What if it wasn't true? What if they were dreaming? And then, when they awoke with their dream arms around his neck, he wouldn't really be there.

There were no words by which Lily could answer their questions. It was no wonder they were frightened. It was true. The worst thing in the world had really happened to Cantor—the final nightmare from which you never awaken. The thing called Death. They had seen it! Cantor had indeed died, and dead was dead.

Until Yeshua came into the Valley of their sorrow.

Throughout the long night Yeshua had healed them all . . . all . . . hands, feet, noses, and ears . . . new faces . . . laughter! Life!

But what of those like Cantor who slept in the dust of Mak'ob's graveyard? Too late for all of them who died before Yeshua came! Too late!

All those living, who were healed, had climbed up the path and escaped from their sorrow. Only Lily had been left below with Yeshua.

After they were alone, Yeshua had called Cantor forth from his grave.

There were stories about others who were raised. Outside the Valley, the stories were retold secretly, in joy and fear . . . so many others. It was not only Cantor who had come back from *olam haba*.

But Cantor was more than a distant story about a widow's son or a girl in Capernaum.

Cantor was real. Cantor taught them hawking. He named the constellations. He sang the psalms of David when their hearts were so homesick for lost families they could hardly breathe. He helped the rabbi instruct them in their alef-bet from the old flat stone that was the bema of Mak'ob's starlit synagogue!

Cantor was not just a story. He was their beloved friend, their elder brother.

And now, unless this was a cruel dream, Cantor had come home to them from the finality of death.

"Children, don't be afraid!" Lily spread her arms to embrace them all. "Yes, it is. It's all true. And more joy yet to come. I'm sure of it!"

Only Yod stepped over her friends in her scramble to reach Cantor and Lily. "Oh, Cantor, it is you! I saw you there, in that moment after my last heartbeat. Before his voice commanded me to come back. I saw you there in *olam haba* . . . in the shining place! But now you're here!" She wrapped her arms around his waist and laughed.

The others remembered Cantor's cold, disfigured body, the clods of earth falling on his face. They did not speak at all now. They did not run to embrace him.

From the midst of the children Rabbi Ahava, spiritual shepherd of the Valley of Mak'ob, rose to his feet. Trembling, he raised both arms and cried out with joy. "I believe. I . . . BELIEVE! This is NOT A DREAM! Blessed . . . blessed be the Eternal!" He clapped his hands. "Look, children. It IS Cantor! He has come back. Back! From very far away to find us!"

The silence broke.

Boys and girls—shining, clean, healthy—squealed and leapt to their feet in a massive cheer. They clambered to surround and embrace Yod, Lily, and Cantor.

Rabbi Nehemiah stepped back from the reunion and grinned. He raised his marbled eyes to the ceiling and shouted over the noise of voices speaking all at once: "So, my brother . . . Ahava! My vision was a true one after all. Thirty-six years I waited for this day! Lamedvov! The thirty-six! Lamedvov! Lamedvov! He who sees us in exile has sent the Lamedvov to teach us. Such a homecoming! Your children . . . all of them. Safe at last. So many new faces, eh? I can see them with my eyes closed!" the blind man quipped.

Lily cupped Yod's smooth chin and kissed her curls.

I'm praying again, Shepherd Who Leads Us from the Beginning to the End. A new face you have given us all . . . all new faces. You have gathered us here in this haven of safety. Present ourselves to the priest, you said, knowing Reb Nehemiah had already seen us coming. I'm thanking you, Lord Who Leads Us. I am praising you! We whom you have given new faces are never lost.

15 CHAPTER

I t had taken some time, much pondering and soul-searching, but by the start of the High Holy Days, Daniel had made up his mind.

Rosh Hashanah, the Day of Trumpets, the celebration of the New Year, came to the Jews of Ecbatana. The city's Gentile populace was a mixture of all forms of paganism: Zoroastrians, devotees of Artemis, even a small sect of Pan followers.

Since the days of Queen Esther, Jews had lived and worshipped freely throughout Persian lands. On this holiday, Jewish trumpets rang at sunset up and down the seven levels of the city. From the white walls of the lowest tier to the battlements of the scarlet height, just below the silver and gold tracery adorning the homes of the Parthian nobles, Jewish trumpeters let the whole city know the High Holy Days of El'Elyon had begun.

It was a time of great rejoicing . . . except in the home of Melchior the Magus.

Daniel saw frozen looks of dismay and disbelief on all his family's faces gathered at supper, but he was determined to not draw back. He repeated his demand: "I said, you have often told me that I am entitled to one-third of your estate. That responsibility has been drummed into me over and over. All right, I believe you. And I want it now."

"Preposterous!" Joshua erupted. "Are you drunk again?"

"He's just angry because he's so incompetent and he cost the family money," Vashti asserted. "This is just a childish way of fighting back."

Esther said nothing, but her face was drawn and grieved. Her hands twisted a napkin into a knotted ruin. Daniel could not bear to look at his mother, lest he lose his resolve.

Instead Daniel peered into his father's eyes, willing himself not to look away. What he saw there surprised him: hurt and disappointment.

Anger would have been easier to bear, but still Daniel persisted. "I don't see that this business concerns my brother or his wife," he said haughtily. "You promised it to me. I am leaving either way, Father, but first I want to see if you are a man of your word."

Daniel heard a sharp intake of breath from his mother. No one ever questioned Melchior's integrity. Melchior had, many times in his life, suffered personal loss rather than go back on a commitment, even when the circumstances had not been his fault.

Mechanically, without emotion, as if speaking by rote, Melchior returned, "Are you determined? Will you not reconsider?"

Daniel could not believe it was this easy. The lift to his pride made it easy for him to be cruel. "I will not stay in this house one moment longer."

"Then my answer is . . . yes."

Joshua exploded. "What? No, Father! You can't mean it!"

Melchior rounded on his elder son sharply. "Silence!"

It was a tone no one had heard Melchior use, not ever.

Then to Daniel he continued, "Since you will not consider reconciliation, and since you believe I have made you a promise, I can and I must make it good. How soon do you demand your inheritance?"

There was no drawing back now, but Daniel's thoughts were reeling. Was this actually happening? "Tonight. I want this settled tonight."

"Very well." Melchior lifted a cautionary hand toward Joshua to head off another eruption. "The olive groves and the oil business represent about one-third of my estate. Will that satisfy you?"

Vashti made a noise like a hissing serpent.

The contempt in her unspoken criticism was enough to harden Daniel's heart still further. "I want cash."

Daniel saw his father bite his lip, then nod, slowly. "Many times Solomon ben Levy has asked to take over the olive oil sales. I have always refused, hoping to keep our family business intact. But now I will sell. Is that agreeable, or do you want to audit my accounts?"

"Audit? I . . . what? No. That will do."

"Very well. If you'll meet me the first day after Yom Kippur at the provincial Hall of Records, I'll complete the transaction. Will there be anything else? I know you won't care to stay under this roof tonight."

Tonight? Daniel had not thought of what the immediate consequences would be. "Just . . . just my things."

"Since I cannot sell the household furnishings or buildings," Melchior added, "and as I do not have the cash equivalent, you may take Lono as the earnest of the rest. I will redeem him at a future date for whatever else is owed you. Do you agree?"

Strangely, Daniel found himself unable to speak. Now that he had gotten everything he asked for, why wasn't he able to feel joy? "After the Holy Days, then," he finally managed to say. "Good night."

Just once as he stalked out of the house did his footsteps falter. It was when he heard his mother rise from her chair and call after him—a pursuit abruptly stifled by a command from his father.

There, Daniel told himself. *I knew it all along. My father doesn't love me. He has never loved me. He has only love enough for Joshua . . . never me. How could he not try to stop me? He expects I won't go through with this. But I'll show him! I'm not an eight-year-old running away from home. I'm really leaving.*

As Lily sat in the Rosh Hashanah services, her thoughts turned to Lord Tannis. He was a man who had everything, yet Lily sensed an uneasiness about him. His smile flashed and faded, on and off, like a signal lamp on a hill. Joy for him was fleeting, as though he had some dark secret he wanted to hide from the world.

After the services concluded, congregants poured out of the tall doors, white and blue prayer shawls billowing in the autumn breeze.

When Cantor and Lily emerged with Yod in tow, Lily saw Lord Tannis, astride his horse across the lane, apparently waiting until the services had ended.

Upon seeing them, Tannis rose up in his stirrups. The smile flashed, faded, then flashed again as Yod waved broadly to him.

"*Shanah Tova!*" he called to the trio.

The air smelled like garlic and roasting lamb with leeks. Lily was amused to see the powerful warlord lick his lips involuntarily.

How long had he been waiting for them to emerge? Lily wondered. And had he truly been waiting? Or had he simply been there by chance?

"*Shanah Tova*, Lord Tannis," Cantor replied.

"May you be inscribed for a good year," Lily added.

Tannis tucked his chin in a gesture Lily had come to recognize. "Inscribed? HaShem, if he exists, would not write my name in his Book. But . . ." He reached into his saddlebag and produced a leather pouch filled with coins. "I brought this. A gift, you might say. For the New Year. For the children who are here . . . all of them."

He faltered as though he wanted to ask a question, then tossed the pouch to Cantor, who caught it with one hand.

Surprised, Cantor hefted it. It had the weight of gold.

Yod cried, "Will you come to supper with us at Reb Nehemiah's house?"

"No, thank you. I am . . . it wouldn't be . . . I can't, you see." Again the gleam of a half smile and the lowered chin. "But you—Yod, is it? Would you answer a question for me?"

Yod placed her hands on her hips. She loved answering all manner of questions. "Sure."

"Well then. Will you tell me . . . Yeshua of Nazareth—the rumor grows, the truth becomes legend—they say he healed many."

Yod was very matter-of-fact. "Not a made-up story."

"Would he heal any child, do you think? Of any . . . any terrible affliction? The worst?"

Yod stuck out her lower lip. She barked a short laugh, letting him know this was a silly question. "Well, what do you think?"

The great man shrugged like a schoolboy who had no answers.

What was behind the question? Lily wondered.

"Perhaps I'll go see him for myself," Tannis replied. "Maybe prevail upon him to return with me. After all, there are sick and hurting here as well. My mitzvah to get my name in the—" he pointed upward—"Book, after all."

There was little left to be said. No other explanation for either the gift or the encounter.

And Lord Tannis rode off to face the New Year as he always had . . . alone.

When the holidays were over, Melchior sent a message to the inn where Daniel had been staying, asking his son to meet him at the Hall of Records at noon. There was very little conversation between the two men.

With great effort Melchior managed to ask, "Will you be staying on in Ecbatana?"

The question posed by his father rang in Daniel's ears like the tolling of a pagan funeral bell. It was a query one would ask a traveler, a merchant . . . a stranger. It thudded against Daniel's heart. It was as a stranger his father now regarded him.

"No," Daniel said, gritting his teeth in an effort to keep the quaver out of his voice. "I'm going to a far country. Perhaps I'll come back . . . someday . . . when I can make you proud of me."

Daniel waited for a response. Surely his father would say he was already proud, that this departure was an unnecessary gesture.

Instead Melchior said, "This is a letter of credit. It allows you to draw against either the mint here in Ecbatana or against funds I have on deposit with the Temple in Jerusalem. Gentiles may require the first; Jewish money changers will accept either." He also took a hefty leather pouch from Lono and passed it to Daniel. "You didn't specify this, but here is also a hundred drachmae with which to travel. Do you know where you're going?"

This was the moment Daniel had been dreading. Where was he going? Babylon? The Parthian capital at Ctesiphon? Someplace truly unknown and exotic, like the Indies? "To a far country," he repeated loftily, as if his destination were no one's business but his own.

"I see," Melchior replied. "Well then. May the Almighty go with you, and keep you in all your ways.[24] If you will permit a last piece of advice: You and Lono take turns sleeping until you're far away from here. A transaction with this much at stake cannot be kept secret. It would not do to be robbed."

Melchior leaned forward as if to embrace his son, but Daniel stepped aside. His father was still giving advice? Daniel was a grown man with a sizable fortune of his own . . . his very own!

"Can't get very far away if we don't stop talking," he said. "Good-bye."

All the way down the hill toward the caravansary, a doleful-looking Lono trudging six paces behind, Daniel ached to turn and see if his father watched him go. But Daniel would not give his father the satisfaction of seeing him look back.

16

sther lay in Melchior's arms, unable to respond to his kisses. Worry about Daniel had pushed every emotion to the side.

Melchior lay back on his pillow and sighed. "Esther?"

"I'm so . . . sorry . . . Melchior."

"Daniel."

"I can't stop thinking about him . . . worried." She turned her back to him. Melchior's sorrow seemed to make him need the comfort of her body more than ever, while her grief consumed her passion until the embers of her desire grew cold.

Melchior got up and wrapped himself in a robe. He went to the window and gazed out at the quiet city and the stars. "Esther, did I do the right thing? Letting him go?"

"What else could we do?"

"I don't know. I was remembering . . . your grandfather. Something he said when I was a young man, a young father. Joshua and Daniel were fighting. I asked him what I should do."

"He knew the hearts of men."

"And the heart of Torah." Framed in starlight, Melchior was silent for a time.

She joined him at the window. The moon was setting in the west. Was Daniel looking up at the same moon? Had he forgotten how to pray and ask the Almighty for help in his eagerness to be his own man?

Melchior sighed and put his arm around her. "I wish sometimes I still had your grandfather here to teach me."

Esther leaned her head against Melchior's chest. "When I was a small girl, just beginning my lessons, Grandfather walked with me beside a herd of cattle. He looked at the herdsman's goad and reminded me that the letter *lamed* is shaped like a cattle goad. *Lamed* is at the heart of the Hebrew alef-bet. *Lamed* means heart. *Lamed* means learning too. And learning must enter a person's heart. *Lamed* is bigger than all the other letters. Reaching up to God for wisdom. It means to teach and to learn. As it is written in Deuteronomy, *These words shall be on your heart.*[25] That wonderful old man! He reminded me that the Hebrew word for the cattle goad means, literally, 'teacher of the cattle.'"

Melchior laughed gently. "So Grandfather would tell me it may take a cattle goad to teach Daniel?"

"I think that's what he would say, Melchior." Her throat constricted with emotion. "But, oh! I wish our son would learn we love him . . . God loves him . . . without such pain!"

Esther buried her face against Melchior. Her shoulders shook as she wept quietly.

At last Melchior said, "Perhaps we will go find our son. Perhaps . . . but not yet. Not now."

Daniel's description of his destination as "a far country" had grown no more specific when he reached the sprawling caravansary on the outskirts of Ecbatana. Anything beyond his hometown spoke of adventure to him.

After confinement within the dreary walls of a countinghouse, travel to anywhere seemed exciting. After tallying olive oil, of all mundane substances, now, suddenly, the world lay spread before him like an oyster teeming with innumerable pearls, waiting to be identified and seized.

His initial notion was to sign on with the first caravan he encountered, no matter what its cargo, no matter what its destination. This idea shifted when it developed that the first camel train leaving was laden with salt for the backcountry villages in the hill country.

Not much glamour in salt.

Daniel reminded himself he was not just looking for travel but for business opportunities as well.

His second choice fell on a pack train of silk heading west from China. The rotund caravan owner was swathed in samples of his wares and sported a diamond earring as big as Daniel's thumb.

Daniel moved to intercept the man, but Lono caught his elbow. "Wait, Mastah. Look at his servants. Look at his beasts."

Grudgingly, because he hated being corrected by a slave, Daniel acknowledged the problems Lono identified. The silk merchant's attendants were poorly dressed and underfed. The same might be said of the camels with their scruffy fur and all-too-evident ribs.

"This man, he make show, but he too cheap, eh?"

Without giving Lono credit for preventing a mistake, Daniel turned away to enter the common room of the caravansary. He sat in a corner, nursing a tankard of barley wine. A handful of small coins encouraged the innkeeper to identify and comment on the different merchants.

"That one's from India." The tavern-master gestured with a nod and spoke behind his fist. "Deals in spices, but he's only a steward and not an owner. The swarthy one who just came in is a Cypriot. He doesn't haul cargo of his own but takes on freight as he can find it."

The first man mentioned was rejected as a possible option because he could not be looking for a partner. The second caravan chief had a lean, hungry look and seemed to be operating on a very thin wallet.

"What about that one?" Daniel indicated a table beside the window. The figure designated was neatly but not extravagantly dressed. Tall and thin, gray-haired, and a bit stooped, he was also evidently weak-eyed, since he reviewed a letter by bringing it very close to his face and squinting.

"That one? Bit of a mystery, that," the caravansary proprietor admitted. "Name's Saul something. Don't know where he hails from, but he keeps his stock and his people well cared for. I see him twice a year . . . once each way."

This seemed to have possibilities.

Daniel approached the man, introduced himself, and asked if he could sit down.

Saul dipped his chin in greeting and swept a broad palm toward a chair. "Are you looking to join my caravan?"

"That depends," Daniel said cautiously. "Tell me about yourself."

Before Saul replied, Daniel felt himself being inspected. He was glad he had spent some of his father's coins—*his* coins, he corrected himself—on a new set of clothing. New boots with silver buckles and a dagger, its leather-wrapped grip chased with silver wire and topped with a silver pommel, bespoke quality and a certain prosperity.

His narrow-eyed appraisal finally complete, Saul admitted, "I am a stork."

The caravan chief did resemble the stalking bird in question, the way he hunched his shoulders about his neck and peered downward.

When Daniel gave no sign of comprehension, Saul continued, "Storks migrate north to south and back again . . . and so do I." The lean man examined the room to see if he could be overheard, then waggled his fingers for Daniel to draw nearer. "I cannot admit this to just anyone," he said softly. "But you impress me as a man of integrity and substance."

Daniel brightened and encouraged Saul to continue.

"In the summers I go north, beyond the Khazar Sea."

The Khazar Sea bordered Parthia to the north. It was an enormous, landlocked body of salt water, without any outlet. Reportedly, it was inhabited on three sides by barbarian hordes. What could possibly be obtained there?

"Amber," Saul whispered. "The finest in the world comes from the ancient land of Caspia. You know Strabo? No? You must read his geography. His writings told me to seek the amber trade where the princes of the Caspians once ruled . . . and he was right!"

Amber—yellow, translucent, valued as gemstones, and said to have magical properties—was found only in a handful of remote locations.

"And south?" Daniel queried, almost holding his breath with anticipation.

"Ivory," was the muted response. "I meet Arab traders who sail the coastal routes. They take my amber to the kings of Axum and beyond. I take their ivory inland. A vast amount of wealth, you see, in each load, without the weight of gold. Of course, both ends pay in gold for my services."

Amber and ivory! Daniel felt his eyes widen, though he tried to control any display of excitement. "And you carry on this trade . . . all alone?"

Saul sighed. "It's not easy to find someone who can be trusted. Someone who is willing to share the financial risk in exchange for great rewards and who does not have family concerns weighing him down, holding him back. I have had partners, but they never worked out."

"I-I might be interested in such a . . . migration," Daniel suggested. "I have recently come into an inheritance. I want to travel and make money."

Saul nodded sagely. "Then you have resources. It is well you chose me to address, Daniel ben Melchior. We are two men of like mind—men of vision, able to carry out big plans." He gazed around the room again, as if to satisfy himself that no one lurked in the corners, listening. "But it is not safe to speak unguardedly. Imagine how I would be pounced on by every bandit between the Strait of Hormuz and the Backbone of the World if my cargoes were known. It is only by dressing modestly and traveling simply that I keep my head on my shoulders. But come, join me in my tent and we'll speak further."

"Hold," Daniel said with belated caution. "I don't know your full name."

"Saul ben Ariyb of Babylon."

"Then . . . you're Jewish?"

"As true a son of Avraham as yourself, Daniel ben Melchior. Now, will you join me?"

PART III

"The stones of the wall will cry out. . . ."

HABAKKUK 2:11

17

CHAPTER

The gift from Lord Tannis was provision enough for the children of Mak'ob to last a year.

Stacks of gold coins glistened on the table before Rabbi Nehemiah, Rabbi Ahava, and Cantor.

Rabbi Nehemiah smiled. "I cannot see it, but the clatter of it clinking together gives me great happiness for the joy the provisions will bring our students."

"A strange fellow, this robber baron," added Ahava. "To deny the existence of the Eternal . . . and yet to make such a contribution to our school."

"A good-hearted fellow," Cantor agreed. "But Lily believes he has some secret about his life that he is hiding."

"Perhaps," Nehemiah agreed. "There are rumors. . . ."

"There are always rumors." Ahava sighed.

"A broken heart," Nehemiah resumed, "an injury he cannot forgive . . . a death he cannot forget . . . a haunting face . . . even stories of the tragic loss of a child. His only child, by some accounts. Born outside the bounds of marriage. He goes alone at times into a walled garden to grieve. In the summers some have heard wailing coming from there."

Cantor replied quietly, "He asked about Yeshua: If he went to fetch him, would Yeshua come back? Does Yeshua really heal all disease? That sort of thing."

"Well then. I see. I see," said the blind rabbi. "His gift to us for the welfare of the children . . . a down payment on hope."

"So we are agreed then?" Daniel pressed. His words were slurred because of the volume of sweet wine he had imbibed, but his spirits had never felt lighter. With each of Saul's anecdotes of mysterious lands and exotic peoples and wondrous riches the young man's excitement increased. Amber and ivory were the trade he must have . . . he would have. Daniel could not bear the thought that Saul might still refuse him.

Summoning Lono in from where he was posted outside the tent, Daniel ordered him to produce the letter of credit. When Lono argued, Daniel was surprised to hear Saul defend the servant's discretion. "You must learn more prudence," the Stork said. "Now I already know more than I should. Your servant carries your valuables on his person. Isn't that so?"

"Around his neck. But, Saul, if we are to be partners . . ."

"Tell me again the amount you have available?"

Daniel named the sum, and Saul whistled softly and stroked his gray beard thoughtfully. "With such an amount I could double my trade within a year. In two, I—we—would have our own fleet of trading dhows and control even more of the merchandise."

"Yes," Daniel agreed eagerly. Words bubbled out of his mouth like liquor from the jar. "It's yours. The money, I mean. I'm a fast learner too. Let's start right now. Teach me how to grade amber. How do you recognize top quality? Show me."

"Gently, gently," Saul warned. "Unlike you, I keep my valuables safely packed and hidden. Later, on the trail, away from prying eyes, then we can examine it all. Your credit document and my amber. I already trust you, you see." Saul stared into the corner of the tent and seemed deep in musing. With a final tug on his lower lip he offered, "All right . . . partner."

Daniel leapt to his feet in profuse thanks, but Saul still had another inquiry. "We leave at dawn. Isn't there anyone to whom you wish to send a message? Tell them of your new plans and our destination, so they won't worry?"

Daniel thought of his father and his brother . . . how they would never believe he had committed his entire fortune so quickly. He grimaced at the thought. It would be envy, absolute envy at Daniel's good fortune.

Let them wonder!

Daniel thought of his mother, then hardened his heart. He wanted no one at home to hear of this venture until he was a roaring success and fabulously wealthy.

"No one at all," he said.

Hawk made his home in the branches of an ancient oak tree that bloomed in the courtyard of the Synagogue of the Exiles. It was said the tree had been there since the days of the Babylonian captivity.

From this lofty perspective the hawk seemed content to observe the comings and goings of a multitude of pilgrims. Descendants of the Jewish exiles of Babylon, hundreds poured through the massive gates each day to bring their tithes and sacrifices and leave their half-shekel Temple tax for the sanctuary of the Almighty in Jerusalem.

Some observed the hawk and commented on his presence here in Narda. There were rumors from the land of Eretz-Israel of a healer who had emptied out the Valley of Lepers and had raised a man from the dead.

The dead fellow, now alive somewhere, was followed by a great hawk, wasn't he?

Others heard the story and said, "It's just a legend. It makes a fine bedtime tale for the children."

All the same, there was the hawk, high in the branches of the oak tree. And strangely, the raptor followed a certain man, a stranger in the city.

When asked about the orphan children taken in by the synagogue, Rabbi Nehemiah said to his congregation, "Listen to no rumors! Orphans from a minor rebellion in Judea, of which we know there are many."

The sun ascended over the flat, arid plain of Silakhow, casting the shadow of Lono's immense hulk upon the thin fabric wall of Daniel's new tent. Daniel saw the subtle movement of the loyal giant's breathing as he slept, like a guard dog, across the entry. With the rising light came the same familiar throbbing in Daniel's temples and the same dull ache in his heart. Unbidden thoughts of Mina came to him again. Wavering between bitterness at her betrayal and a pitiful longing for her return, he recalled the lesson from the book of Proverbs. His father had used the passage to suggest a warning about the girl. How he wished he had listened then.

The lips of an immoral woman drip honey.[26]

Such sweet, sweet lips.

"You must be careful, my son," Melchior had warned. "True love and loyalty will be earned. One who gives affection so freely to you will not withhold it from others either."

Her speech is smoother than oil.[27]

How he ached to hear her voice.

"She is a flatterer, Daniel," his father discerned. "Such constant expressions of admiration are not genuine."

But in the end, she is bitter as . . .[28]

"Wormwood." Daniel cringed as he unintentionally spoke the word aloud.

"Mastah?" Lono called softly.

Daniel rose from his cot and donned his robe. "Yes, yes. Patience, Lono. I'm just finishing my morning prayers." He spat the words, pretending to be angry. Presenting anger to those around him, he reasoned, was preferable to displaying the anguish he actually felt. *Much more virile,* he thought, as he flung back the tent flap and strode into the harsh morning glare, trying to look, but not feeling, the part of a strong, confident businessman.

"Wine, Lono," Daniel demanded, his gaze fixed on the white peaks of the mountains to the distant south, as a commander surveys his battleground. Five or, at the most, six days' travel, and Daniel would be a wealthy man. Then he would pay his father back. He wanted nothing from the family that thought so little of him. To Daniel, the credit carried around Lono's neck was a loan . . . no more.

The servant hesitated only briefly before going about the task. It was enough. Daniel recognized Lono's disapproval in that moment but resolved he would not acknowledge it. For as long as Lono had been with the family, he had been Daniel's constant companion and conscience. Lono was not Jewish and, as far as Daniel knew, had no faith of his own, so he did not keep Sabbath with other servants of the Melchior household. But through quiet observation, Lono *knew* it all, every rite and ritual, and never failed to remind Daniel of his obligations, or of the inconsistencies between his actions and the law of Moses.

Whatever pang Daniel might have felt would be drowned soon enough as he untied the mouth of the leather wineskin and drank heavily of the tart ruby liquid within.

Roused by the activities of Daniel and Lono, Saul ben Ariyb emerged from his own tent. At the sight of Daniel and the wine pouch, he laughed lightly and beckoned for his own attendants to fetch him water for washing and a small loaf for breakfast.

"Will you join me in celebrating our new partnership?" Daniel called across the camp, his arm outstretched with the wineskin. He would feel no guilt at all, he thought, if someone else were to drink with him.

"If you start every day like that," ben Ariyb responded, scrubbing his hands and forearms vigorously under a steady stream of water poured for him by a slave, "you'll shrivel your insides."

Already feeling the first warm wave of the wine in his stomach now spreading to his head, Daniel sneered and drank more deeply himself. Behind him, Lono set about collapsing the shelter, readying for the journey.

As Lono worked, Daniel surveyed the modest treasure he had amassed in preparation for the journey. Lono himself was included in that treasure, Daniel thought. In addition to being Daniel's conscience, the enormous slave with fearsome striped tattoos on half his face and covering most of the rest of his body also served as Daniel's protector. No bandit, unless mad or accompanied by an army, would dare set upon Daniel with Lono by his side. As frequently annoyed as he was by the giant's moral judgments, Daniel was grateful to have him along as he began this new venture that would take him to strange and, no doubt, dangerous lands.

Lono labored to pack away the next of Daniel's treasures, his tents.

Reasoning that his was now also a migratory life, Daniel had purchased no fewer than three canopies with varying densities of fabric, to accommodate the different climates the caravan would travel through. The heat of this valley floor was already unbearable, and the day was yet young. But the mountains, Daniel knew, were even now still capped with snow. With a new cot, blankets, and skins of various weights to accompany the tents, Daniel thought his present accommodations much more comfortable even than his old home.

To the silent dismay of Lono, Daniel also purchased enough wine to last through the entire trip, if he were providing it to the whole caravan.

He was not.

The thought of such a large stock of wine all for himself made him giddy, and he drank again from the skin he held.

"No accidents, now," Daniel called as Lono packed the skins away, though he knew the warning was unnecessary. The slave would no more harm his master's possessions than he would the master himself.

Two new camels Daniel had also purchased for the journey lay patiently nearby as Lono harnessed and burdened them again. *They must not understand*, Daniel mused, as he found shade from the low sun beside a squat desert palm and gulped more wine. *They don't know what is expected of them in the days to come, or they would not bear this time so stoically.*

Captivated by the idea, Daniel strolled somewhat unsteadily toward the nearest one. Taking the beast by the ear, he leaned in to whisper, inhaling its acrid, musky scent. "Camel," he slurred. Daniel could see the animal's other ear flick around as he spoke. "Camel, you ought not be so optimistic. You will never be free of such oppression unless you rise up!" With those words, he gestured broadly with his hands and, in that moment, the camel did just that, throwing Daniel flat on his back across a heap of stones.

His breath knocked from him, his head spinning, Daniel lay still, staring into the cloudless blue sky until Lono darkened his view with a disapproving look and hefted him upright again.

"Mastah," he grumbled, "you drunk."

Daniel stood erect, looking straight into the servant's face, realizing and pleased with the fact that wine had once again replaced his pain with humorous moments. "Lono," he said, "you right."

18

The air was perfumed with spices and incense. Carrying a small clay lamp, Lily passed through the gloomy, narrow corridor. Low doors led to rooms housing the scholars who studied at the School of Hillel and members of the community. It was dark and silent. A strict curfew was maintained. Her hair was damp from her bath, and her feet were cold on the stone floor.

Lily and Cantor occupied a sparse chamber with a sleeping mat, a blanket, one chair, and a square study table big enough for one leaf of a scroll to be opened. The only ventilation came from a window set high in the wall.

The hinges of the door squeaked when she opened it. "Home," she said.

"It is . . . beautiful. And the air. Can you smell it?" Cantor was already beneath the blanket.

"A miracle, Cantor. A miracle, this place is."

He smiled and patted her place next to him.

She sank down beside him and started to blow out the lamp.

"No. Don't put out the light." He set it to one side. "I want to look at you." Then, holding the blanket for her, he asked, "Cold?"

She lay on her back, his arm beneath her head. She warmed her feet against his leg and he laughed. "Cold, eh? You offered to warm me up, but you didn't know what you were getting into."

His gaze hardened with desire. "Yes, I knew."

Lifting her face to his, she kissed his mouth. A wave of warmth surged through her. "So tonight, you'll tell me about heaven?"

He pulled her closer. "Yes. But no words. . . ."

What had first looked like a solid ridge of mountains just a few hours before was gradually taking shape as two. One lay to the southwest of the caravan, the other to the southeast, narrowing to a low valley between, due south of their position. The heights also grew considerably; lifeless brown below an elevation of snowy peaks now filled the majority of the view.

What little Daniel knew of the southern lands was useless for the caravan's proposed route. Had he been asked to cross the Zagros, he would have set out due west from Hamadan, relying on the conventional route through Kangavar and Bakhtaran. But because of the secrecy of their trade and the value of their cargo, ben Ariyb insisted they travel as far south as Dow Rud before turning west. There the mountains would be drastically more difficult to cross, the southern end of the range rising sharper than the north. But ben Ariyb said he knew the way, having passed that way many times.

"I will not take any other," he told Daniel as they got under way that morning. "I have been attacked too many times by thieves and brigands near Bakhtaran. When we at last turn to the mountains, we will pass only poor nomads who want nothing to do with us. Unfriendly, yes," he chuckled, "but not dangerous."

In the meantime, the caravan would travel with the towering, snowy heights at their shoulders, remaining on the scorching valley floor. Though it was still a few days away, Daniel could not wait to reach those cooler regions. Several hours into their first day the good humor born of the novelty of travel had worn off from his outlook. While the rest of the travelers were often drinking quantities of water, Daniel maintained his devotion to the wine. Now the disjointed, pounding gait of the camel combined with the intense heat of midday to make consciousness unbearable. As he clamped his eyes tight to shut out the harsh, painful light, nausea washed over him.

"Stop, stop," he called weakly down to Lono, barely keeping his churning stomach from interrupting the brief plea.

Lono glanced over his shoulder from where he walked, leading the pair of camels over the barren terrain. It was plain he knew what troubled his master, but he made no sign of disapproval. Concern seemed his only response. Quietly, gently, he coaxed the camel into a kneeling position on the scorching earth, lifting Daniel easily from the saddle with one massive tattooed arm. With the other he unfastened the cloak from his neck and laid it, and Daniel on it, in the tiny line of shade cast by the humped profile of the beast.

The rest of the caravan trudged slowly on, as yet unaware of the absence of two of their number. Lono hurried to the second of their camels, fetching a skin of water for Daniel. "Drink, Mastah," he said, pouring a trickle over Daniel's lips. Far from refreshing, though, the water was hot, and Daniel could swallow very little of it.

His world began to spin, and he attempted to raise himself and crawl away from the camel, lest he vomit where he lay. But his elbows gave way and he collapsed, doing just that, soiling Lono's garment with sour-smelling bile.

"No mattuh, no mattuh," Lono reassured him, shifting him back into the shade against the camel. "You bettuh soon." He wet another corner of the cloak with water and patted Daniel's forehead gently.

"Good, Lono," Daniel croaked, watching a small stream of his sick trickle away to smooth, shiny pebbles nearby. "I do not deserve such a good friend."

"You bettuh soon," Lono said again, and Daniel fell asleep.

Instantly, visions of Mina came to his mind. Severe, violent color surrounded her soft face, and she laughed loudly at him, reaching for Bartok behind her. Then his friend was laughing too, pulling Mina close to his chest the way Daniel used to do. Bartok kissed her deeply, all the while staring at Daniel with a mocking smile in his eyes.

In the vision Daniel tried to strike Bartok, but his fists flew through empty space, and then the pair of faithless friends was gone.

The air echoed with the words of Daniel's father: *"Her feet go down to death; her steps lead straight to the grave."*[29]

A few minutes later Daniel awakened to approaching hooves as a camel carried a servant back from the caravan to determine the cause of their delay. At first Daniel could not make out the words, only recognizing the voices of Lono and ben Ariyb's slave, Muti, as they apparently argued. As their debate became more intense, though, Daniel could hear it clearly.

"Your buffoon of a master causes us much trouble," Muti sneered. "Master ben Ariyb will not tolerate this another time."

"Do Muti's mastah know you speak like this?" Lono's tone was incredulous. "Silence now. Tell ben Ariyb, Mastah Daniel come soon, by night."

"You are as much a fool as your master if you think that drunk has the right to *tell* ben Ariyb anything. Saul ben Ariyb leads this caravan, and if that child wishes to remain a part of it, he will collect himself immediately and return to his place." Muti paused to add extra offense to his next words. "At the rear."

Daniel found strength in the anger he felt at the affront and pulled himself upright by the camel's saddle. His eyes locked with Muti's in a stony glare; then the slave whipped his camel, wheeling it away toward the south.

"I can go on now," Daniel said, cutting short a protest from Lono as he remounted the saddle. Another wave of nausea hit him with the exertion, but less than the first, and he successfully fought the urge to vomit again.

Lono cast a handful of loose dirt over the stain on his cloak, then wiped the resultant mud from the fabric. As he urged Daniel's camel into motion again, he looked back often to be sure his master would not fall from his perch.

Muti is right, Daniel mused, trying to keep his mind off feeling ill. *Though such coarse speech from a slave is unexpected.* He began to wonder if Muti's words must be a reflection of his master's true feelings about Daniel. *He would know,* Daniel thought, *that I would complain to ben Ariyb of his insolence, so he must not fear his master's response. If he does not fear his master's response, then surely ben Ariyb holds the same disagreeable view.*

The thought made Daniel angry. *I am as important to this venture as he. Without my capital, ben Ariyb's quantities are much reduced; so too, then, is his profit. It may be true I don't have the contacts in the goods we seek, but he ought to be grateful I chose to expand this business. I could just as easily breed pigs for Gentiles. If that's what ben Ariyb thinks of me, then I won't acknowl-*

edge it at all. I won't complain to him. I won't punish Muti. But neither will I behave any differently. After all, he reasoned, *if I will not reform for my father, then who is this stranger to tell me how to behave?*

As the caravan made camp at the end of their first day of travel, Daniel opened, upended, and emptied another skin of wine, despite disapproving glances from all the other members of the group, including Lono.

From the moment of their reunion Yod would not be parted from Cantor and Lily. It might be said she fixed her heart more on Cantor than Lily. It was also true that Cantor did not wish to be parted from Yod.

Was it that one moment the two souls had shared together in *olam haba*?

Yod said to Cantor, "I saw you there when I first arrived. And I knew he would call you back. I wasn't afraid to come back to this sad world after that. Because I knew my friend Cantor would be there too."

So it was that Yod became their child. Life was just as she had always dreamed in the Valley of Sorrows.

Those who had seen the face of the Lord knew how tragic life was beyond His care, so their hearts remained fixed on the Lord, who had given them life.

It was true among all the children whom Yeshua healed. More than mere flesh had been made well.

There were three classes, divided by age, and consisting of eleven students in each class. Lily taught music. Cantor soon recognized that their students sang with a harmony he had only heard among the angels of *olam haba*. So this heavenly gift of joyous song was given to the Children of Sorrow.

Rabbi Ahava instructed the eleven- and twelve-year-olds in Torah. Hebrew text was comprehended by his pupils as if they were scholars who had long studied in the School of Hillel.

Cantor taught science, mathematics, and astronomy. He discovered the ability of the children of the Valley to comprehend difficult concepts exceeded that of grown men educated in the renowned schools of Alexandria.

The smallest star shone the brightest by far.

It seemed to Daniel he was not the only one pleased to reach the cooler temperatures of the lower peaks. Tensions between him and the other travelers eased somewhat. Ben Ariyb rode at his side and they talked pleasantly.

Even Muti seemed respectful as he offered water to Lono several times during their slow, winding ascent out of the valley. "Sir," he acknowledged Daniel with a slight bow and averted eyes before riding back to his place among ben Ariyb's train.

When Muti had gone, ben Ariyb said, "I had a word with him after your . . . illness . . . yesterday."

Daniel looked at him with interest. He regretted the incident completely but blamed the heat and would certainly not apologize, he decided.

"Muti," ben Arriyb continued, "is a good fellow. Loyal. Imagines himself somewhat of a business manager for me. Always looking for slights against my interests, you see. A bit too eagerly, perhaps."

"He told you, then? What he said to Lono?" Daniel was sure Muti hadn't told the whole story, but he was curious now.

"I scolded him severely for it," ben Ariyb answered quickly. "It is not his place to challenge you. He is but a lowly slave and has no say in how you behave."

A long pause followed, during which Daniel gazed up at the mountains now towering to either side of the caravan. They shaded the trek for all but a few hours of the day, bathing the valley floor in cool blue light the rest of the time. The broad pass they traveled was littered with enormous, smooth red boulders, out of place in the otherwise brown terrain. Daniel imagined this must have been a powerfully flowing river once, carrying the stones from high peaks, polishing away sharp edges in the journey. His eyes locked on one such egg-shaped rock, and as their camels sauntered past, he asked, "And you?"

Ben Ariyb had not lost the thread of their conversation, despite the long pause. "Inasmuch as it might affect our business, I request, humbly . . ." He glanced at Daniel. "Yesterday's delay was not such an incident."

Daniel was placated. He returned to his wine with vigor as they continued deeper, higher, into the wondrous, foreign terrain. At last he was feeling as he thought he should. He was visiting new lands and had the prospect of great wealth, respect from others, and a good, steady drunken haze that kept him from dwelling too much on Mina.

Ah, Mina. He sighed. *I will return to Ecbatana a wealthy man. And what will she have? Bartok.*

He chuckled, and ben Ariyb eyed him with interest.

"I was just imagining," Daniel explained, "how someday I'll return to my home and purchase groves and groves of olive trees. We will press the finest oil in all Parthia, and the king's patent will someday—"

"Master!" Muti shouted, loping his camel back toward Daniel and ben Ariyb. "Riders approach!"

They'd passed other caravans in the last few days, but no one had ever gotten so excited. Muti must have seen the question on Daniel's face as his camel bawled and jerked to a stop.

"Slavers!" Muti exclaimed.

Ben Ariyb groaned, and the pair whipped their camels to the front of the caravan once again.

Daniel had never seen the slave trade up close, only heard the horrific stories of the slaves' brutal treatment until they were sold into employment in a house like Melchior's. Lono himself had scars as evidence of such treatment—broad tan stripes across his back and around his neck that blurred the once-crisp lines of his native tattoos. Daniel sensed his tension as they continued at a greater distance behind the others.

"Not to worry, Lono," Daniel assured him. "We are propertied men, this is a well-traveled pass, and ben Ariyb is knowledgeable. He is no doubt having a friendly conversation with the men this instant. No harm will come to you, I promise."

Beyond a stand of young, wispy trees in the middle of the pass, Daniel could just make out the line coming toward them. A rider on horseback before, and one behind, each on a black steed. The guards, wearing scimitars and turbans, shepherded a string of twenty men in misery far worse than Daniel had imagined.

As they drew nearer, Daniel saw each man was shackled by his ankles to the wrists of the one behind, causing them to hobble awkwardly down the slight incline. Their bindings were so tight and the action of the rope so abrasive that a thin snail's track of glistening black blood soaked into thirsty dirt behind them.

The last of their number, a male child no more than six, was perhaps most pathetic of all. His captors had long ago given up forcing him to keep rhythm with the rest; he was clearly too small. Instead, he was tied around the neck of the man in front of him, his ropes also bloodied.

Most astounding to Daniel was the boy's face. His left eye was black and swollen beyond recognition, as if from a brutal kick. Both his cheeks were covered from the dust churned up by the men's shuffling feet, except one streak, washed perfectly clean by the little boy's silent crying.

When he saw this, Daniel jerked the reins from Lono's hand and wheeled the camel toward the front rider.

"Mastah?" he heard Lono call as he went. "What do you do?"

"Sir," Daniel called to the slaver, "sir, I beg you, speak with me a moment." Daniel caught up with the man in front, halting his progress. The rear rider also came, his sinister curved sword drawn in defense of the other.

Examining Daniel with coal-black eyes, a slight smile parting his lips, the slaver dismissed his attendant with a wave.

"Forgive me," Daniel said, "I am unaccustomed to the ways of your business, but I wonder if you might part with one of your captives now." His next words came in a rush. "This young boy—" he gestured—"he cannot be much use to you. I'm sure he slows your travel, and I could use—"

To Daniel's chagrin, the man laughed.

That was his only response.

The slaver's amusement grew as he motioned for the little column to move again. He laughed louder still when Daniel tried once more to negotiate the sale. The guffaws echoed off the ragged peaks above them as Daniel rode, bewildered and defeated, back to his own caravan.

It seemed to Daniel that he could still hear the wicked laughter echoing throughout the pass even as his own camel train made camp that night. The memory died away at last as Daniel finished another skin of wine, forgetting also the optimism of earlier.

19 CHAPTER

After rising early and reciting his prayers as he was accustomed to do on Sabbath mornings, Daniel then returned to his tent to sleep off his hangover. He knew his laziness wasn't *exactly* honoring the Sabbath, but he felt especially worn from their recent travel. *If I asked our rabbi, he too would prescribe this extra sleep,* Daniel thought.

He would not have told Rebbe Sheramin, though, nor did he let himself dwell on the fact that his constant drunkenness was really to blame for his weariness.

Instead, as he drifted off, he thought of Lono and how the faithful servant also deserved a day of leisure. *If I sleep longer,* he reasoned, *Lono also enjoys more rest this day.*

There were parts of the ritual of the day that Daniel had always found difficult to comply with. The prohibition on the kindling of fire always meant a cold meal, or one that had been prepared the day before and kept warm over low coals. No travel, unless by foot, and then only a certain distance, meant he rarely saw friends.

As he slept, he dreamed he rose high above their camp, floating slowly up to the very height of the snowy peaks above. Far, far below, he recognized Lono, wandering away to the north. As he went, Lono carried a stick, drawing a line in the sand. He seemed to walk deliberately, measuring his paces as he went. Somehow Daniel knew Lono was marking an Ehuv, the line an observer of the Sabbath could use to remind himself of the acceptable distance of travel that day. As he watched, he expected Lono to circle around the camp, providing a perimeter in which they could move, but he walked on.

Surely, Daniel thought, *he has already traveled much more than a Sabbath day's journey.*

On and on Lono walked, returning to the blistering valley and continuing north toward Ecbatana, toward home.

What a foolish dream, Daniel told himself. *A faithful Jew could never travel such a distance on the Sabbath.*

"*Pikuach Nefesh*," Daniel heard his father say. "Any law, save only three, *must* be broken to save a life."

And Daniel awoke.

It was nearly midday, and his tent was growing warm with the direct exposure to the sun. As he emerged, he saw ben Ariyb's tents had been dismantled and packed onto his camels.

"A later start than is usual, even for you," ben Ariyb joked, but Daniel could see he was truly annoyed. "Shall we be on our way now?"

"What of the Sabbath? Will we not rest today?" Daniel glanced at Lono, who sat on a carpet near their camels and scowled at ben Ariyb.

Muti stifled a laugh and ben Ariyb smiled. "I am sorry, Daniel," he said. "Business takes precedence in this caravan. You have rested quite enough." With that, he mounted his camel.

Daniel hurried to ready for travel, even assisting Lono in collapsing the tent and packing the belongings onto the camels again.

Muti seemed amused by the sight and watched the activity with interest until ben Ariyb instructed him to take the caravan on ahead.

"I'll ride with Daniel again today," he said. "Wait for us at Dow Rud." As Muti rode off, ben Ariyb explained to Daniel, "Dow Rud marks our path into the Zagros. By tonight, we will be halfway across the mountains!"

Without an audience, Daniel felt he could better question ben Ariyb on his refusal to keep the Sabbath. "Why must we hurry so? What is one more day to our business? Surely we will not lose anything by waiting until tomorrow to resume?"

"Daniel," said ben Ariyb, "as I have said many times before, our cargo is very valuable. A thief confronted with so much to gain will not honor our law when considering whether to cut your throat to get it. Shall we sit and endanger our own lives? Surely this is not the intent of God's Holy Day."

"Is there still so much danger in this route?" Daniel asked. "I thought that was the reason we came by this lesser-known way."

Annoyance translated into a rough handling of the lead rope of his camel, and ben Ariyb's beast shifted impatiently. "There is always danger," said ben Ariyb. "I will not lose my life *or* my profits to the whim of a boy who keeps the Law only when it is convenient for him to do so." He seemed to enjoy the look of surprise on Daniel's face as he turned, suddenly, quite angry, and railed, "Is your drunkenness and sloth acceptable to God all the other days of the week? Then why will you obey his commandment today? Come! I have no more patience to spare." With that, he turned the camel harshly and whipped it to a run.

As the clatter of ben Ariyb's mount faded, Daniel stood in silence, staring blankly at the ground, feeling as he always had when similarly chastised by his brother. The guilt raised by the bare truth of the accusation made his anger impotent, his frustration complete. Sober for the first time since the journey began, memories of recent events flooded back all at once: His "perfect" brother and sister-in-law, their self-righteous abuse. The love of his life, his only friend, their cruel betrayal. *Did they think of me when they touched? Did they speak of their deception and laugh? Do they laugh still when they remember my utter destruction in the discovery?*

"Oh, God!" he cried out, and tears streamed from his eyes. "Why? Why?" He collapsed and Lono came to comfort him.

The servant did not need to ask what had broken his master's spirit. It was plain ben Ariyb's angry words were not the sole cause of this episode. He knelt next to Daniel and patted his back. "Now, now," he said simply. "Dere, dere."

Daniel faced him, tears still streaming. "I am so weak, Lono," he said, apologizing. "I am nothing like my father or my brother. They would bear any such abuse in silence. They would never break so."

Another discouraging thought struck him with such force he could hardly breathe. "These things would never happen to them. If I were a stronger man, Mina would not have—"

"Now you stop dat!" Lono commanded. "Dat girl do what she do because a' her, not because a' you. She all broke . . . in dere." He tapped a thick finger on Daniel's chest. "You 'member, Mastah Daniel, I know you since dis high." Lono flapped a meaty palm toward his knees. "I see evuh'ting. You perfec'?" He laughed. "No, no. But you fadda perfec'? You brudda? No, dem nee'duh.

"We none perfec', Mastah Daniel. Only him." Lono pointed upward. "Only him perfec', an' we jus' do evuh'ting we can try be perfec' too. But dat between me an' him. You fadda an' him. You brudda, him wife, dat Mina. You—" he tapped Daniel's chest again—"an' him." He helped Daniel to his feet. "You jus' need find him again."

Walking toward the camel, Daniel sniffed, wiping his eyes and his nose with the hem of his robe. "What do you mean 'again'?" He climbed into the saddle, and Lono coaxed the animal up.

"You don' 'member, Mastah Daniel?" Lono spoke over his shoulder, leading the camels. "*You* tell *me* 'bout him, long time 'go. Sometimes afta I come you fadda's house way back, I cry jus' like you. Long, long ways dey bring us, beat an' whip, but most I hurt *inside,* jus' like you, for the *people* I lose. An' you see me cry one day an' you tell me all about him. You tell me about you family, belongin' to him, an' you tell me I part you family now, so his family too. An' I ask how I can see him. Oh, you jus' giggle. You say, 'Only talk to him in you heart, an' you see him someday.' I belee dat, Mastah Daniel." Lono stopped and turned, looking up to Daniel in earnest. "An' I talk to him in here ever' day. Thas' how you find him again."

For a long time they moved on in silence, Daniel contemplating what Lono said. *But how,* Daniel pondered, *can it apply to me? I was a child then. I'm just starting to prove myself, to assert myself as a man. Now is not the time for childishness, especially spoken by a slave . . . even if he's quoting me!*

Rabbi Nehemiah sat beside the fire in his chambers, his grandson at his right and his brother Rabbi Ahava on his left. The aged scholar fixed his glassy eyes on the warmth of the fire.

He said to Cantor and Lily, "Warmth is my light now. For a dozen years I have not been able to see the letters of the sacred scrolls dancing beneath the lines." Raising his head as if to see them with his hearing, he asked. "Do you think you could?"

Lily and Cantor exchanged glances. The power they had felt three times, compelling them to speak the name of their Healer and command illness to vanish, had not been present since they entered Narda.

Cantor said apologetically, "Rebbe Nehemiah, it was children the Lord brought to us, children which the speaking of his Name cured."

"And yet my aged brother Ahava," the old man said, "himself a leper in the Valley many years . . . Yeshua healed him. With all the others." He pivoted to where he knew Ahava sat. "How many lepers, Brother? How many did Yeshua heal that night?"

Ahava's head bent as he spoke the answer. "Six hundred and twelve." Ahava's eyes, as clear and bright as those of a man of twenty, glanced at Cantor. "And then Yeshua made 613. The number of the commandments. But, my brother, Cantor was beyond the sickness of earth when he was called back."

Nehemiah's hands trembled. "Yes! And thirty-six of you came here. Refuge from Herod Antipas and from the rulers in Yerushalayim . . . the Lamedvov, the thirty-six righteous." He raised his right hand, imploring. "I ask myself, what is it? Why have thirty-six *tsara'im* come here to this Synagogue of Exiles to be purified? Why did Yeshua send you to us?"

Ahava knit his brows together. "Children and their teachers. No more."

Nehemiah shook his head slowly. "And yet, you . . . Cantor? Lily? You whom he sent out with the command to heal and cast out and raise? You cannot heal my old blind eyes that I may see and read the light of Torah once again?"

Cantor clasped Lily's hand and inquired of her with his expression. She shook her head.

Three times they had prayed over the rabbi of Narda and recited the Name of the Great Healer. They had attempted to cure the blindness that kept him in darkness. Should they now attempt to heal the old man's blindness again?

Cantor answered him, "Honored rebbe, your vision is not for us to give. We don't understand the . . . failure . . . any more than you. It is by the command of Yeshua and by his Name alone that we received this commission."

Nehemiah challenged, "Yet three times as you journeyed here, some child was healed . . . as you only prayed and spoke the Name. Why not me? Am I not a man who loves the Lord? Why only three children whom you will never meet again?"

The disappointment of the old scholar nearly crushed Lily's heart. *I'm praying again, You Who See Everything. He wants to see your Word so badly . . . wants to see the flames of your Word leap from the page to warm his soul. Why not? Why not?*

The silence of the old rabbi's sorrow was thick like smoke in the room for a long time. The fire crackled. No one could answer him. Why this one was healed. Why another was not.

Rabbi Ahava inhaled deeply. "My brother, Yeshua sent us here to you, the children, the teachers. He said to me, 'Your brother will protect them.' So, we have come to you. We are thirty-six . . . Lamedvov, the righteous, you say. And the people of this city hear rumors about miracles, but no one is sure about what happened to us. They don't know where we come from. There has not been one cured of sickness in the Name of Yeshua within the walls of Narda. Yeshua said you would protect us . . . and so? Perhaps your blindness protects us."

"I don't understand," Nehemiah protested.

Ahava finished his thought. "And what would the people say if Rabbi Nehemiah was cured of his blindness? They would know something miraculous was afoot. Our brothers in Yerushalayim despise the very one who worked this miracle for us. They claim he cures only by the power of Satan. You know and have heard they seek his life. And so? Perhaps it is not safe for our little ones for anyone to know for certain."

The possibility that Nehemiah's sightless world was for the safety of the little ones cheered him somewhat.

His head bobbed and bobbed as though the words were striking his brain one at a time. "So," he said. Then again, "So. So. So, it makes a kind of dark sense." Then to Cantor: "It is the season when the Temple tax will be collected here and taken back to Yerushalayim. The Herodian Guard and the Temple guards will come to fetch the taxes soon, as they do every year. They will come here. They will see that Rabbi Nehemiah is still blind. They will think, No miracles here. But, perhaps after they have gone? Then you will pray for this old man once again?"

20

CHAPTER

Dow Rud was little more than a ring of goatherds' shanties, but according to Saul ben Ariyb, it marked their passage over the Zagros Mountains. Arriving there much later than the rest of the caravan, Daniel was surprised to find the number of waiting travelers more than doubled.

"A wonderful blessing," ben Ariyb called to Daniel in explanation. "An old friend finds himself traveling this way as well. We shall ride together."

Pleased as he was that ben Ariyb had apparently forgotten their earlier row, Daniel was nonetheless confused as to his business partner's delight in the addition. *Wasn't the small size of our caravan part of our defense?* he thought, but he would not question ben Ariyb again this day.

"Wonderful," he said simply, looking over the ten other travelers. *But which of these is ben Ariyb's "old friend"?* Each of the new additions rode his own camel, each carried a gleaming blade prominently displayed at his side, and none seemed more remarkable than another. Lono seemed to notice this as well and exchanged a brief look with Daniel as he pulled the camel to its knees for Daniel to dismount.

"No, no!" ben Ariyb directed. "They have been waiting all day. We ride for the mountains immediately."

Without further word, the group urged their camels on, half of the extras riding ahead of the group, half falling into line behind Lono and Daniel. Ben Ariyb returned to his own string of camels and servants, leaving Daniel to his thoughts once again.

From Dow Rud the thin trail ascended sharply into the mountains. The caravan moved single file. Switchbacks were sharp and frequent, and Daniel rarely saw more than one other rider in front of him. Twice in the first few minutes of travel, Lono left the reins of Daniel's camel to guide the second animal around a particularly precarious bend. The stone was darker and rougher than what they'd traversed in recent days, and Daniel worried for the camels' feet.

The peaks above them were invisible in the waning sunlight as a swirling mist materialized on their supporting slopes. The mountains rose so vertically on each side of the narrow pass, Daniel thought it less a way *over* the mountains and more a crack *through* them. Indeed, there were parts of the trail that passed under an outcropping from one side or the other.

"Odd," Daniel said aloud, and Lono nodded as the word whined away in reverberation off the walls. "One heavy winter's snow would fill this crevasse, and no one would know it was here."

"Or caravan in it," Lono joked, though Daniel had already thought an avalanche would accomplish as much in summer too.

After a pause, Daniel said, "The Red Sea could not have looked more frightening to the Israelites before it fell upon the Egyptians." He idly wondered to which group this caravan belonged. The thought made him laugh nervously to himself.

The sun would have been well below even a flat horizon, and the sky emitted only the faintest, intangible light, before the trail straightened and opened into a comparatively spacious expanse. *Meadow* was the description that came to Daniel's mind, but the terrain was as barren as the path they'd come by, and he dismissed it.

The ten or so members of the party ahead of them were already dismounted and making camp as Daniel and Lono approached. Even the camels seemed relieved to be in open space again, grunting happily at the sight of the other animals.

As Daniel climbed from the saddle and Lono began unpacking, ben

Ariyb approached with a grin and clapped him on the shoulder. "Pleased to arrive, Daniel?"

Pleased seemed too enthusiastic a word. Daniel looked across the clearing to where the trail led away again, narrowing immediately to another constricted, sinuous passage. "I should say we're safe from thieves here. No one could come into this camp unbidden. Tell me," he asked as another thought suddenly struck him, "the passage is so narrow and the walls so steep, what will we do when another traveler comes from the opposite direction? Surely you cannot pass in there?"

"There will be no others," said ben Ariyb. "The beauty and safety of this route. Now come." He led Daniel by the arm toward a growing campfire. "Warm yourself. And when your man is finished with your shelter, let him bring our new companions some of your wine."

Daniel frowned. After his conversation with Lono earlier, he had planned to abstain from wine for a while, thinking it might actually be doing more harm than good to his outlook. But it would be rude and churlish not to drink with the others.

"Just a little," he agreed.

Ben Ariyb said, "You've enough wine to supply us *all* for this journey several times over, and you'll share *'just a little'*?"

"No," Daniel protested in the face of ben Ariyb's criticism, "I only meant—"

Ben Ariyb interrupted, "Well, *I* only meant to allow you one final night of blissful ignorance before your life changes forever, but I see now that's unnecessary!"

"What do you mean?" Daniel asked, hearing a scuffle behind him. He turned in time to see three of the last riders attempting to wrestle Lono to the ground. "What is the meaning—?"

It was suddenly horrifyingly clear: only glimpses of their trade goods, a little-known route, traveling on the Sabbath, passing a slaver and his captors! Ben Ariyb had never meant to do business with Daniel. Daniel and Lono *were* his business, and these extra additions to the caravan were more than coincidence; they were there to ensure all went as planned.

Someone grabbed Daniel from behind in a firm headlock and began choking him.

"So now we will just *take* your wine," triumphed ben Ariyb. "And everything *else* you own!"

Daniel struggled but was helpless against the more powerful man who held him and laughed in his ear. As his sight grew dim in the choke hold of his attacker, Daniel saw Lono shake two men from his back as easily as a wet dog drying his coat. Lono brought his elbow down sharply on another who gripped him around the waist, and the man slipped limply to the ground at his feet.

Nearly free, Lono moved to help Daniel as well, dragging the last attacker across the rough stones as the assailant clung to Lono's left ankle.

Good, Lono, Daniel thought, *you will save us!*

Two more men ran at Lono from both sides, colliding with each other as he squatted beneath their attack just before they struck. In the same motion he grabbed the hair and lifted the head of the man who clutched at his legs and smashed his nose with the heel of a fist.

With a fearsome, deep scream, Lono spun in place to free himself from the four attackers, now recovering from their impact and punching and scraping at his face and ears. All but one was thrown to the ground, striking the bare stone hard. The last continued hitting Lono with a closed fist in the right ear as he balanced on Lono's back, his left hand wrapped in the giant's cloak.

Lono stopped struggling to glare at ben Ariyb, whose face betrayed some fear at the sight of this lone man beating back his whole small army. Lono laughed maniacally.

His ear became bloody and mangled as he endured the repeated blows from the man on his back, but he reached calmly over his shoulder with his right hand and grabbed the man's wrist. With little effort Lono passed the wrist to the grip of his own left hand, and pivoting his body down and to the left, he pulled the man over his shoulder into a whirling arc and solid impact with the ground. Another blow from the heel of his right fist splintered the man's nose in an audible explosion of blood.

Now fully free from his attackers, Lono snarled and lunged and laughed at the remaining men who circled around him, afraid to engage.

"Stop!" yelled ben Ariyb, striding to where Daniel struggled against his captor. Pulling the silver-hilted dagger from Daniel's belt, he unsheathed it and held the point to Daniel's throat.

Daniel instantly chastised himself for forgetting he had the weapon. *I could've used it myself. I was depending on Lono to save me.*

Lono did stop then, afraid ben Ariyb might slit Daniel's throat. At that moment Muti approached the giant from behind with a club, both hands lifting the weapon high as he struck.

His eyes locked with Daniel's in apology, Lono winced at the first blow, fell to his knees with the second, and lost consciousness with the third.

The choke hold tightened, and a moment later, Daniel's world went black.

A single grain of sand nearly filled the vision of Daniel's left eye. One facet gleamed like a gemstone, reflecting red from a nearby campfire. Daniel lay facedown on his right side and, for a long moment, could not remember where he was or what was happening. Forcing his focus upward, he saw Lono lying unconscious, a shadow behind his mangled, bloody ear dancing crazily in the flickering light.

Daniel tried to reach for him but found he could not move his arms. Something held both wrists fast behind his back. Trying to move his legs to sit up was equally ineffective; his knees and ankles were also bound. Bending at his waist, dragging his face across the ground, he was able to get a view beyond his servant and suddenly remembered all.

Saul ben Ariyb stood at the edge of the firelight drinking from one of Daniel's wineskins. Another man was with him, but Daniel could not make out his features. The two laughed blithely as though the violent quarrel had happened long ago, making Daniel wonder how long it *had* been. When a footstep sounded behind him, he closed his eyes again, hoping to convince the intruder he was still unconscious, but it was too late.

Muti's harsh voice announced Daniel's awareness to the camp. "The young prince lives, Master ben Ariyb." He grabbed Daniel's forearm, hefting him into a sitting position. Daniel gasped as the lift put painful pressure on his shoulders. Muti chuckled and leaned close, snarling in his ear, "Welcome to your new life, Prince Daniel."

"Why have you done this?" Daniel panted as ben Ariyb walked closer. Ben Ariyb's companion stayed back in the shadows.

"Something you'll quickly learn," ben Ariyb responded, "is that the mere sound of a slave's voice will sometimes anger his master." He struck Daniel in the cheek, hard enough to knock him over. Again Muti lifted him by his tethered arms.

Daniel gritted his teeth hard to avoid crying out. "Please," he begged, "I can pay you. My credit—"

"How slowly you learn." Ben Ariyb kicked Daniel over this time, stomping at his unprotected face as Daniel tried to roll and twist away from the attack. Unseen members of the caravan snickered.

"Stop!" a heavy Arab accent called from the darkness at last. From the corner of Daniel's eye he saw the black-clad figure of ben Ariyb's companion emerge. "Saul, you damage the merchandise." Then he guffawed and Daniel realized where he had seen the man before.

The slaver they'd passed a few days earlier assisted Daniel to the sitting position again. Daniel spat dirt from his mouth.

"I am Faisal," he said, with a beaming grin set into his handsome, olive-toned face. "And you won't ask any more questions, will you?"

Daniel only shook his head and grimaced as Faisal knelt and gently brushed gravel away from his cheek. "A pity," said the slaver, almost under his breath, "the abuse of such finery." Daniel shuddered as Faisal drew his index finger backward down Daniel's temple and under his nose, wiping away the blood there. Holding it up for Daniel to see, he continued, "The value of punishment is to break the will." He tapped Daniel's forehead, leaving a red spot. "Not the body." With that he wiped his finger along the length of Daniel's left sleeve and stood.

Faisal snapped his fingers at an attendant who brought a jug of water for him to wash off the remaining blood. As he rubbed his hands under the trickle of water, he said, "You are a slave now. One I *plan* to purchase." Turning toward ben Ariyb, he said, "But I have not yet and *will* not if you are crippled!"

"Just a little sport," ben Ariyb protested. "And he must be taught quickly."

Faisal looked back at Daniel. He shook the water from his hands and took a cloth from the shoulder of the servant. "Leave the teaching to me. And have your *sport* with that ox."

Without a thought for Lono, Daniel screamed in his mind, *My God, my God, help me.*

"I remember you," Faisal said to Daniel. "You showed much compassion for that little straggler in our train. He is dead. And so shall you be if you do not learn your place. You are a slave now; that is your entire being. If you think of yourself as anything but property, you will die."

Oh, God, Daniel thought again, *please help me!*

"That is what I mean, Daniel!" Faisal chastised in a disappointed tone. "Where was your mind just then? Praying?" He turned away and snapped for another servant. "A selfish prayer, the wish for a better life— these are dangerous things. You would do better to pray for me, Daniel. Petition my god, Allu, to prosper me, for when I am happy . . ."

Daniel glanced nervously from Muti to ben Ariyb as they huddled together in seeming expectation. Faisal's servant trotted to his side, carrying a short, iron staff with some sort of ornament on the end.

Faisal laid the ornament in the fire where the coals burned white-hot. "I believe one way to help you forget yourself is to give you a constant reminder that you are now the property of someone else."

"No, please," Daniel began but was silenced by a kick from ben Ariyb.

"Some men will brand a slave on the shoulder." Faisal spun the brand in the embers, sending a small shower of red sparks into the air. "But this can be concealed. No, I find that if you want a faithful slave, you must mark him where he himself can see it at all times."

"Please," Daniel sobbed again, "please, I will be faithful. I swear it."

"But you have already broken your word, Daniel." Faisal sighed and turned to his little audience. "It is always the same. They promise silence but show them a brand, and listen . . ."

Snickers sounded from around the camp. Daniel began to cry. "Oh, God," he repeated between wracking sobs. "Oh, God, please."

Abruptly, Faisal turned. "You know what to do," he called to someone behind Daniel, and walked away.

Several sets of hands grabbed Daniel all at once; he was lifted in the air and dropped onto his stomach. After regaining his breath, he cried for Faisal, begging for his mercy. But the screams went unanswered.

As Daniel watched in horror, the brand was drawn from the fire and brought near. Unseen assailants braced against his struggles, roughly turning his right forearm upward.

"No, no!" he panted.

He heard it first—a terrible, strange whistling and popping as the iron first boiled then charred his flesh, and still they held it there.

He screamed violently, and his vision yellowed with nausea from the pain. Before he passed out, Daniel heard ben Ariyb's voice.

"Faisal," he said, "does not like violence."

Aram, the captain of the Herodian Guard detachment, was brusque and used to being obeyed. It galled him to defer to Shinar, the Levite in charge of tithes. Shinar was envoy for the high priest, as Aram was for Herod Antipas. Since arriving in Narda, they had been kept waiting for two days.

Today's appointment had already been delayed two hours. Time dragged in the antechamber to Narda's judgment hall. The Herodian officer strode up and down the paving stones, eager to get this business concluded.

The Temple official—older, grayer, and much more phlegmatic in dealing with petty chieftains and desert warlords—counseled patience. He muttered to his counterpart that any show of impatience would only drive up the price of cooperation, but the soldier could not help himself and resumed pacing.

Just as Aram was ready to storm out in frustration, an unseen gong clanged loudly. The doors swung outward to reveal a double file of black-robed, sword-bearing soldiers, forming a living corridor. A tall, thin man, bearing a gold-headed staff of office designating him Narda's steward, escorted the envoys.

On the raised platform at the far end of the chamber sat Hannel and Tannis, Jewish mercenaries, robbers turned caravan protectors and Lords of the Marsh, rulers of Narda. "Greetings to the representative of our brothers from Judea," Tannis exclaimed after the two envoys bowed.

After preliminary diplomatic pleasantries had been exchanged, the matter of transporting the Temple tax was raised. As protocol demanded, the brothers protested that it was a pleasure for them to be of assistance—the fulfilling of a mitzvah for them to keep the Almighty's tithe secure.

Shinar replied with profound appreciation but noted that, naturally, the brothers would incur certain expenses, which it would be Lord Caiaphas' pleasure to reimburse.

Many protests later, the sum of reimbursement was mentioned—

a small increase over previous years—and accepted with a show of reluctance. It was then Shinar said, "There is another matter in which the high priest would like your assistance."

Tired of being purely decorative, Aram interjected, "And my lord Herod Antipas directs . . ." The officer halted at the frown that appeared on Tannis' face. "Tetrarch Antipas is also interested in this . . . other matter," he concluded lamely.

"Truly, it must be significant if the reverend high priest and the famed ruler of the Galil both desire our humble aid," Hannel suggested. "What is it?"

Shinar explained about the sudden desertion of the Valley of Mak'ob and how the circumstances pointed to either black magic or rebellious plotting—or both.

"But what has any of that to do with us?" Tannis demanded gruffly. "If Antipas or Caiaphas can't keep even impoverished beggars from running away, what do they expect us to do about it?"

Aram's face displayed the anger he was now barely able to control.

"Mak'ob . . . lepers . . . a Galilean healer . . . rebels . . . locate and detain . . . I think I've got it," Hannel said with an air of polite assistance. "We—"

"What my brother means to say is that we will retire to discuss this matter and give you our reply shortly," Tannis abruptly interrupted.

With that, Aram and Shinar once more found themselves waiting in the antechamber, perhaps no nearer their goal than before.

21

Alone in the private study behind the judgment chamber, Hannel congratulated his brother. "Thank you for stopping me," he praised. "I was too eager. If we give them a show of reluctance, we can ask for a much bigger price!" Hannel's eyes widened in pleasurable anticipation. "Fifteen percent of the taxes? Even twenty? And to have both that old bag of guts, Antipas, and that old windbag, Caiaphas, beholden to us! Magnificent!"

"Narda has always been a place where Jews fleeing persecution have come for sanctuary," Tannis observed.

"That's the way. I always knew you were a better negotiator than me, but I see I have so much more still to learn! Remind them how far beyond the reach of Roman tyranny we are here. How difficult what they ask will be."

Tannis fixed his younger sibling with a cold stare that froze Hannel's words on his lips and momentarily his blood in his veins as well.

"You're . . . you're serious, aren't you?" Hannel asked.

"Since the days of the exiled King Jeconiah, Narda has been a haven. We have pilgrims from all over the world who come to visit the

Synagogue of the Exiles. What would Narda's reputation become if they were sold out? What would our reputation become?"

"When you were a brigand, jumping out at lonely travelers and slitting throats for pennies, you weren't concerned about your 'reputation,'" Hannel returned scornfully.

Tannis swelled up in anger. "Do you want to oppose a true miracle of HaShem?"

Hannel snorted.

Changing the ground of his opposition for his skeptic brother, Tannis argued, "Or can you recognize someone from Mak'ob, now healed, who doesn't want to be known? Think what evil will be unleashed! Everyone with an old score to settle will denounce his enemy for ten silver pieces. Do you want to sell them all to Herod Antipas?"

"Not all," Hannel countered. "Just enough to satisfy him. Among the ones who have recently arrived we can find a few likely rebels, a handful with wild tales of a healer from . . . what foolish place was it? Nazareth? What does that sound like to you? They're crazy. It doesn't mean we should be!"

Tannis scanned his brother up and down. "You only see the money. Not the people."

"And you . . . o-ho! You already have someone in mind!"

"That's enough," Tannis snapped. "I forbid it. No deals with Antipas. He makes too good an enemy to turn him into an ally."

Tannis was surprised when Hannel acquiesced. "Let's not quarrel about this anymore," Hannel replied. "I'll follow your lead, since you feel so strongly about it. Let's not make the envoys wait longer. We'll appear together and tell them no."

When Aram retired for the night, he was groggy from the amount of wine he'd consumed over the meal provided by the Lords of the Marsh. As if to apologize for their refusal to aid Lord Antipas, the brothers had spread a lavish feast.

The taste of the food and wine had been sour in Aram's mouth and remained so in his stomach. Antipas disliked failure at all times, but to be refused something by anyone lower in rank than Caesar himself would drive the tetrarch wild with wrath.

Aram had seen this happen often enough before to know the sequel: The messenger was the first to be punished for Antipas' disappointments.

Aram reeled toward his bed, pulling his tunic over his head. With the garment half off, he viewed the coverlet at the end of a kind of tunnel. There, directly beneath his gaze, was a scrap of parchment.

How had it come there? Aram had not left it there. No one in his retinue would communicate in such a fashion. His own guard, posted outside this room, had strict orders to admit no one.

Snatching his sword from its sheath, Aram made a circuit of the room, stabbing tapestries for vacant spaces and hammering with the hilt on seemingly solid walls to search for hidden passages.

Finding none, he returned to his bed and used the point of the weapon to flip the message open.

Keep this just between us, it read. *For our own reasons of state, we cannot openly agree to your proposal or discuss it. But we will do as you ask for . . .* Here the note mentioned a sum that made Aram whistle even as he calculated that it was within the margin he was authorized to pay. *Speak to no one, but wait 'til you hear from me next.*

It was signed, *Hannel.*

Searing pain woke Daniel before the sun as Lono awkwardly dressed the wound on his arm. "Sorry, Mastah," Lono whispered. "Only have da cloth. No water to clean, no poultice."

The two men were now bound as Daniel had seen the slave train days before: their wrists tied together, linked by a braided cord to the closely shackled ankles of another.

Daniel saw several more men had been added to their ranks. He was now merely one of the additions to the string of misery.

"Where have all these men come from?" Daniel asked, wincing as Lono cinched the crude bandage around his arm.

"Come in da night. Dem already branded, an' come wid two more Faisal men."

Daniel was suddenly bitter. "And how did *you* escape the branding, Lono?" He pronounced the servant's name harshly.

Lono looked hurt. Slowly he maneuvered his bound arms to present his right forearm to Daniel's view. There, untreated and uncovered, was a large scorched mark in the shape of a triangle surrounded by a circle.

Daniel didn't have time to apologize. Ben Ariyb bellowed from his tent for Muti, and the entire camp was soon in motion. The other slaves were on their feet at the first command, and Daniel and Lono followed their example.

One of Faisal's men untethered the first three of the line, ordering them to dismantle the camp. Daniel watched with growing anger as more guards emerged from *his* tent. Then he heard Faisal's voice behind him.

"Poor Daniel," Faisal said, walking toward the slaves. "Missing your things already? I'll tell you another secret that will help you forget."

He stopped in front of Daniel and reached out as though he might take Daniel's hand in his. Instead, he gripped Daniel's forearm, pressing his thumb hard into the center of the bandage covering the brand. "Remember the pain," Faisal hissed through a smile as tears came to Daniel's eyes. "Yes, remember the pain, and you will forget everything else."

He pushed Daniel's arm away and summoned a servant for water to wash in. "And you—" he nodded toward Lono—"will help him forget."

At first Daniel did not know exactly what Faisal meant when he said Lono would help him forget. Was he assigning a special task to his former servant to teach him the rules of being a slave?

But as the line of men was whipped into motion, he suddenly understood. Tethered as they all were to one another, each man's movement was affected by the others. Daniel's bound wrists were tied to Lono's ankles, and as the bigger man shuffled along, the cord alternately tightened and slackened, pulling Daniel's arms forward and extending his elbows. The wound on his arm cracked and chafed under the bandage with each movement, and soon his only thought was of shadowing Lono so closely that the cord remained slack.

Using short, sideways glances, Daniel noticed the mountain pass widening away from the trail they walked. The walls receded and flattened into gentle slopes once again and they were in the middle of a large valley. The peaks were nearer now, the snow seemed close enough to run to, and his breath grew short in the thinner air.

The caravan stretched out lazily on both sides, riders of camels and horses traveling in groups of twos and threes. Counting all of Faisal's men and ben Ariyb's, there were as many free men as there were slaves. One guard for each captive.

"Good!" Faisal smiled down at him, riding comfortably alongside, but Daniel did not look up. "You see? Soon you will not remember who you are, much less what you had or where you came from. Wonderful!"

But I'll always remember this, Daniel thought. *I'll always remember this, and I'll always remember you. And someday* . . . "I'll kill you." Daniel was so lost in the daydream, he did not realize he had said the last words aloud.

"What did you say?" Faisal screamed, and the line of men stopped abruptly, each one plowing into the back of the next.

Ben Ariyb rode hastily to Faisal's side. "What is the matter, my friend?"

"When I have been so helpful to you, Daniel?" Faisal scolded. "How can you misuse me so? Untie him!"

The other riders circled around the slaves as Muti used Daniel's dagger to cut him free from his tether to Lono.

"And what shall we do with you, Daniel?" Faisal asked loudly, looking more to the assembled watchers than to the slave. "For such an offense as threatening your master with death, I should cut your tongue from your head." The guards cheered, and Daniel saw Lono's shoulders sag in sadness at the idea.

"But your education is of value to your future master," Faisal continued, "and your ability to speak a necessary part of that. No, we cannot cut out your tongue." The onlookers were disappointed, and there were several groans.

"Another brand might help you remember your place." Another cheer began but was cut short when Faisal remembered, "But we are not in camp. We've much more travel this day, and to build a fire would take far too long."

Again groans of disappointment resounded, as if the onlookers thought there might not be any violence at all.

"Whip him," Faisal said at last, almost too quietly to hear. "Yes, take all his clothes, flay his back open, and let him walk naked until we camp tonight."

Then, as an afterthought, Faisal added, "And, Saul, have at least two of your party ride next to him for the rest of the day. Their laughter can teach a better lesson than any whip will." With that he spurred his horse away, leading part of the caravan with him.

"You heard," Muti jeered and began stripping Daniel's clothes.

When Daniel resisted, Muti simply cut the cloth away until Daniel stood naked among a pile of rags, surrounded by hostile, laughing faces.

Even as he screamed in pain when the first lashes scored his bare back, deep in his mind Daniel thought, *He is right. My shame is my suffering.* And then, *What a fool I was to call on God. There is no one to hear. There is no one there at all.*

22

CHAPTER

he Synagogue of the Exiles was different from any house of worship Lily had ever seen. A geometric pattern of ten circular stones
was set in the foundation of the assembly hall. The shape of the
building was constructed along the same pattern.

Each stone was inlaid in lapis lazuli, trimmed in silver, with a word
written in Hebrew.

Through the lattice of the Women's Gallery Lily saw the pattern
plainly. A series of twenty straight lapis lines linked the circular stones
into a Star of David pattern.

She fingered the ten smooth pebbles, the stones of Israel, still in her
pockets. But where had the pattern set in the floor come from?

Beneath her high view, Cantor and Rabbi Ahava made a circuit of
the markers. They hovered over each, contemplating the inlaid words
as one might gaze at the name of a loved one engraved on a headstone.
They murmured the inscriptions, recalling the faces or remembering
the voices of those long gone.

Rabbi Ahava asked, "Surely now we who have been healed understand the meanings?"

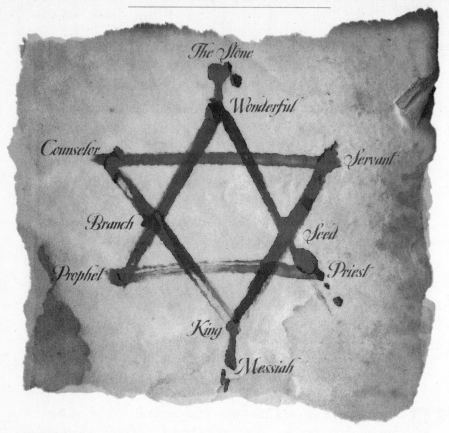

Cantor exhaled slowly. He stooped and traced the letters of the word *Messiah*. "He is Messiah, the Anointed One. The One the prophets foretold. But who will believe us? They don't believe we were lepers, healed by his word."

Rabbi Ahava tugged his lower lip in thought. "That's true. Still, even healing a leper seems a small thing compared to . . . to . . . you. Being called back to this world from such a far place."

Cantor replied quietly, "It was not so far, Rebbe. Not so far. Very near, in fact. Near enough that I could . . ." He stopped and frowned. "Ah, well. They wouldn't believe me if I told them."

On the balcony, Lily suppressed a cough. She did not want Cantor to know she was looking down at him, that she could see and hear him. Did he not know she believed all that he had told her?

I'm praying again, Lord Who Brings the Dead Back to Life. Remind Cantor that I will believe him. Remind him I was there. I saw the grave open and felt the wind that blew away the dust from his eyes. I saw the color climb to his face. It was my face above him when he opened his eyes. I am praying again, Lord of Life. Tell his heart to speak to me. I will believe him.

As if hearing her prayer, Cantor turned his face to the lattice. He raised his hand as if in acknowledgment of someone's presence above him.

He spoke quietly to Rabbi Ahava. "It was something like that . . . like the gallery. I could look down, see Lily through the lattice. Hear her voice and pray for her and cheer her on. Though she could not see me or hear me."

Ahava's eyes grew wide. "You could . . . see?"

"I could love," Cantor answered. "And now back here I know. They who lived before us are witnesses of the race we run."

"Well then. Not what I imagined."

"No. If I speak to the exiles of my . . . journey . . . they won't believe me. Or what I saw."

The old rabbi clasped his hands behind his back. "You were called back for a reason. There are others whom he called back from the land beyond death. A girl in Capernaum.[30] The only son of a widow in Nain.[31] Others. The list is long, and people come from everywhere to meet them. Perhaps they have fled the territory of Herod Antipas as well. All such witnesses Antipas and the Sanhedrin would prefer silenced. As Antipas silenced the Baptizer."

"I'm not afraid. I would have stayed there, if not for Lily's longing. Yeshua knew her heart. Yeshua's mother asked him for this miracle. For Lily's sake. And I'm glad for Lily. Even though time had passed, and my mortal self was returning to the dust. I would have been content to watch her through eternal windows and pray for her . . . until she came to join me."

Cantor's words cut Lily to the heart. How could he say he had not wanted to come back to live his life with her? to give her children and spend the years loving one another?

Rabbi Ahava said, "It was more wonderful than life?"

Cantor smiled sadly. "It's this life that's the shadow. This is the dream. I died and woke up in Paradise. And . . . well, what does it matter? I'm still longing for a distant home."

"The names inscribed here . . . they are all about himself. So many generations in exile. They have forgotten the meaning of the stones. They have forgotten that the prophets wrote about him before he came. If we could tell them, then they would believe."

Cantor clamped his mouth tight. "Ten stones. Ten names of Messiah. Yeshua clearly fulfills them all—each name. He is the cornerstone. But they don't believe him. In Yerushalayim the leaders of Israel plot how they can kill him, even though his miracles speak louder than words. If those who have seen him face-to-face won't believe, can these exiles of Israel believe what they haven't seen? The people come to him for bread. They come for comfort. But they don't come because they want to know him."

Cantor swept his hand over the ten stones. "These tell who he is. They are the prophecies fulfilled in our time, and they tell the future. If the people won't believe him, even after seeing proof for themselves, then how can we convince them?"

"He sent us, and you and Lily, here to the exiles of Israel. To the place where Gan Eden was lost. To proclaim what you saw." The old man looked toward the ceiling. "I will tell them of the day we laid you in the grave."

Exhausted from days of constant marching, little water, and poor rations, Daniel was near the end of his strength. Lono offered to carry Daniel. When he was told to shut up and get back in line or he would be killed, he responded, "Soon Mastah Daniel die. If he die, I no care if I killed or not. Two dead or two living . . . which make you more money?"

The slavers relented.

Even with Lono's assistance, Daniel was more unconscious than awake when they reached an oasis with a pool of brackish water. On hands and knees Daniel crawled to the edge of the pond and drank deeply without raising either head or body from the dirt.

Then he was chained to a palm tree with his elbows interlinked with another slave's, who was seated back-to-back with him. Lono, whose girth and massive arms made such pinioning to another impossible, was shackled facing Daniel across the pool. "Courage, Mastah Daniel," Lono called. "You not fear terror by night nor arrow by day.[32] Remember!"

For his encouraging prayer, Lono was slashed across the mouth with a riding crop and then gagged.

All of the prisoners were blindfolded. Why this extraordinary step was taken, Daniel did not know, unless it was to cow them into deeper submission. It was truly terrifying to be bound into immobility and deprived of any warning when a blow might fall.

The last sight Daniel had before a stinking rag was secured over his eyes was of a waxing crescent moon centered in the setting constellation of The Lion.

Where are you, God of my father? Daniel prayed. *Lion of the Tribe of Judah, as they say you are and as my father believes. Where are you tonight? How could this be happening to me?*

The sliver of moon, so like a smile blazoned in the western heavens, mocked him. Even after the cloth was knotted across his forehead, the image laughed at him in his thoughts.

Either you do not exist or you are impossibly cruel. What did I do to deserve this? Why me?

Then, unaccountably, Daniel thought, *I wonder if they're praying for me, or if they've given me up for dead?*

Somehow the thought that he was already forgotten and abandoned by those who had claimed to love him made him more bitter than ever at his fate.

On this angry, resentful note, Daniel fell asleep.

23

The Herodian troopers arrived outside the Synagogue of the Exiles very early in the morning . . . but after a minyan had already assembled for prayer. Captain Aram stood beside Shinar, the Temple official, who had advised Aram not to enter the synagogue by force.

So the encounter became an improbable stalemate.

A dozen gruff, battle-hardened, and unfeeling Samaritan soldiers confronted nine elderly Jews and their leader, Rabbi Nehemiah.

The soldiers stood in the street before the house of worship.

The elders stood silently on the steps, facing them.

Like ten living stones, the scholars in prayer shawls represented the foundation of the synagogue. They were the most spiritually responsive of all the Jews of Narda. These ten hobbled every morning as fast as bowed backs and weak knees and canes could carry them, in order to share in the honor of being counted in the minyan.

Since the days of Abraham, when the Almighty agreed to spare Sodom if ten righteous men could be found therein, it was a watchword that a half score was enough to fulfill righteousness. No matter how many more attended a service, be it one or a hundred beyond the ten, they added not one bit to the acceptability of the gathering as worship to the One God.

Just as the nine and their leader understood morning worship to be a sacred mitzvah, they felt no less serious about confronting the threat today. Neither were they any less confident in HaShem's commitment to deliver them.

Aram barked, "We know you have fugitives here. Rebels. Give them up at once, by order of Herod Antipas."

Wisps of Nehemiah's fine white beard stirred in the thinnest of breezes blowing down the length of the Euphrates. "The son of Herod the Butcher has no authority to command here," he responded.

A dozen latecomers to morning prayers arrived during this discussion, forming a rank behind the Herodians. The troopers, glancing around, fingered the hilts of their swords.

Shinar laid his hand on Aram's arm, lest the officer do something rash. Shinar had no desire to be clapped into a Parthian prison or hanged for inciting a riot. "The captain spoke hastily. We want your cooperation in locating these wanted ones, these runaway lepers. Lord Caiaphas would take it kindly if you would assist us. He is the high priest, so he does have authority, even here."

Another twenty Jews of Narda arrived from all parts of the Jewish Quarter of the city. The unusual circumstance had to be communicated to these late arrivals, so the air behind the soldiers buzzed with commentary and speculation.

Nehemiah's sightless eyes, the color of robins' eggs, turned unerringly toward Shinar. The Temple official quaked as if the blind gaze bored into his soul. "There are no lepers here," Nehemiah said bluntly.

"But you harbor a man who . . . who has a hawk . . . and a wild tale. A tale used by insurgents to stir up trouble," Aram countered. "We want him."

Nehemiah pivoted slowly in place as another fifty worshippers arrived, thoroughly hemming in the Herodians on all sides. A few of the latest to come carried clubs. Others hefted chunks of stone pulled from the pavement.

The rabbi's unnerving stare roamed over the officials and the rank of troopers, pausing without error on each face as if recording the features.

More Nardean Jews arrived, some muttering angrily.

Aram fidgeted. His men were now outnumbered ten to one.

At last Nehemiah spoke. "You must be mistaken. I see no such man. I see no hawk. You must tell your master. You must tell Lord Caiaphas what I said."

Frustrated and flushed with anger, Aram nevertheless looked relieved when, at Nehemiah's command, a corridor opened through the crowd, allowing the Herodian retainers and Shinar to depart.

Daniel was drenched in sweat. His arms had no feeling below the elbows; above that they were a solid mass of aching flesh. Two especially focused points of pain throbbed with each beat of his heart: his birthmark and the burn that branded him a slave.

A trail of ants marching around the palm's trunk found Daniel's neck a convenient shortcut as they went about their business. If he moved his head to rub them off, they bit . . . not hard, just an annoyed pinch.

Despite the heat, Daniel shivered.

And when he heard footsteps, he shivered again.

Torchlight, blazing orange, illuminated the muted confines of his blindfold. Who was this coming at night to the slavers' camp? What could it mean?

Daniel's thoughts leapt to the idea of a rescue . . . but by whom and for what cause he could not guess. He wanted to cry out for help, to protest his treatment, to beg for release. These others . . . perhaps they were born to be slaves. Perhaps it was their lot in life. *But not mine. Not me!*

The recollection that, bound and blindfolded as he was, Daniel would never see a blow descending before it landed kept him silent.

A pair of muffled voices reached Daniel's ears. One was unmistakably the rasping tones of the slaver—obsequious, but demanding at the same time, bargaining. "Surely my lord knows the penalty for selling outside the market. The governor and the king must have their duties paid, eh?"

"And that tiny risk is why I sweeten the deal," was the reply. "So I get my pick before the auctioneer, paid by the Babylonian governor, runs up the price."

That voice! It was familiar to Daniel, but where? Who? He knew no one in the slave trade . . . in the trafficking in misery and degradation that was the sale of human flesh.

"It is even as your lordship says," the slaver agreed. "I am but a poor businessman."

Lord of what? A noble, or simply someone the slaver flatters with this title?

"That one there," the familiar but unplaced voice said. "The one with all the heathen markings on his skin. Where did you get him?"

Lono?

The pair must have turned away from Daniel at that moment, because he could not make out the response. When next he comprehended the murmuring voices, he shuddered yet again, because the commentary seemed to be about him!

"Was there someone with him? Someone with a dark mark here . . . just on his cheek?"

The torches bobbed nearer. The footsteps grew louder, until their flare filled all Daniel could see. When one of them bent closer, he heard the crackle of the flame and felt the heat scorch his cheek.

When he ducked his head and pulled away, a hand roughly seized his chin and yanked it upward, toward the light.

"Ah! I'll have that one as well."

"He is . . . special," the slaver whined.

"Spare me your haggling techniques, Faisal. We have already agreed on the price . . . and the fact that I spare your head in spite of your dubious activities."

"As you say, my lord," the slaver agreed as light, footsteps, and voices bobbed away into the night. "As you say."

"Deliver them in the usual manner" was the last comment Daniel overheard.

He did not sleep that night.

Shinar, envoy from the Jerusalem Temple, paced angrily within the Jerusalem stone pattern of the Star of David.

Cantor, the object of Shinar's tirade, stood on the stone named *Eben*, set in the floor just in front of the bema.

Shinar raged, "This fellow . . . he matches the description."

Rabbi Nehemiah asked gently, "But, Shinar, where are the witnesses to the crime? Where are his accusers? Our law requires two witnesses."

"We will take him back to Yerushalayim, and there we shall see! He matches the description, I tell you. An itinerant healer . . . blasphemes! Uses the name of Yeshua of Nazareth to work his miracles! And the hawk—"

Nehemiah interjected, "Yet you say the child was healed?"

"A fraud! Or, if true, then certainly performed by the powers of darkness."

The council of the synagogue appeared to listen attentively. Rabbi Nehemiah asked, "And the identity of this healer? this perpetrator of evil? he who used the anathema name of Yeshua?"

Shinar was certain of his facts. "The woman he traveled with called the healer Cantor. In every case he was called Cantor. Now we find that this very fellow—" he shook his finger at Cantor—"is the cantor of the Synagogue of Golah. And he owns a hawk."

Nehemiah inhaled deeply and sat back. "Well then, you see, his innocence stands upon a firm foundation. The name is Eben, which means 'Stone.' Stone comes from a family of exiles from Yerushalayim. Therefore, the name is Eben Golah. Stone of Exile. And Eben Golah is there before you."

Shinar fumed. "And how long have the ancestors of Eben Golah been a part of this synagogue?"

"Since the first stone was laid in this place," Nehemiah replied.

Shinar glared at Cantor. "You have bewitched them. But what am I to do?"

Nehemiah answered, "You see our cantor there. He stands before the Almighty. That is the heritage of Eben Golah. No sir. No. A case of mistaken identity if ever there was one. You shall not take our cantor with Holy Days upon us."

Nehemiah turned his body to address the council. "Why, all of us know the coruler of our city himself trains hawks and falcons and the like. Not unusual for this province . . . mistaken identity."

The vote was unanimous. Shinar, angry and certain he was being deceived, strode from the sanctuary.

24 CHAPTER

aniel was alone in a damp cell. For days he had seen no other human face. At least Daniel thought it had been a passage of some days. The spaces in the ventilation grill brightened and darkened on an almost imperceptible cycle.

Sunrise and sunset?

The only thing audible besides his own moans had been a single high-pitched shriek, so full of agony and terror that, afterwards, Daniel shivered for hours.

The only sign anyone knew he existed was twice each day: once when the door panel slid open to exchange water and waste buckets, and once again when a plate of rice and gristle and a loaf of gritty barley bread were thrust in the same way.

On one occasion he tried to plead with his unseen jailors: "It's a mistake. I'm not a slave. I don't belong here."

The response had been to withhold his food and water for a day, accompanied by the shouted threat of another beating.

Daniel was once again dreaming of home: food, clean clothes, servants to fetch whatever he wanted.

The cell door flung open with a crash and rebounded with a clang.

Before Daniel uttered more than an uncomprehending gurgle, three figures set on him. Two pinioned his arms while the third flung a black hood over his head, yanking it down and securing it around his neck.

Once more his hands were tied behind his back.

The point of a spear nudged him just above where his wrists were secured. "Get up and move."

Stumbling over every jutting stone in the floor and running face-first into archways made his tormentors laugh. Other times they jerked him roughly to the side or thrust him through passages.

No light reached the inside of the hood and precious little air.

Where was he being taken? What had he done? Was he about to be killed? Had they verified his identity and were now going to dispose of him to hide the evidence of their crime?

Up and up he was prodded, banging his knees when he fell across uneven heights of steps. Gradually the air that did seep in around the noose grew fresher, less fetid. Daniel had no shoes, but the slapping of the sandaled feet of his guards against the pavement grew louder. Daniel sensed without seeing it that he had been led into a larger, vaulted room.

Just as he made this discovery, he was shoved to his knees and warned, "Stay there and don't speak."

On his knees, his breath roaring in his ears, Daniel waited for the stroke that would end his life.

Booted footsteps walked around him, stopping immediately in front of him.

No one spoke.

"Who are you? Who's there?" Daniel begged.

The footsteps resumed their circuit. Without warning, a thumb-nail jabbed between the angle of his jaw and his ear. He flinched and ducked away.

"And just like that, you're dead," said a voice close behind him. "Life is so fragile and so easily taken. The point of a long, thin blade here—" the thumb poked him again—"and all is over in seconds."

"Who are you? What do you want?"

Daniel heard the panic in his voice but could do nothing to control it. He tried to rise, but guards he had not even known were close by forced him back.

"Who?" he gasped.

"Don't you know me?" his tormentor inquired. "Forgotten me already?"

The tone was vaguely familiar, but who? Where?

"Why are you doing this?"

The reply was laden with boredom, the cruel sport already exhausted. "Show him."

Without untying the cords securing the hood the head covering was removed. The jerk seemed to almost pull Daniel's head from his body. The sudden pain made him dizzy and made the room sway around him.

The burst of light dazzled his eyes, darkening all the shapes. His eyes struggled to focus on the features of one looming over him. It was . . . Lord Hannel!

"Welcome to Narda," Hannel offered sarcastically. "But then I forgot. You've already been enjoying our hospitality for some time."

Daniel did not understand, could not comprehend what was happening. "Thank you! Thank you!" he said, believing rescue had come. He tried to reach for Hannel's hands, almost toppling forward from his bound ankles and wrists.

The Lord of the Marsh chortled. "A first! Do you hear that, Karek? A first! I've never been thanked by one of my prisoners before!"

It was Karek behind Daniel's back. A chill ran from his toes to the top of his head.

"Prisoner? I don't . . . ," Daniel babbled.

"Don't you? Let me help. Wasn't I respectful of your father's fame? Didn't I promise to make a great man of him? But your father refused my offer of employment. Very well, but he should be made to pay for ignoring me. But how? How to make that happen? Then, like an answer to my prayers, Karek here spotted you in the train of . . . slaves. How droll. Young Master Daniel of Ecbatana! So eager to prove himself a man! So anxious for fame. So ambitious. It's too perfect, isn't it, Karek?"

The tavern bully moved to confront Daniel. "Places reversed now, eh, boy?" He fingered the stump of his ear. "Guess I have reason enough to remember you."

"You want ransom? But my father . . . he . . . I . . ." He stopped abruptly, biting down hard on his lower lip. Daniel's thoughts were spinning, but even as confused as he felt, this was no time to suggest

Melchior would not pay a ransom. If Daniel had no value, he would soon be dead.

"What else?" Hannel replied. "Karek here will take good care of you until the payment arrives. How hard your life is until then is entirely up to you."

What would happen next?

Lightning illuminated the plains beyond Narda. Thunder boomed moments later as a heavy downpour pummeled the tile roof of the synagogue.

Lord Tannis did not remove his sword, even in the inner chamber of the synagogue. He had come alone this evening. His eyes moved constantly, searching for clandestine movement of the thick brocade curtains. He listened for the footsteps on the stair. He spoke to Rabbi Ahava and Rabbi Nehemiah with a hushed urgency.

"... So. My brother holds hostage Daniel, son of Melchior the Magus. I tell you there will be no ransom returned by one of our brigands. None are to be trusted with such an errand beyond the gates of Narda."

"Ransom of a captive?" Rebbe Nehemiah turned his marbled eyes skyward. "What is that to us? We here at the Synagogue of the Exiles ..."

"We are beyond such matters," Ahava finished.

Tannis fixed his gaze on Cantor. "You know what I am talking about, eh?"

Cantor nodded. "The Herodians. The Temple guard."

Tannis snapped his fingers. "They are seeking one who they say claims to have died and returned. He who is followed everywhere by a hawk. Cantor, word reached the Sanhedrin in Yerushalayim. Maybe just a rumor. A legend. But there are others whose lives have been blessed by miracles. They have fled the territory of Herod and Rome. Now the Sanhedrin sends documents. They are seeking the master of the hawk ... he who took refuge here in my walled city. They mean to kill the man raised from death. Or torture him until he confesses his story is a fraud."

Cantor finished, "They have come for me."

"My brother has made a deal with the Herodian captain. I will not risk civil war in my territory, but I came with this warning: You will not survive for long if they discover you here. Kidnappers at best. Assassins at the worst. Brother, master of raptors, they seek to shoot you down before you fly away again to safety."

"So." Ahava comprehended the reason for Tannis' visit. "Why should we trust you? Might you not also take Cantor from us and hold him for payment by the Herodians?"

"A good question." Nehemiah stroked his beard. "Why have you come to warn our Cantor?"

"I have come here to warn you, to help you, because . . ." Tannis faltered.

"Speak up!" Ahava demanded as though reprimanding a school-boy.

Tannis replied, "If it is true, Cantor . . . if what they say of you is true . . . it's more than being healed of leprosy. It's being healed of death." He searched Cantor's face. "So. Is it? Is it true what they say?"

Cantor replied with a single downward stroke of his chin.

The dark eyes of Tannis widened with fear. "It is whispered. We hear it among our servants. Slaves say this Yeshua of Nazareth has raised others besides you and that they have returned with stories of a fantastic world beyond this."

Again Cantor answered by inclining his head in the affirmative.

Tannis exhaled loudly. "Then could I let them murder you? And keep silent? If what you have seen is real? And you have come to tell us about this place, this Eden . . . then I must hear of it. I want to know."

"There are no words to describe . . . ," Cantor began.

"But something . . . you must speak. Some hope, perhaps, even for a man like me." There was a moment—an instant, really—when another question appeared in the eyes of the Lord of the Marsh.

Then it vanished as suddenly.

Silence. Rain dripped from the eaves.

Cantor raised his eyes toward heaven, as though listening to another voice. "Fear not," he whispered.

"Then it is true." Tannis did not express joy at the revelation. Rather, fear filled his eyes. "Leave . . . at once."

"I will go, then. I'll go to Ecbatana," Cantor said.

Tannis agreed. "And I will send my most trusted men with you."

Despite Hannel's promises that the harsh treatment would be changed, it was several days before Daniel was released again from the depths of the dungeon. He stood once more before Hannel, this time in the courtyard of Hannel's private rooms. Daniel blinked and swayed in the harsh daylight, peering through squinted eyes at his surroundings.

Arrayed against him were Hannel and Karek. To Daniel's surprise, Lono was present as well, though bound and gagged and chained between two guards.

"Are you ready for better housing?" Hannel asked wryly. "By now you should have no doubt that I'm completely serious. No one could ever find you in my cells. From what I hear, no one even knows in what city to look."

This sally produced a loud, harsh laugh from Karek.

"Beyond that, bodies wash up all the time downstream from here . . . sometimes with their throats cut. Am I clear?"

Daniel nodded mutely.

"But I've decided to be merciful. If you will give me your pledge not to try to escape, I'll find a room in my servants' quarters for you and your ape. He is too much trouble to be of any use, always breaking someone's head or getting his own thick skull clouted . . . waste of time and effort. It's up to you to keep him in line, or you'll be the one to suffer for it. Is this arrangement clear to you? Leave my palace grounds and back in the hole you go. Do you swear?"

Daniel nodded, now so afraid to speak he could not utter a word.

A crooked smile splayed across Hannel's ferretlike features. "So you can be taught! Very good. But this time I want to hear you say it: 'By the Temple of HaShem in Yerushalayim I swear to not attempt escape.' Say it!"

"I-I so swear."

"On my life, I swear it!"

"On my life," Daniel added dully.

With a backhanded gesture Hannel ordered Karek to remove Lono's gag. "Careful . . . his bite is poison. He's already maimed several of my other retainers." Then, addressing Lono, Hannel said, "You heard your master swear. He is spineless and would never run anyway, but here's what you must know: His life depends on your behavior as well. Will you swear by your heathen gods not to attempt escape or to harm any more of my men?"

"I believe in the One God," Lono said, "but I make oath on Mastah Daniel's life. This enough?"

Hannel studied Lono's impassive features. "Yes, I believe it is. What do you say, Karek? As one who never, ever worries about oath-breaking, how do you judge this tattooed monster?"

"He would die for ben Melchior, though Ba'al alone knows why. Yes, I believe him."

"Then here I will leave the matter," Hannel finished. "It will not be long before we have word from your father. And he will surely choose to reimburse me and repay my expenses for *rescuing* you. But in the meantime, you must continue in your service to me, as I have paid fairly and dearly for that service. Otherwise, you will continue your life as slaves, tethered and guarded, like any other."

Hannel smiled. "Good. Wait here. One of my servants will explain your duties and provide you a cot in their quarters. You shall share their food as well. It is not much, but certainly a better lot than of any *slave* in Narda. You will serve my household. Your cumbersome friend will as well, but I mean to also use his strength where it's needed."

Hannel grasped Daniel's hand, elaborately and unconvincingly wincing at the sight of the healing branding scar.

"Do you hear?" Daniel hissed to Lono, when Hannel and the guards had departed and they were alone. "I was never supposed to be a servant *or* a slave! Am I some stupid savage sold because of a village famine? I come from a wealthy family in a civilized land. I have an education."

"Patience, Mastah Daniel. You won' be slave too long now."

"Oh?" Daniel scoffed. "And then what? Return to my father . . . to my brother and his shrew wife, like a starving dog begging for scraps? I am as much a slave there as here. If I want to live free, it will not be there! But I'll not be a slave here either!"

"Mastah Daniel, please, we give Lord Hannel our word. We swear we stay an' serve 'til you fadda send for us."

"And what of his promise to us? Do you really think he'll allow us to go free once he has what he wants? And what makes you think my father will agree to his terms anyway?"

For the first time in the conversation, Lono grew angry. "Stop an' speak right!" he shouted. "You fadda love you more than him own self. He tell me on our leavin' day, 'Lono, you take him good care. I give him dat money an' thousand time more, long as him safe.' Of course he buy you back!"

Daniel narrowed his eyes and sighed heavily. "Such a simpleton you are, Lono. These are things my father tells himself, no doubt every day, to justify his ill treatment of me. I am second-born, and half-loved. And I won't return to him as a beggar . . . not ever!"

"I give my word, Mastah Daniel," Lono said at last, resting against one wall, weary from Daniel's constant griping. "I give it an' I not break it. An' if you care 'bout Lono, you keep you word also."

"So be it," Daniel said. "Stay, keep your precious word. And what good will it do you? Abuse and humiliation await you here, and all for your silly honor."

"Mastah Daniel," Lono said, turning once again to his work, "I a slave. Honor all I own."

25

The sun had not set, yet the highest clouds already glowed in bright fuchsia flames. The distant mountains of Parthia were purple.

Lily and Cantor walked along the parapet of the synagogue. Beneath them the courtyard and the pack animals were lost in shadow.

A camel bawled, as if to protest the weight it must carry in the journey.

Cantor pulled Lily close against him. "The angel said, 'Fear not.'"

"This will be our first night apart since you awakened."

"We will travel by night. While you sleep, I will be awake beneath the stars . . . following the stars. Thinking of you."

"Then I'll stay awake all night. Every night. I'll climb the steps to this place. I'll look toward the mountains and know—"

He kissed her hard and long. His mouth lingered on hers. It was a kiss that must perhaps last for weeks. "No. Sleep at night. And dream of me. Dream of the day when I'll come back to you."

A sudden fear seized her. "They won't follow? Herod's men? They won't come after you?"

"'Fear not,' the angel said."

"I didn't hear him. Tell me, Cantor. Will they follow and take you back . . . or worse?"

"Lily, what you're afraid of . . . it's a small thing."

Now her anger flared. "If they are going to kill you . . . and me . . . and all of us . . . then what was the point? What? Why did Yeshua come? Why heal us? If it would all end so horribly in some dungeon, remembering a few months of happiness?"

He told her what she wanted to hear. "I'm only a messenger. Carrying word to Melchior of Ecbatana. Herod's men wouldn't dare follow— not in Parthian territory, against Lord Tannis' guards. Lily, please. I need you to be brave. The children need you to be brave. I'm coming back. I am . . . I know . . . this parting is not forever."

She wept silently against him. Her ear against his broad chest, she listened to his slow and steady heartbeat. "I know you say there's more for us, more waiting. But I love you so. I love being alive with you . . . here. And I didn't know if I should tell you. But . . . Cantor? You're going to be a father. Spring." She guided his hand to her slightly rounded stomach. "There. You. Growing within me."

"Well then." He sighed. "Then part of me stays with you even as I go . . . and I have so much to come back to."

Melchior and Esther embraced Joshua and his wife. Three small granddaughters gathered round them. The children cried that they wanted to go on the long journey as well. Esther did not shed a tear openly, though her heart felt like it would crack open. How long would she and Melchior be gone?

How hard it was to say farewell to her grandchildren!

Melchior offered this explanation to his eldest son: "Joshua, you will be in charge of everything while I am gone. Your mother and I must make this journey to the West before we are too old. The infant whose star we followed thirty years ago has grown. Yeshua's reputation as Healer, Prophet, and Messiah has now reached us even here in Ecbatana. We must see Yeshua, Lion of the Tribe of Judah, with our own eyes."

Both Melchior and Joshua knew the tales of Yeshua of Nazareth in the faraway land of Judea were not the true reason Melchior and Esther were setting out on such an arduous journey.

Caesarea Maritima had been the ultimate destination of young Daniel's caravan. Melchior had gleaned that information by relentlessly quizzing tavern owners and caravan suppliers until the facts about Daniel's goal were discovered.

Though the truth was unspoken, Melchior's quest was not to find the Son of the Living God. Melchior was, in fact, searching for his own lost son.

Aram's horse was breathing hard after the galloping ride from the Herodian encampment outside the city. The guard captain had wasted no time in responding to Hannel's summons, knowing a word from him could mean capture of his quarry.

Returning to Herod Antipas successful could mean promotion to the rank of the royal entourage and rooms within the walls of the palace.

Aram waited for Hannel to join him near the main gate.

"Excellency." Aram bowed as Hannel emerged. "I came soon as I received your message. Tell me what you've discovered."

Hannel guided the Herodian away from the gate and any potential listeners. "My brother is away until tomorrow, midday. He left with his troop of men to escort a caravan north, away from Narda, but news of his journey only just now reached me. That should make it easy for you to pounce on the one you seek: the man with the hawk."

"That's the one!" Aram exulted. "A blasphemer! A charlatan . . . and an irritation to my lord Antipas."

Hannel nodded sympathetically. "If you will go there just after first light tomorrow, I will see to it the city guards along your route are not at their posts, and the arrest will be unimpeded."

By now the pair of men had made a full circle in their stroll around the front grounds and stood again by Aram's horse, tied to a hitching post near the gate. He loosed the reins and climbed into the saddle, thanking Hannel. "If your information is correct, you'll be rewarded as agreed," he promised.

"Indeed I will," Hannel concurred. "Indeed I will."

When Hannel's houseboy, Jacan, had shown Daniel and Lono to their quarters, he recited a long list of duties the new additions to the staff would be expected to perform.

Daniel heard none of these. He took note only of doors, windows, and other things along the way, including potential weapons, which he might use to escape: chairs, pottery, even a stick of firewood that could be used as a club in case someone tried to stop him. Such thoughts of preparation gave him comfort and confidence, and he was sure he could menace any servant Hannel might throw in his way.

Karek and the guards were another matter.

Daniel reminded himself that if he acted compliant, the guards would soon tire of watching his every move and leave him alone.

Then he would make his escape.

In the servants' quarters an open hearth stood at each end of the long narrow room. Each servant had a cramped enclosure defined by cloth screens. Every stall contained a woven carpet over the earthen floor, in the middle of which sat a single cot.

When Daniel started to protest the conditions, Lono interrupted: "I sleep on ground, Mastah Daniel. Same I do you fadda's house."

Daniel had forgotten that. He was thinking only of his own case and suddenly realized that perhaps the House of Hannel was no worse for Lono than Ecbatana. There the islander had been a servant and not a slave, but was that distinction significant to someone raised as a slave? Perhaps comfort was all that mattered.

Daniel had never given any thought to Lono's needs. All the Ecbatana servants acted happy and well cared for.

"Report to the household steward," Jacan ordered, "to be assigned your duties. Most likely the big fellow will be put to work on construction. You. . . ." He looked Daniel over and sniffed doubtfully. "Housework? Kitchen help?"

Daniel squinted. Scrubbing and cleaning?

Jacan added, "I almost forgot. Wash and put on the *clean* clothes laid out on your cot before meeting Steward. You stink!"

Daniel had a mind to cuff the boy but remembered Hannel's warning.

Lono did as he was told, donning the fresh robe and preparing for work. "Come, Mastah Daniel, pretty soon we go home, eh? You smart. Learn fast. No trouble, eh?"

"Right," Daniel retorted. "Servant here or slave there. What's the difference?"

Lono eyed him curiously but made no further comment.

PART IV

*The stone the builders rejected has become the capstone;
the LORD has done this, and it is marvelous in our eyes.*

PSALM 118:22-23

26

With one hand Lily brushed an errant strand of blond hair back underneath her head scarf. The other hand was firmly clamped onto Yod's tiny wrist. The little girl's red locks faithfully bobbed alongside Lily's stride at all times, but in the Narda market-day crowd, Lily took no chances.

Lily was grateful when Rabbi Nehemiah asked her to undertake replenishing the supplies for the school's larder. Anything that kept her busy and required planning helped the hours apart from Cantor pass more quickly. Lily reflected that she had vowed to never, ever be separated from Cantor again since his return from *olam haba*, but she understood and agreed with the wisdom of making him the envoy to Ecbatana.

Today's expedition was to refill the rice bins for the school. The marshy lands around Narda normally produced the grain in abundance, but this year the crop had failed and the quantity available was very limited and expensive.

Lily had heard a rumor that a shipment of Egyptian rice had arrived, poled up the river on barges just one day earlier. If true, she had the authority to spend synagogue funds to acquire enough for immediate needs and to provide a reserve.

Yod tugged at her sleeve. The girl was wide-eyed at the clamor and bustle of the marketplace, but mostly at the shapes, sizes, and attire of the people. "Look," she said, gesturing toward a pair of clean-shaven, gray-haired men wearing trousers beneath short tunics.

All the Jewish men of Yod's acquaintance were bearded, if old enough to have gray hair, and none wore trousers.

"Yes, dear, but it's not polite to point," Lily instructed.

A Parthian soldier strode by, conical helmet and quiver of arrows betraying his occupation. His bowlegs announced that he did not usually travel afoot.

A grand lady in a palanquin, carried by a quartet of sweating black slaves, leaned out from her curtained litter to give imperious orders to a rug merchant.

Despite her kind heart, even Lily could not forbear staring at the enormous dark-brown-skinned man across the square from them. He was in a party of workers unloading paving stones from a cart, but he towered over them all. If his size were not enough to draw attention, the tracery of blue-black lines that adorned his face would.

As if he sensed their gaze, he looked up and caught Lily's eye.

She looked quickly down, only to see Yod staring boldly at the man. When a bright smile lit Yod's face, Lily lifted her gaze enough to see that the giant was grinning too.

They had arrived at the rice merchant's awning. Lily set herself to negotiating the best deal for the synagogue she could. Though from Egypt, the tradesman was also Jewish. He belonged to a synagogue in Alexandria and was already familiar with the famous Synagogue of the Exiles in Narda. He was more than willing to assist Lily and pleased to deliver so much of his cargo to a single purchaser.

The discussion would have concluded even faster had not Lily and the seller needed to shout to make themselves heard. This was not due merely to the uproar of the market but more especially to the pair of soldiers in green livery at an adjoining dealer in dried fruit.

"And I tell you these dates are spoiled," one of them barked in Aramaic at the merchant. Grabbing a handful, he squeezed them into a glutinous mass and dropped it on the display table.

Lily transferred Yod to her side, away from the ruffians, but had to speak still louder to complete her transaction. She was so absorbed in finishing her business that she didn't notice when the nearby argument abruptly ceased.

Suddenly a pair of olive drab tunics flanked her on either side. "Where are you from?" the taller of the two demanded.

Lily ducked her head and said nothing.

"Don't pretend you don't understand," the other soldier added. "We heard you just now. . . . Galilee by your accent, sure as I'm standin' here, eh, Zimri? How'd you come to be in Narda, eh?"

"Why are you bothering this lady?" the rice merchant demanded in a quaking voice. "You are not soldiers of Narda."

"No, we ain't," the first replied. "But it's our business because Lord Herod Antipas and Rome says it is, see? We was sent to arrest heretics. We've got warrants for arrest of same, according to the High Council of Yerushalayim. A number of criminals is fled here to escape judgment. And you'd be smart to keep out of this."

Herodian soldiers!

The only recourse for Lily was to brazen it out. "You're mistaken. My daughter and I belong to the Synagogue . . . the School of the Exiles here. Let us pass, please."

"Not so fast. Maybe you live here and maybe you only just come. Wasn't there some description of a pretty blond 'un and a little red-headed girl, Zimri? Come along quiet-like. We'll get our captain to sort this out, see?"

Before Lily could protest further, the tall soldier swooped Yod up and flung her, kicking and crying, over his shoulder. "Now you'll come quiet, won't you? And tell your brat to keep still too, so I don't accidentally drop her in the river as we cross the bridge. Come on, Bana. I'm thinkin' there's ten silver pieces for each of us in this."

The paving stones carted to the section of road on which they worked were broad and thick. Each required two men to carry and set into position.

Except for Lono.

He carried one himself each time, tilting it on edge against his chest. Wrapping his arms around the stone, he clasped his hands tightly, as if embracing an old friend. When he had carried it to its place, he knelt, hunched his shoulders, and let the massive slab fall into the sandy roadbed. If it needed repositioning, he simply stood over it, dug his fingers beneath one side, and spun it easily, according to the overseer's direction.

Throughout the day, whenever the supply of stones was exhausted, Lono was responsible for fetching more. He wheeled a large wooden handcart up the avenue and around the corner behind a shop. There the entire day's supply had been stacked neatly out of the way by the quarry workers the day before.

As he labored, Lono amused himself by watching the people in the marketplace while they bartered and bargained for purchases. One pair of shoppers, in particular, caught his attention: a stunningly beautiful blond woman and a little auburn-haired girl. They seemed out of place to Lono, like the sprout of a flower through a crack in gray stone.

He soon realized he was not the only one to think so. As he watched, armed men approached the lady and her little companion, grabbing them roughly and speaking to them harshly. He did not recognize the livery, but he knew soldier bullies, whomever they served.

Lono could not hear what was said, but after a moment they began dragging the pair away, up a side street. Onlookers stood silently by as they went, afraid to interfere with the armed men. The city guards were nowhere to be seen.

Lono decided he must help them. Dropping a stone in place, he returned to the cart. Passing a pair of his coworkers, who grunted with the effort of carrying another, he began to wheel the cart away.

"Get more," he called to the overseer.

"There are still two more slabs in your cart, Lono. What's the rush?"

Without answering, Lono tilted both stones up and hefted them, growling with the effort, as he stamped in short steps to the end of the road. After laying them in place, he ran panting back to the cart and pushed it away without another word to the astounded men.

As Lily and Yod were led away, Lily continued to protest, asking for help.

"What are you lookin' at?" their captor spat at a rug merchant. "Mind your own business."

The merchant's curious stare quickly turned to fear. None of the Narda citizens could take on Herodian soldiers, and none of the Nardean troops were nearby. Bana dragged Lily by the wrist. With a slight twist on her arm he growled, "One more word from you, and I'll break it."

Zimri stalked on ahead with the child. "And one word out of you and Bana here'll break your ma's wrist."

They strode from the market square and entered a warehouse area between the river and the center of the city. "Not that way," Bana protested when Zimri pivoted to the right. "This way's quicker." He turned left into a narrow, deserted alleyway.

Oh, God who has saved us from so much and protected us so far . . . where are you right now?

"They don't look like no lepers, do they?" Bana pondered aloud. The reminder of the supposed origin of the fugitives made Zimri take Yod off his shoulder and hold her at arm's length like a dangerous viper.

It was just past the next corner that an enormous apparition loomed out of a shadowed doorway. One fist the size of a carpenter's maul hammered into Bana's face. His head snapped back and bounced against a protruding stone. His grip turned nerveless in an instant. By the time he toppled onto his chin in the dirt, Lily had already pulled free and was clawing at the arm holding Yod.

Zimri, unbalanced in his awkward posture anyway, spun clumsily at the extra weight and commotion. Lily snatched Yod away and stepped back just in time to see the tattooed giant bring clasped fists downward onto the bridge of Zimri's nose.

Like his compatriot, Zimri collapsed, moaning.

"You belong synagogue?" the rescuer confirmed with Lily.

"Thank you, yes! Thank you! Thank God!"

"Yes, thanks be to God. Lono take you there, but we go before more soldiers come." To Lily's delight, not only had Yod stopped crying, but she positively beamed to be atop Lono's broad back, her tiny fingers twined in his mass of curly hair.

It seemed another miracle that the trio arrived back at the gate of the synagogue compound so quickly. "Lono," Lily begged, "won't you please come in? You can stay here. You'll be safe here too. If those Herodian men recognize you, they'll kill you."

Lily watched the tattooed face struggle with several emotions.

"I cannot," he said. "Lono make oath not to run away, not to hide. Must go back. But you pray for me, eh? Pray Lono an' Daniel, an' the good God let us see each other again."

And he was gone.

27 CHAPTER

D aniel's excitement grew minute by minute. His strategy had worked perfectly! He had been cooperative, acted complacent, been no more than mildly incompetent in his chores, and had not talked back to the Steward.

As a result, none of Hannel's other servants or guards paid him the least attention as he went about his duties hauling firewood and buckets of water and dumping trash. Everyone seemed to believe Daniel was content to await the ransom coming from his father.

How little any of them understood how he was seething inside. *No one can keep me against my will . . . and I'll not live beholden to my father, either.*

So it was with huge excitement, barely contained, that Daniel received the news: "Master Hannel expects you to serve at supper tonight."

Jacan droned the words of the announcement quickly in monotone as he had said them many times before, since he served as Hannel's page. "There's to be a feast to celebrate Lord Hannel's new treaty with the king of Armenia to provide caravan escort within that territory." With that he spun on his heel and walked away. Over his shoulder he called,

"And tell your pet elephant he's serving too. Warn him not to break any plates, or it'll be his head broken next."

The time for my escape is tonight, thought Daniel, as Hannel's guests began to arrive. *Soon there will be enough commotion that no one will know whether I am here or not.*

Chariots, horse carts, slave-carried litters approached the main house one by one, depositing men and women of power and privilege upon Hannel's doorstep. It seemed to Daniel that the man had invited all of Narda to attend. "Anyone with money, anyway," he muttered to himself.

Daniel had been a part of such rituals once, attending lavish gatherings held in the name of some celebration or other. Now he resented the spectacle, condemning the banquet as a thinly veiled pretense for Hannel to flaunt his wealth and display his power. *How many servants will the wealthy walk past tonight, without casting a single look in their direction?*

"Daniel!" Hannel shouted from the courtyard behind where Daniel stood, observing the procession, "why are you glaring at my guests? Get back to work!"

Daniel apologized and scurried back to the kitchen outbuilding where Lono assisted the evening's cooks, lifting, carrying, and fetching. He had always been that way, Daniel remembered. As a child, Daniel had often watched the staff at work in preparation for one of his father's own parties, and though Lono's duties always involved heavy labor, performed from first light until evening, he never hesitated to lend a hand to the domestic staff in their work as well.

Daniel would miss him when he ran away, but Lono's disappearance would surely be noticed. Nothing must jeopardize Daniel's own escape. He rationalized that his need was greater than Lono's.

"Mastah Daniel," Lono cried with a smile when he saw him in the doorway, "come'a talk wid Tovi. Dis nice lady feed you good if you good help."

Standing next to Lono, comically dwarfed in comparison, stood an elderly woman with tight gray curls on her head. The new cook mopped her brow with her sleeve and smiled at Daniel. "The peelings and rubbish on that cloth will make good food for Master Hannel's hogs. Gather the corners up and carry the bundle down the path to their troughs."

When Daniel delayed, realizing he might never see Lono again,

Tovi said, "And yes, Lono is right. You will be fed well tonight . . . *if you do your share of the work. Now run!*"

Given orders by an old crone, a servant herself, and expected to obey them!

"Yes," Daniel stammered, giving one last glance to Lono and hefting the load. He wanted badly to tell Lono good-bye but knew he must not act out of the ordinary, lest his escape be discovered and the alarm raised. So without a word, he walked from the stifling kitchen into the cool evening air.

The curving path cut through a thicket of tall, dry canary grass, obscuring Daniel's view of anything more than a few paces ahead. He barely noticed the weight of the load he carried, but he was breathing heavily, and his heart beat wildly with the excitement and fear of his purpose.

Since he had been brought to Hannel's estate blindfolded, he was unsure of the size of the property or whether it was walled all around as it was in the front. His best hope was that the animals—nasty, unclean things—were kept near one border so he might slip out in the same direction he was already moving.

Though he was sure no one followed him, he nonetheless imagined he was being stalked, and the feeling made his vision swim. At last the path opened into a clearing where the hog pen sat, bordered on the far side by a large stone-and-earth berm at shoulder height. Beyond it was more tall brush, which Daniel would have to push aside to see through. Quickly scattering the vegetable scraps for the animals, Daniel climbed the wall and made a part in the grass. There, across a narrow beach of pebbles, a wide swath of the River Euphrates gleamed in the setting sun. Beyond the far bank, a few dwellings stood, already lit here and there with torches and lanterns.

Daniel knew nothing of the current and depth of the river; if it was too swift or too deep, he was sure he would drown. He spent only a moment more deciding whether he should wade in to see. He knew if he found it impassable and had to turn back, his wet clothes would raise suspicion in the minds of anyone he might encounter as he ran another way. Turning from the sight, he sprang from the wall, back toward the interior of Hannel's estate.

He was suddenly paralyzed with fear when he saw a figure standing where he had left the rubbish cloth. "Quite a sight, eh?" the man called to him. "I came to enjoy the color of the setting sun. You also?"

Daniel tried his best to act calm and unconcerned, but the violence of his heart beating in his throat made his voice quaver as he replied. "Indeed, yes, I just slipped away to have a look myself." *Too guilty*, he thought. *The man didn't ask for an explanation. . . . Offering one makes me seem guilty.*

The man approached slowly, grasping the stone fence of the swine enclosure as he came. "Of course, I'm too old to climb to the view you've just had, but still . . ."

Daniel could see now the man was elderly. "Well, I must return to my work," he lied, retrieving the cloth at the man's feet.

"Work?" the old man queried. "You are not a guest of Lord Hannel's?"

Daniel froze, half bent toward the ground. He had not thought the man assumed he was a visitor. *And if I'm not*, Daniel thought, *he'll wonder what I'm doing up here.*

It never occurred to Daniel to just say he had been sent to feed the pigs and had stopped for a moment to enjoy the sunset.

The trip-hammer action of his pulse prevented him from reasoning clearly.

"Are you a servant?"

It sounded like an accusation.

By Daniel's hand lay a short, stout stick. He reached for it and spun, breaking it over the old man's head.

The pass through the mountains had widened. A fresh, cold stream ran down the center of the canyon, but there was room enough for the westbound caravans to use one side of the creek while the eastward-laden followed the other.

Cantor and Lord Tannis' men, not slowed by camels or burdened with freight, traveled much faster than other parties they encountered. Still, men and horses and hawks must stop for rest and food at times, and this was a likely spot.

It was just evening. Jupiter, bright and glowing, hung in the west.

A near full moon was rising in the east. Cantor viewed the sight and the setting with satisfaction and a twinge of loneliness that he did not have Lily to share it with him.

At the encampment across the stream a man and a woman stood together, also gazing at the sky. Cantor envied their togetherness. As he watched, the man enfolded the woman in an embrace, pulling her close.

Suddenly bothered by the sense that he was spying on them, Cantor turned away toward the guard sergeant in charge of Tannis' men. "Beautiful night," he remarked.

"Aye," the sergeant agreed. "Better if there was a pretty woman about to share it with." He gestured toward the other camp. "But even there it ain't all pleasantries, I reckon."

"What do you mean?" Cantor inquired. The man and woman over the way reentered their tent. "How can you know that?"

The officer shrugged. "Call it an old soldier's instinct, if you like. That man there—" the sergeant jerked his chin—"he watched us make camp. Looked us over good, you might say. So much so I kept an eye on him." The man shrugged. "But he done that to every party passing by. Never did find what or who he was after, though. Just now give up tryin'."

Hannel ripped a giant mouthful of meat from a chicken leg and continued his conversation with the guest seated to his left. "Oh yes, quite plain. It's a mark one doesn't easily forget."

"And did he also recognize you?" the astonished guest asked.

"That was the beauty." Hannel chuckled and accidentally spat a small glob of chewed meat at the listener. "He was blindfolded. They were *all* blindfolded. He had no idea who was negotiating his purchase."

"Amazing," said the guest.

"What a find," offered another. "And will his father really pay you what you ask?"

"I'm sure he would pay that and more," Hannel bragged and gulped down an entire goblet of wine, which Lono refilled when Hannel snapped his fingers. "After all, didn't I rescue the second son of the House of Melchior from the hands of slavers? And here is *his* slave."

Hannel laughed. "Lono, where is Daniel? I wish to introduce him to my guests."

Lono only shrugged.

Hannel frowned. "What do you mean?" The warlord imitated Lono's gesture sarcastically. "Bring him to me at once."

Lono bowed and left the hall where Hannel and his guests dined, headed toward the kitchen building. He suspected Daniel had made his escape but would perform a diligent search for him as Hannel commanded.

Leaning in the cookhouse doorway, he called to Tovi, "Where Daniel? Mastah Hannel ask him to come."

"Why, I haven't seen him, Lono," she said, pausing from her cleaning.

After checking the servant quarters, Lono returned to the main house. He knelt at Hannel's side to whisper the report that he had not been able to find Daniel.

28 CHAPTER

caling a section of the south wall of Hannel's estate, Daniel found himself on an empty cobbled street. He ran east along the road. The direction would eventually take him near the front entrance of Hannel's fortress. Several streets branched off ahead; he would turn up one when he estimated he was getting close.

He slowed to a walk as a horse cart rattled past, carrying just one rider and a load of hay. When they had disappeared in the dusky gloom behind him, he raced across the street and around a corner.

As he ran, he wondered how long it would be before they discovered his absence. He hoped it might be morning before they knew he was gone, but he also knew he must nonetheless move as if they were right behind him.

Daniel hoped to be out of the city long before the dawn, and far enough into the country to the north that no one who might be questioned by Hannel would have seen him. While he wore the plain garments of a servant, the sleeves of the robe at least covered the brand that would absolutely identify him as a runaway slave.

Two more times he passed people in the street but did not bother slowing now. *I am far enough*, he reasoned. *No one will know what I'm running from, or where I am going.*

His headlong sprint did attract disapproving stares.

As he approached the courtyard of a building on his right, he slowed to a walk again, long enough to read the letters carved into the cornerstone.

In Hebrew they announced that this was the Synagogue of the Exiles.

What luck! he thought. *I might just be leaving evening prayers. And that is what I'll say if I'm questioned.*

Lily led prayers in the girls' dormitory at bedtime. Each one of the thirteen offered petitions for Cantor on his long, arduous journey. They had all known too many farewells in their short lives to accept this parting without fear. Except for Yod.

Red curls fanned out on her pillow, she clasped Lily's hand in her fingers. Lips curved in a faint smile, she whispered, "They're all afraid. They think Cantor won't come home."

Lily fought back emotion. Did Yod see Lily was also afraid? "We haven't been parted since . . . since he woke up."

Yod's expression did not falter at the admission of Lily's sorrow. "I heard an angel say . . . he said, 'Fear not.'"

"An angel?"

"Yes."

"But . . . an angel? Yod, how can you tell it was an angel?"

The child giggled. "Can't you tell?"

"Where?"

Yod's expression changed to bewilderment. "But look!" She pointed behind Lily. "He's there. And another . . . there. And them . . . over there by the door and . . ."

Lily blanched. "How many?"

Yod counted to thirteen, pointing to an unoccupied place in the room as if some noble being stood there. "The others left with Cantor." Again Yod smiled and waved at nothing. Then she spoke to no one. "Shalom. Yes, I told her. Fear not, I told her."

A faint breeze carried the scent of lavender through the high window. "Yod?"

The child looked through Lily, into her. Chiding gently, she instructed, "But you don't see them, do you?"

Lily shook her head. She kissed Yod and by the light of the guttering lamp made her way to the steep steps leading up to the Women's Gallery of the synagogue.

Her own breathing seemed to fill the empty space. And yet, were there angels around her now? Had an angel followed her out of the dormitory? Did some heavenly being watch over her now?

I'm praying again, You Who Command the Angels I Can't See. Did you tell them to remind Yod we shouldn't be afraid? Herodian soldiers in Narda. Come to find us and drag us back. And Cantor gone. But you say to a child's heart, "Fear not"? I'm praying again. Afraid. Missing Cantor. Afraid he won't come back to me this time. Afraid he will come back and we will be gone. I AM. I AM, you call yourself. "Be still," you say "and know."[33] *But even when I am still . . . I am still afraid.*

"Mastah Hannel," Lono said stoically through bloodied, swollen lips, "Mastah Daniel no tell when he go, no tell where."

"Lies!" Hannel hissed and struck Lono again. "And if you call him 'Mastah' once again, you will not live to see him captured!"

The banquet had been cut short by the discovery of Daniel's absence and Hannel's embarrassment. The guests quietly skulked away from the scene as Hannel dismantled the arrangement in the courtyard with violent rage.

Though Lono was not resisting, Karek and another guard held him by the arms as Hannel issued the beating. "If you are blameless," Hannel continued, "why don't you fight?" He struck him again. "It's because you knew he would run! You share the blame for his escape!"

He was interrupted by the shriek of the little cook as she ran into the courtyard. "Master Hannel," she cried, "my husband . . . someone has attacked my husband! Help!"

"Karek, see to it that *Goliath* here is shackled securely and assemble your riders."

Hannel took two more guards and followed Tovi to the swine pen, where they found her husband lying prostrate, drying blood covering a large wound to his scalp.

"Where did he go, old man?" Hannel demanded.

A gesture was the only reply, waving vaguely in the air.

Hannel barked orders to his guards in rapid succession. "You, help her get him back to the house. You, get torches. I'll have my property back before sunrise or I'll have all your hides in payment."

Daniel was afraid.

At the end of the street he had followed, he had only run into another river, or so he believed.

He did not know the horseshoe bend in the Euphrates surrounded the Old City.

Am I on an island? Daniel thought crazily. He was sweating despite the coolness of the evening. He tried to slow his pace, but panic gripped him and he began a slow trot, which quickened gradually to a full run as he retraced his footsteps.

Panting, and ignoring the possibility of onlookers, Daniel allowed himself a small whimper with each exhalation.

"Is something the matter, young sir?" a concerned pedestrian tried to ask, but Daniel bolted past, ignoring him completely.

As he came to each break in the road, he stopped briefly, looking wildly around for some clue as to the correct way to go to leave the city. *Ask someone, fool!* he chastised himself, but quickly thought better of it. *They will only know I'm running from something. They'll think I've committed some crime.*

You have! came another voice in his head. *You killed an old man, and now they'll crucify you!*

A man on the opposite side of the road stared at him.

Running from something? the voice came again. *You're not moving at all at the moment!*

Daniel began trotting again, moving blindly in a city he knew nothing of, in the one direction he was sure was wrong.

Where are your big plans now? the voice scoffed. *Branded just to show you're a slave, imagine what will happen to you when they catch you now!*

Then he saw them. Faint at first, orange glows winked in the distance like stars crisscrossing the darkened earth.

Torches! Carried by riders, the flames grew and flared in the wind with each stride of the galloping horses.

It would not be long before they were upon him.

"Oh, God," Daniel cried, clutching his palm over his mouth. "Where can I go, God? Please!"

Then he suddenly realized he had his answer. "The synagogue!" he shouted. He would beg for sanctuary from the rabbi there. He had not much time. The band of riders grew closer every second.

Lily dreamed she stood above Cantor as he lay awake in the open grave of Mak'ob. She saw him wrapped in a tangle of roots from an ancient tree. He was a prisoner, unable to move. Though she tried, Lily could not free him.

"Help me," Cantor called. "Open the door, Lily. Help me!"

Lily pounded hard against the gnarled roots of the ancient tree. She tried to tear him loose but could not. As she gaped into the yawning chasm, suddenly Cantor's face was changed. Cantor, the leper of Mak'ob, became Daniel, the hostage of Ecbatana for whom Cantor was risking his life.

Water began to seep into the grave, threatening to cover young Daniel's torso. Murky liquid inched up over his arms.

"You're drowning," Lily told him. "I don't know how to help you."

The prisoner whimpered. "Help me. Fetch my father! Tell him I'm . . . so sorry."

Lily watched as Cantor disappeared on the highway. Hawk flew above him, following him on his mission to Ecbatana. In her dream Lily knew Cantor would return too late to save Daniel.

She cried, "Cantor, you must hurry!"

But Cantor seemed not to hear her.

The pounding grew louder. More frantic.

"Cantor," she cried out in her sleep. "Cantor!"

Her voice echoed in the chamber. She awakened. "Only a dream," she whispered in relief.

Then the pounding exploded on the doors of the synagogue. "Help me! Refuge! Refuge!" a terrified voice called out.

Lily lay a moment longer where she had dozed off on the floor of the Women's Gallery. Was she still dreaming?

"Please! Open the door!" The boom of fists echoed in the empty auditorium.

This was no dream!

Lily sprang to her feet and peered down through the lattice. The golden censer hung above the ark where Torah scrolls were kept. The lamp burned low. The ten stones of Jerusalem were lost in shadow.

Massive doors were bolted and locked. Who kept the keys? The watchmen had left long ago. Who could open the doors for her at such an hour?

The fugitive pleaded, weeping as he begged to be let in.

Lily rushed to the window overlooking the entrance and the street. Faint light from the city illuminated the scene. A dark shadow pressed against the portals. "Please, it's Daniel . . . son of Melchior!"

Lily gasped, recognizing the fugitive. "Daniel! Daniel! What are you doing? I have no key," she shouted.

"Please, you must! They're coming. It's Karek—he's behind me!" Torches bobbed at an ever-quickening pace toward where Daniel cowered. "Help me! Don't let them take me back."

The ring of riders surrounded Daniel with his back to the locked doors of the synagogue. Each carried a torch in his right hand, pointed as a weapon at their prey, obscuring Daniel's view of their faces. He thought he might dart past the blockade, along one wall or the other, but every slight movement he made seemed anticipated by the horsemen. They reined their mounts in precise side steps to keep him contained, like a wild animal brought to bay.

At last, convinced of his defeat, Daniel stood in silence. The flames' pattering dance atop the oil-soaked tow of the torches was the only commentary to be heard.

"You are quite an annoyance, Daniel ben Melchior." The rider in the center finally spoke, and Daniel recognized the voice.

"Karek," he said tonelessly. "Please. I can pay you. . . ."

The captor raised his torch, illuminating his face and missing ear. "Not enough . . . not for this."

At a sharp motion of Karek's hand three riders dismounted, dropping their torches and retrieving a coil of rope each. They came slowly, warily, uttering soft reassurances as men approach a dangerous beast.

"Come easy now."

"No one means to hurt you."

"Just relax."

Daniel wanted to believe that what they said was true—that he would not be tortured in his recapture—but he knew it was false. Fingering the burn scar on his arm, he knew he would be punished severely and painfully for his flight. He might even be executed for killing the old man.

He also knew he would be beaten badly if he tried to resist now. He sank to his knees and began to cry, broken by his bleak prospects.

The riders, at least, were true to their word. Continuing their soothing patter, they bound his wrists, shackled his ankles, and leashed him to Karek's saddle to be led back to Hannel, sobbing as he went.

When they reached the main gate, Daniel tried in vain to resist, pulling against the inevitable, forceful strides of the horse.

"Be a man," Karek scolded. "For once in your life."

I'm not a man! Daniel wailed inside. *I'm only a bad son of my father, and I need someone to save me!*

Hannel met them at the columned portico with a scowl. "Your word!" he bellowed, grabbing Daniel roughly by the elbow. "You gave your word to me. I expected better from the line of Melchior."

Daniel found some courage in his anger at the insult. "I'm sure you would. An extortionist relies on the trustworthiness of his victims."

Hannel slapped him hard in rebuke and stormed into the house, shouting over his shoulder as he went, "Bring him to the stable. Let him witness his punishment."

Daniel's knees felt weak as the guards untied the knot of his leash and pulled him around the side of the house. "You don't have to do this. I don't want to die!"

Karek laughed. "Die? We're not going to kill you. Count yourself lucky the cook's husband survived your cowardly attack."

"The cook's . . ." Daniel was dumbfounded. He didn't know whom he had attacked, only fearing the man might've stopped him from escaping.

"Yes, Daniel. But what is in store for you is a thorough lesson."

As they rounded the corner and the stables came into view, Daniel tried pulling against the ropes again, digging his heels into the gravel path and twisting his wrists in futile effort against his bonds. Karek stamped his boot down hard on Daniel's toes and kicked him, sending him sprawling forward, and they dragged him.

The barn's door stood open a crack. Daniel saw the dim orange light of a lantern illuminating the interior.

He moaned again.

The peak of the barn's roof loomed menacingly over him the way a gallows platform must look to a condemned man. When the group of men reached the door, Hannel threw it wide on its hinges, revealing a horrible sight within.

Unconscious, beaten bloody, hanging limply by the wrists, tied between two opposite posts of the horse stalls, was Lono. His knees were bent beneath him and, were it not for the bindings on his arms, he would have slumped to the floor. His head lolled forward and to one side, and as the men pulled Daniel farther into the barn, he could see Lono had been flogged severely. His shoulders seemed grotesquely misshapen, as his own weight all but dislocated them. Daniel knew they must have been at him for quite a while—hours, perhaps.

Daniel's own restraints went lax. The guards stood around him, smirking, as if revealing a surprise gift to a friend and awaiting his reaction.

"Why?" Daniel whispered, tears brimming in his eyes.

Hannel scoffed. "We know he knew of your escape and did nothing to stop it or warn us." Before Daniel could protest the point, Hannel continued, "Besides, we can't very well send *you* back to your father in that state, can we?"

Karek looked disappointed.

"Is he . . . ?" Daniel couldn't finish the horrifying thought. Then he heard a faint gurgling, a bubbling of air through liquid as Lono breathed shallowly through his broken, bloody nose. "Please!" he said, "cut him down. For pity's sake, cut him down. He didn't deserve this; *I* did!"

"And you might dwell on that," Hannel agreed, "as you nurse him back to health. But mark me, Daniel ben Melchior. He is worth very little to me compared to your ransom. If you try to escape me again, he will not survive. It will be your doing."

With that, Karek hacked away the rope attached to Lono's right hand, and the giant fell solidly to the barn floor, rolling slightly on his side. The guards also freed Daniel, and he dropped to the ground beside Lono, wiping away dirt and straw that stuck to the servant's bloodied face when he fell.

The guards and Karek and Hannel left them there, amused by Daniel's gasping apologies to a man who clearly couldn't hear them.

30

CHAPTER

It was some time before Daniel could bring himself to leave Lono's side. The giant's condition seemed so grave that Daniel feared he might die any moment. He did what he could to aid with what he had immediately at hand. He covered Lono with the least soiled horse blanket he could find. Daniel gingerly cleansed the face and back wounds with a bucket of water Lono himself had toted earlier that day.

That thought in particular upset Daniel for some reason, more than any other. *If I had concentrated on my duties . . . if I had worked with Lono and taken his advice . . .* But Daniel knew his self-reproach was useless to the injured man. He also knew he was not capable of really taking care of him.

When he was sure Lono's condition was not worsening, Daniel ran to look for help in the servants' quarters.

Jacan, the houseboy, stopped him at the door with an angry look. "You nearly killed old Efran!" His voice was harsh, but he whispered to avoid waking anyone else. "Now you expect our help?"

"That wasn't Lono's fault," Daniel said. "He doesn't deserve to suffer because of something I did."

"You've been a blight on this house since you came here," the boy replied. "Go away and watch him die!"

He moved to shut the door on Daniel, but a voice called from behind him, "Wait. He is right." The shuffling tread preceded the appearance of the cook's husband, his head bandaged neatly in a continuous strip of clean linen. "I will fetch Tovi. Your friend is too large for us to move, so she will have to tend to him there in the barn."

"Thank you! Oh, thank you," Daniel said. "I cannot say how sorry—"

"Hush, now," the old man interrupted. "How my head aches! We'll talk more later. Go to him and wait there for my wife."

Daniel did as he was told, and a few minutes later the little cook arrived in the barn, accompanied by the houseboy. The look of joy Daniel had always seen in her face before was replaced with scorn, but she seemed determined to focus on Lono's care.

"I didn't want to help you," she said, "but my husband insisted. I don't know you and I don't trust you, but for his sake, I will tend to your friend's wounds. Don't speak to me unless I ask you to, and do everything I ask without question. Now—" she knelt by Lono—"how bad is it?"

She winced when she pulled the horse blanket back and saw the deep, jagged gashes in his back. "Horrible," she said under her breath.

There was so much revulsion in the single word that Daniel was not certain if she meant the wounds, the one who inflicted them . . . or Daniel himself.

Perhaps all three?

To Daniel she said, "These are the worst of his injuries. His face looks terrible, but at least he can breathe. But this—if we do not clean these properly, they will poison him and he will die. And this will not do." She threw the horse blanket away from Lono. "I can tell you tried to clean his wounds. What did you use?"

Daniel gestured to the bucket nearby and the piece of cloth he had torn from his own clothes.

"No, no . . . that won't do either." She turned her attention to the houseboy. "Jacan, run back to the hearth and stoke it high. You—" she nodded to Daniel—"fetch more water . . . two buckets, and take them in to boil. When you are through, Jacan, show him to the salt bin. Add one jarful to one bucket of water and bring both buckets to me. Fetch two fresh blankets from your quarters and ask Efran for five rolls of linen bandage."

Then she paused. "And, Jacan, also ask Efran for my lavender oil. He knows where it is hidden. Wake him if you have to," she added as the pair trotted out. "There's no reason he should sleep comfortably when he's sent me to work all night."

And through the rest of the night Daniel stood a solemn watch as the old woman sponged warm salt water over Lono's lacerations, then washed them out with fresh. Several times Lono stirred and moaned as the procedure surely added to his pain, but he did not wake.

When the last stripe was clean the old woman took the vial of expensive, fragrant oil, soaked one corner of a bandage, and dabbed it along the length of each wound.

"This will lessen the pain . . . a little," she explained, "and help fight the poison."

As the sun began to rise, piercing the narrow cracks between the planks of the barn's east wall, Tovi knotted the last bandage in the tidy wrapping around Lono's torso and covered him. The houseboy had fallen asleep in an empty stall, and she covered him also with a horse blanket.

"I will check on your friend throughout the day," she whispered to Daniel as she collected the jars and buckets. "But now I have to return to the kitchen. The master will expect his breakfast soon."

"Thank you. God bless you," Daniel said, hoping his words conveyed as much gratitude as he felt for the woman's unexpected and extraordinary kindness.

"Don't thank me yet." She let a little smile cross her lips as she nodded to the houseboy and added, "A barn is a filthy place to lie in good health, never mind with wounds such as Lono has suffered. We'll know by tonight if these measures are enough to save him. Until then, I suggest you pray."

Daniel had been praying, begging in fact, for Lono's healing since Tovi had begun her work, and he would not stop until he knew his friend was safely mending. "I will," he said, as she left the barn. "But tell me . . . why? Why did you do all this?"

Her face softened still further. "In the Synagogue of the Exiles, a rabbi from Judea has been telling us of the words of a great Rabbi there, one who commands, 'Love your enemies and pray for those who persecute you.'[34] I'm trying to obey this. Now, I must go."

Daniel knelt beside his friend. *God Almighty, Creator of all. You know the depth of this injustice I've helped to inflict on Lono. You know his good heart and his innocence. Mine is the body that should be bleeding. His scars should be mine. It is too late to change that, I know, but I beg you, more than anything I could ever ask for, please don't take him from this world. Ease his pain, Merciful God. Heal his wounds.*

His next thought caused tears to flow freely down his cheeks, and he cried the words aloud. "And don't let him hate me when he wakes! Please, let him forgive me for this horrible thing. I know I don't deserve it. I know I don't deserve such a faithful friend, but please, let him forgive me."

There was a stirring in the barn. Excitement welled in Daniel. He opened his eyes and wiped his face, almost expecting to see a miraculous healing. But it was the houseboy, awakened by Daniel's plea.

He walked to Daniel's side, putting a hand on his shoulder. "He will," Jacan said.

Daniel had forgotten the youth was there and was embarrassed by his tears, but could not keep them from flowing. The boy was less than half his age, but Daniel wanted desperately to believe his words were true, that Lono's forgiveness was assured. "How can you know?" he asked. "This man has done more for me in my life than I can remember, yet I've led him to this ruin. God!" he cried again heavenward. "How can I have done this? Why did I stray so far?"

The boy patted Daniel's shoulder but had no more comforting words to offer.

Lily removed the ten small stones from their leather pouch and placed them on the window ledge of the tiny room. Was it not said that the land of Israel was planted thick with angels? that everywhere the dust of the land blew, the angel armies of the Lord flew with them?

So these small pebbles were a foothold for her unseen guardians while Cantor was away, she thought.

The river where the sole of Jacob's foot had trod flowed in her imagination like a barrier against encroaching evil. The Spirit of the

Lord resided at the foundation of the walls that surrounded her and the children of Mak'ob.

What did Yeshua teach about the smallest child in His Kingdom? "The smallest, the youngest child, the *tsaowr*, the most vulnerable of all in the kingdom of *olam haba*, is greater than the greatest prophet."[35]

Lily's heart understood what he meant. *Tsaowr*, the word for "child," was so close to the word *tsara*, the word for "leper."

Yeshua had proven that those little ones the world labeled valueless were of the most value to Him in heaven. Meanwhile, they were here on earth to try the metal of every man's heart. All the wealth and knowledge and position in the world were of small value compared to the worth of a child . . . a child like Yod, the smallest and least valued in all of Israel.

Lily touched each stone on the window ledge. The blessings and promises of Israel were hers, even in this place of exile.

I'm praying again, You Who Number the Stars and Number the Grains of Sand and Count the Stones of Zion among Your Treasures. We who are valueless in the eyes of the world are worth the world to you. Protect us as we wait for the return of our Hope. Let us live to see the face of your Son once more.

The Syrian hogs were lumpy black beasts covered in stiff, wiry bristles. The males sported curving tusks that sprouted from their lower jaws. With these they sliced each other and any human foolish enough to come between them and their feed.

The females were not so good-natured.

Daniel's first approach was from downwind. It was a mistake. The rank, pungent smell made his eyes water and made him gag.

"You get used to it," said the hog boss, Portus.

A condemned career criminal, Portus had lost the tip of his nose in an earlier punishment. It gave him a very swinish appearance . . . and perhaps explained why the smell did not bother him.

Daniel could not believe he was reduced to tending the most unclean of all unclean animals according to the Law of Almighty God. Not only was he a swineherd, but he took orders from a convict. "I won't ever get used to this," he said through gritted teeth.

Portus looked offended. "You want me to tell the Steward you refuse?" he demanded.

Daniel remembered the sight of Lono hanging like a side of slaughtered beef. "Don't," he protested. "Just tell me what to do."

"In that wagon is the swill from the palace," Portus said. "Get to slopping the hogs."

The wagon was heaped with refuse. The tools Daniel had were two wooden buckets with rope handles. While Portus lounged in the shade of a stunted acacia tree, he gave orders as if directing a battle. "Hurry up! If you don't dump those buckets faster, they'll start fighting."

When Daniel rushed to comply, Portus piped, "Did I say dump them all in one spot? Are you trying to make them fight? One bucket in each corner, then go on to the next pen. Hurry it up!"

The garbage from the palace was a jellied mass of rice, gnawed bones, fruit rinds and pits, all glued together with grease. On his third trip Daniel made the mistake of leaning too far into the pen to dump the load. A boar lashed out at him with a savage jerk, opening a bloody wound the length of Daniel's forearm, from burn scar to wrist.

"You do want to put some salve on that or it'll mortify," Portus said helpfully. "Had a helper eat up that way 'til he was covered in sores."

"What happened to him?"

Portus rubbed the end of his stub and blew snot into his palm. "Fell into the pen. Hogs eat him up."

"Where do you keep the salve?" Daniel asked, setting down the buckets.

"Not now! Can't stop work for a scratch. Get back to it."

Two hours were required to unload all the garbage into the pens. Daniel's arms were covered in black muck to the elbows. Congealed fat squished between his toes from drips that fell during the countless trips.

When the wagon was empty, Daniel stared in disbelief at his hands. He desperately wanted to wipe the stinging sweat from his eyes but not with those hands. "Rags?" he asked hopefully.

"Use your tunic, swineherd." Portus laughed. "But what're you stopping for, anyway?"

"The food's all gone."

"So? Watering time. The well's down by the creek bed . . . over there. By that carob tree."

By peering through greasy and swollen lids Daniel barely made out the indicated location. It was about a quarter mile away. "Nothing closer?"

"Had one. Dried up. Hop to it. Two buckets for each trough. Four troughs in each pen. Twenty pens. Better get moving. Hogs is mighty thirsty after they eats."

31

After reaching Ecbatana, getting directions to the home of Melchior the Magus was easy. Within an hour Hawk was perched in the branches of a pomegranate tree outside the front door, awaiting Cantor's return.

A household servant ushered Cantor into an office and told him he would be helped shortly.

The man who joined him there was prosperously dressed and sturdy of build, but too young to be the father of the now twenty-three-year-old Daniel. Cantor decided he must have made some mistake and said so.

"What is your name and business?" the other demanded.

"I think both are my own, unless there's some reason I should tell you," Cantor returned.

"I am Joshua ben Melchior. My father is away, and I am in charge in his absence."

That explained it. "My name is Cantor. I come from the Synagogue of the Exiles in Narda. It's about your brother, Daniel."

"So?" Joshua returned coolly. "Does he owe you money? Because if he does, you'll get none here."

"Not that, not at all," Cantor explained. "He was captured by slavers. He and his man, Lono. But they're safe now," he hastened to add. "Rescued—recovered, anyway—by Lord Hannel of Narda."

Joshua nodded and stuck out a thick lower lip. "Lord Hannel I know of. So why hasn't Daniel returned with you?"

Cantor frowned. "There were certain . . . *expenses* connected with redeeming your brother. Lord Hannel would like to be reimbursed before . . . you understand?"

Joshua grimaced. "Completely. Instead of you, it's Lord Hannel he owes money to."

Cantor let that comment pass.

"So we're really talking about ransom here. How much is the demand?"

"The figure for redeeming Lono is one thousand drachmae."

"And for my brother?"

"Twenty talents of silver."

The former number was three years' wages for a man—not an unreasonable price for a good, strong slave.

The latter figure represented nearly fifteen hundred pounds of precious metal. Enough to pay ten men all their wages for five years . . . or one man for a working lifetime.

Cantor saw Joshua's eyes narrow, but the fleeting, crafty look was quickly replaced by a jovial smile. "This must be attended to at once," Joshua said. "Give me a moment. I'll write out the order right now."

Grasping a sheet of parchment and a quill pen, Joshua scratched his ear for a moment with the feather, then began to rapidly scrape out a reply. When it was complete, he folded it carefully, melted wax over the fold, and pressed the crown of his ring into the seal.

Before handing it to Cantor, he said, "Take good care to keep this confidential. We both know what's happening here. Can't let the word get out or we might spark a rash of kidnappings for ransom, eh?"

Cantor vowed complete secrecy and the personal delivery of the order to Lord Hannel.

In contrast to Joshua's former manner, now he seemed much more relaxed, grateful, and pleasant, even inviting Cantor to spend the night. "We wondered where Daniel had gone. We were terribly worried about him . . . not Father so much, but I was. Can't we at least thank you by offering you a meal and a bed?"

Cantor declined, saying that since his mission was accomplished, he would be camping with his escort and leaving again for Narda at first light. He thought he again saw something odd in Joshua's eyes at his refusal to remain in the house, and once more at the mention of the accompanying guards, but Cantor dismissed it as imagination. Probably he was just thinking about the danger from the Herodians he faced back in Narda.

In any case, Joshua had met the requirement promptly and without discussion. He bowed Cantor out of the house with a profusion of compliments and abundant expressions of gratitude.

Over time a famine's grip on Narda strengthened. Not only had the rice crop failed, so did the barley . . . then the wheat. Those who could move away did so.

Those who remained in the region tightened their belts and prayed for relief.

Daniel staggered as he toted the buckets from well to pen. After the evening feeding he set aside the last pail, allowing it to sit in whatever shade he could find until full dark. By then some of the suspended dirt had settled out, leaving a couple inches of mostly clear, drinkable water.

This was not only needed to quench his thirst; the dry crusts of bread he ate morning and night had to be moistened before they could be swallowed. Even then they were hard to choke down.

The amount of garbage shrank as well. The wagonload no longer overflowed, but the hogs remained as ravenous as ever. "Don't let 'em lose no weight," Portus cautioned before scuttling under his shelter. "Hannel won't like it. It'll be your hide."

"What am I supposed to do?" Daniel protested. "I can't feed them what I don't have."

Portus reemerged briefly, perhaps only because he feared he would share the blame for any skinny pigs. The aggrieved look, added to his already deformed features, made him look truly demonic. "Do I need to tell you everything?" he whined. "You know that carob tree? Loaded with them black pods? There's a whole hillside of them trees about half a mile farther on. Strip them pods and feed 'em to the pigs."

So now, twice each day, after dumping what garbage still came and watering his charges, Daniel hauled the wagon nearly a mile. He filled it up with the black, wizened seedpods, then returned and fed those to the hogs as well.

There was no longer a midday respite from labor. Feeding, watering, and gathering occupied hours and hours. By the time the morning chore was complete, the afternoon swill arrived, and the entire process began all over again.

It was without summons or invitation that Aram returned late to Hannel's estate, waiting impatiently at the gate for an audience. Hannel's guard was plainly intimidated by the Herodian as he did not speak during the delay, only avoided eye contact. Once, when his gaze did meet Aram's face, he nodded curtly, then looked quickly away again. Aram snorted.

"What is the meaning of this?" Hannel asked, descending the gravel path.

"Your information has been useless," Aram said curtly, "as has your assistance. The transfer of the Temple tax is already late. I am overdue in reporting back to Lord Herod Antipas. Not only is there no man with a hawk anywhere in the city, there is no hawk. Both have flown the coop!"

Hannel looked embarrassed as his guards observed the conversation and gestured angrily to quiet the Herodian captain.

"May I suggest," Aram continued bluntly as he remounted his horse, "if you wish to please the tetrarch or collect this reward, find the courage to tell your brother your plans or arrest such criminals yourself. As for us, we have wasted enough time here already."

With that he spurred the steed away into the night, leaving Hannel cursing and Hannel's guards trying to achieve invisibility.

32

CHAPTER

The morning hours at the Synagogue of the Exiles were more hectic than usual. Yod's red hair glistened like copper in the sunlight streaming through the windows of the synagogue. The children of Mak'ob gathered around Lily in the Women's Gallery to watch the procession as the representatives of the Jerusalem Temple gathered in the auditorium to collect the Temple tax.

A large contingent of armed Herodian guards remained outside, blocking the street as numerous chests of Temple shekels were loaded onto camels for transport back to Jerusalem.

In turn, men and beasts and treasure were surrounded by the cutthroat army of Lord Tannis and his brother, Hannel.

Resentment flashed in the eyes of Shinar, the Temple envoy, as he raised his eyes toward the lattice screen of the gallery. He seemed to fix his gaze on Yod. Had he glimpsed the copper sheen of the child's hair through the openings?

Lily overheard Shinar's words to Rabbi Nehemiah: "If ever such evildoers, followers of the imposter Yeshua, do appear in this place, claiming healing by this so-called miracle worker, you are instructed to report it immediately to Caiaphas in Yerushalayim."

Shinar turned his face toward the observers in the gallery and raised his voice so they would hear his unsheathed threat. "Rabbi Nehemiah! I leave this warrant with you, as the elder of Ha-Golah, this outpost of Zion's ten stones. At your word, a troop of Temple guards will be sent here from Yerushalayim to arrest any who claim Yeshua is Messiah and bring them back to Yerushalayim for trial. Yeshua will be dead by summer, they say, and all this will be finished."

Lily met Shinar's stare as his angry look grazed all the children behind the lattice. Her fingers closed around Israel's ten pebbles in her pocket.

I'm praying again, You Who Sent the Redeemed to the Safety of Exile. From the smallest stones of Israel to the largest, all are precious to you. This man, he knows . . . he knows the truth of the foundation stones. It doesn't matter to him that these little ones are healed and well and cut from the same quarry as the patriarchs and the prophets. He cares only that the high priest has declared the healing of any illness in the Name of Yeshua a blasphemy. Oh, Lord, God of Exiles, Guardian of Ha-Golah, the exiled Stones of Zion, so it has come to this. You, our Redeemer, are in Exile with us all.

Rabbi Nehemiah replied to Shinar with a raised hand and this vow: "The Lord grant that Caiaphas, or any high priest of Israel, may live so long as to see the day I send such a message."

Lily restrained herself from laughing behind a grim smile at the clever wording of Nehemiah's vow.

Yod asked, "Lily? Are those men talking about our Yeshua? calling him a bad name?"

Lily replied, "Yes."

"And us?"

"Yes."

"And Cantor?"

"Yes."

The child tossed her curls. "Look, Lily. See? The Shining Ones behind those men? Angels . . . standing on the stones from Yerushalayim."

Lily, not seeing and yet believing Yod's vision, asked, "How many?"

"Ten."

"A minyan of the righteous." For a moment Lily thought she glimpsed a light behind the Temple envoy as the last of the treasure was carried out.

"The letters on their belts match the letters set in the ten stones they stand on," Yod said softly.

The heavy presence of holiness made Lily's knees suddenly weak. She locked her fingers in the lattice to maintain her balance. She managed to whisper, "Did the angels speak to you, Yod? When Shinar said what he said . . . about Yeshua being dead before summer?"

"No. But when Shinar said Yeshua's name, the Shining Ones drew their swords . . . and the ten swords have the same words as on the ten belts and on the ten stones."

"Where are their swords now?" Lily asked.

"They hold them with the sharp edge above the heads of the Temple guards."

The sound of something hitting the stone floor roused Lily from her slumber. The blue light of predawn filled the sleeping chamber. It was too early to willingly awaken, yet there was something stirring on the window ledge above her. One by one the stones she had placed there were falling to the floor.

Lily rolled over and leapt to her feet in almost one motion. "Hawk!" she cried.

The raptor playfully picked up the last pebble in his beak and dropped it at her feet.

Like a herald, the noble bird had flown ahead of his master to announce Cantor's homecoming to Lily!

A feast of celebration for Cantor's safe return was held that night at the synagogue. Bathed and anointed with fragrant perfume, Lily and Cantor were sung to the door of their chamber by the children as though they were newlyweds.

The stars that had guided Cantor to Ecbatana and back again shone through the open square of the window. A nightbird sang in the garden outside. Cantor softly sang the Song of Solomon to her and they made love, slept, then awoke to satisfy their longing once again.

Lily lay in Cantor's strong arms and sighed with contentment.

Cantor kissed her hair. "I often woke up beneath the stars and wondered what you were doing."

"Every night. The same. Dreaming of you."

Her answer pleased him. "What are you thinking now?"

"That I'm glad you're not a dream."

He said, "I waited on the hill beyond the river. Watched until I saw the soldiers from Yerushalayim leave the city . . . heading west. I couldn't come back to you 'til then."

"Hmmm. I was afraid for you. Afraid they'd find you on the road."

"Fear not," Cantor whispered. "Remember what I told you, what I know above all things: Fear nothing. Fear no man."

"I have not seen what you've seen, Cantor. You have seen *olam haba*. My world is still only this world. And I never want to live in this world again without you."

Cantor's reply was filled with wonder. A revelation. A glimpse of *olam haba*. "I spoke with Elijah, or rather, he spoke to me. . . ."

So many men were named Elijah. Did Cantor mean *Elijah* . . . the prophet? "Cantor?"

"Yes. It was himself. Before I heard the Voice call me back. This is the lesson Elijah sent with me." Cantor stroked her face as he spoke. Soothing. Quiet. Filled with a vision of what was to come. "From the earliest days, the Lord has taught his ways to Israel through the prophets. We can understand every event—past, present, and future— through the language of God's Word. Without prophecy, we can only guess at God's will by the outcome of events as we perceive them. We may only see a fragment of his plan and misunderstand . . . and always, the events continue to unfold beyond our short lifetimes."

Cantor pointed at the stars gleaming through the window. "See that? The light from that star began its journey to your eye perhaps ten thousand years ago. So it is with everything set in motion on this earth. Solomon wrote that in each life there is a *time* for us to be born and a time to die.[36] There were twenty-eight things Solomon wrote as the Times in our lives between birth and death. But I tell you the truth, Lily: When we follow and believe the master plan within God's Word, we are beyond the reach of time."

"What if you had not come back to me?" she asked. "What if I had gone on alone?"

"Every step is marked out for you . . . just walk. What you and I do now for God is like the light of that star. To someone yet unborn you are a distant star. What good you do now may shine forth, yet it may not be seen or received by anyone during your lifetime. But then your act of kindness will someday change the destiny of someone far in the future. A thousand or two thousand years from this moment. What we do now matters *eternally*. The written Word of the Almighty lets us study and see how the eternal picture is unfolding through generations. Whatever we suffer now? We can have faith that, in the end, even our suffering will be golden thread in the eternal tapestry."

"How would I live without you?"

"Our destiny is already recorded in the Book. This is what I learned in heaven. Everything matters. Every word. Deed. Thought. Prayer. Fear not! It is time that makes us fear. Fear of running out of time. Lily, there is no time where we are going. The prayer we pray today . . . the prayer we think God does not hear? It may yet be answered for our grandchildren . . . or their grandchildren. Do you understand what I am telling you, Lily?"

She considered his words. "Elijah told you this?"

"Elijah is the prophet who never died." He cupped her face in his hand. "So I tell you: God is the God of the living, not the dead. No matter what happens in this life, Fear not."

33 | CHAPTER

ews of the envoy's arrival had reached Daniel's ears even before Jacan was sent to fetch him. A tremendous sense of relief filled him as he followed the boy back to the main house and into what Hannel referred to as his "audience chamber."

A grand name, thought Daniel, *for such a tiny space*.

The room had one door and no windows. It was cluttered with stacks of parchment, placed in no particular order around the walls and on top of the one small table and chair. Now, as Jacan opened the door, the room was also crowded with seven other people, including Hannel, all standing awkwardly over and around the parchment pillars.

Hannel wore a thin smile as he introduced the others. "Welcome, Daniel," he said. "Welcome at last. These gentlemen are from the synagogue. They've come to bear witness to this transaction. Rabbis Ahava and Nehemiah." He gestured to two men, both old, one blind and leaning against a younger man for guidance. "This is Cantor and Lily. They've come with your father's message and—" he licked his lips— "the money. And Karek, of course you know."

Daniel stood in silence during the greetings, only nodding at those he did not know and avoiding eye contact with Hannel and Karek.

Hannel cleared his throat. "To the business at hand."

Cantor retrieved the sealed document from his cloak and held it out, unsure whom to hand it to. Rabbi Ahava stepped forward and thanked him, wasting no time in breaking the seal and reading the contents.

Odd, thought Daniel, *the blind man faces Rabbi Ahava as though he watches him like the rest of us.*

Everyone saw the puzzled look on Ahava's face, but it was the blind man who commented, "There is something wrong. What is it, my brother? What have you read there?"

"It is . . ." Ahava paused, looking toward Daniel. "Strange." And he passed the letter to Hannel.

Hannel read the note quickly, grunted, and dropped it to his desk. "Jacan, go and fetch Lono also. *He* will be returning to Ecbatana. Daniel will not."

"What?" Daniel and Cantor exclaimed in unison.

"How can this be?" Cantor asked, reaching for the paper.

"It is there," Hannel said, all pretense of kindness gone. "Read it yourself. It seems the House of Melchior wishes to be rid of Daniel as much as we do. Unfortunately for us all, it means he'll be staying here."

Daniel felt ill as Cantor read the letter aloud.

Esteemed Lord Hannel,

We thank you for bringing the matter of the recent ill fortune of our son and our servant, and your kindly rescue of them, to our attention. Unfortunately, a recent error in business accounting has badly reduced our assets, and we are therefore unable to send the total amount you've requested to redeem them.

Instead, we send the lesser of the two amounts you specified—enough only to free the man called Lono.

Thank you for his prompt release and safe passage away from Narda. Please see that he also receives the few drachmae extra we've included, to provide for his travel needs.

Yahweh's blessing upon you all, most sincerely.

For the House of Melchior of Ecbatana

Cantor looked confused and apologetic as Hannel dismissed Daniel. "Back to your work then, young ben Melchior. Karek, go with him and see that he does not do anything foolish. He is still my property, after all."

Daniel was stunned beyond thinking. The world outside seemed harsh, too bright, and he trudged lamely back toward the stables. Karek walked behind Daniel, mocking him, but he heard none of it.

Only when he saw Lono step from the servants' quarters, shuffling along at Jacan's side, did he emerge from his dulled state.

"Good-bye, my friend," he called to Lono. "Tell my father I understand, and I do not blame him."

Then Karek shoved him hard from behind, and Lono was lost from view. The words of the slaver Faisal came back to Daniel as he marched down the curving path to the hog pen: *"You're a slave now. That is your entire being. If you think of yourself as anything but a servant to me, you will die."*

Daniel believed he now truly understood the meaning of the words and the advice they contained. *Hope is my enemy*, he thought. *I must resign myself to this new life or I cannot survive.*

Even though exhausted, Daniel could not sleep. A blasting wind swept down from the mountains separating him from home. The thin walls of his shed offered no protection against the dust. He coughed and sneezed into his rags.

Then, just as he had sneezed himself into a stupor, a blazing full moon rose over the Zagros Mountains, boring directly into his dazzled eyes. Blinking stupidly, he woke again.

In that moment of recognition Daniel suddenly hated the carob trees. He hated feeding the pigs. He hated watering the pigs. He hated his life.

But he hated the carob trees most of all.

They seemed to him to represent everything he had left behind and now could never have again.

In his father's house he had never been a servant, much less a slave, still less a swineherd. His father would have shuddered at the thought.

What a change from last year.

On every holiday in Daniel's memory dried and candied fruit of every kind had been spread on platters throughout the house. Honeyed figs, moist dates, sweet apricot rounds, apples slices . . . and dried carob fruit.

This year Daniel huddled miserably in his rags in a shelter not even as sturdy as the worst of the pigsties, starving . . . and the carob pods were for the pigs!

Two days ago Lord Hannel had placed a pair of his guards in the carob orchard. They were there to prevent anyone stealing the pods. In a year of no grain and no grass, all flocks of sheep and herds of goats were moved to distant pastures because there was no fodder.

But hogs could not be driven like sheep or goats. To feed them Lord Hannel relied on the carob trees, and no one except the swine could have any.

Each time Daniel returned with a load of husks for the hogs a guard rode with him to see that no one—not even Daniel—took so much as a single black, wizened pod.

No one at home was praying for him anymore, Daniel thought. They had not come to seek him, they would not redeem him, and now they had given up praying for him.

Perhaps this very night they were celebrating: gathering with friends and neighbors to gorge themselves on sweet morsels, laughing and singing. . . .

Daniel groaned and, hugging himself around the middle, rocked himself to sleep.

He hated the carob trees.

It was the dry season again. This year the Euphrates dropped to barely a trickle. The canals were empty, the wheat and barley fields abandoned.

Added to his other labor, Daniel spent exhausting hours inside the well. He dug it out deeper, extracting one painful shovelful of muck at a time. When two buckets were full, he tied them to a line and climbed a rickety ladder to the top. Hand over weary hand he hauled them up to be dumped in a stinking heap; then back down into the ooze he went.

By this toil, water collected to the depth of Daniel's knees overnight. It was barely enough to meet the needs of the hogs.

There were fewer animals now. Lord Hannel stopped selling his pigs. Those that remained were for the tables of the palace alone.

Not many sows littered that year. Those that had savaged their young, and only a handful of piglets had been rescued.

The air in the bottom of the well was stifling, even though cooler than the surface.

Daniel had a recurrent nightmare of passing out and drowning in the mud. In his dream no one bothered looking for him until someone else was dispatched to clear the well. In his vision he saw his body recovered from the mire . . . and fed to the hogs.

At that moment he always woke up, screaming.

He asked himself repeatedly why he did not run away. If caught, he could beg them just to kill him.

The honest answer was, it was too late.

He had no strength to go even one day's journey without food. There was nowhere to beg. To stay was to suffer and barely survive.

To leave was to not survive at all.

At home, the worst of his father's servants had plenty to eat. None of them went hungry. The orchard and vineyard workers were treated to holiday feasts and their midday meals were provided by the House of Melchior.

If only Daniel could get home again, he knew what he'd say: *Father, I have sinned against the Almighty and against you. I was stupid and arrogant and prideful. I wasted my inheritance. Lono was punished and almost died because of me. I know I can't be your son anymore, but could I just . . . work for you? If I could just be your servant . . .*

But there was no way to go home.

34 CHAPTER

annel sat behind his cluttered desk, scribbling busily with a quill on a roll of parchment. When Karek entered without knocking, Hannel jumped, spilling his inkpot.

"A day's work ruined!" Hannel shouted. "What is it this time?"

"I've come to tell you, Daniel's work—"

Hannel sighed heavily. "Spying on Daniel again, Karek? We've *sold* most all the swine; there's no feed for them anyway. It occurs to me, he's likely *finishing* the work that's required of him. But what about your own duties? Why are you spending your time spying on the servants?"

Karek stammered as Hannel continued, "I know you enjoy bullying him, but I have servants to spare and without a herd of pigs for him to tend, his presence here is just an annoying reminder of the money I lost on the ransom. I think it's time we parted company with Daniel ben Melchior."

Karek smiled sinisterly as he grasped Hannel's meaning. "How shall I do it, Master? Will you have me slit his throat? Or will we—"

"Fool!" Hannel interrupted. "I don't want you to kill him. I want you to take him to the common market and have him auctioned. He's no good to me here, but even less if I can't recoup some of my money."

"Yes, my lord," Karek said. "I'll see to it immediately."

"And, Karek," Hannel added, "see to it that he's not *accidentally* harmed along the way. An injured slave fetches far less than one in good health. If you should return with less than two hundred drachmae, I shall know why, and I will hold you responsible."

Melchior and Esther were weary as they arrived in Jericho. Since leaving Ecbatana, they had sought Daniel all the way to Caesarea Maritima on the seacoast, but without success. Neither had there been any reports of such a caravan as he had joined.

It was as if all had vanished.

Feeling no one else could be of assistance, Melchior pinned his hopes on Yeshua of Nazareth.

There again they were frustrated. When they sought the Teacher in the Galil, He had left for Judea. When they reached Judea, He was teaching in the countryside.

Now, just as they were en route to Jerusalem to pray at the Temple before giving up and going home, they found Him!

At the Jericho synagogue they asked for news of their son. It was a common practice when traveling for Jews to leave messages for each other at synagogues along the route.

There was still no word about Daniel, but the place buzzed with the news that Yeshua was approaching. In fact, throngs of people had already gathered, lining both sides of the highway connecting the Old and New Cities.

It was Yod's fifth birthday and she requested a journey into the vast market square of Narda. She held tightly to Lily's right hand and Cantor's left as they made their way through the crowds.

The clouds were low, heavy, and gray. Expressions on shoppers' faces reflected the brooding sky. Yod's excitement was undiminished. She searched each face and seemed to hear songs when none were sung.

In the clamor and crush a blacksmith struck a hammer upon his anvil. Different notes clanged out a sort of tune as he shaped the glowing metal into links of chain.

Yod stopped outside the shop and exclaimed, "Oh, listen! So beautiful. Remember, Cantor? The music. Like his Spirit. Oh, the colors in the notes!"

He quietly translated for Lily. "You see, music has color. Or, maybe color makes music. You not only hear it; there is a fragrance in the notes, like a garden. Each note like a different flower. Music is different—bigger—over there." He smiled wistfully at the memory.

Bunches of lavender hung drying in an herb shop. The air was redolent with the aroma. It seemed right somehow to Lily that music in heaven made color and fragrance. She imagined what Eden must have been like when it was planted here in this very soil. Music, color, perfume . . . all combined. What had it been like to hear the Voice of the Lord as He walked in the cool of the day?

The Lord walking . . . heavenly music . . . where the souk of Narda now stands . . .

Could it have been? Eden? Paradise? Here?

Yod raised her hands to Cantor, who picked her up and swung her onto his shoulder. She perused the scene of buying and selling from this high vantage point like the sharp-eyed Hawk, taking in every detail of the bustling scene.

Cloth merchants. Spice sellers. Grain and wine and oil. Every sort of fruit and vegetable was offered in the souk.

Suddenly Yod's smile vanished. The child wailed in horror. "Oh, Lily! I see men all chained together. There—on the other side of the marketplace. People for sale. Look!" She turned to glance at the coil of new chain on the floor of the blacksmith shop.

Was it a vision of what had been or what would be? Lily wondered. Or was it something in the present reality?

"Put me down, Cantor!" Yod cried, slipping off his shoulder and springing to the pavement like a kitten. Then, in an instant, she darted past a plump housewife with two children and a loaded basket and vanished into the mob.

35 | CHAPTER

In front of the Jericho synagogue, drawn up in a solemn row, was a file of officials. In contrast to the jubilant, excited mood of the crowd, these men seemed austere and self-important. Their attitude indicated they felt it entirely proper for Yeshua to come and pay His respects . . . to them.

Not a welcoming committee so much as a receiving line.

Melchior approached the men. "I need to speak with Rebbe Yeshua," he addressed the one garbed as a priest.

"Everyone wants something from him," the priest sniffed.

"Yes, but we've come so far! Ecbatana in Media. I hope to get news of my son Daniel. Twenty-three. Slim. A dark mark here, on his cheek."

The priest had already turned aside and was deep in conversation with the rabbi. He had not listened to Melchior at all.

Another man, who identified himself as the Chazzan of the synagogue, said, "Don't get your hopes up. Look at the way the rabble are ready to mob him! Disgusting, really. And just look there."

The Chazzan indicated a sukomore fig tree so large it topped a nearby wall and even shaded part of the road. Its leaning trunk and larger branches were festooned with children scanning the crowd for Yeshua's arrival. "What a spectacle," the Chazzan remarked. "All defiled, every one of them. That tree belongs to Zachai the Publican—a terrible sinner, worse than a leper. The most hated man in Judea." He viewed Melchior's travel-stained clothing with disdain. "No interviews today. We've got to give this Yeshua a break from all insignificant demands. Try again tomorrow."

The central square of Narda's New City was surrounded by date palms. The flagstone-paved courtyard also boasted a trio of fountains drawing water from the King's Canal through lead-lined conduits.

The largest of these was a representation of two colossal bronze male statues, each holding massive amphorae from which gushed cool, clear liquid. The figures depicted the Assyrian god Euphrates and his Sumerian brother, the creator of the Tigris. Tigris was lithe where Euphrates was brawny, but with their backs they supported a model of the city of Narda.

Since Narda's wealth and security depended on the two rivers and the marshes and canals they birthed, it was natural to honor them. Devotees tossed flowers and coins into the clear pools.

Beside the monument Babylonian priests of the cult of the goddess Anahita poured goblets of water drawn from one of the spouts over the heads of expectant mothers. On the opposite side of the shrine a priest of Mithra slaughtered an ox being offered in birthday celebration, then washed away the blood from his hands in the fountain.

The very depiction violated the Jewish prohibitions against making graven images and worshipping pagan gods. It seemed even here in this place of exile caused by violating those very commands, the descendants of those exiles still had not learned the lesson. Among the crowd thronging the square were many Nardean Jews, none of whom seemed dismayed by the setting.

Cast out of Eden. Cast into exile. Enslaved to sin. And all because of pride—setting human will against the commandments of Almighty God. What had humans gained? And what had they lost? And how could the eternal cost in consequences ever be paid in full?

O Lord, God of my salvation,
I have cried out day and night before You.
Let my prayer come before You;
Incline Your ear to my cry.[37]

Daniel recited the psalm in his mind as he stood half-naked and shackled upon the platform of the slave auction in the Narda market, waiting his turn to be sold.

For my soul is full of troubles,
And my life draws near to the grave.[38]

Three other slaves were to be sold before him. The delay was unbearable as he stood, ashamed by his nakedness, before the crowd gathered there. Above the breechclout that was his only covering, his ribs protruded.

I am counted with those who go down to the pit;
I am like a man who has no strength,
Adrift among the dead,
Like the slain who lie in the grave,
Whom You remember no more,
And who are cut off from Your hand.[39]

"What am I bid for this new slave?" cried the auctioneer, pushing another young man to the fore. "Sure to be a true hand in the field, eats very little I'm told. An easy keeper, friends. An easy keeper."

You have laid me in the lowest pit,
In darkness, in the depths.
Your wrath lies heavy upon me,
And You have afflicted me with all Your waves.[40]

Daniel shivered, though the day was very warm. A trickle of sweat rolled down his back.

You have put my acquaintances far from me;
You have made me an abomination to them;
I am shut up and can't get out.[41]

Then Daniel spotted Lono moving through the throng . . . and was torn between joy at the sight of a single friendly face and deep shame at where Lono found him.

36

CHAPTER

ily and Cantor threaded through the crush of the marketplace in pursuit of Yod. Hawk soared above them in a tight circle as if to pinpoint the exact location of the child.

"The slave auction!" Cantor called over his shoulder when Lily fell behind, her hands protectively clasped before the slight bulge of her pregnant belly.

A passing herd of goats separated the couple. Lily waded through the animals and barely noticed the angry curses of the herdsmen. A beam of sunlight burst through the clouds as she broke through the wall of shoppers into the packed circle of the slave auction.

In the slave pen dozens of young men, naked from the waist up, were shiny with oil meant to accentuate their muscles.

Lily spotted Cantor, Hawk on his shoulder, working his way toward Yod. The child clung to Lono's meaty hand. The brown-skinned giant stood outside the slave cage, weeping like a little boy at the sight of Daniel being shoved toward the stage.

"Mastah!" cried Lono, reaching through the bars with his right hand. "I no leave you. All time I work on roads. Save money . . . mebbe buy you freedom."

Daniel turned an expressionless face toward his former slave. "Whatever you have, it can't be enough. My father has chosen my punishment."

Lono pleaded, "I no believe you fadda do this. You fadda has great love for his son! I know he forgives. I know he stands to search the highway for some sight of you."

Daniel replied, "Tell Mother I'm sorry."

"It no their will you be sold. They would not!"

"This is just."

"Sir! What shall I do?"

"Go home, Lono. To Ecbatana," Daniel instructed. "Home to my mother and my father. Tell them I love them. That I'm sorry for all the pain I have caused."

The noise of the crowd swelled like the roar of an incoming tide. An exuberant crash of praise and wonder broke over the synagogue like thunder. The excitement poured out on Yeshua of Nazareth reverberated and echoed around the hilltop of Jericho until it seemed to come from everywhere at once.

Through all the commotion the rank of religious leaders remained calm, complacent. The country preacher was coming to pay his respects. Entirely proper . . . entirely their due.

Despite the Chazzan's refusal to allow a meeting, Melchior waited, alternately fearful and in hope. What if this Yeshua was not the same person he had only met as a baby all those years ago? Even if He were the same, grown into manhood and fame, what if He refused to help?

What if He could not?

Once pounced on by this self-righteous set of synagogue elders, would Melchior even be allowed to present his need?

Then suddenly, there He was! Flanked closely by a man dressed in the rags of a beggar and surrounded by an anxious crowd of talmidim, Yeshua's face beamed as He looked up at the waving children in the tree.

The Teacher walked directly toward the waiting officials.

Melchior's heart sank.

In the lane formed by the wall of the publican's compound, Yeshua neared the religious authorities . . . neared, and passed by without stopping or speaking.

Halting directly under the largest branch of the sukomore fig, Yeshua looked upward, and Melchior noticed for the first time that a man and a woman were also amid the foliage, like ripe fruit ready to be plucked.

"Zachai!" Melchior heard Yeshua shout boisterously up at the tree. "Hurry and come down. For I must stay at your house today."

Melchior and Esther slipped away from the shadow of the synagogue into the pleasant shade of the sukomore tree . . . but not before Melchior noted the outrage and outright hatred on the faces of the Chazzan and the rest of the slighted officials.

"Sold!" the auctioneer cried.

Then Daniel was shoved roughly to the front of the platform.

Lord, why do You cast off my soul?
Why do You hide Your face from me?[42]

Karek stood directly below the auction block, sneering at Daniel's embarrassment.

"Why is he being sold?" cried a man from the crowd. "I have heard he was defiant in the House of Hannel!"

"A spirited slave," replied the auctioneer. "In need of constant labor to expend such energies. What am I bid?"

I have been afflicted and ready to die from my youth;
I suffer Your terrors;
I am distraught.[43]

Daniel closed his eyes as a few potential buyers ascended the steps, pinching the muscles of his arms and legs, pulling his hair, even prying open his mouth to look at his teeth.

Your fierce wrath has gone over me;
Your terrors have cut me off.
They came around me all day long like water;
They engulfed me altogether.[44]

"Thirty drachmae," one of those inspecting Daniel said, pulling one eyelid open and looking closely at the white.

"Fifty," called a voice from the crowd, and Daniel looked to see who it was. A stocky, gray-haired man with upraised arm caught his eye. Daniel quickly looked away.

"Excellency," the auctioneer replied with a bow. "Your presence here is an honor. Surely you do not want this . . . er, skinny and spirited slave. I have no doubt we could find you another, better suited to your esteemed house. The bid stands at thirty. Are there any others?"

"Fifty," the man called again. "Perhaps my brother lacks the ability to properly train his slaves." The man continued, as he approached the platform, "That is, the *will* to discipline his servants. I'm sure I can handle this boy, even if he cannot. Fifty drachmae, I said. Are you refusing my offer?"

"Lord Tannis," groveled the auctioneer, kneeling to whisper to the man, "you must realize that not a soul in Narda will bid against you for anything you desire. This slave can fetch three times as much for Hannel as you offer. Please, tell me what it is you require, and I'm sure we can find a slave better suited to your need. Even one sold by . . . someone else."

"And you must realize," Tannis replied, "I do not care for a better-suited slave. I have no need of a slave at all. If my treacherous brother's profit is diminished by my purchase of this slave, then my trip to the market is a success, and my day is complete."

Then he addressed Karek, who stood nearby. "And you may tell him you heard me say so . . . with your own ear."

Turning his attention back to the auctioneer, Lord Tannis said, "I'll either have this boy for a slave . . . or *you*. Decide."

The auctioneer sprang back to Daniel's side, announcing to the crowd, almost in warning, "The honorable and esteemed coruler of Narda, Lord Tannis, desires this slave for his own and has offered fifty drachmae. Are there any other bids?"

The crowd was silent.

"Sold!" the auctioneer shouted, wiping his brow and giving every evidence that having lost any additional commission was still a very good thing.

Daniel was led off the platform to be introduced to his new owner.

37 CHAPTER

ily saw a blank mask of resignation on Daniel.

In her husband's face she read confusion and frustration and sorrow. How could this be happening? Had Cantor not risked his life to restore Daniel to his family?

I'm praying again, God Who Sees Further than Me. How can this be the right outcome? Where is the message of mercy today?

Cantor showed nothing but resolution as he approached Lord Tannis. "What will you do with him?" Cantor asked curtly, with no attempt at subservience.

"He's my hostage."

"But what use is he to you?" Cantor boldly inquired. "If his family won't redeem him, what earthly use do you have for him? What will redeem him? How much will you take?"

"Hope," Tannis replied without explanation. "My price is . . . hope." Brusquely turning to the auctioneer, he gave orders for Daniel to be delivered to his home.

But what hope was there?

Then to Cantor, Tannis added, "Come to my house this evening around sunset. Your wife and the giant should come as well."

And he strode away.

When Cantor and Lily arrived at Lord Tannis' home, they were ushered into the dining salon. Lord Tannis rose to greet them and show them to their places.

The only other person present was Daniel.

To Lily's surprise, not only was he clean and dressed in new clothes; he reclined at table like a guest.

The questioning look on her face must have been correctly interpreted by Daniel, for he returned a glance of confusion and suspicion.

Fingering the pouch of stones in her pocket, Lily thought, *I'm praying again, You Who Know the End from the Beginning. What is happening here? Is this an answer or a new form of cruelty? Is this the hope Lord Tannis spoke of or a deception? Help me not confuse facts with Truth.*

Supper was pleasant but subdued. The conversation seemed to deliberately avoid any discussion of Daniel's fate. It centered instead around the perfect timing of Cantor's return when the Herodian guards had given up waiting for him and left Narda.

Only once did Daniel even attempt to speak. When Cantor spoke of reaching Ecbatana and Melchior's home, Daniel could not resist asking whom Cantor had met there.

At his first words, Tannis corrected, "Stop. You are still my property. You are still my hostage."

So the discussion changed to a series of pointed inquiries about Yeshua of Nazareth.

"I want the truth," Tannis demanded. "Who is he?"

Lily loved speaking of the lives she had seen Yeshua touch . . . cures for leprosy of the soul as well as of the body.

Tannis bore in like a falcon swooping on a dove. "Yes, but what authority do you have to speak in his name? Eh? What?"

Cantor replied, "He told us: 'Heal the sick. Raise the dead. Cleanse those who have leprosy. Drive out demons.'"[45]

"Yes," Lily agreed eagerly, "we are to tell everyone, 'The Kingdom of Heaven is near.'[46] Then she added, "He said, 'Go to the lost sheep of the House of Israel.'"[47]

Tannis snorted. "I think that description applies to me."

Quietly Cantor added, "He also said, 'I am sending you out like lambs among wolves.'"[48]

"So you have the authority to act in his name?" Tannis demanded again, abruptly.

Cantor gazed at Lily before replying. When she nodded, he declared, "Yes."

"Then this will be your chance to prove it." Tannis addressed Cantor and Lily but stared at Daniel while speaking.

During supper the light streaming into the hall had changed color from yellow to orange to pastels to violet as the sun settled. The progression was most noticeable through an arched window above a door. Beyond the portal Lily glimpsed the topmost branches of a tree, so the exit must lead to a private garden.

As the purple shadows deepened, Lily heard moaning. It was soft at first, almost undetectable, but grew in volume and intensity as the light fled and darkness settled across Narda.

"Behind these walls is my greatest treasure—the one thing in this world I love above all else. Also my greatest sorrow. Daniel," Tannis instructed suddenly, "open the garden door."

The hinges of the gate groaned. From within the garden a steady wail, like that of a wounded animal, pierced the night.

It was Mary, the mother of Yeshua, who recognized Melchior and Esther at the gates of Zachai's estate. She spread her arms wide to embrace and welcome them to the banquet.

It had been over thirty years since they first met Mary and Yosef in the Beth-lehem home of Zadok the shepherd. Yeshua had been an infant in His mother's arms.

Now the beloved son of Mary, the One for whom the stars had rejoiced, was grown and celebrated by the *am ha aretz*, the common folk of the land. And yet, even as Herod the Great had sought the life of the infant Yeshua, now Herod's son Antipas and others were also determined to kill Him. How would this end? Melchior wondered, as they sat down at the long tables in Zachai's courtyard.

It seemed to Melchior as if no time had passed. The old shepherd bore the scars of Herod's massacre of the sons of Beth-lehem. There were a few others in the company who looked familiar to Melchior, but of all expressions, Mary's smile was like being welcomed home.

And it was in her embrace that Esther finally let her tears spill out. ". . . and his name is Daniel . . . my heart . . . breaking . . . so worried . . . my son . . . my son."

Mary listened and listened, saying little to Esther but providing a safe place in her eyes.

Melchior did not express his doubts aloud. Had he done the right thing? Should he have let Daniel leave? Could he have soothed the troubled waters between Joshua and Daniel before their rivalry became so destructive? There were a thousand little what-ifs in Melchior's life. All were summed up in one question: Could he have been a better father?

He heard his own silent heartache expressed in Esther's outpouring to Mary. Two women, two sons. Was Mary's heart breaking as well? Melchior knew Mary had every right to fear for her son's future.

The dome of the synagogue of Jericho loomed above the walls of Zachai's estate. Melchior knew the leaders who remained outside the celebration even now were plotting harm to Yeshua. Envoys had been sent to Jerusalem with the news he was traveling there for Passover.

Behind Mary's smile was a solemn concern.

The night wore on as the waxing moon settled in the west like the sail of a ship on pilgrimage to Jerusalem for Passover. Would Daniel be among the throngs of the festival? Melchior wondered. Would they find their son in Jerusalem so they could tell him he was loved and would be welcomed back home?

Yeshua seemed to know Esther and Melchior at a glance, though He had been too small to have any memory of them. Mary leaned close to her son's ear and whispered something to Him. An explanation of why they had come? A search for their lost son that had, by chance, led them here to Yeshua . . .

He came to them as they stood beneath the giant fig tree in the courtyard. He was tall, lean, and bronzed by the sun of Israel. His warm brown eyes were flecked with gold. He smiled broadly as He clasped Melchior's hand.

"And you are Esther," He said, touching Esther's shoulder. "Mother told me so much about you . . . your journey from the East. The way you helped us."

Esther seemed unable to speak in His presence. At His touch, her tears began again.

Yeshua closed His eyes a moment and nodded slowly as though He could see it all . . . everything from the beginning.

Melchior said, "His name is Daniel." There was a catch in his voice. "My son, my child, the thing I love most in my life. And also my greatest sorrow. Yeshua, we were not searching for you when we went out to search for our son. But alone we are helpless to find him. Hopeless to help him. Can you give us hope? Can you help us regain our lost son?"

Within the confines of the torchlit garden, a howling boy child of about seven crouched in a sandbox. A pale, haggard woman in her midthirties hovered over the boy. She looked up sharply as the gate swung open.

Wild-eyed, the boy bared his teeth at the figures in the portal. Sinking down, he clutched his knees and rocked back and forth, moaning . . . moaning.

Tannis' voice caught with emotion as he spoke. "My son. His name is Daniel. My son, my child, the thing I love most in all the world. His mother was killed in our camp by brigands. He saw her die and has never stopped living that horror from that moment 'til this. I have been alone and helpless to find a way to bring him home. Hopeless to help him. Can you—in the name and by the authority of this One, Yeshua of Nazareth whom you serve—give me hope? Can the One who healed the exiled lepers of Mak'ob now redeem the son I have lost?"

And so it had come to this. Five hundred miles separated Yeshua of Nazareth from the two lost sons of Israel, yet the distance between freedom and captivity, joy and sorrow, health or sickness, life or death could be measured in the space of ten heartbeats.

Yeshua drew Esther and Melchior close against Himself.

Cantor and Lily wrapped their arms around the boy.

Esther felt the breath of Yeshua against her hair.

Lily cradled small Daniel close beneath her chin.

Melchior heard the steady heartbeat of Yeshua, Son of the Most High God.

Cantor encircled small Daniel and Lily with his arms, lifted his eyes, and began to pray.

As the gates of heaven swung wide, there was no distance between the home of a warlord in Parthia and the garden of a tax collector in Jericho.

Ten beats of Yeshua's heart.

Ten words proclaimed the healing, restoration, and redemption of two beloved sons.

Yeshua whispered quietly, "I . . . praise . . . you, Father, for . . . redeeming . . . lost . . . sons! Daniel! Return!"

Five hundred miles away, at that instant, a mighty wind sprang up. Cantor raised his face to heaven and cried out loudly, "In the Mighty Name of your Son, Yeshua! Our Savior!"

On the distant plain in the land of the two rivers, lightning flashed and thunder followed. Hawk cried and rose on the updraft. He soared above their heads as Daniel, the son of Tannis, joyfully cried out, "Oh, Papa! Papa!" The child rushed into the open arms of his father.

It began to rain as Cantor and Lily and Daniel, son of Melchior, returned to rejoin Lono at the Synagogue of the Exiles.

Letters of warning came that week from members of the Sanhedrin in Jerusalem to Rabbi Nehemiah and his brother Ahava. These few secret followers of Yeshua wrote:

Tell no man. Do not speak openly of what you have witnessed. The chief priest and the elders conspire with Herod Antipas and with Rome to silence Yeshua of Nazareth forever. They seek also the lives of those He has healed, and they seek to kill those who have tasted death and returned from olam haba at the command of Yeshua. My brothers, we must do what we can. For every circumstance beyond our power to change, we must trust in the will of the Almighty. If this is founded upon the Law and the Prophets of the God of Avraham, Yitz'chak, and Isra'el, then the Kingdom will remain forever until every prophecy is fulfilled and every foundation stone is in place!

There were rumors that Herodian soldiers would return. Agents of the religious hypocrites who sat in judgment on the High Council were on the march with a dark purpose. Those whom Yeshua had healed would continue to be in danger of their lives. Herod Antipas desired that all who had been touched by Yeshua would be silenced quickly.

The plan to end the life of Yeshua, son of David, born the true King of Israel, was undiminished from the time of Herod the Great.

Yet in this Jewish outpost there was certainty that Yeshua was the stone the builders had rejected. Yeshua was the chief prophetic cornerstone of the Kingdom of God.

Because their very lives were proof of who Yeshua was and is, there was an ever-present danger to the thirty-six exiles from Mak'ob. For this reason, through centuries to come, the identities of the exiles would remain hidden until all was fulfilled. This was understood by all present in the synagogue that day.

Rabbi Ahava stood to the side as Cantor taught the lesson of the names of the ten stones set in the foundation of the Synagogue of the Exiles. The children of Mak'ob gathered round the Star of David and traced the lapis letters with their eyes. Motes of dust spun on shafts of sunlight beaming down. The polished gilt and gold leaf of the ancient Temple artisans exiled here four hundred years before glistened as if the building had been constructed recently.

"Everything means something," Cantor said to the children, touching each of the ten stones in turn with his staff.

The students recited the ten names aloud as he tapped each one: "The Stone. Wonderful. Counselor. Servant. Branch. Seed. Prophet. Priest. King. Messiah." Each name contained a prophecy recorded in the Law and the Prophets.

"Upon these foundation stones are engraved what the Law and the Prophets declare about Israel's Messiah. We who were the lepers of Mak'ob know him. We met him. He healed us all, and we know his names are true."

And then Cantor swept his staff over the six points of the Star of David. "On each of the ten stones from Yerushalayim that make the mosaic of David's shield, there is a hidden word." Cantor smiled at the intense concentration of all. "How do you spell the Hebrew word *stone*?"

"*Alef, bet, nun*," the children replied in unison.

Cantor repeated the sequence. "*Alef, bet, nun* spells the word *Eben*, Stone. Now here is the secret. Here is the wonder of the holy language of Torah. Children, what happens when you read the word *Eben* in reverse?"

Yod raised her hand. "The letters are *nun, bet, alef*. This makes the word *Naba*."

Cantor winked at Lily as gasps and cries of delight rose throughout the group. "And *Naba* means?"

Daniel, son of Tannis, blurted out in excitement, "Eben, Stone, spelled backwards, is Naba. Which means, 'To prophesy . . . to speak by inspiration.'"

Cantor seemed pleased. "Well spoken. *Eben* equals *Naba*. *Stone* read in reverse commands *proclaim prophecy*. And so you see why it is spoken by the sages that even if the voices of men refuse to proclaim praise and thanks and glory to the name of our Messiah, Yeshua, the stones of Israel will cry out that our Messiah, the Son of David, has come to redeem Israel." He smiled as the young ones clearly comprehended the meaning of David's Psalm 118: *The stone which the builders rejected.*

Cantor, who had seen the power of Torah in *olam haba*, continued, "Everywhere, in all of Scripture when you read the word *Stone*, read it also in reverse: *Eben. Naba*. Examine the meaning closely and ask if that Scripture also proclaims a prophecy. The *prophecy* which the builders rejected has become the chief *prophecy* by which God's living Temple is built."[49]

The religious leaders in Jerusalem had indeed rejected and reinterpreted every ancient foundational Scripture foretelling details about Israel's Messiah.

"His name is Yeshua! Which means 'Salvation'!"

Lily grasped the ten small stones in her pocket. *I'm praying again, You Who Command That the Stones of Israel Praise the One Who Fulfills Your Covenant. Help us, the healed lepers of Mak'ob, to be Living Stones, proclaiming that prophecy has been fulfilled in you! May our voices be heard in all the world! Oh, redeem us quickly, Son of David! Corner Stone, Wonderful, Counselor, Servant, Branch, Seed, Prophet, Priest, King, Messiah! Yeshua, you alone are Redeemer of exiles! Even so, come quickly! Amen!*

And he arose and came to his father.
But while he was still a long way off,
his father saw him and felt compassion,
and ran and embraced him and kissed him.
And the son said to him,
"Father, I have sinned against heaven and before you.
I am no longer worthy to be called your son."
But the father said to his servants,
"Bring quickly the best robe, and put it on him,
and put a ring on his hand, and shoes on his feet.
And bring the fattened calf and kill it,
and let us eat and celebrate.
For this my son was dead and is alive again;
he was lost . . . and is found."

LUKE 15:20-24

Epilogue

Shimon Sachar was alone in the secret Chamber of Scrolls beneath Jerusalem's Temple Mount. He had found the scroll of the exiles of Mak'ob, just where Eben Golah had promised him during their first meeting on a wintery afternoon in London.

Tenth jar. Tenth row. First room.

But who was Eben Golah? How did he figure into the centuries of guardians who had protected the Chamber of Scrolls? And why had Moshe not explained his connection with a man he had fought beside in 1941 during the Nazi offensive in Iraq?

Shimon rewrapped the Scroll of the Ten Stones as he wondered about the destiny of all those who had been exiles from Mak'ob. They had fled to the land that had begun its history as the location of Eden. For centuries Narda had remained the haven of Jewish exiles and scholars.

Now the stones of Jerusalem carried away during the Babylonian Exile were hidden beneath the dust of Iraq. Eden, Narda, was known to the world as the Muslim terrorist stronghold of Fallujah.

In these fierce last days, the fertile land between the rivers had deteriorated from Paradise to a battleground of demons.

"An ancient war," Eben Golah had warned Shimon.

Shimon tipped the clay jar. A small leather pouch spilled out from the bottom of the amphora. A scrap of parchment and a hawk's feather were tied to it.

As he carefully opened the bag, ten small smooth stones spilled out onto the table. Shimon placed them in the palm of his hand, imagining Lily and Cantor and little Yod with them. Then he unrolled the parchment and read the Hebrew words, written in the same neat hand as the scroll:

Many who were with us in Mak'ob from the beginning have fallen asleep in the Lord. They await the final resurrection, when the voice of Yeshua will call them from the dust.

There are yet some who remain in this world to bear witness to each new generation of the world to come. We who live on sometimes envy those who passed through the gates before us. We comfort one another when we meet together in each new generation.

I have hope that in our exile from olam haba, the Lord is teaching and guiding, and, as He promised, the Ruach HaKodesh is within the Living Stones of His Kingdom.

It is written by our brother Paul that to live is for the sake of Messiah, but to leave this world is a treasure to be gained.[50]

At the passing of my beloved, I once asked El'azar his opinion of the length of days for those who died and yet were raised. When would our final redemption, GEULaH, put an end to our exile, GOLaH.

He thought perhaps that we who died and were raised to life at the command of Yeshua would not sleep in the dust of earth again. The length of our exile from our true home will not end until Israel is once again a nation. Then it is written that our Redeemer will return from olam haba to reign in Jerusalem for eternity.

Wherever the Jewish people are exiled from their homeland, we are not there by chance. The Commander of all History has exiled us to teach the nations the prophecies that mark the End of Time and the Beginning of Eternity.

The exiles of Israel will return to their homeland. Then we, along with all the world, must look up! For His return and our redemption are near!

Fear Not!
Testimony of Eben Golah
Council of Ephesus
Anno Domini 431

Yeshua answered,

"If I want him to remain alive

until I return,

what is that to you?

You must follow Me."

JOHN 21:22

Digging Deeper into
TENTH STONE

Dear Reader,

Have you ever wondered what your worth is to the Creator of the universe? if He would stoop to help somebody like you? Have you ever grieved for the path a loved one has taken? Or for the path you yourself have taken, and all the hurt you've caused others? Do you wonder if you could ever rebel against God so much that He'd stop caring for you? Do you fear your present circumstances—or the future?

If you've had these questions and thoughts, you're not alone.

In *Tenth Stone*, Yod, Lily, Cantor, Rabbi Ahava, and other former lepers leave the Valley of Mak'ob after they are healed by Yeshua. Yod, the littlest of the lepers, is considered of no value in society, yet to Yeshua, she is of the greatest value! He holds her in His arms as she dies and brings her back from heaven to become part of Lily and Cantor's family. Lily, who would have died in the Valley, and Cantor, who died and was brought back to life by Yeshua, were entrusted with the most important of all missions—to take the good news of Yeshua's transforming touch and redemption to those who need His hope and the freedom from fear.

Melchior and Esther grieve for Daniel, their rebellious son. They wonder what they have done wrong . . . what they could have done differently. Should they have let him go his own way? Where could he be now? Is there any way to regain their lost son? any miracle great enough to bring him back to their arms?

It is only when Daniel, the arrogant young rebel, realizes that his undisciplined, selfish behavior has caused Lono, his devoted friend, to be beaten nearly to death that he becomes broken. How far Daniel has strayed from his childhood faith. Is it possible his life can be redeemed? Will he ever be able to return home?

Lord Tannis, who has done so much wrong in his life, harbors a secret sorrow. Would the Healer—if that's truly who Yeshua is—stoop to help someone such as him? Even if it is to restore his son, Daniel—an innocent victim of a horrible evil?

Dear reader, what plan might be unfolding in your life? Do you think God has enough grace and mercy for you, and for those you love?

Following are six studies. You may wish to delve into them on your own or share them with a friend or a discussion group. They are designed to take you deeper into the answers to these questions:

- Does God really see and hear me? Does He care? How much am I worth to Him?
- Is Yeshua who He says He is? How can I know for sure?
- Can God still love me, even if I've chosen to walk away from Him? Can I be forgiven, no matter what I've done? no matter whom I've hurt?
- How can I break free from fear?
- My heart is so broken; how can I find hope again?
- Is heaven real? And if so, what will it be like?

What are you longing for? searching for? Why not come home, as Daniel and Lord Tannis did, to Yeshua's embrace of love, warmth, and acceptance? He's waiting, just for you. In *Tenth Stone*, may the promised Messiah come alive to you . . . in more brilliance than ever before.

1 THE LEAST OF THESE

The Lord did not set His love upon you and choose you because you were more in number than any other people, for you were the least of all the people.
— DEUTERONOMY 7:7

What people do you consider to be "important" in today's society? What people do you consider to be "least"? What qualifications do you use to decide "important" or "least"?

_____

_____

_____

On a scale of one (being of no importance) to ten (being of great importance) to God, where would you place yourself, and why?

_____

_____

_____

In the days when *Tenth Stone* took place, leprosy was greatly feared. All those who showed even a beginning spot of leprosy—even children—were sent to the Valley of Mak'ob to live out the end of their days. All who came to the Valley knew they could not leave . . . except through death. Yod, the smallest citizen of the leper colony, had never known anything but Mak'ob, since she was born there.

Yet in spite of the continual reminder of death that surrounded her, she dreamed of being Cantor and Lily's daughter—of being part of a family. Then Cantor died . . . and those in the Valley lost hope. When Lily left the Valley to take a baby boy to safety, Yod weakened and was carried to the Dying Cave. Only heartbeats remained of her life when Yeshua entered the Valley. . . .

READ

"Messiah! Healer of Lepers! . . . He is here! On the stone of the bema. Teaching! Healing!"

"He has come to heal us all!" . . .

Yod heard the shuffling of feet near where she lay. Did they not see her?

There was a rustle of tattered blankets as those who shared the darkness with her moved toward the light. . . . But Yod was alone. Forgotten. Left behind in the darkness. . . .

   —P. 5

[Yeshua] asked, "But is this every one of us? All the lepers of Israel?"

The old rabbi frowned and scanned the ranks. "Everyone?"

Yeshua questioned him. "One little lamb is missing. Counting from the smallest to the largest. *Yod* to *lamed*. All of Israel." . . .

Ahava's eyes widened. "But where has she gone? There is a little girl, you see. Yod is her name . . . our little one! Our youngest child! She was in the Dying Cave. Did anyone carry Yod here?"

No one answered. A moan arose from the congregation. Had the littlest in Israel perished just before the moment of deliverance? Had they left this one precious soul behind?

   —P. 6

ASK

If you were Yod, what would you be thinking? Would you be resigned to the fact that everyone has left you? Would you still hope in the stories of the great Healer? Why or why not?

_____

_____

_____

Have you ever felt forgotten by God? In what circumstance(s)? How has that time influenced the way you think of God now? the way you live?

_____

_____

_____

If you were one of the people in the Valley who had suffered so greatly and you just realized little Yod was missing, would you be most concerned with your own healing? finding Yod? Both? Something else? Explain.

_____

_____

_____

READ

All the people of Mak'ob watched in silence as the light of Yeshua's torch fell on every rag and mound of blankets in His search for the child. . . .

The Great Shepherd cried, "Yod! It's Yeshua! I have been looking for you, little one! Searching . . ."

Yeshua gathered Yod into His arms and held her close. . . .

He kissed her bloody cheek and stroked her hair. Tiny stubs that had been feet protruded from his arms. Moments passed as he held her.

—PP. 6–7

"The letter *yod* hangs above the other letters like a little bird. *Yod* begins the word *Israel* . . . Yis-ra-el. . . . So Israel begins with what is smallest. . . . Israel ends with the largest letter, *lamed*. This proves that the Almighty, blessed be he, loves all of Israel from the smallest to largest. From the youngest to the eldest. And everyone in between."

—PP. 3–4

ASK

Why do you think it was so important to Yeshua to find this *one little child* in the midst of the crowd?

_____

_____

_____

Do you believe the Almighty loves *everyone*, from the smallest to the largest? From the youngest to the eldest? And everyone in between? Why or why not?

_____

_____

_____

Do you believe the Almighty loves and values *you*, specifically? Why or why not? What has happened in your life to bring you to that conclusion?

_____

_____

_____

READ

Hawk perched on the highest window ledge of the classroom. A flock of children laughed and pointed and called out. One cry rang like a bell above the others: "It's Cantor's hawk, I tell you!"

Lily recognized the voice of little Yod, child of the last thousand heartbeats! But she did not recognize the little girl—with curls now the color of cinnamon and bright, clear eyes a slightly darker shade of brown.

Lily gasped with joy. Cantor grasped her hand.

Yod exclaimed, "It is! Cantor's hawk come all the way from Sorrow!"

A boy, a year or two older, agreed. "Hawk! He's followed us here and found us!"

Children, beautiful and perfect, discussed the identity of the speckled raptor who observed them solemnly. . . .

I'm praying again, You Who Are the God of the Living . . . you who love us in this world and love us in olam haba. *You saw these children always. You knew what they looked like beneath their ragged flesh and suffering. You remade them what they would have been if . . . if only there were no sickness or sorrow or death. Beautiful! . . .*

How many had been destined for the Dying Cave before the evening Yeshua entered the Valley of Sorrows? Blind from leprosy, they had lost the ability to see. Robbed of speech, they had been unable to laugh . . . until Yeshua came into the Valley of their sorrow.

Throughout the long night Yeshua had healed them all . . . all . . . hands, feet, noses, and ears . . . new faces . . . laughter! Life! . . .

—PP. 103–104

What did Yeshua teach about the smallest child in His Kingdom? "The smallest, the youngest child, the *tsaowr,* the most vulnerable of all in the kingdom of *olam haba,* is greater than the greatest prophet."

Lily's heart understood what He meant. *Tsaowr,* the word for "child," was so close to the word *tsara,* the word for "leper."

Yeshua had proven that those little ones the world labeled valueless were of the greatest value to Him in heaven. Meanwhile, they were here on earth to try the metal of every man's heart. All the wealth and knowledge and position in the world were of small value compared to the worth of a child . . . a child like Yod, the smallest and least valued in all of Israel.

—P. 211

I was hungry and you gave Me something to eat. I was thirsty and you gave Me something to drink. I was a stranger and you invited Me in. I needed clothes and you clothed Me. I was sick and you looked after Me. I was in prison and you came to visit Me. . . . I tell you the truth, whatever you did for the least of these brothers of Mine, you did for Me.

—MATTHEW 25:35-36, 40

ASK

When has a child taught you a lesson about life? What was that lesson?

_____

_____

_____

How do you naturally respond when you pass by one of "the least of these" on a street corner?

_____

_____

_____

The next time you encounter a child who needs help, a lonely elderly person, a hungry street person, a disabled person, or anyone else considered "the least of these," in what way(s) could you respond like Yeshua? How will you put those good intentions into action in the next few months?

_____

_____

_____

WONDER . . .

Lily touched each stone on the window ledge. The blessings and promises of Israel were hers even in this place of exile.

I'm praying again, You Who Number the Stars and Number the Grains of Sand. . . . We who are valueless in the eyes of the world are worth the world to you. Protect us as we wait for the return of our Hope.

—P. 211

Do you see your worth through the eyes of other imperfect humans or through the eyes of a loving Lord? No matter your "value" in society, your value is inestimable in God's eyes. If you lived every moment in the light of that Truth, how would your life and relationships change?

2 | SEARCHING FOR PROOF

"Test every spirit," [old Balthasar] said. "Search the Scriptures and see if everything—every single signal— agrees with all the prophets have said. If he fails in one thing, he is a false prophet and not Messiah."
—P. 23

If you turned on the TV and someone was claiming to be the "messiah" of the world, would you believe that person's claims or not? Why?

_____

_____

_____

What kind of proof would you need to believe that someone is indeed the Messiah of the world? Explain.

_____

_____

_____

Throughout the centuries, many have claimed to be the Messiah—the one sent to save the world. Such claims abounded in the days of Melchior the Magus, and they still abound today. So how can you know who is real and who is a false prophet?

Thirty years earlier, Melchior, court astronomer to King Phraates of Parthia, had followed the stars that led him (and his bride-to-be and her

grandfather) on a life-changing journey to meet an unusual baby in Beth-
lehem. Now he's convinced, by the signs he sees in the heavens, that the
plan he became aware of years ago is progressing.

"It's happening now," Melchior tells himself. "It must be. He is in his
thirties. By now he must be about his Father's business" (p. 11).

But who will believe Melchior? Could this baby—now a grown man—
indeed be the Healer who has transformed so many lives and hearts?

READ

Quizzical blue eyes regarded Melchior from over a prominent hooked
nose. Hasdrubal spread his hands in deprecation. "With all due respect to
our host, surely we have seen messianic pretenders before this. Always they
come to a bad end. Always they cause tumult. Always misguided and foolish
commoners lose their lives to no purpose. Why does the good Magus think
this occasion any different?"

Ben Levy spoke up on behalf of his friend. "Have you forgotten what
occurred thirty-some years ago? It wasn't only Melchior who followed the
miraculous conjunction and saw the babe, but also Balthasar of this city—a
great Magus and man of great faith. Joining them were men of many distant
lands . . . the Indies, Africa, Tarsus in Pamphyllia. . . . Surely you do not say
they all agreed on the same false tale or dreamed the same dream?"

"No, no," Hasdrubal argued. "I mean no disrespect to Melchior, or to
the others you name. But where is the proof the one they found survived?
Did you not say Herod the Butcher King murdered the babies in Beth-
lehem? How do you know if the one you met still lives?"

Melchior tapped his chest. "I know it . . . in here."

"But where is he, then?" Sheramin demanded. "Why has he not
declared himself?"

—PP. 20–21

ASK

If you were Melchior, Balthasar, or one of the men from distant lands and had seen a miraculous joining of stars that pointed the way toward the birthplace of a baby, would you think there was something unusual about that baby? Why or why not?

_____

_____

_____

If this baby was reported to be murdered, would you believe that he could have lived, like Melchior did? Or would you be dubious, like Hasdrubal? Why or why not?

_____

_____

_____

Have you ever known something in your heart that you couldn't prove? What was the circumstance? Were you proven right, in the long run? Tell the story.

_____

_____

_____

READ

"Tell us, Melchior, what you saw in the sky tonight. I heard wonder in your voice as you described it to us. I confess I am no student of the stars, though I honor their Maker. What does it mean?"

"More than ever," Melchior returned thoughtfully, "I miss the wise counsel of my wife's grandfather, Old Balthasar. He was a true sage . . .

a wise man in the tradition of the ancients. But since you ask, here are my thoughts: The amazing conjunction we saw tonight—five of the seven lights of the menorah—was entirely contained within the sign of the Bull . . . what the Egyptians call Apis and the Greeks Taurus. What we call Shor. Disregarding what the heathen do, what use do we make of bullocks?"

"They are sacrificed as thank-offerings," Sheramin replied. "When the Almighty has answered our prayers, delivered us from danger, forgiven us great wrongs and restored our lives, or when a task of great importance is complete, then we give him a bullock as a thank-offering."

"Just so," Melchior agreed. "When something of great significance has been completed, there is still a sacrifice to be made."

"I do not understand," Hasdrubal argued. "What has this to do with Messiah?"

"I think his mission is already coming to its climax," Melchior said. "He who is the Splendor of the Almighty, The Lord of the Sabbath, the Heavenly Adam, and the Divine Messenger, empowered by the *Ruach HaKodesh*—combining all those titles in himself, just as we saw tonight—for him, the thank-offering of conclusion is coming soon."

"But, good friend," Sheramin disagreed, "your sign would seem to say not that the Chosen One would make a sacrifice, but that he would *be* the sacrifice."

"I know," Melchior replied softly. "I do not yet understand, yet I see the same conclusion myself. What does the prophet Isaias say? *He was pierced for our transgressions, He was crushed for our iniquities. . . . By His wounds we are healed.*"

"But this Yochanan, called the Baptizer. He's already been killed," ben Levy said flatly.

Melchior put his hands flat on the table in front of him. "I have had word . . . of another. Let me tell you about him."

—PP. 21–22

ASK

When you think of a "messiah," what images come to mind? What kind of person would "save the world"? What qualities would he/she have? What would he/she look like?

_____

_____

_____

Look back in history at some of the false messiahs.

- Just after Yeshua walked the earth, a man who called himself Simon bar Kokhbah (meaning, "Simon, son of a star") was announced as the Messiah. But he led a rebellion against Rome that led to the final destruction of Judea and to the Diaspora (the dispersal of the Jews throughout the world).
- In the late 1800s in Sudan, a warlord named Muhammad Ahmed announced himself to be the "Mahdi"—a messiah figure in the religion of Islam. He and his armies slaughtered his opponents, including the inhabitants of Khartoum, before he finally died of typhus.
- In the 1900s, Adolf Hitler rose to power in Germany. While setting up what he called the Thousand Year Reich (Germany's domination of Europe), he massacred countless Jews in his diabolical mission to rid the world of the Jewish "vermin" and establish a pure German race. He was responsible for the deaths of over 46 million Europeans in WWII and the destruction of much of Europe. He committed suicide just before Berlin fell to the Soviet army.

Was personal sacrifice for the cause a part of the lives and thinking of these three false messiahs? Why or why not? How did their claims turn out? What was the result to the people left behind?

_____

_____

_____

What makes the Messiah in the prophecy by Isaiah so different from others who have claimed to be a messiah?

_____

_____

_____

READ

"The sun of righteousness will rise, with healing in its wings," Melchior murmured. . . .

Motioning with his right hand, Melchior drew an imaginary circle around the wandering star called The Righteous. "The prophet Malachi," he explained. "You recall I told you last night that only Tzadik and Holy Fire—the Sun—were missing from the menorah we all saw in the sky? But see where the Sun and Righteousness rise together!" . . .

Hasdrubal concurred. "The Anointed One, the Messiah, will have such power and authority that just touching the hem of his garment will cure disease. . . . And this Yeshua of Nazareth, of whom you spoke—does he have the gift of healing?"

"Miracles follow him wherever he goes," Melchior confirmed.

"Someone must go and investigate," Sheramin ventured. "This matter is too important to rely on the gossip of pilgrims and the hearsay evidence of camel drovers."

—PP. 22–23

ASK

Is Melchior's search of the skies the same as looking for astrological signs? Why or why not? If not, how would you distinguish the two? What is the purpose of Melchior's search? the purpose of searching for astrological signs?

_____

_____

_____

If a supposed messiah did miracles, would you be more tempted to believe him, or not? Explain. What kind of proof would convince you?

_____

_____

_____

READ

"Why not you, Melchior?" Hasdrubal suggested. "You were witness to him as a baby. Shouldn't you be the one to seek him again?"

Melchior frowned as he tugged his beard thoughtfully. "I intended to leave a year ago, but I am not allowed to. King Artabanus says he needs my advice in dealing with the civil unrest in Media, and as envoy to the Lords of the Marsh . . . that he cannot spare me for such a long journey."

"You think this is an excuse to keep you from going? Why?"

Raising his chin, Melchior stared at Jupiter. "The king read my report of the babe. He knows I am a convert to our Jewish faith. He knows I went to worship beside the cradle three decades ago. Herod, may his name be blotted out of all memory, is not the only king who fears for his throne. Artabanus knows Messiah will command the loyalty of all the Jews in Parthia when he comes."

"And he's right," Hasdrubal agreed. "Though I think Lord Caiaphas, high priest in Jerusalem, looks more to Rome than to heaven for his obedience."

—P. 23

ASK

What did Artabanus and Caiaphas have to lose if they believed in the claims of Yeshua as Messiah? What did Herod have to lose?

_____

_____

_____

Why do you think people today choose to not believe in Yeshua as Messiah, in spite of all the well-kept records speaking of His miracles and confirming that He has fulfilled every prophecy in the Old Testament?

_____

_____

_____

WONDER . . .

The students recited the ten names aloud as he tapped each one: "The Stone. Wonderful. Counselor. Servant. Branch. Seed. Prophet. Priest. King. Messiah." Each name contained a prophecy recorded in the Law and the Prophets.

"Upon these foundation stones are engraved what the Law and the Prophets declare about Israel's Messiah. We who were the lepers of Mak'ob know him. We met him. He healed us all and we know his names are true."

—P. 251

Yeshua did many other things as well. If every one of them were written down, I suppose that even the whole world would not have room for the books that would be written.
—JOHN 21:25

Have you met Yeshua? Do you know Him? If not, why not investigate the prophecies and Truths about Him in the Bible for yourself?

3 | MORE THAN JUST A STORY

There was a man who had two sons. The younger one said to his father,
"Father, give me my share of the estate." So he divided his property
between them.

Not long after that, the younger son got together all he had, set off for
a distant country and there squandered his wealth in wild living.
—LUKE 15:11-13

Have you ever done something bad just for the sake of adventure? When?
How did that adventure work out for you? for others? in the short term? in
the long term?

_____

_____

_____

How have you learned from your own past mistakes? Explain.

_____

_____

_____

On a scale of one (I can't believe you'd do *that*) to ten (there but by the grace of God go I), where would you place your understanding of, and empathy for, others' bad choices? Why?

_____

_____

_____

Check out any newspaper, magazine, or TV or radio talk show, and you'll find plenty of stories about people who have made poor choices that have led to their downfall. Or perhaps you know personally about taking a bad direction in life, because you've reaped the consequences in the past or you're reaping them now. Can you ever rebel against God so much that He stops caring for you? Can you run so far from Him that He can't find you?

The Parable of the Prodigal Son (read the entire story, with all its highs and lows, in Luke 15:11-32) is more than a good story. It shows that *anyone*—no matter how far they've fallen—can be restored. Look at Daniel, who grew up in a home with two godly parents, yet went so very, very wrong.

READ

"Be home in time for the New Moon supper," Daniel's mother had warned him. *"Important visitors coming. Rabbi Hasdrubal from Babylon will be here."*

Daniel snorted, then wiped his nose with the sleeve of his robe. Important? Stuffed and pompous, probably. All his father's visitors ever seemed able to discuss were politics, astronomy, and religion. Boring beyond belief. No music. No women. It was bad enough to be stuck here in a backwater place like Ecbatana. But when guests arrived from someplace exciting like Babylon or Ctesiphon, did they ever talk of exciting things? Never!

—PP. 13–14

ASK

How does Daniel view his life—and why? What kind of life does he adopt as a result? Does this life satisfy his craving for excitement?

_____

_____

_____

Has there been a time in your life when you could empathize with Daniel? If so, tell the story.

_____

_____

_____

READ

Joshua squeezed a little harder than necessary and dragged his brother a little faster than Daniel's stumbling steps could match. "I don't understand you," he scolded. "Ten years ago, when I was your age, I—"

"You were already running the family olive oil business . . . had a wife . . . went to synagogue every morning . . . I know, I know. Stop talking, won't you? My head is splitting."

With Joshua's greater height and greater strength it was easy for him to grab Daniel's other elbow and shake him. "You embarrass _me_!" he hissed. "Why can't you grow up?"

Daniel felt as if the dice were now inside his head, rattling around. "Why? Just because you were a grumpy old man at age thirteen, should I give up my friends?"

"Your friends?" Joshua sneered, dragging Daniel again. "Your friends only care about you because you buy them drinks and lose money to them. . . . I think Father should cut off your allowance until you prove you deserve it. You need to be taught a lesson. This is the last time you'll come home drunk!"

"Just . . . just stop shouting, will you?" Daniel asked. "Let me go to bed. Fix my miserable life tomorrow, but tonight leave me be."

—PP. 16–17

Daniel said, "I'm sorry, Father. I lost track of the time. You know how it is."

"No," Melchior corrected, "I don't know how it is. But I do know this cannot go on."

This level tone worried Daniel. There was no anger in Melchior's voice, just frustration and firm resolution.

"You are old enough to take an active role in the family business, but can I trust you with the simplest duty? Your sisters are married and provided for. Joshua is proving that when the time comes, he will preserve the two-thirds of my estate to which he is entitled. But what about you? How long would it take you to go through your third of the property?"

This was serious. His father was talking about dying. Daniel turned over and sat up, propping his head against the wall. "You aren't . . . you're not sick?"

"Nothing like it," Melchior replied. "Unless worried sick about you counts as an illness. Ever since losing the twins, your mother and I have doted on you. Clearly we've done you more harm than good."

"Don't say that, Father," Daniel begged. "I can do better."

"I'd like to believe that," Melchior said doubtfully. "What happened to the boy who was stuck to my side every observation night? The one who could name all the constellations without missing any? Where has he gone, and who is this . . . drunken lump who has taken his place?"

There was no response to this, and Daniel did not offer one.

—P. 29

"I've let you down, Daniel," Melchior asserted. "I don't know when it happened, but you've lost direction in your life."

"It's not . . . I mean, I can do better. . . ."

"Please don't interrupt," Melchior said sternly. "I see now that giving you tasks to do for me but not supervising the results has brought you to this point. You think it's all pointless make-work and can be ignored. I hoped by sending you out on different errands you'd find the part of my business you liked best and wanted to pursue. Instead you have gotten lazy, careless, and foolish. All that will stop today."

—PP. 30–31

ASK

Contrast the responses of these two men to Daniel's lifestyle:

- Joshua, his brother

_____

_____

_____

- Melchior, his father

_____

_____

_____

In your opinion, should Melchior feel responsible for his son's drinking, gambling, and irresponsibility? Why or why not?

_____

_____

_____

READ

"Dogs!" Karek chuckled at the pair of single dots facing upright. "You lose." He raked over the last of Daniel's coins.

Gaze fixed on nothing, Daniel slurred, "You cheated me. You're a cheat."

—P. 14

"What's happened to you? Here I am, bearing the most exciting news ever to reach Ecbatana, and you can't be bothered? . . . Hannel is here!" Bartok pronounced triumphantly.

"Who?" Daniel returned absently. His gaze strayed back across the last tally of oil jars. He spotted a place where he had made an extra mark. Was that five or six?

"Lord Hannel of the Marshes, that's who. The greatest Jewish warrior since Zamaris . . . maybe since Judah Maccabee."

"The one who rules Narda between the rivers?" Daniel queried, his interest growing in spite of himself.

—P. 42

It was close to midnight again when Daniel at last gave up his attempt to locate the accounting mistake. After another week's effort, he still had not found the error and his thoughts wandered so far from extra jugs of oil that at last he quit trying.

—P. 48

"You were working on the accounts of the First Pressing Oil, weren't you?"

Daniel admitted this, adding, "Vashti asked me to double-check some figures and copy them over into the permanent record."

Husband and wife exchanged a look Daniel immediately interpreted as meaning trouble. . . .

"Aha!" [Joshua] said, jabbing a forefinger like a knife. "Two months ago! Look! . . . Can't you do anything right? . . . You transposed the count! See that? Instead of 135 you wrote 531! Idiot!"

"Wait just a—"

"You don't understand, do you?" As if Daniel were not even present, Joshua faced Vashti and announced, "He doesn't even know what he's done wrong. How can anyone be so careless? so brainless? You! You? You are to have a third of Father's estate? Ha! Your error made me sell oil already promised to someone else . . . to the king! Don't you understand? Our jars wear the king's seal! Suppliers to the royal household! It's worth thousands of drachmae . . . and now we'll lose it because of your carelessness!"

—PP. 81–82

Great scholar, famous man, successful merchant—none of Melchior's well-deserved reputations impressed Daniel tonight. Daniel was tired of being disrespected and disregarded, and he blamed his father for allowing it to continue.

—P. 93

How Daniel arrived at the Jeweled Peacock that night he could never remember. Neither did he immediately know how he came to be propped in the corner by the fireplace, soaking wet, though that came to be clear soon enough.

He remembered hitting Bartok in the jaw and seeing him fly backwards into a wall and slide down it. He had a perfect recollection of Mina screaming, then yelling that she never, ever wanted to see him again.

—P. 97

ASK

How do the above seemingly small events in Daniel's life escalate, propelling him toward ruin?

_____

_____

_____

How could a different response and/or attitude in each of these events have changed the course of Daniel's life?

- Gambling with Karek and calling him a cheat

_____

_____

_____

- Going with Bartok to see the famed warrior, Lord Hannel

_____

_____

_____

- Looking for the accounting mistake

_____

_____

_____

- Vashti and Joshua finding Daniel's mistake

_____

_____

_____

- Blaming his father

_____

_____

_____

- Finding Bartok with Mina and his fight with Bartok

_____

_____

_____

What small events, if any, have added up to bigger trouble in your own life, or in the life of a loved one?

_____

_____

_____

When you look back at those events, in what way(s) could you have changed your own response and/or attitude toward them?

_____

_____

_____

READ

By the start of the High Holy Days, Daniel had made up his mind. . . . Daniel saw frozen looks of dismay and disbelief on all his family's faces gathered at supper, but he was determined to not draw back. He repeated his demand: "I said, you have often told me that I am entitled to one-third of your estate. That responsibility has been drummed into me over and over. All right, I believe you. And I want it now. . . . I am leaving either way, Father, but first I want to see if you are a man of your word."

Daniel heard a sharp intake of breath from his mother. No one ever questioned Melchior's integrity. Melchior had, many times in his life, suffered personal loss rather than go back on a commitment, even when the circumstances had not been his fault.

Mechanically, without emotion, as if speaking by rote, Melchior returned, "Are you determined? Will you not reconsider?"

Daniel could not believe it was this easy. The lift to his pride made it easy for him to be cruel. "I will not stay in this house one moment longer."

"Then my answer is . . . yes."

—PP. 107–108

There, Daniel told himself. *I knew it all along. My father doesn't love me. He has never loved me. He has only love enough for Joshua . . . never me. How could he not try to stop me? He expects I won't go through with this. But I'll show him! I'm not an eight-year-old running away from home. I'm really leaving.*

—P. 109

Daniel ached to turn and see if his father watched him go. But Daniel would not give his father the satisfaction of seeing him look back.

—P. 112

ASK

How does Daniel go out of his way to hurt his father—and why?

_____

_____

_____

Have you ever hurt someone you love because of pride, insecurity, or jealousy? What happened?

READ

After confinement within the dreary walls of a countinghouse, travel to anywhere seemed exciting. After tallying olive oil, of all mundane substances, now, suddenly, the world lay spread before him like an oyster teeming with innumerable pearls, waiting to be identified and seized.

—P. 114

It was suddenly horrifyingly clear: only glimpses of their trade goods, a little-known route, traveling on the Sabbath, passing a slaver and his captors! Ben Ariyb had never meant to do business with Daniel. Daniel and Lono _were_ his business, and these extra additions to the caravan were more than coincidence; they were there to ensure all went as planned.

—P. 143

"You're a slave now. That is your entire being. If you think of yourself as anything but a servant to me, you will die."

Daniel believed he now truly understood the meaning of the words and the advice they contained. _Hope is my enemy_, he thought. _I must resign myself to this new life or I cannot survive. . . ._

In that moment of recognition Daniel suddenly hated the carob trees. He hated feeding the pigs. He hated watering the pigs. He hated his life.

But he hated the carob trees most of all.

They seemed to him to represent everything he had left behind and now could never have again.

In his father's house he had never been a servant, much less a slave, still less a swineherd. His father would have shuddered at the thought.

What a change from last year.
—PP. 227–228

ASK
Compare Daniel's initial expectations with the realities of his life just a short while later.

_____

_____

_____

Have you (or a loved one) ever chafed against the restraints of home and family, wishing for life to be different? What happened as a result?

_____

_____

_____

READ
"Please!" [Daniel] said, "cut him down. For pity's sake, cut him down. He didn't deserve this; *I* did!"

"And you might dwell on that," Hannel agreed, "as you nurse him back to health. But mark me, Daniel ben Melchior. He is worth very little to me compared to your ransom. If you try to escape me again, he will not survive. It will be your doing."
—P. 206

Daniel knelt beside his friend. *God Almighty, Creator of all. You know the depth of this injustice I've helped to inflict on Lono. You know his good heart and his innocence. Mine is the body that should be bleeding. His scars should be mine. It is too late to change that, I know, but I beg you, more than anything I could ever ask for, please don't take him from this world. Ease his pain, Merciful God. Heal his wounds.*

His next thought caused tears to flow freely down his cheeks, and he cried the words aloud. "And don't let him hate me when he wakes! Please, let him forgive me for this horrible thing. I know I don't deserve it. I know I don't deserve such a faithful friend, but please, let him forgive me. . . .

"This man has done more for me in my life than I can remember, yet I've led him to this ruin. God!" he cried again heavenward. "How can I have done this? Why did I stray so far?"

—P. 210

ASK

Why did this one event, more than anything else, break Daniel's heart?

_____

_____

_____

Do you think you can ever rebel against God so much that He'll stop caring for you? Can you ever run so far from God that He won't be able to find you? Why or why not?

_____

_____

_____

Can you point to any circumstances in your life where God has used difficulties to restore, rebuild, or strengthen His relationship with you? If so, explain.

_____

_____

_____

WONDER . . .

"You say, 'Only talk to him in you heart, and you see him someday.' I belee dat, Mastah Daniel." Lono stopped and turned, looking up to Daniel in earnest. "And I talk to him in here ever' day. Thas' how you find him again."
—P. 138

If you have been a prodigal, what is keeping you from the healing touch of the Lord? Being restored to a loving relationship with God is only a matter of saying to Him, "Father, I know I've sinned against you. I've hurt others. Please forgive me." So why not take that step today? Come home to your heavenly Father!

If you, like Esther and Melchior, have grieved for a prodigal and wondered if you did the right things (or if you could have done anything different), what can you do to soothe the troubled waters? to help the prodigal want to come home?

> *While he was still a long way off, his father saw him and was filled with compassion for him; he ran to his son, threw his arms around him and kissed him. . . . The father said . . . "Let's have a feast and celebrate. For this son of mine was dead and is alive again; he was lost and is found."*
> —LUKE 15:20, 23-24

4 | BLESSED BY MIRACLES?

"Maybe just a rumor. A legend. But there are others whose lives have been blessed by miracles."
   —LORD TANNIS, P. 172

"Miracles follow him wherever he goes."
   —MELCHIOR, P. 23

"His miracles speak louder than words. . . . Don't be afraid. . . . He who sent us knows every step we take before we ever took the first. . . . No matter what happens in this life, Fear not."
   —CANTOR, PP. 160, 40, 223

What fears keep you awake at night—or wake you up? How do you handle those fears? To whom or to what do you turn to put those fears into perspective?

_____

_____

_____

What is your definition of a miracle? Does it have to be a big thing, or can it be a small thing? Have you or a loved one ever experienced what you'd call a miracle? If so, share the story!

_____

_____

_____

According to *Merriam-Webster's Collegiate Dictionary*, a *miracle* is "an extraordinary event manifesting divine intervention in human affairs." In *Tenth Stone*, Lily and Cantor experienced miracles. They were healed of their leprosy by the loving touch of Yeshua. Cantor, who had died and was in the grave, was raised to life again. Talk about miracles!

Still, as life moved on from the Valley of Sorrows, fear crowded into Lily's mind . . . fear of going outside the boundaries of what she had known in the Valley, fear of losing Cantor again, fear of the Herodian guards and how she and Cantor might be harmed.

Yet from the beginning of their journey from Mak'ob to their arrival and experiences at the Synagogue of the Exiles, miracles continued to mark their path.

READ

The heap marked one of the boundary points defining the Valley of Mak'ob.

Beside the warning mound was another stack, but not of rocks and stones. Inside a makeshift hutch of fallen branches and ragged cloth was a supply of unleavened bread, dried fish, preserved figs, and a round of hard cheese.

It was one of the donations friends of those condemned to Mak'ob sometimes left outside the Valley for those confined within.

"Look, Cantor," Lily exulted. "There's no one left in the Valley now! We can use this as provision for our journey."

"Too much for us, really," Cantor noted. "We can't even carry that much."

The clatter of hooves picking through loose stone made them turn. The newcomer was only a man leading a donkey on which rode a small boy. . . .

Without even pausing for breath, the man launched into an inquiry.

"Did you . . . see him?" he panted. "Is he nearby? Yeshua, the Healer? Do you know where he is?" . . .

Cantor smiled at the boy. He was about eight, Lily thought. Then Lily saw her husband's smile freeze on his face. Following the line of his wrinkled brow, Lily's gaze took in the child's legs. One was sound and whole.

The other was withered and the foot turned inward. . . .

Aaron patted his father's arm, the child doing the consoling. "It's all right, Father. You'll see."

I'm praying again, God of All Mercies. You see how much this father loves his son. Is there no miracle left for them? . . .

Abruptly Cantor said, "Lily. Come here and stand beside me." When she complied, wondering what was in his thoughts, he suggested, "Didn't Yeshua commission us to be his witnesses?" Without waiting for her response, he said, "But we were wrong about our duty beginning in Narda. Our job begins . . . here. Hold my hand. Put your other hand on Aaron's left shoulder and I'll do the same on the right." . . .

The boy looked down at his now perfectly strong, matching limbs and a wide, gap-toothed grin spread across his features. "See, Father! Pick me down."

And then, as if to prove it was no dream, Aaron jumped from the donkey's back and ran a quick circle around the animal before rushing to give his father a hug. "Thank you. Thank you for believing what I said about Yeshua! Thank you for taking me."

"But, Son, thank these . . ."

Cantor shook his head. "Not us. Give glory to God and praise him in Yeshua's name. But tell no one outside your village," he cautioned. "It might be dangerous for the boy."

"I understand . . . yes, certainly. But what can I do for you? Is there no need of yours I can meet? Anything at all?"

Cantor began to shake his head again, then stopped abruptly. Lily followed his gaze to where it rested on the beast of burden.

Minutes later, from the top of the next knoll, Lily turned back to wave to the father and son as they skipped and danced the path toward home. Lily walked alongside as Cantor led their new donkey, loaded with all the provisions of Mak'ob—a donkey now perfectly sound, and not lame at all.

—PP. 25–28

ASK

List all the miracles that happened in this story.

_____

_____

_____

Which miracles do you consider to be the most important, or biggest, and why?

_____

_____

_____

In what way(s) did Cantor's obedience to the commissioning of Yeshua lead to a further miracle?

_____

_____

_____

To whom did Cantor give credit for the healing? Why is this clarification important?

_____

_____

_____

Have you ever done something that didn't make any logical sense, just because the Lord prompted you to do it? If so, when? What happened as a result?

_____

_____

_____

READ

A patch of blackberries grew beside the highway. "Just for us," Lily said as they waded into them.

Cantor plucked one and held it up to examine the geometric pattern of the berry. "A miracle." He held it to his nose and inhaled the scent, then brought it to his ear as if it could whisper a message.

"What is the berry saying to you, Cantor?"

He did not hesitate. "Fear not. Fear nothing. Fear no man. Fear no moment. That is what the miracle of one blackberry or one blade of grass or . . . well, look." He swept his hand across the horizon. "Fear not."

—P. 39

An hour later, as they drew near the border crossing, Lily clutched Cantor's arm. Her anxiety increased with each passing step. Why was she so frightened? Was it because her only previous trip out of the Valley was so filled with danger and heartache?

But then she had still been a leper. That journey, fearful as it was, ended in triumph, not tragedy, at the feet of Yeshua of Nazareth. . . .

A guard, wearing armor but no helmet, lounged against a lean-to shelter, taking advantage of the only shade. He looked bored and barely straightened from his slouch at their approach. He did not bother to retrieve his spear from where it lay in the dust.

"Where are you going?" he demanded perfunctorily.

Cantor replied for them both. "My wife and I are going to Narda."

"Narda, eh?" the guard repeated. "Why Narda?"

"To show ourselves to the priest there," Cantor replied truthfully. . . .

"Pass," he said, jerking his thumb over his shoulder. . . .

Lily heard the approach of a galloping horse. A rider, dressed in Antipas' livery, scattered the band of pilgrims with the violence of his arrival. With a savage tug on the reins, he skidded his mount to a stop beside the guard, who jumped to attention.

"New orders," Lily heard the courier bark. "Pay attention to anyone mentioning Mak'ob or leprosy. To anyone talking of healing or miracles or such claptrap."

"And do what?" the border sentry demanded, hastily donning his helmet and grabbing his spear.

"Detain them and notify your captain. Fail and it's your neck."

—PP. 40–41

Still far from the city, Cantor and Lily were halted at another checkpoint by a thin, sour-faced little toll collector. "I have no need of duck eggs. Nor do I have pity. If you cannot pay to pass over the bridge, how will you prevent yourselves from becoming beggars and a burden to the government? You may not pass until you have the money. I would take the donkey."

Cantor shook his head.

"Then you'll never pass, because you will never have the money."

So Lily and Cantor dangled their feet in the water and remembered days and nights of waiting in the Valley of Ma'kob, when they had no provisions and no hope except in God.

I'm praying again, Provider for the Birds of the Air. Dresser of Flowers. You have no need of my praise. It adds not one measure to your glory. Still, for the sake of my own heart I praise you in my poverty. If you feed the birds and clothe the flowers, as Yeshua teaches, and you heal the lepers of Mak'ob, then surely you will make a way to the city where Yeshua commanded us we must go.

Lily's prayer was answered suddenly. It was the hawk that gained them favor and passage through a whole series of toll gates. A charioteer on the highway riding with a single attendant noticed Hawk as he swooped down at Cantor's command. The man, strong and in his midforties, with grizzled hair and beard, reined up his fine team of horses. He grinned broadly as Cantor scratched the top of Hawk's head.

"I favor falcons m'self," commented the charioteer. . . . Aye. Spend my days in the mews talking to my birds. Where are you going?"

"To Narda. The synagogue." Cantor did not mention his need for the toll payment.

"Well then. I'm not the religious type. No arguing Torah and the like. But I can use the company of a fellow who appreciates falconry. Will you and your woman ride along to the city? My man here will bring your donkey."

Lily and Cantor joined him gladly.

—PP. 82–83

The herald cried, "Make way for Lord Tannis! Gracious and terrible. Elder brother, to be feared among all warriors. Coruler of the province of Narda!"

Cantor considered their host with renewed curiosity. Lily almost laughed.

I'm praying again, Lord Who Knows All Things. Where and When and Who and How. So you sent one of the infamous rulers of this place to help us enter. The kinder of the two brothers, they say. You know such details. Things we could not know.

—P. 88

ASK

In the passages above, how did the miracles of the Lord pave the way for Lily and Cantor to continue their journey?

_____

_____

_____

What does the miracle of finding the berries say to Cantor, especially? In what situation could you take Cantor's message to heart right now?

_____

_____

_____

Look back over the last year. What miracles has God done in your life that you haven't identified as miracles and thanked Him for? Share the stories to encourage others!

_____

_____

_____

READ

Cantor pointed at the stars gleaming through the window. "See that? The light from that star began its journey to your eye perhaps ten thousand years ago. So it is with everything set in motion on this earth. Solomon wrote that in each life there is a *time* for us to be born and a time to die. There were twenty-eight things Solomon wrote as the Times in our lives between birth and death. But I tell you the truth, Lily: When we follow and believe the master plan within God's Word, we are beyond the reach of time. . . .

"Every step is marked out for you . . . just walk. What you and I do now for God is like the light of that star. To someone yet unborn you are a distant star. What good you do now may shine forth, and yet it may not be seen or received by anyone during your lifetime. But then your act of kindness will someday change the destiny of someone far in the future. A thousand or two thousand years from this moment. What we do now matters *eternally*. The written Word of the Almighty lets us study and see how the eternal picture is unfolding through generations. Whatever we suffer now? We can have faith that, in the end, even our suffering will be golden thread in the eternal tapestry."

—PP. 222–223

ASK

Do you believe that everything on this earth was set in motion by a creator? What life experiences or teachings have led you to that conclusion?

_____

_____

_____

Do you believe there is an appointed time to be born and a time to die? Why or why not?

_____

_____

_____

How can you be, right now, that "distant star" that shines forth for generations to come? In what way(s) can you show kindness for eternal good?

_____

_____

_____

WONDER . . .

"Our destiny is already recorded in the Book. . . . Everything matters. Every word. Deed. Thought. Prayer. Fear not!"
— CANTOR, P. 223

When you're in the midst of difficult circumstances, remember that everything that happens to you matters greatly. It's part of the Lord's eternal tapestry, and your star will shine brightly for generations to come if you choose to do what is right. Fear not—and stop along your life's journey to look for the miracles God is doing.

Lord of All the Angel Armies . . . you are the Good Shepherd. You rescue from danger, and all your paths are true. As David, the man after your own heart, wrote: I will fear no evil, for you are with me.
— LILY, P. 40

5 | A DOWN PAYMENT ON HOPE

Those who hope in the LORD will renew their strength. They will soar on wings like eagles; they will run and not grow weary, they will walk and not be faint.
   —ISAIAH 40:31

A wise man, St. Paul, once said that the three most important things of life are "faith, hope, and love" (1 Corinthians 13:13). Would you agree? Why or why not?

_____

_____

_____

In what or in whom do you place your hope? How does this influence your attitudes and life choices? Give an example.

_____

_____

_____

Lord Tannis was a strong man. A man people feared . . . and obeyed. Yet behind the scenes of his tough "bad boy" reputation was a lonely, hurting, hopeless man. A man who harbored secrets that haunted him every day, every moment. And none dared to enter his world until the Lord sent Lily and Cantor, former lepers who would never have associated with such a man, to Narda.

READ
"[They] gathered an army of Jews, built forts in the marshes of the Euphrates, and beat the governor of Babylon in battle. . . ."

The Jewish brothers, sons of a weaver-woman, had carved out a kingdom for themselves. Instead of eradicating them, King Artabanus, the Parthian monarch, bribed the Hebrew warriors to keep a check on his Babylonian subjects' ambition. For ten years the brothers had plundered and robbed passing caravans, but for the last decade they had been paid—handsomely, it was said—to provide protection for those same trade routes. They lived like kings, defended by handpicked Jewish archers, multistoried stone walls, and a network of canals and embankments that augmented the natural swamp. The story ran that no one, not even King Artabanus himself, could enter their domain without their permission. It was also said no one could find his way out again unassisted.

—P. 43

"Tannis has some military savvy. Hannel is all bluster and show. They will come to a bad end one of these days."

—MELCHIOR, P. 51

Tannis and Hannel gathered, stored, and guarded the Temple funds from all of the east . . . for a percentage of the revenue. Caiaphas justified this expense as needed to protect the balance from bandits.

—P. 73

ASK
What was Lord Tannis' reputation, based on the above passages?

_____

_____

_____

Would you want Tannis for a friend? a business partner? an enemy? Explain why or why not.

_____

_____

_____

READ

A charioteer on the highway riding with a single attendant noticed Hawk as he swooped down at Cantor's command. The man, strong and in his midforties, with grizzled hair and beard, reined up his fine team of horses. He grinned broadly as Cantor scratched the top of Hawk's head.

"I favor falcons m'self," commented the charioteer. . . . Spend my days in the mews talking to my birds. . . . I'm not the religious type. No arguing Torah and the like. But I can use the company of a fellow who appreciates falconry. Will you and your woman ride along to the city? My man here will bring your donkey." . . .

The man did indeed talk falconry nonstop, even through every checkpoint. Tolls were waived for him. Officials greeted him, bowing as he passed. . . .

I'm praying again, Lord Who Opens Gates When Every Way Seems Barred. Thank you for sending this brash fellow to us. A pleasant enough sort. A fine judge of men and of hawks.
—PP. 82–83

The fields were carpeted with lavender flowers. Millions of stalks, acres of blossoms, gave the region its name. . . . The charioteer inhaled appreciatively and thumped his chest with a clenched fist. "Smell that?" he demanded unnecessarily. "No wonder they say this is where Gan Eden stood."
—PP. 83–84

Every eye was on them as they drove through the city of Narda. The wealthy nodded. The poor bowed low. Who was this fellow? Lily wondered.

The charioteer pulled up his team and allowed them to drink at the fountain in the central square. He scowled and searched the faces of the crowd, as though he was looking for someone.

Moments later a herald and five armed servants dressed in elegant blue livery pushed through the crush of citizens, approached, and bowed at the waist.

"Lord Tannis."

"You're late," the charioteer growled. "You were told to be here when I returned."

"Only a minute or two."

Tannis cuffed the herald on the side of the head, then mounted his chariot again. Two servants took position on each side of the vehicle and two behind.

The herald cried, "Make way for Lord Tannis! Gracious and terrible. Elder brother, to be feared among all warriors. Coruler of the province of Narda!" . . .

Lord Tannis brought the reins down on the backs of his team of horses. It was not difficult to picture a whip in his hand snapping on the backs of the servants who ran beside them.

Tannis sneered as he drove, and now people scrambled out of the way. "So. This is my city. Now you know it. These are my slaves. I am their master. Though they are late."

—pp. 87–88

ASK

Compare the views of Lord Tannis' character shown in the scenes above.

_____

_____

_____

What do these contrasting views say to you about what's going on inside Lord Tannis?

_____

_____

_____

Have you ever dealt with a person who seems to change who they are, depending on their circumstances or the group they find themselves with? How do you handle that person?

READ

Tannis narrowed his dark eyes. "Our city has seen a flood of exiles from Judea these months past. Many are accused of heresy by the council in Yerushalayim. Are you heretics?"

"No, Lord Tannis."

He fixed his fierce gaze on Lily. "Then why do you come here to offer your sacrifices? I expect the truth."

"We were lepers in the Valley of Mak'ob," Lily replied.

Only an instant of surprise registered in his expression. "Were . . . you were . . . lepers? So you claim to be among those healed by the prophet we have heard so much about? This Nazarene prophet?"

Lily nodded.

"I'm not a believer. I am a Jew, but unwelcome in the synagogue of my own city. But I tell you, it is well you have fled from Herod Antipas. He beheaded the Baptizer . . . the prophet who proclaimed doom upon him for adultery. And he will kill the Nazarene as well before the story is finished."

Cantor replied, "We hope not, Lord Tannis. We pray not."

"Pray all you like. Politics and Money are the twin gods who rule Yerushalayim, Rome, and the whole world." The reins cracked down on the horses. "And the sword and the whip in the hands of men are the voice of the gods."

Cantor said, "Yeshua is stronger than death."

"No mere man is stronger than death. Death requires that all men must pay the sacrifice." He shook his head. "So . . . you claim to be former lepers of Mak'ob. Healed by a prophet. And he sent you here with the others? Where are your sacrifices, then? What do you bring to the God of Avraham, Yitz'chak, and Ya'acov?"

"The Lord will provide our sacrifice."

Tannis snorted. "The Lord is a businessman. Two doves and a lamb, is it? That is what is required? Money must first be produced before God provides such an expensive thank-offering. You will stay at my home. Inspect my raptors. Tour my mews."

The invitation of Lord Tannis was a command.

"The synagogue. Pressing business," Cantor explained.

"It can wait, I think." Tannis gazed appreciatively at Lily. "You're concerned about entering the house of an apostate? accepting my hospitality? No, don't deny it. I see it in your eyes. *Apostate*, you're thinking. But never mind. You will sleep in a tent . . . like Avraham and Sarai. All silk and brocade. A pavilion like the patriarchs. You'll not be defiled by entering my home."

Lily and Cantor had no choice in the matter. It was settled in the mind of Lord Tannis, and Lily knew that to object or refuse his offer would be dangerous.

—PP. 88–89

I'm praying again, Lord Who Knows the Hearts of All Men—rich and poor, proud and humble. See how he surveys his slaves and sweeps his hand over all and says, "Mine." Tannis is a lone tree, claiming every wind that touches him is his own. He is lonely, I think, Lord.

—P. 90

Tannis scratched the owl's head. Then he asked, "You like them? My little family?"

"Very much," Cantor replied.

"Good. I am in need of a falconer. A trainer. These birds are only the best. Acquired by me from around the world." He paused. "There is a falconry competition each year. Renowned. Romans. Greeks. The ruler of Parthia himself. My falconer died unexpectedly last month. He was a wise old bird, but now he's dead. So, it may be the fates at work. I find you on the road . . . and here you are."

Lily considered Tannis' words. Even the dead falconer had been "his."

Cantor replied cautiously. "I–I'm flattered, but I must have some time to consider."

"There are quarters above this room. A dwelling above the mews for a man with a family. A salary for a freeman. A good place to live. I have slaves who learned enough to carry on, yes, but I need a man who will live here . . . work with my birds for the love of the sport."

Lily caught a flash of some unnamed emotion in Tannis' eyes. It was dangerous. Somehow the offer of employment implied ownership.

—PP. 91–92

ASK

Based on the passages above, what views of God and life does Lord Tannis have?

_____

_____

_____

What does Lily discern about Lord Tannis' attitudes and emotions? Have you ever sensed such attitudes and emotions in a loved one's life? in your own life? How have you dealt with them?

_____

_____

_____

READ

Lily looked toward the big house, where Tannis lived. There was the glimmer of a light and stirring behind the curtain of his bedchamber. Was he watching to see their response?

"The Lord has provided our sacrifice, Cantor," Lily said quietly. "Everything we need."

Cantor joined her in the cool morning air. He stroked the head of the lamb. "He means us to offer this sacrifice . . . not only for ourselves . . ."

Lily nodded. "If he met Yeshua, he would know."

"It is written in Leviticus that the Lord dwells with his people even when they are unclean with transgression. It is the haughty and proud he cannot endure."

Lily gazed toward Tannis' window. "Better a sinner in need of mercy than an arrogant man."

I'm praying again, Provider for Our Needs. You command us to fulfill the law of lepers, and you provided the sacrifice. I'm praying for Lord Tannis, so far from your courts, but near to your heart. Ashamed of his sins—not proud. What word did you whisper that made such a man give the gifts of a leper to offer back to you? He is not proud, Lord, and so, I'm praying. Asking. Look at the healing sacrifice we offer today for our own leprosy as healing also for the leprosy of sin in the soul of Lord Tannis.

—P. 99

ASK

What does this passage reveal about Tannis' heart and his longings?

_____

_____

_____

Leviticus 26:11-17 and Psalm 101:5 say that God dwells even with sinners, but the proud he can't endure. Why do you think that is? Explain.

_____

_____

_____

READ

[Lord Tannis] was a man who had everything, yet Lily sensed an uneasiness about him. His smile flashed and faded, on and off, like a signal lamp on a hill. Joy for him was fleeting, as though he had some dark secret he wanted to hide from the world. . . .

Lily saw Lord Tannis, astride his horse across the lane, apparently waiting until the services had ended. . . .

Tannis rose up in his stirrups. The smile flashed, faded, then flashed again as Yod waved broadly to him.

"*Shanah Tova!*" he called to the trio. . . .

How long had he been waiting for them to emerge? Lily wondered. And had he truly been waiting? Or had he simply been there by chance?

"*Shanah Tova*, Lord Tannis," Cantor replied.

"May you be inscribed for a good year," Lily added.

Tannis tucked his chin in a gesture Lily had come to recognize. "Inscribed? HaShem, if he exists, would not write my name in his Book.

But . . ." He reached into his saddlebag and produced a leather pouch filled with coins. "I brought this. A gift, you might say. For the New Year. For the children who are here . . . all of them."

He faltered as though he wanted to ask a question, then tossed the pouch to Cantor, who caught it with one hand.

Surprised, Cantor hefted it. It had the weight of gold.

Yod cried, "Will you come to supper with us at Reb Nehemiah's house?"

"No, thank you. I am . . . it wouldn't be . . . I can't, you see." Again the gleam of a half smile and the lowered chin. "But you—Yod, is it? Would you answer a question for me?"

Yod placed her hands on her hips. She loved answering all manner of questions. "Sure."

"Well then. Will you tell me . . . Yeshua of Nazareth—the rumor grows, the truth becomes legend—they say he healed many."

Yod was very matter-of-fact. "Not a made-up story."

"Would he heal any child, do you think? Of any . . . any terrible affliction? The worst?"

Yod stuck out her lower lip. She barked a short laugh, letting him know this was a silly question. "Well, what do you think?"

The great man shrugged like a schoolboy who had no answers.

What was behind the question? Lily wondered.

"Perhaps I'll go see him for myself," Tannis replied. "Maybe prevail upon him to return with me. After all, there are sick and hurting here as well. My mitzvah to get my name in the—" he pointed upward—"Book, after all."

There was little left to be said. No other explanation for either the gift or the encounter.

And Lord Tannis rode off to face the New Year as he always had . . . alone.

—PP. 109–111

ASK

Why do you think Lord Tannis brought a gift to the children for the New Year? And asked Yod a question?

_____

_____

_____

What do these statements and question reveal about Lord Tannis' thoughts and secrets?

- "HaShem, if he exists, would not write my name in his Book."

_____

_____

_____

- "No, thank you. I am . . . it wouldn't be . . . I can't, you see."

_____

_____

_____

- "Would he heal any child, do you think? Of any . . . any terrible affliction? The worst?"

_____

_____

_____

- The great man shrugged like a schoolboy who had no answers.

_____

_____

_____

- "My mitzvah to get my name in the—" he pointed upward—"Book, after all."

_____

_____

_____

READ

The gift from Lord Tannis was provision enough for the children of Mak'ob to last a year. . . .

"A strange fellow, this robber baron," added Ahava. "To deny the existence of the Eternal . . . and yet to make such a contribution to our school."

"A good-hearted fellow," Cantor agreed. "But Lily believes he has some secret about his life that he is hiding."

"Perhaps," Nehemiah agreed. "There are rumors. . . ."

"There are always rumors." Ahava sighed.

"A broken heart," Nehemiah resumed, "an injury he cannot forgive . . . a death he cannot forget . . . a haunting face . . . even stories of the tragic loss of a child. His only child, by some accounts. Born outside the bounds of marriage. He goes alone at times into a walled garden to grieve. In the summers some have heard wailing coming from there."

Cantor replied quietly, "He asked about Yeshua: If he went to fetch him, would Yeshua come back? Does Yeshua really heal all disease? That sort of thing."

"Well then. I see. I see," said the blind rabbi. "His gift to us for the welfare of the children . . . a down payment on hope."

—PP. 121–122

ASK

How does the above information influence your thoughts and feelings toward Lord Tannis? What do you think Lord Tannis is really seeking in his actions and questions?

Who in your life is a Lord Tannis? How can knowing what might be going on behind the scenes help to change your perspective and actions toward that person?

READ

"Since the days of the exiled King Jeconiah, Narda has been a haven. We have pilgrims from all over the world who come to visit the Synagogue of the Exiles. What would Narda's reputation become if they were sold out? What would our reputation become?"

"When you were a brigand, jumping out at lonely travelers and slitting throats for pennies, you weren't concerned about your 'reputation,'" Hannel returned scornfully.

Tannis swelled up in anger. "Do you want to oppose a true miracle of HaShem?" . . . Tannis scanned his brother up and down. "You only see the money. Not the people."

—PP. 151–152

Lord Tannis . . . spoke to Rabbi Ahava and Rabbi Nehemiah with a hushed urgency.

". . . So. My brother holds hostage Daniel, son of Melchior the Magus. I tell you there will be no ransom returned by one of our brigands. None are to be trusted with such an errand beyond the gates of Narda. . . . [The Temple guards] are seeking one who they say claims to have died and returned. He who is followed everywhere by a hawk. Cantor, word reached the Sanhedrin in Yerushalayim. Maybe just a rumor. A legend. But there are others whose lives have been blessed by miracles. They have fled the territory of Herod and Rome. Now the Sanhedrin sends documents. They are seeking the master of the hawk . . . he who took refuge here in my walled city. They mean to kill the man raised from death. Or torture him until he confesses his story is a fraud."

Cantor finished, "They have come for me."

"My brother has made a deal with the Herodian captain. I will not risk civil war in my territory, but I came with this warning: You will not survive for long if they discover you here. Kidnappers at best. Assassins at the worst. Brother, master of raptors, they seek to shoot you down before you fly away again to safety."

"So." Ahava comprehended the reason for Tannis' visit. "Why should we trust you? Might you not also take Cantor from us and hold him for payment by the Herodians?"

"A good question." Nehemiah stroked his beard. "Why have you come to warn our Cantor?"

"I have come here to warn you, to help you, because . . ." Tannis faltered.

"Speak up!" Ahava demanded as though reprimanding a schoolboy.

Tannis replied, "If it is true, Cantor . . . if what they say of you is true . . . it's more than being healed of leprosy. It's being healed of death." He searched Cantor's face. "So. Is it? Is it true what they say?"

Cantor replied with a single downward stroke of his chin.

The dark eyes of Tannis widened with fear. "It is whispered. We hear it among our servants. Slaves say this Yeshua of Nazareth has raised others besides you and that they have returned with stories of a fantastic world beyond this."

Again Cantor answered by inclining his head in the affirmative.

Tannis exhaled loudly. "Then could I let them murder you? And keep silent? If what you have seen is real? And you have come to tell us about this place, this Eden . . . then I must hear of it. I want to know."

"There are no words to describe . . . ," Cantor began.

"But something . . . you must speak. Some hope, perhaps, even for a man like me." . . .

Cantor raised his eyes toward heaven, as though listening to another voice. "Fear not," he whispered.

—PP. 172–173

"Excellency," the auctioneer replied with a bow. "Your presence here is an honor. Surely you do not want this . . . er, skinny and spirited slave. I have no doubt we could find you another, better suited to your esteemed house. The bid stands at thirty. Are there any others?"

"Fifty," the man called again. "Perhaps my brother lacks the ability to properly train his slaves." The man continued, as he approached the platform, "That is, the *will* to discipline his servants. I'm sure I can handle this boy, even if he cannot. Fifty drachmae, I said. Are you refusing my offer?"

"Lord Tannis," groveled the auctioneer, kneeling to whisper to the man, "you must realize that not a soul in Narda will bid against you for anything you desire. This slave can fetch three times as much for Hannel as you offer. Please, tell me what it is you require, and I'm sure we can find a slave better suited to your need. Even one sold by . . . someone else."

"And you must realize," Tannis replied, "I do not care for a better-suited slave. I have no need of a slave at all. If my treacherous brother's profit is diminished by my purchase of this slave, then my trip to the market is a success, and my day is complete." . . .

Turning his attention back to the auctioneer, Lord Tannis said, "I'll either have this boy for a slave . . . or *you*. Decide." . . .

Daniel was led off the platform to be introduced to his new owner.

—P. 242

ASK

How does Lord Tannis try to right his past wrongs in these passages? Why do you think he does so?

_____

_____

_____

Have you ever tried to make right something you've done wrong? What steps did you take, and what was the outcome?

_____

_____

_____

When someone else tries to make right what they have done wrong to you, how do you respond? After seeing into Lord Tannis' heart in *Tenth Stone,* will you respond differently in the future? If so, how?

_____

_____

_____

READ

The discussion changed to a series of pointed inquiries about Yeshua of Nazareth.

"I want the truth," Tannis demanded. "Who is he?"

Lily loved speaking of the lives she had seen Yeshua touch . . . cures for leprosy of the soul as well as of the body.

Tannis bore in like a falcon swooping on a dove. "Yes, but what authority do you have to speak in his name? Eh? What?"

Cantor replied, "He told us: 'Heal the sick. Raise the dead. Cleanse those who have leprosy. Drive out demons.'"

"Yes," Lily agreed eagerly, "we are to tell everyone, 'The Kingdom of Heaven is near.'" Then she added, "He said, 'Go to the lost sheep of the House of Israel.'"

Tannis snorted. "I think that description applies to me."

Quietly Cantor added, "He also said, 'I am sending you out like lambs among wolves.'"

"So you have the authority to act in his name?" Tannis demanded again, abruptly.

Cantor gazed at Lily before replying. When she nodded, he declared, "Yes."

"Then this will be your chance to prove it. . . . Behind these walls is my greatest treasure—the one thing in this world I love above all else. Also my greatest sorrow. Daniel," Tannis instructed suddenly, "open the garden door."

The hinges of the gate groaned. From within the garden a steady wail, like that of a wounded animal, pierced the night.

—PP. 244–245

Tannis' voice caught with emotion as he spoke. "My son. His name is Daniel. My son, my child, the thing I love most in all the world. His mother was killed in our camp by brigands. He saw her die and has never stopped living that horror from that moment 'til this. I have been alone and helpless to find a way to bring him home. Hopeless to help him. Can you—in the name and by the authority of this One, Yeshua of Nazareth whom you serve—give me hope? Can the One who healed the exiled lepers of Mak'ob now redeem the son I have lost?"

—P. 249

ASK

What secrets were behind all the questions that Lord Tannis was asking about himself? about his son? about Yeshua of Nazareth?

_____

_____

_____

What questions would you like to ask Yeshua right now? In what situation(s) do you feel helpless? long for hope?

_____

_____

_____

WONDER . . .

> Find rest, O my soul, in God alone;
>   my hope comes from Him.
> He alone is my rock and my salvation;
>   He is my fortress, I will not be shaken.
> —PSALM 62:5-6

My hope is built on nothing less
Than Jesus' blood and righteousness;
I dare not trust the sweetest frame,
But wholly lean on Jesus' name.

On Christ, the solid rock, I stand,
All other ground is sinking sand;
All other ground is sinking sand.
"MY HOPE IS BUILT ON NOTHING LESS"
WORDS BY EDWARD MOTE, 1834

In what or in whom do you place your hope?

6 | CALLED BY NAME

"When the time is right, he will call them each by name. . . . And they will also hear and come forth healed from their graves."
—CANTOR, P. 8

He sent forth His Word and healed them;
 He rescued them from the grave.
—PSALM 107:20

What do you think life after death will be like? What images come to mind?

_____

_____

_____

Do you believe that heaven exists? Why or why not? What experiences have led you to that conclusion?

_____

_____

_____

Do you fear the end of your life on earth or look forward to it? Why?

_____

_____

_____

Lily had lost her beloved Cantor once through death. Then, by a miracle of Yeshua, who took the leprosy of those in the Valley of Sorrow upon Himself, Lily was healed. She was freed from her life of death in the Valley and given a new purpose—to tell others about the redemption and healing of Yeshua.

Even more miraculous, Cantor was raised from death to life. Little Yod, too, when she took her last breath on earth, was taken to heaven and then returned to earth. Their brief glimpses of heaven and eternity with God would forever transform their view of life on earth.

READ

"It's not what you think it is."

"It?"

"*Olam haba*. The World to Come. A strange name for it, because it already exists. It is not the world to come. It is . . . already." . . .

"But what did you see?" She tried to guide his memory of Paradise.

"I . . . it's easier if you ask me *who*. I can put an answer to that."

"All right, then. Who?"

"So many. From the Valley. There to welcome me. All well. Beautiful. All about the same age. No matter how old they were when they flew away, they seemed to be my age. They came and gathered around me. Embracing. Laughing. Singing. It was a celebration. You know?"

Lily named a dozen she had known in the Valley of Mak'ob. Some, Cantor had seen. But not all.

He continued his story. "Music. Songs I knew mixed in with some I had never heard. They could not be sung on earth because they are too beautiful. There was light. And color all around. Like this . . ." He swept his hand up from the water toward the sky. "Only much more . . . much more."

Lily leaned forward eagerly. "And who else? Anyone else?"

He nodded. "They walked with me. We were on a path the color of sapphire. The Lord loves color. Greens and blues. And water—the water has a scent, so wondrous. Beyond . . . oh! I don't know what it's like."

"Who else? Any of the old ones? from the stories?"

"Yes. Many. Abel, who died at the hand of his brother. And Enoch, who never died at all. Noah in the midst of a herd of deer. . . . His family all around him. Still work to do, you know. And they worked."

"Work in *olam haba*?"

"But not as we work here. Joy in their work. And Avraham and Sarai. All the patriarchs. At a great distance I saw Mosheh too, among a council of the prophets. King David . . . all of them. I heard a voice say, 'Those who by faith subdued kingdoms, administered justice, obtained blessings, closed the mouths of lions, extinguished raging fire' . . . Some who were tortured for their faith had suffered greatly. Their wounds were still on them, but they were like shining gems. Battle awards. Heroes and heroines. I knew them, though they did not say their names at first. And they knew me. From first to last. There were so many. They kept coming. I would think of one great one and suddenly—" he snapped his fingers—"suddenly I would see him and know. I understand why we will need eternity."

—PP. 73–75

Yod stopped outside the shop and exclaimed, "Oh, listen! So beautiful. Remember, Cantor? The music. Like his Spirit. Oh, the colors in the notes!"

He quietly translated for Lily. "You see, music has color. Or, maybe color makes music. You not only hear it; there is a fragrance in the notes, like a garden. Each note like a different flower. Music is different—bigger— over there." He smiled wistfully at the memory.

Bunches of lavender hung drying in an herb shop. The air was redolent with the aroma. It seemed right somehow to Lily that music in heaven made color and fragrance. She imagined what Eden must have been like when it was planted here in this very soil. Music, color, perfume . . . all combined. What had it been like to hear the Voice of the Lord as He walked in the cool of the day?

P. 233

ASK
How does Cantor describe these aspects of heaven?

- the people

_____

_____

_____

- the animals

_____

_____

_____

- the music

_____

_____

_____

- the colors

_____

_____

_____

- the work

_____

_____

_____

What, if anything, about his description matches your own musings about heaven? What things surprise you?

_____

_____

_____

If you could ask questions of one person from ages past, who would it be—and why?

_____

_____

_____

What would you ask that person?

_____

_____

_____

READ

"It was something like that . . . like the gallery. I could look down, see Lily through the lattice. Hear her voice and pray for her and cheer her on. Though she could not see me or hear me."

Ahava's eyes grew wide. "You could . . . see?"

"I could love," Cantor answered. "And now back here I know. They who lived before us are witnesses of the race we run."

—P. 159

Therefore, since we are surrounded by such a great cloud of witnesses, let us throw off everything that hinders and the sin that so easily entangles, and let us run with perseverance the race marked out for us.
—HEBREWS 12:1

ASK

Think about the loved ones you've lost through death. Do you believe they can see and hear you? that they are still thinking about you? Why or why not?

_____

_____

_____

If you thought of them as "witnesses" even now of everything you say and do, would your words and actions change in any way? If so, how?

_____

_____

_____

READ

Lily stared at the mounds of the cemetery. She fixed her gaze on the open grave where Cantor had lain. She said, "What was here . . . and who we were before he came . . . it will be forgotten, I suppose."

Cantor nodded, testing his voice. "When the time is right, he will call them each by name, like he called me. And they will also hear and come forth healed from their graves. Better than healed. They will walk up the steep path to where we stand now." He stretched his hand up to Hawk in a signal that it was time to go. "Or maybe on that day we will all know how to fly."

Lily smiled softly. "Will you tell me . . . everything?"

Cantor nodded. His eyes reflected light from a distant place. "There is no death there."

"And where he is sending us now? The land where Eden once existed? The land he said is waiting to hear our story—that the Redeemer of Eden has come back?"

Cantor frowned for the first time since he awakened from the long sleep. "It was perfect once. I saw it as it was . . . before. There was no death until there was a murder of brother by brother."

Lily asked, "What was it like?"

"Too much to tell. Beyond beauty . . . beyond fear. Lily, I will never be afraid again. They are all there, waiting for us, and waiting for him to return home."

—p. 8

"It is time that makes us fear. Fear of running out of time. Lily, there is no time where we are going. The prayer we pray today . . . the prayer we think God does not hear? It may yet be answered for our grandchildren . . . or their grandchildren. Do you understand what I am telling you, Lily?"

—CANTOR, p. 223

ASK
Do you agree that we fear because of time? Why or why not?

_____

_____

_____

Is it important to you to be remembered after you die? Why or why not? How can you develop a legacy that will last for generations?

_____

_____

_____

READ

Cantor smiled sadly. "It's this life that's the shadow. This is the dream. I died and woke up in Paradise. And . . . well, what does it matter? I'm still longing for a distant home."

"The names inscribed here . . . they are all about himself. So many generations in exile. They have forgotten the meaning of the stones. They have forgotten that the prophets wrote about him before he came. If we could tell them, then they would believe."

Cantor clamped his mouth tight. "Ten stones. Ten names of Messiah. Yeshua clearly fulfills them all—each name. He is the cornerstone. But they don't believe him. In Yerushalayim the leaders of Israel plot how they can kill him, even though his miracles speak louder than words. If those who have seen him face-to-face won't believe, can these exiles of Israel believe what they haven't seen? The people come to him for bread. They come for comfort. But they don't come because they want to know him."

Cantor swept his hand over the ten stones. "These tell who he is. They are the prophecies fulfilled in our time, and they tell the future. If the people won't believe him, even after seeing proof for themselves, then how can we convince them?"

"He sent us, and you and Lily, here to the exiles of Israel. To the place where Gan Eden was lost. To proclaim what you saw." The old man looked toward the ceiling. "I will tell them of the day we laid you in the grave."

—PP. 159–160

ASK

When do you tend to pray to God? When you need comfort, when you need a miracle, or because you love Him and want to know Him? Explain.

_____

_____

_____

Have you ever felt out of place in this present world? Have you longed for a distant home? In what situation(s)? In what way(s) is this life a "shadow"?

_____

_____

_____

WONDER . . .

Do not let your hearts be troubled. Trust in God; trust also in me. In my Father's house are many rooms; if it were not so, I would have told you. I am going there to prepare a place for you. And if I go and prepare a place for you, I will come back and take you to be with me that you also may be where I am.
—JOHN 14:1-3

"'Tell them the wonders you have witnessed.' He said, 'Tell them I am here.'"
—P. 66

If you don't yet believe in Yeshua, what is stopping you from accepting Him and the promise of life forever with Him in heaven?

If you believe Yeshua is the Messiah who came to earth to redeem all who trust in Him, how can you proclaim what you've seen? What stories of God's love, grace, and mercy could you share?

"May it please the Lord, who sent us out to bring good news to the exiles of Israel, to also bring us home one day soon!"
—P. 32

Dear Reader,

You are so important to us. We have prayed for you as we wrote this book and also as we receive your letters and hear your soul cries. We hope that *Tenth Stone* has encouraged you to go deeper. To get to know Yeshua better. To fill your soul hunger by examining Scripture's truths for yourself.

We are convinced that if you do so, you will find this promise true: *"If you seek Him, He will be found by you."*
—1 CHRONICLES 28:9

Bodie & Brock Thoene

Scripture References

[1] Deut. 7:7
[2] Isa. 53:3
[3] Isa. 53:5
[4] Ps. 107:20
[5] Ps. 136:1
[6] Hab. 2:11
[7] Isa. 53:5
[8] Mal. 4:2
[9] 1 John 4:1
[10] Gen. 32:22-30
[11] Deut. 6:4
[12] Ps. 23:4
[13] Isa. 49:16
[14] Matt. 2:1-12.
   Also see *Sixth Covenant*, in
   the A.D. Chronicles series.
[15] Matt. 11:5; Luke 7:22
[16] Exod. 20:8

[17] Heb. 11:33-34
[18] Matt. 6:25-30
[19] Lev. 26:11-17
[20] Ps. 101:5
[21] Lev. 14
[22] 2 Kings 5
[23] Ps. 103:3
[24] Num. 6:24-26
[25] Deut. 11:18
[26] Prov. 5:3
[27] Prov. 5:3
[28] Prov. 5:4
[29] Prov. 5:5
[30] Mark 5:35-43; Luke 8:49-56
[31] Luke 7:11-17
[32] Ps. 91:5
[33] Ps. 46:10
[34] Matt. 5:44

[35] Matt. 18:3-4
[36] Eccles. 3:1-8
[37] Ps. 88:1-2
[38] Ps. 88:3
[39] Ps. 88:4-5
[40] Ps. 88:6-7
[41] Ps. 88:8
[42] Ps. 88:14
[43] Ps. 88:15
[44] Ps. 88:16-17
[45] Matt. 10:8
[46] Luke 10:9
[47] Matt. 10:6
[48] Luke 10:3
[49] Ps. 118:22-23
[50] Phil. 1:21

Authors' Note

The following sources have been helpful in our research for this book.

- *The Complete Jewish Bible.* Translated by David H. Stern. Baltimore, MD: Jewish New Testament Publications, Inc., 1998.

- *iLumina*, a digitally animated Bible and encyclopedia suite. Carol Stream, IL: Tyndale House Publishers, 2002.

- *The International Standard Bible Encyclopaedia.* George Bromiley, ed. 5 vols. Grand Rapids, MI: Eerdmans, 1979.

- *The Life and Times of Jesus the Messiah.* Alfred Edersheim. Peabody, MA: Hendrickson Publishers, Inc., 1995.

- Starry Night™ Enthusiast Version 5.0, publishing by Imaginova™ Corp.

About the Authors

BODIE AND BROCK THOENE (pronounced *Tay-nee*) have written over 50 works of historical fiction. That these best sellers have sold more than 10 million copies and won eight ECPA Gold Medallion Awards affirms what millions of readers have already discovered—the Thoenes are not only master stylists but experts at capturing readers' minds and hearts.

In their timeless classic series about Israel (The Zion Chronicles, The Zion Covenant, and The Zion Legacy), the Thoenes' love for both story and research shines.

With The Shiloh Legacy and *Shiloh Autumn* (poignant portrayals of the American Depression), The Galway Chronicles (dramatic stories of the 1840s famine in Ireland), and the Legends of the West (gripping tales of adventure and danger in a land without law), the Thoenes have made their mark in modern history.

In the A.D. Chronicles they step seamlessly into the world of Jerusalem and Rome, in the days when Yeshua walked the earth and transformed lives with His touch.

Bodie began her writing career as a teen journalist for her local newspaper. Eventually her byline appeared in prestigious periodicals such as *U.S. News and World Report*, *The American West*, and *The Saturday Evening Post*. She also worked for John Wayne's Batjac Productions (she's best known as author of *The Fall Guy*) and ABC Circle Films as a writer and researcher. John Wayne described her as "a writer with talent that captures the people and the times!" She has degrees in journalism and communications.

Brock has often been described by Bodie as "an essential half of this writing team." With degrees in both history and education, Brock has, in his role as researcher and story-line consultant, added the vital dimension of historical accuracy. Due to such careful research, the Zion Covenant and Zion Chronicles series are recognized by the American Library Association, as well as Zionist libraries around the world, as classic historical novels and are used to teach history in college classrooms.

Bodie and Brock have four grown children—Rachel, Jake, Luke, and Ellie—and seven grandchildren. Their children are carrying on the Thoene family talent as the next generation of writers, and Luke produces the Thoene audiobooks. Bodie and Brock divide their time between London and Nevada.

For more information visit:
www.thoenebooks.com
www.familyaudiolibrary.com

THOENE FAMILY CLASSICS™

✪ ✪ ✪

THOENE FAMILY CLASSIC HISTORICALS
by Bodie and Brock Thoene

*Gold Medallion Winners**

CP0064

THOENE FAMILY CLASSICS™

✪ ✪ ✪

THOENE FAMILY CLASSIC AMERICAN LEGENDS

LEGENDS OF THE WEST
by Bodie and Brock Thoene

Legends of the West, Volume One
Sequoia Scout
The Year of the Grizzly
Shooting Star
Legends of the West, Volume Two
Gold Rush Prodigal
Delta Passage
Hangtown Lawman
Legends of the West, Volume Three
Hope Valley War
The Legend of Storey County
Cumberland Crossing
Legends of the West, Volume Four
The Man from Shadow Ridge
Cannons of the Comstock
Riders of the Silver Rim

LEGENDS OF VALOR
by Luke Thoene

Sons of Valor
Brothers of Valor
Fathers of Valor

✪ ✪ ✪

THOENE CLASSIC NONFICTION
by Bodie and Brock Thoene

Writer-to-Writer

THOENE FAMILY CLASSIC SUSPENSE
by Jake Thoene

CHAPTER 16 SERIES
Shaiton's Fire
Firefly Blue
Fuel the Fire

✪ ✪ ✪

THOENE FAMILY CLASSICS FOR KIDS

BAKER STREET DETECTIVES
by Jake and Luke Thoene

The Mystery of the Yellow Hands
The Giant Rat of Sumatra
The Jeweled Peacock of Persia
The Thundering Underground

LAST CHANCE DETECTIVES
by Jake and Luke Thoene
Mystery Lights of Navajo Mesa
Legend of the Desert Bigfoot

THE VASE OF MANY COLORS
by Rachel Thoene (Illustrations by Christian Cinder)

✪ ✪ ✪

THOENE FAMILY CLASSIC AUDIOBOOKS

Available from
www.thoenebooks.com or
www.familyaudiolibrary.com

CP0064

the middle east

FIRST CENTURY A.D.

Mount Hermon +

GALILEE

Mediterranean Sea

• Caesarea Philippi

Chorazin •
Capernaum •
Magdala •
Sepphoris •

• Bethsaida
Sea of Galilee
• Tiberias

• Beth Shan

Jordan River

SAMARIA

Jericho •
Jerusalem • + Mount of Olives
• Bethany
Bethlehem •
• Herodium

PEREA

JUDEA

Dead Sea

IDUMEA

N

← to Alexandria, Egypt